THE URBANA FREE LIBRARY
W9-BBQ-486

THE GALILEAN SECRET

THE GALILEAN SECRET

EVAN DRAKE HOWARD

Guideposts
New York, New York

For Paul D. Sanderson with deepest gratitude

The Galilean Secret

ISBN: 978-0-8249-4794-1

Published by Guideposts
16 East 34th Street
New York, New York 10016
www.guideposts.com

Distributed by Ideals Publications, a division of Guideposts
2636 Elm Hill Pike, Suite 120
Nashville, Tennessee 37214

Acknowledgments are on pages 443–444.

Library of Congress Cataloging-in-Publication Data

Howard, Evan Drake, 1955–
Galilean secret / Evan Drake Howard.
p. cm.
ISBN 978-0-8249-4794-1
1. Christian antiquities—Fiction. 2. Jerusalem—History—Fiction. 3. Israel—Fiction. I. Title.
PS3608.O917G35 2010
813'.6—dc22

2010003090

Cover design by Kathleen Lynch
Cover images by Veer and Corbis
Interior design by Lorie Pagnozzi
Typeset by Nancy Tardi

Printed and bound in the United States of America
10 9 8 7 6 5 4 3 2 1

From The Day the World Changed
Copyright © 2063
by Karim Musalaha

CALL ME ANYTHING, BUT NOT A LIAR. A man would be a fool to lie about something this big. Something that the media covered all over the world. What no one knows is how it happened, or who started it, and certainly not why.

No one but me.

I kept the secret because it's so hard to believe.

I believe because I was there. I saw the events take place, and who was behind them, and how they affected everyone involved.

Now it's time to tell the story.

Before the change came, I only believed in hate—and the anguish and despair it caused. That's all anyone believed in. On either side. But they wouldn't admit it, because no matter how wrong they were, they declared that their religion made them right. This kept the tears flowing so long that no one knew how to stop them.

Or how to quench the thirst of the blood-soaked earth.

But that was long ago now, and anyone still alive today can hardly remember back then. Back before peace finally came between my people, the Palestinians, and our sworn enemies, the Israelis. Back when the world thought it was impossible.

And no one had ever heard of Karim Musalaha.

PRESENT DAY

CHAPTER ONE

The Dead Sea
Wednesday, March 5

THE FOOTSTEPS WERE GAINING ON KARIM MUSALAHA.

Desperate to escape, he scrambled toward a cave midway up the sculpted limestone cliff, his heart pounding in his throat. He wiped sweat from his forehead and stumbled across jagged rocks. When he climbed into the cave, bats flew out with raucous, high-pitched squeals, as if mocking his distress. His insides lurched as he dove for cover and began to crawl, careful to avoid the pitted walls of hardened sand and the scorpions that patrolled them. As he scraped hand and knee against stone, a thought—more oppressive than the thick darkness—struck him: If he died here, no one would care. His decision to run away had left him utterly alone, as bereft of human contact as the Dead Sea was of life.

He paused and listened, afraid that the footsteps belonged to Abdul Fattah, a soldier of the Palestinian Patriotic Alliance intent on capturing and returning him to Nablus. Under his breath he cursed Abdul's loyalty to Sadiq Musalaha, Karim's father and the political leader of the alliance. When Karim reached the back of the cave, he knelt and took off his pack.

His jeans and T-shirt were covered with dust. Three days earlier he had dropped out of graduate school at Birzeit University and fled with his refunded tuition. His body reeked from not having had a shower since he left Ramallah.

Never would his father understand, let alone forgive. Karim despised Sadiq Musalaha's use of suicide bombers against Israel and refused to join the PPA militia. The words of a music video broadcast on Palestinian TV haunted his thoughts: "How sweet is the fragrance of the *shahids*. How sweet is the scent of the earth, its thirst quenched by the gush of blood, flowing from the youthful body." A ribbon of sweat slithered down Karim's back. The best way to express his outrage was to join the Palestinian-Israeli peace movement. He had come here, a kilometer south of the Qumran visitors' center, to seek spiritual guidance, as the Prophet Muhammad had in a cave on Mount Hira, outside of Mecca. Karim also hoped that a sojourn in the desert would throw Abdul off his trail. But he only now realized the cost: a life as barren as the sun-scorched peaks of Qumran.

Still hearing footsteps outside, he ducked behind a section of rock that jutted from the wall. The Islam he had learned at Birzeit condemned both suicide and the murder of innocents. He twirled the gold band on his little finger. The ring had belonged to his deceased mother and bore the inscription "True Islam is peace." To him, those words affirmed the saying in the Qur'an, "Do not throw yourselves to destruction with your own hands." The inscription also echoed a powerful Hadith of Muhammad: "If people do good to you, do good to them; and if they mistreat you, still refrain from being unjust."

He searched the floor with a hand, feeling for a stone to throw. As he probed in the dark, his fingers brushed something smooth and round protruding from the floor of hard-packed sand. With no time to explore, he kept searching and probing until he found several sharp stones, which he then held in his palms. He remained still, vowing to fight if necessary, while wondering about the smooth object.

The clatter of falling rocks caused him to recoil. He pressed his shoulders against the jagged back wall of the cave, the air dusty. A scorpion crawled down his arm, but he dared not move. The footsteps neared the entrance. He held his breath and waited, sweat stinging his eyes. So this was the price of freedom—to suffer terror and exhaustion in a desolate cave as he pondered a lonely future.

Yu Allah! Please don't let Abdul find me. Karim believed that Allah answered prayers and would protect him, as Allah had protected the Prophet Muhammad and Ishmael and Hagar in the desert. The Islam he practiced honored Jews and Christians, as well as Muslims, as children of Abraham. The thought of murdering twenty-three of his brothers and sisters and injuring seventy-six more, as his older brother Saed had done on a bus in West Jerusalem, repulsed him.

Karim dreamed of becoming a journalist, of marrying and raising a family. But what hope did he have of marriage now? Very little. And yet he yearned to find a wife who would be more precious to him than the seventy-two virgins who awaited a *shahid* in heaven. If he could only survive, he would flee to Bethlehem, far from his father and the militants in Nablus, and support the movement for peace.

Flashlight beams darted into the cave. Voices murmured. He squeezed the stones, realizing that two people were pursuing him. As he held his breath and waited, ready to defend himself, his blood ran colder than a desert night.

"Over here. Look over here!"

"Okay, but quickly. Then I'm leaving."

The two voices grew louder, the light flashes closer to him. He exhaled in relief as he realized that the people were speaking English. Abdul Fattah, Sadiq Musalaha's chief lieutenant, spoke Arabic and also wouldn't have traveled with a partner. Karim had successfully eluded Abdul, at least for now. The voices probably belonged to tourists or researchers of some sort. Still . . . he continued to grip the rocks, prepared to fight if necessary.

"It's dark inside, and steep and rocky. I'm going home with Dr. Jordan."

The footsteps began to fade along with the male voices. Karim dropped the stones and waited for the haunting stillness of the desert to return. Then he began to feel around for the smooth object. His fingers probed the crusty, jagged surface until he grazed the object again. He thought it was probably a stone and tried to pry it loose, but it wouldn't budge.

The hardened sand resisted his attempts to dig with his fingers. Only by taking the pocketknife from his pack and jabbing deep did he make progress. He dug all around the object and then scooped the rocks and sand away. Finally he was able to unearth it. To his amazement, the object was tall, perhaps fifty centimeters, and round like a ceramic vessel. He remembered the Bedouin shepherds who had discovered the Dead Sea Scrolls in these caves in 1947, and wondered if he, too, had stumbled upon treasure.

His pulse throbbed in his ears as he listened for footsteps. When he heard none, he put on his backpack and carried the object to the entrance. Only then could he see what it was—a tall, round clay jar sealed with a cork. He pried the crumbling cork loose, reached inside, and to his surprise, withdrew something that looked like a cylinder wrapped in linen. He unfurled the linen to find what appeared to be a scroll made of fragile papyrus.

Brittle and soiled in places, the scroll reminded him of his life—a relic of its earlier promise, fighting a losing battle against decay. At least the scroll was in fair condition. The top part of it contained a document written in black and signed boldly at the end. Below the signature was another section of writing, equally long, but written by a different hand. The script of both sections reminded him of Hebrew, only less cluttered and with fewer dots. It was square in appearance and probably read from right to left.

The scroll must be ancient and was no doubt valuable. He hoped that finding it was a sign of Allah's favor. His friend, Brother Gregory Andreou, a Greek Orthodox monk and visiting professor at Birzeit University, lived in Bethlehem. As a scholar of Near Eastern languages and civilizations, he might be able to translate the scroll.

Karim gazed at the barren beige cliffs, which were turning gold from the setting sun. Under different circumstances, he would have found the sight exhilarating, but it would take more than the discovery of a scroll for that to happen. The salt of the Dead Sea smelled pungent and burned his lungs. He formulated a plan as he gazed down at his GMI 104 motorbike parked in a grove of date palms below the cliffs. He would lock the jar in the fiberglass carrying case on the back and ride for Bethlehem.

After rolling up the scroll, he placed it inside the jar. The sun was almost all the way down, but he could still see. If he didn't leave soon, he would have to spend the night in the cave. He rose and peeked outside the entrance. Seeing no one, he climbed out, the jar tucked under an arm.

He started down the rocky slope and had gone no more than a dozen meters when he heard footsteps behind him. He turned and saw a middle-aged man, well built, with wire-rimmed glasses and a full head of sandy hair, rushing toward him, trowel in hand.

The man wore an army-green shirt and pants. "I'm the only one who has permission to excavate these caves. You'll need to give me that jar."

Karim bristled at the order. "No, I don't. I found it. I'll decide what to do with it."

"I'm afraid you don't have a choice." The man lunged at him with the trowel. Karim sidestepped and narrowly escaped the thrust. He spun away from the man and started down the moderate incline, half sliding, half bolting down the hillside. The man continued pursuing him, his steps quick and determined, his breathing heavy. Karim darted right and then left so he wouldn't fall headlong onto the ground below. He struggled to keep his balance, his loaded backpack shifting, his feet slipping on the pebble-strewn limestone.

"I said give me the jar!" The man neared to within a couple feet of Karim and stabbed at him, tearing the sleeve of his T-shirt. But the thrust threw the man off balance and Karim lurched past him. If he could beat the man to the limestone plain beneath the ridge, he could get to his motorbike. But the backpack and the jar were slowing him down. Just then he felt the man grab his T-shirt from behind, which made Karim fall. When he hit the stone, the jar broke into pieces, exposing the scroll. Karim scooped it up as he scrambled to his feet.

"Give me the scroll," the man said.

"I found it, and you're not going to—"

Before Karim could finish, the man charged. Karim parried the man's thrust with his free arm. He then set the scroll down and grabbed the man's wrist, pulling and twisting. The trowel hit the ground as Karim slammed a knee into the man's gut and shoved him down. As the man lay groaning, Karim kicked the trowel away, grabbed the scroll, and started zigzagging down the sloping cliff face.

Once on the open limestone plain, he broke into a sprint. A fast runner, he took advantage of the head start by racing toward the grove of palms. He glanced over his left shoulder to see the man gaining on him. Karim would have to lock the scroll in the carrying case and kick-start the motorbike in one motion.

As he reached the bike, Karim dug in his pocket for the key, the footsteps pounding closer. He laid the scroll in the carrying case and slammed it closed. Then he swung his leg over the bike and brought his weight down on the kick-start pedal.

Nothing.

He kicked again.

A sputter.

The thudding footsteps were bearing down, strong as hoofbeats. Karim kicked one last time with frenzied determination.

The engine roared to life.

He gave it gas as the man reached him and latched onto the carrying case. Karim swerved right and then left to shake him loose.

The man coughed on the swirling dust, his breathing choked. "I'll kill you!"

Karim revved the engine and the motorbike surged forward. The man's weight shook the bike, causing it to swerve wildly. Karim fought to keep his balance, steering straight and accelerating until he broke the man's grip. Glancing over his shoulder, Karim saw him hit the ground. When Karim reached the road, he watched him get up and start running. Turning left, Karim passed a gray Chevy Impala parked on the shoulder. The man must be running toward it.

As Karim guided the motorbike up the highway, he saw that the Impala was following him. He decided to ride through the desert, where no car could follow.

Tires squealed behind him.

He turned and glimpsed the Impala catching up. As he left the road and steered into the desert, he wondered who the man was and why he was prepared to kill for the scroll. Even more, he wondered about the writing. Whose hand had etched it onto the papyrus? What did the writing say? These questions were impossible to answer, but thinking about them sent excitement snaking through him as he sped into the desert.

CHAPTER TWO

***Jerusalem*, AD 33**

ON THE MORNING OF HER WEDDING, JUDITH OF JERUSALEM KNEW SHE COULDN'T GO THROUGH WITH IT. She woke up before dawn drenched in sweat. Stomach churning, she put on her tunic and sandals and felt her way to the bedroom window. *Oh, why am I not attracted to Gabriel?* The lament that had haunted her for months now sounded like a scream. She stared into the darkness that draped Jerusalem like a shroud, her breathing short, her head throbbing.

She liked and admired Gabriel ben Zebulun but could not marry him. She stumbled toward the nightstand beside the bed. On it stood the candle in the brass holder that she had set out the night before. The candle that she must light and place in the window.

The candle that would signal Dismas, Gabriel's older brother, that she would elope with him instead.

Judith hesitated. How could she do it? If she ran away with Dismas and they were caught, they would be stoned to death as adulterers. When her quivering fingers touched the candle, she drew back, terrified. She tiptoed into the hall to listen for the steady breathing of her parents, her older brother and his wife, and her two younger sisters. Relieved that no one was stirring, she paused by the lamp outside her parents' door and caught a whiff of the flame's oily scent.

She thought of Reuben, her brother who had died a year earlier at age four. He should have been here too. But he was gone—because of the Romans. Because they had murdered him as sure as she was standing here. Her throat tightened, as it did whenever she remembered Reuben and how his death had occurred. Fighting back tears, she returned to her room and sat down on the bed.

Oh God, Oh God, what should I do? She wiped sweat from her forehead and groped for the candle again. Her hands shook like those of a leper. She glanced out the window to see the stars glittering in the silent purple sky, beckoning her. If Dismas didn't come before the sun rose, she would be forced to marry Gabriel, the man her father had chosen for her a year earlier. The man she did not love, but couldn't bear to hurt.

When she again reached for the candle, she quickly withdrew her hand. Her passion for Dismas had so consumed her these past few months that she never questioned her decision to run away with him. Until now. Gabriel offered her the security she had always known as the well-educated daughter of a wealthy spice trader. She considered him handsome in an understated, approachable way. Not only did his boyishly endearing features frame the most serene brown eyes she had ever seen, but he was also a gentleman and a successful merchant like his father, with his own food and clothing market.

Dismas, on the other hand, had shunned business to become a stonemason and to join the *Sicarii*, the dagger-wielding Zealots intent on overthrowing Roman rule. Suddenly the thought of abandoning her learning and comforts for a vagabond life in the desert made her gasp, as if winded after a footrace. *It is not too late to back out,* she told herself. But how could she? As kind and good as Gabriel was, she felt nothing for him.

She swallowed hard and buried her face in her hands. Tears stung her eyes; she struggled to catch her breath. Looking up, she peered through the gray-black darkness and made out the candle on the nightstand. She thought of the girls who accepted loveless matches as if they were mandated by God, and she thought of the Jews—her own family included—who had nothing but contempt for the Romans but did nothing about them.

She could no longer live with such hypocrisy. With the wedding only hours away, she had to flee what she feared most—a passionless marriage. *I must go and fight the Romans with Dismas,* she told herself. *In his arms I become the woman I long to be.* The thought of making love to him calmed her trembling. Her heart leapt. She grimaced and reached for the candle. This time she seized it and held it tightly. Tiptoeing into the hall again, she approached the lamp, lit the candle from its flame and then quietly returned to her room.

She strode to the window and placed the candle on the ledge; then she went back to the bed and reached under it. After retrieving the long rope that she had hidden there, she returned to the window, tied the rope to its frame and peered out. Where was Dismas? She moved away and rummaged through her bag. Made of homespun cloth, it was full of clothes from the oversized wooden chest in the corner of the room. Her mind was full of questions. *Had Dismas reneged on his promise to elope with her? Had bandits robbed and beaten him?*

Assured that she had packed everything, Judith lifted the bag onto the bed and sat to brush her long chestnut hair. Comforted by the scent of pine, a gift from the trees along the street, she heard footsteps below. *Dismas!* She threw the brush into the bag and ran to the window. His gaze was directed upward, his hair windblown, a faint smile on his ruggedly handsome face. A shudder ran through her; she gripped the ledge, hesitating.

He waved. "Please hurry!"

Judith froze, unable to bring herself to climb down the rope. How could she betray her betrothed, shame her father, ruin her mother's wedding plans, disrupt the lives of two families and more than one hundred guests? But then, as she gazed into Dismas' expectant eyes, she wondered, *How can I* not *go with him?*

He was pacing nervously. Before she could decide what to do, he seized the rope and began to climb up, his muscular arms moving in tandem with his sure steps on the wall. In an instant, he had entered her room. She brushed away a tear and put a finger to her lips.

He met her gaze and whispered, "What's wrong?"

"I am not sure I can do this," she said.

He studied her, as if admiring her glinting hazel eyes, and when he spoke his voice was low. "After all our planning, are you going to back out now? What about the anguish we've known under the Roman fist?"

She turned away. "What about Gabriel's anguish?"

"He'll get over it." Dismas reached for her arm. "But if you marry him, I never will. And neither will you."

Taking the measure of his sculpted athlete's frame and tight-set jaw, she said, "I am afraid of the desert, of what might happen to us."

"That's why you need me. I'm strong enough for both of us, and where I want to take you is the only place worth going." He said nothing more, but took her in his arms, whispering her name.

Then he was kissing her, igniting a flame that rose from the soles of her feet, up her legs, through her torso, to the place where their lips met. His sweet scent, combined with the pine and traces of lemon and hibiscus from the garden below, enveloped her in what seemed like a dream. The night became luminous, as if possessed by a hidden radiance that only he controlled. She held perfectly still, savoring each shared heartbeat.

Her rage at the Romans surfaced like oil in a boiling cauldron of water. *Dismas understands that love is more than doing your parents' bidding, and that freedom must be fought for.* She saw him as an idealist, a man on a righteous mission. That is why he had volunteered to go to the caves at Qumran, near the Dead Sea, to serve under the fierce and heroic Zealot commander, Barabbas.

The first splashes of dawn were reflecting pale light into the room. She gazed into Dismas' steely dark eyes, which were focused like a warrior's. A thud from the hall interrupted her thoughts. Dismas tensed, shifting his weight onto the balls of his feet, preparing for a fight. After she waved him toward the wooden chest, he lifted the lid and ducked inside. She stuffed her bag under the bed and slid beneath the blanket, pretending to be asleep. Her heart throbbing, she expected her brother or father to storm into the room.

Perhaps this is an omen. An omen of the trouble that will fall on us. If her burly brother searched the room and found Dismas, the two would fight. Her father, Nathan, would rush to Gideon's aid and help him to prevail. She and Dismas would be publicly humiliated and severely punished, if not stoned. Not even Gabriel would want her then.

But no sound followed the thud. Then there were plodding footsteps. Were they headed toward her room? She braced for a confrontation, but the footsteps stopped. Her heart beat easier as she realized what had happened: Her sixty-six-year-old father had gotten up to relieve himself, as he often did in the early morning. Lying perfectly still, she waited until the soft, barefooted steps signaled that her father had gone back to bed.

Dismas poked his head out of the chest, glanced around the room, and then dashed to the window. Judith was close behind. One leg over the ledge, he paused to face her and said, "As a Zealot I am determined to return Israel to the true worship of God. I've never met a woman who shares my two great passions—love and freedom." He cupped her face in his hands. "I would never pressure you to come with me, but I want you to. I want you to be my wife and fight for freedom with me."

She could not resist the wildness she saw in his eyes. It was as if a dam had broken and a river was sweeping her downstream on whitewater rapids. She had tried to forget about Dismas, but she could not help herself. At twenty-one Dismas was four years older than she, and had the confidence and life experience that she lacked. His strength made her more secure than money ever could. She pulled the bag from under the bed. *I must go with him,* she told herself, reaffirming her passion for the Zealot cause and Dismas. "You are my future now, Dismas," she whispered under her breath. "Promise you'll never disappoint me."

The first rays of sun were painting the horizon pink as a cock crowed in the distance. When Judith saw Dismas on the ground, she tossed her bag down, took the rope and boosted herself over the window ledge. Her feet dangled precariously until they found the outer wall and pushed against it. Not daring to breathe, the rope chafing her hands, she leaned back as a burning ache shot from her shoulders to her fingertips. Suddenly her foot slipped and her knee hit the wall, cutting the skin.

"Who's there?" Her father's demanding voice came from his window. She froze, dangling against the stone.

"Hurry!" Dismas said.

She could hear people rushing into her room.

"Go ahead and jump! I'll catch you." Dismas held out his arms.

She fought to hang on, her body swaying wildly from side to side as she slid down the rope. As her feet neared the ground, she let go and Dismas caught her. "Let's go!" He tucked her bag under his arm and took her hand. She broke into a sprint, pulled forward by Dismas, who was guiding her toward a heavily loaded horse that she could see up the street.

"Judith!"

She heard her father shouting but did not look back, the image of his slender frame and stern features etched in her mind. He sounded frantic, desperate. Dismas boosted her onto the horse, threw her the bag and then climbed up himself.

"Judith, come back!"

"Please, Judith, don't do this!"

Recognizing the voices of her sister Dinah and her mother, she stole a backward glance. Expressions of terror creased their still sleepy faces. Her brother Gideon had flown down the stairs and out the door.

"Come back with my sister!" Gideon's deep voice boomed as he sprinted to within feet of the horse, cursing Dismas.

Judith closed her eyes tightly, determined to shut out all doubt. She clung to Dismas as the horse began to gallop into the morning, leaving her family and their futile shouts behind.

CHAPTER THREE

THE POUNDING ON THE FRONT DOOR WOKE GABRIEL BEN ZEBULUN WITH A START. Certain that someone was breaking into the house, he rolled his lanky frame out of bed, grabbed his tunic and the dagger that he kept for protection, and ran toward the door, dressing on the way. His father met him in the broad central courtyard that led to the front. A large man with a nimbus of white hair around his bald head, Zebulun's face was contorted with alarm.

Gabriel recognized the voice of the man outside. Nathan, Judith's father, was shouting that he must talk to them, that something terrible had happened. When Gabriel opened the door, Nathan burst in, red-faced, hands gripping his heart, an anguished expression on his strong features. Without taking a breath, he related how Dismas had run away with Judith. The two had met when Nathan hired Dismas to repair his courtyard.

Gabriel felt the color drain from his sun-bronzed face and made no attempt to hide his shock and dismay. His father led Nathan into the sitting room and offered him a chair. Gabriel paced back and forth, head throbbing, feelings numb. "How can this be true?" As he struggled to grasp the terrible news, his hazel eyes became teary. "You gave me your daughter's hand. Today is our wedding day. Does your word mean nothing?"

Zebulun could barely contain his rage. "You knew that Dismas was estranged from us, yet you hired him! How could you?"

"I needed a good stonemason, and Dismas is one of the best in Jerusalem." Nathan fidgeted nervously. "I had no idea that he was seducing Judith. If I had known, I would have fired him immediately." He buried his face in his hands. "This was supposed to be the happiest day of my life. Now it's the saddest."

While the three men were discussing the appalling turn of events, Gabriel's slightly rotund mother came in, her gray hair tied back. "What is all this commotion about?" When Nathan told her, she appeared faint. "What are we going to do? We have more than a hundred guests coming for the wedding feast."

Gabriel's mind raced furiously. *Why would Judith do this to me? How could she be so cruel?* He had sensed her reluctance to marry him, but he assumed that she would love him after the wedding. The power of his infatuation allowed him no other conclusion.

Since his father had introduced him to Judith a year ago, she had consumed his thoughts. He dreamed of their wedding night, of freely expressing his love for her with body and soul. He longed to have her as his wife, to greet her each morning and come home to her at night, to build her a spacious home and to father her children. But now his dreams lashed at him like a sandstorm. And who had initiated this lashing? His own brother!

Gabriel abruptly slipped the dagger inside the belt of his tunic and hurried toward the door. Nathan shouted after him. "Where are you going?"

He neither answered nor looked back. He fled up the street, his sandaled feet barely touching the dusty stones. To his relief, few people were out that early. As he moved faster and faster, desperate to get away, he berated himself for failing to win Judith's heart.

The streets seemed rougher and the hills steeper, as if conspiring to trap him. Gabriel turned north toward the Temple, drawn by the first blasts of the ram's horn, yet he was oblivious to the sound. He kept running until his lungs burned, his legs grew weak, and the labyrinth of streets grew longer and more inescapable.

Images of Dismas flooded his mind: their footraces and wrestling matches, their archery duels and mock gladiator contests as boys. Whether studying, working, or playing, they were sparring partners constantly pitted against each other. And Dismas, the older and stronger, usually won. He always got his way, the favored one. Gabriel slowed to a walk. He had received little recognition or affirmation until Dismas left home, and by then it was too late; his image of himself was irreparably damaged.

Still he craved approval, hungering for it like a beggar invited to a feast but not allowed to eat. Succeeding in his father's business became his only outlet for satisfying the craving. Dismas was better at working with his hands, and it galled him to see his younger brother excel in the family trade. When Dismas left home to join the Zealot resistance, Gabriel wondered if he had done it because he was no longer the favored son.

Did he run away with Judith to get revenge? Was this Dismas' last desperate attempt to assert his dominance? To Gabriel, the reasons didn't matter, just the rejection and shame. Judith was the only woman he had ever loved; without her, life lost all meaning. He might as well be dead.

Gabriel was nearing the Temple Mount, its massive platform rising high above the city, its majestic courts and altars surrounded by a sixty-foot marble wall that, even in the gray of dawn, shone dazzlingly white. If he jumped from there, it would be his end. He looked up at the Temple's enormous Corinthian columns, filigreed with gold on top of the capitals, and thought, *What better place to end my life than here? I would rather die than go home to face the wedding guests.* Everything that gave meaning to his life had been taken from him—the woman he loved, his honor, his hope for the future. Today the holiest place in Israel served only as a reminder of God's indifference to his pain. His self-inflicted death here, resulting from the treachery that had been visited upon him, would publicly embarrass God for allowing it. All of Jerusalem would see a Jew spurn a weak and indifferent deity!

The blasts of the ram's horn rang in his ears. The Gates of Hulda stood open; lepers and beggars were clustered on the ground nearby, still asleep. A few pilgrims were already entering the Court of the Gentiles with doves, goats, and lambs for sacrifice. He was determined to climb to the walkway atop the wall, where he had seen trumpeters stand during festivals.

Gabriel watched as a family of five, pushing a cart loaded with wheat, dates, pomegranates, olives, figs, and grapes, headed for the gates. He followed close behind, as if he were a family member, and once inside the Temple's outer court, strode up the stairs to the walkway, undetected by priests on their way to assist with the sacrifices.

Roman soldiers patrolled the walkway and policed the gates at the bottom, but at this early hour, Gabriel saw no one. He climbed onto the ledge and looked down. Then he withdrew his dagger and held its tip against his stomach. *One step and my misery will be over,* he told himself, rocking precariously on the balls of his feet.

He was breathing hard, lips quivering, heart pounding. He gazed at Jerusalem's dusty streets and rounded hills, and at its one- and two-story stone houses, tawny like a lion's coat. Glancing down, he became dizzy and fought to keep his balance. When he finally stabilized, he bent his knees, ready to jump. Then he noticed the rising sun. Streaks of red were blazing on the horizon as if enormous torches had been flung across the sky. Gabriel hesitated. *If I jump, I'll never see another sunrise. How can I give up all this?*

The answer throbbed in his mind: He could give it up because life without Judith was no life at all. The rejection churned in his stomach like a sickness that only death could cure. He whispered farewell to the gentle morning, rocked back on his heels, and bent his knees, prepared to leap. But before he could spring forward, he heard a shout behind him.

"Don't!"

Startled, Gabriel turned to see a heavyset man, slightly taller than medium height, with shoulder-length white hair and kindly dark eyes. The man was wearing a purple robe and a black turban. Around his wrists he had the cords of phylacteries—the small leather boxes that contained verses of scripture. Obviously a Pharisee, the man reached out a hand. Gabriel froze. *Just jump!* Yet the hand beckoned, trembling, stretched to its limits.

"You there! Get down at once!"

Gabriel looked to his left. A hefty Roman soldier had rounded the corner on patrol. He was running toward Gabriel, yelling in Greek. Startled, Gabriel stepped back, putting him within the Pharisee's grasp.

The Pharisee seized his tunic and yanked. Gabriel fell onto the walkway, losing control of his dagger as he lay sprawled across the rough stone surface. His skin burned as he scraped it from his elbows to his ribs and knees. He scrambled to his feet, scarlet-faced as he picked up the dagger and hid it inside his tunic, backpedaling. The soldier bore down on him, red and gold regalia flapping with each step. He grabbed Gabriel and twisted an arm behind his back. "What kind of stunt were you trying to pull?" The soldier wrestled Gabriel toward the stairs. "I hope you enjoy Pilate's prison because that's where you're going."

Gabriel's shoulder throbbed with pain, as if someone were beating it with a hammer. Afraid his arm would break, he drew a quick breath, dug in his heels, and slammed his body against the soldier, stomping on the Roman's foot with his full weight. Stunned, the soldier let go and Gabriel began to run, but after only a few steps he felt something sharp hit his shin. As he stumbled and fell, he realized that the soldier had tripped him with his javelin. The soldier then pounced on him and held the javelin to Gabriel's neck. "I'll teach you to—"

The Pharisee rushed over and grabbed the Roman's arm. "Please don't hurt him! My son was just admiring the sunrise." He was yelling in Greek and trying to pull the soldier off. "I'll make sure it never happens again."

The soldier wrestled Gabriel upright and held the tip of the javelin against Gabriel's back. "I *know* it won't happen again—not where he's going."

Gabriel stood still, amazed at the Pharisee's lie.

"There has been enough trouble between the Jews and Romans," the Pharisee said. "I want peace, but you will have a fight on your hands if you throw my son into prison."

The soldier spun Gabriel around and then eyed the Pharisee scornfully. "Why should I show your boy mercy after he nearly broke my foot? He's a troublemaker and must be taught a lesson."

"Please, sir, he has never been in trouble before. He's a good boy and I will make sure he stays away from here."

The soldier glared at Gabriel and then turned back to the Pharisee.

"All right," the soldier said. Then he pushed Gabriel aside and began to walk away. "But if I catch your boy climbing here again, I'll show no mercy."

Gabriel dusted himself off and turned to run away, his neck and ears red with shame. He had forgotten why he wanted to jump; all that mattered was fleeing from the man who had seen him try.

The Pharisee called after him in Aramaic, "I saved your life and lied to keep you out of prison. You owe me an explanation!"

Gabriel wanted to keep going, but the urgency of the man's words stopped him. He faced the Pharisee and said, "I didn't ask for your help. You had no right to stop me from jumping."

The Pharisee approached him, brow furrowed, close-set auburn eyes flashing. "You were about to commit a grievous sin. It was my duty to stop you."

"Was it your duty to lie for me?"

"Of course not. But I could no more let you get thrown into a filthy Roman jail than I could watch you kill yourself."

Gabriel heard compassion in the Pharisee's voice and this surprised him. He had always thought that the Pharisees lived up to the meaning of their name—"separated ones." They avoided contact with anyone who didn't strictly obey Jewish law and they bitterly opposed the Sadducees, the Temple priests whose compromises with the Romans and whose unorthodox beliefs offended them. He knew the Pharisees as severe men who cherished their privileged status in the Jewish caste system.

The Pharisees prided themselves on being members of the *chaburah* or brotherhood. Obsessed with the minutiae of God's law, they strove to honor every regulation—the Sabbath, the dietary laws, the requirements of ritual purity—and to monitor who complied and who did not. Gabriel respected the Pharisees' learning and dedication, but he saw them as wearisome meddlers. This man's sensitivity took him aback. "Why would a Pharisee care about someone he doesn't even know?" Gabriel asked.

"I *do* know you." The Pharisee reached out and squeezed Gabriel's shoulders. "Are you not Zebulun's son? You are the mirror image of your father; I have known him since before you were born."

Gabriel's mouth gaped open in disbelief. "Who *are* you?"

The Pharisee extended his hand. "I am Nicodemus ben Gorion, a member of the Sanhedrin. I often seek quiet on this wall before beginning my duties in the Temple."

"The Sanhedrin!" Gabriel stepped back in awe. He revered the Sanhedrin as Judaism's Supreme Court. Composed of distinguished priests, scribes, Pharisees, and their elitist rivals, the Sadducees, the Sanhedrin's seventy members ruled on the fine points of Jewish law. Not only did they determine the verdicts and punishments of those accused of violations, but they also advised Caiaphas, the high priest, and Pontius Pilate, the Roman governor, on religious matters.

Those who served on the Sanhedrin were often wealthy and always influential. Gabriel hesitantly took Nicodemus' hand and said, "Yes, I am Gabriel, Zebulun's son. It doesn't surprise me that you know my father. He has many important friends." Gabriel paused and stared at the ground for a moment; then he met the Pharisee's eyes. "It's partly because of my father's friends that I wanted to jump."

"How could they make you so desperate?" Nicodemus asked.

Gabriel again turned to go, ashamed.

Nicodemus tightened his grip on Gabriel's hand. "Sometimes problems seem unbearable. May I help?"

Gabriel felt tears burning in his eyes. He had attempted to end his life and never expected to meet such a kind man. He didn't want to talk because he feared breaking down. But the sincerity of Nicodemus' concern emboldened him, and he decided to try. "I lost the woman I loved," Gabriel said, clearing his throat and withdrawing his hand. "She has run off with my brother. Now I have nothing to live for." Gaining confidence, he took a deep breath and his story came pouring out—how he had dreamed for months of marrying Judith, and how she had run away with Dismas and left Gabriel to face their wedding guests alone. "Can you understand why I want to die? How can anyone recover from such humiliation?"

Nicodemus didn't answer right away. When he finally spoke, his voice was reassuring. "You have suffered a deep wound, my son. I can understand why you feel your life is over. But what if it is just beginning? What if this terrible loss takes you where you never dreamed of going? I know a great comfort for heartbreak. If you let me, I will share it with you."

Gabriel suddenly felt hot, as if he were standing in the midday sun. He wiped his tears on his tunic and said, "I have nothing to lose."

It was still quiet, and Nicodemus spoke softly but with deep emotion. "The trouble with being a Pharisee is that I am expected to live the law perfectly, but, of course, no one can. Even the wisest of us has questions and makes mistakes; I have made many, especially in my marriage. I was miserable as a Pharisee—and as a husband and father—until I met a Galilean rabbi named Jesus of Nazareth. Late one night I spoke at length with him, and he told me how to be born anew. It happens through opening one's heart to God's love."

Gabriel waved a hand dismissively. "I don't want to hear anything about God ever again."

Nicodemus waited for him to calm down. "Please hear me out. This rabbi describes God's love in a new way. By meditating on this love daily, I have found a depth of serenity that I never imagined possible. It's serenity not only about my own life, but also about a glorious future for our people, a future without war. I am willing to explain further, but only if you promise not to tell anyone that I have shared these insights with you. Jesus' teachings have offended many of the Pharisees. If they found out about our friendship, I would be thrown off the Sanhedrin and shunned."

Gabriel studied Nicodemus. "My customers from Galilee have told me about this Jesus of Nazareth. They say that the masses flock to hear him by the sea and that he preaches about a coming reign of peace." He paused to consider the man's words. "I'll keep your secret. But tell me—how could this rabbi make such a difference?"

Nicodemus looked from left to right and then leaned closer. "He is like no other rabbi I have ever known. He speaks truth, not just words. When I meditate on his teachings, I feel God near."

Gabriel shook his head and frowned. "I have lived as a faithful Jew and don't deserve this heartbreak. I meant to jump off the Temple, to get even with God."

Nicodemus nodded, acknowledging the gravity of Gabriel's words. "Jesus discusses heartbreak but without blaming God. He emphasizes that in this imperfect world, where the sun rises and the rain falls on the evil and the good, heartbreak is inevitable. Relationships end, tragedies strike, dreams turn to ashes, sickness and death come to us all. As a result, everyone suffers. But if we treat our suffering as sacred and learn to trust because of it, we can become new people, for suffering exists to perfect us in love. This is true not only for individuals but also for our nation."

Gabriel made an angry face. "I don't want perfection—I want Judith back."

Nicodemus put an arm around him and began to walk toward the stairs. "You must go after her. Murder and insurrection will ruin her life and destroy our people. Jesus of Nazareth challenges the ways of the Zealots. His growing spiritual movement is our people's best hope for freedom and peace."

They went down the stairs, with Nicodemus leading. The singing and shouting that reverberated throughout the Court of the Israelites was carried on air that smelled of incense, roasting meat, and popping fat. The Temple was coming to life. Money changers were at their booths; pilgrims were bringing in their sheep, goats, and doves; priests were leading the bleating and cooing animals toward the altar.

Gabriel followed Nicodemus into the Court of the Gentiles. Surrounded by the surging crowd, the Pharisee pointed toward the Gates of Hulda and said, "Before you ride after Judith, you must go home. It will not be easy, but you have no other choice. By facing the wedding guests, you will win their respect—and your own. It takes more courage to live with suffering than to leap from the Temple wall. If you listen, the pain will become your wisest teacher, and you will find new life beyond it."

Gabriel forced a smile. "You speak with deep conviction. I hope you are right."

Nicodemus drew him close and lowered his voice. "My conviction comes from the heart, where Jesus of Nazareth changed me. He teaches that love, not the Zealots' violence, is the hope of the future. He is gaining followers daily, and many of us believe he is the Messiah. Soon I will go to Galilee to see him. Perhaps you can come with me."

Gabriel ran a hand through his hair, mulling over Nicodemus' invitation. He had heard that the rabbi called Jesus had offended some Pharisees in Jerusalem, that he had performed healings, and that the Romans feared his growing popularity. Jesus' opposition to the Zealots made Gabriel eager to help him. This murderous group had corrupted his brother. Now Dismas had run off with Judith and ruined Gabriel's life. He wanted to settle the score. Perhaps the movement that Jesus was leading was the only force powerful enough to stop the Zealots. He said to Nicodemus, "I will travel with you to Galilee, but first I must go after my betrothed." He reached inside his tunic and withdrew the dagger. "And I'll take this with me." He narrowed his eyes. "Dismas is not the only one who knows how to use one of these."

Nicodemus held up a hand, his expression grim. "Violence is justified only when you must defend yourself or another. Jesus teaches that those who live by the sword will die by the sword."

Gabriel studied the dagger for a moment. With the words of caution echoing in his thoughts, he put the dagger away and shook Nicodemus' hand. He thanked him, said good-bye, and hurried toward the gate, squinting against the sun's expanding brilliance. At the street he turned south and walked briskly through Jerusalem, now bustling with merchants, tradesmen, and pilgrims. He would face his parents and all their friends unafraid. It was not his fault that Judith had run away. She should be ashamed, not he. As for his rage at her and Dismas, it would embolden him to go after them, but he knew that he must control it or the rage would destroy him.

Entering his neighborhood, he found the familiarity of the modest homes comforting, and his thoughts turned to Nicodemus. The possibility of seeing him again and learning from him set Gabriel's heart racing. As he turned onto his street, he thought of going to meet the rabbi from Nazareth, and hope rose in his breast.

CHAPTER FOUR

JUDITH HAD NEVER RIDDEN A HORSE BEFORE, LET ALONE GALLOPED ON ONE. She clung to Dismas and held her breath between strides, her heart pounding drumbeats in her ears. As they galloped through Jerusalem, he didn't say a word. She pressed her cheek against his back as they sped through the Tyropoeon Valley and passed the Pool of Siloam.

Everything is going to be all right, she told herself, squeezing him tighter. But she was choking on dust, hungry and exhausted. She had to fight the urge to turn back. Only the feel of Dismas' strong body and the thought of making love to him kept her looking ahead.

When they reached the Judean Desert, he slowed the supply-laden horse. Glistening with sweat, its charcoal coat appeared as black as midnight. Judith sat up and arched her back, the sound of the galloping hoofs still echoing in her mind. The horse was walking now, but her legs had become so accustomed to conforming to its body that she couldn't relax them, and her arms ached from squeezing Dismas' waist.

She looked around and gasped. Never had she seen such jagged hillsides, the land pockmarked as if diseased with leprosy. Rocks—from enormous boulders that dwarfed the horse to pebbles sharp enough to cut leather—filled the landscape. Judith closed her eyes to escape the desert's incandescent monotony. *What have I done? How will we survive in this barrenness?*

She tried to console herself, but the memory of her mother's anguished face tormented her. She couldn't get her father's shouts or her brother's grasping hands out of her thoughts. Everything had happened so fast—the rendezvous with Dismas, the escape from the house, the ride into the desert. Now she couldn't go back. Her stomach felt as if it had stones in it, clashing and grinding against one another.

She opened her eyes and blinked to clear them of dust. Only when she thought of her four-year-old brother Reuben did her stomach begin to settle. A year earlier, she and Reuben had been returning from the market near the Temple Mount when they took a shortcut through an alley across from the Antonia Fortress, the stronghold of Roman military power. As they crossed back into the street, a horse-drawn chariot carrying two Roman soldiers sped around a blind corner, and Reuben, instead of stepping backward, ran ahead. The driver didn't even try to stop as he crushed Reuben. She scooped up her brother's mangled and bloody body and ran home. He was dead before she got there. She would never forget the cruel arrogance of the Romans who ran over him. *How dare they treat Judeans like maggots!* She shook a fist. *How dare they!* Her resolve to avenge Reuben's murder became a sacred vow.

Glancing around again, Judith saw the landscape as less threatening. Suddenly the horse came to an abrupt stop. As Dismas let the tired animal rest, she thought about Gabriel. How could she have married him? He wouldn't understand her rage. It was better to betray him than Reuben. Going through with the wedding would have been a sin against her murdered brother—and against her own dreams of justice and love. She tightened her hold on Dismas' waist. *It doesn't matter how foreign this place is or what threats I face; I am with Dismas now, and we will drive the Romans from our land!*

At Dismas' urging, the horse began to walk again, and they kept going until the road descended sharply into the desert. Then he stopped the horse and helped her down. She sat on an oblong boulder as he gave the horse water from a wineskin and offered Judith bread and cheese. When they had finished eating, Dismas took the reins and said, "We must find a place to rest." His words came as a relief to her. After waking so early, she was exhausted and craved sleep. He helped her back onto the horse and led it up onto a ledge that overlooked the road. When the path leveled off, he spotted a thicket of scruffy pines. "This will be a safe place," he said, beginning to unpack the horse.

Judith pitched in and spread two blankets on the ground. After Dismas had laid the remaining supplies on them, he tied the horse to a tree nearby. Before he returned, she was asleep.

More than an hour later, Judith woke when Dismas shook her arm and whispered, "I think I hear hoofbeats." Concern clouded his face; determination flashed in his eyes. He took her hand and led her behind a large boulder, where they hid to watch the road below. The hoofbeats grew louder, and in time a group of men on horses approached. Judith's heart was beating as fast as the hoofs, her breathing strained and shallow. Gabriel, along with his father and hers, and her swarthy, heavy-set brother Gideon were just below them.

Dismas pressed a finger to his lips and pulled her behind the boulder as the horses passed. "What should we do?" she asked.

He kept his voice steady. "We'll camp here tonight and then head for the Dead Sea, near Qumran, where Barabbas and the Zealots are hiding. There are so many caves there—no one will ever find us."

When the men were gone, Dismas began to gather wood for a fire. Judith arranged some stones in a circle and, still tired, lay down and closed her eyes. By the time he returned with his arms full, the sun was setting. She placed the wood inside the circle as darkness descended, and with it, the chill of the night. Shivering, she moved close to him as he got the fire going.

"We're finally together," she whispered, leaning against him. He turned and kissed her tenderly, his earthy scent as intoxicating as fine wine. She felt him against her and, aching to receive him, reached beneath his tunic to stroke his back. But when she nudged him to lie down, he gently pushed her away.

"Not until we're married," he said. "Remember, I am a Zealot. We must obey the law."

Judith sat up and moved away from him. "But how can we marry? There are no rabbis in the desert."

He took her hands and stood up. "We don't need a rabbi, only each other and a sacred pledge of our love." He gazed down into her eyes. "From this day forward, I want you to be my wife. Do you promise to be faithful and honor me as your husband?"

She froze, her legs paralyzed beneath her. As she met his gaze, she thought of how much she had given up—the dignity of a public wedding, the breaking of the ceremonial glass, the cheers of the guests, the dancing and wine and song. Even more, she thought of Gabriel. Of the secure life he could have provided her. Of the sadness and confusion he must be feeling. It all gave her pause.

Dismas wanted a commitment, but marrying him would mean renouncing forever everything that had given her life meaning—her family, her learning, her social standing. Was Dismas worth it? She searched his eyes for the security and closeness she craved. Her legs still would not move, and she worried that he would hear her heart booming and sense her fear.

To her relief, she finally glimpsed sincerity in his eyes, the same yearning for lasting love that burned within her. She remembered why she had come this far—the hope of happiness that he offered. A happiness that would heal her of the guilt of not saving Reuben. A happiness that she could attain by helping the Zealots defeat the Romans.

Dismas gently squeezed her hands. The strength of his hands assured her. These were the leathery, callused hands of a warrior and tender lover, and she decided that she must completely give herself to him. The feeling returned to her legs, and she pulled herself up, never looking away.

"I promise," she said, her voice shaking with emotion.

"And I promise to be your husband, to cherish and protect you always."

He kissed her gently and she closed her eyes, secure in his arms. Savoring the kiss, she didn't want it to end. When it did, she gazed up and studied him intently, as he studied her, nodding his satisfaction. She felt his reluctance when he finally pulled away and dug into the saddlebags for the food he had packed. Judith smiled when he laid out some bread, cheese, figs, and olives, and poured two cups of wine from the skin he had brought.

"You prepared a feast," she said as he joined her on the blanket near the fire.

Dismas withdrew his long, slightly curved dagger from the sheaf on his belt and sliced some cheese. "It's not every day that a man marries the woman he loves. You deserve a real feast, with guests and music and dancing. I hope to give you that"—he admired his dagger briefly—"as soon as we drive the Romans from our land." He handed the dagger to her, which she pushed away. But he insisted that she hold it, and eventually she did take it from him. The dagger was heavier than it looked, its blade as sharp as cut glass. Examining it made her feel both terrified and powerful.

"Have you used this on the Romans?" Judith asked, not really wanting to hear the answer.

"Yes. And I plan to use it as often as necessary until we triumph. The dagger is the only language they understand."

"After what they did to my brother, they deserve the dagger."

"Until we drive the Romans from our land," he said, toasting her with a cup of sweet wine. She took a sip and began to eat the bread and cheese and olives. But before she could finish, he reached over and ran the back of his hand down her cheek. His touch felt hot, as if a flame were burning inside his fingertips, igniting her desire and reaching into her very bones.

When she diverted her eyes shyly, he rose on one knee and took her face in his hands, kissing her with abandon. The night lay still, the only sound an occasional pop or crackle from the fire. His dusty scent blended with the smoke to create a kind of desert incense. Judith received his kisses as if she had no need of air, as if their breathing and heartbeats had become one. The night sky was an illuminated dome, its glimmering stars reflecting her joy, as the silver moon watched with envy.

She leaned into him, her movements fluid, choreographed by the power that seeded the clouds with rain and turned winter to spring. In that moment, her concerns about her parents, the Romans, the future, all faded into the crevices between the desert stones. Only Dismas was real. Lost in his arms, she wanted to remain there forever, for she had never felt so loved. As Judith gave herself fully to him, she prayed that he felt the same and told him so. But her words sounded strangely discordant, as if they had betrayed the sacredness of the moment by sullying it with human speech.

Afterward she sat by the fire, wrapped in his arms, staring into the luminous desert night. She glimpsed a pair of eyes, just beyond the flames, staring back. Burrowing closer to Dismas, she pointed. "Something's out there." As Dismas rose, she heard a growl. The eyes began to move toward them, in a semicircle around the fire. Now she saw clearly what was lurking in the dark. A leopard.

Its steely eyes riveted on them, its fangs bared, the leopard appeared monstrous and enraged. Dismas sprang toward the fire and grabbed a thick tree branch from the flames, one end of it burning like a torch. He held his ground, crouching low, and brandished the flaming branch at the leopard.

The leopard turned and fled.

Dismas came back, threw down the branch and held her again. "Don't worry. It's gone."

She clung to him, her spine taut.

She relaxed as he kissed her tenderly. "I'll keep watch," he said, pulling away. "You rest."

Lying there, staring into the starlit sky, she sensed that she had crossed into a new land—a land from which she could not return. Dismas had brought her to this wilderness, this desolate place of bliss and terror, in which she had found her womanhood. Now she was totally dependent on him.

Shuddering at the thought, she felt panic sweep over her. Only when she stole a glimpse of his eyes and saw the passion burning there did the panic subside. As she fell asleep, she prayed that the passion wouldn't prove more dangerous than the leopard he'd scared off only moments ago.

CHAPTER FIVE

WHEN GABRIEL SAW THE LIGHTNING, HE GRABBED NICODEMUS BEN GORION'S ARM AND STEERED HIM TOWARD THE PROTECTION OF THE HILLSIDE. They were traveling to Nain, in Lower Galilee. After Gabriel had failed to find Judith and bring her back, he was glad for an excuse to get out of Jerusalem. Walking with a cane, Nicodemus stumbled momentarily on the rocky ground. Gabriel steadied him and then took the old man's bag, carrying it with his own. A glance at the darkening sky told him that they had to move fast. If they didn't, fist-size hailstones could pelt them or they could get swept away by a flash flood, common during Galilean winters.

They needed to shelter. Gabriel regretted that they had taken four days to travel from Jerusalem to Galilee through Samaria. It usually took three. Though spry for his age, Nicodemus walked slowly. They had hoped to reach Nain by nightfall. Now, at twilight, it was impossible.

Gabriel knew that Nicodemus' old friend Simon ben Ephraim would be worried about them. The two Pharisees had met during their rabbinical training in Jerusalem and remained friends. Simon had invited

Nicodemus to a meal he was hosting the next afternoon for Jesus of Nazareth. Thankfully Nain was now less than five miles away.

The gusting winds whipped up a cloud of dust, but no storm could dampen Gabriel's burning need. He would meet the Galilean rabbi and ask for his help against the Zealots. He believed that Jesus might be able to sway large groups to stop Dismas and Judith from causing a slaughter of the Jews. And if the tide turned against the violence, perhaps Judith would see her folly and come back to Gabriel.

He cupped one hand over his eyes; with the other he held on to Nicodemus. Massive clouds now rolled in, turning the sky almost totally dark. When the rain started, it came down in torrents. As Gabriel nudged Nicodemus toward a cave in the hillside, he caught a whiff of wet dust, pungent and arresting. Fierce winds created updrafts that sent them stumbling forward. Gabriel fought for his balance and led Nicodemus toward the cave. "You go ahead," the old man said. "I will be fine."

Gabriel clung to him. "No. I won't leave you." His words were drowned out by thunderclaps so loud that he felt them resound in his bones. In the dim light he could see beads of water streaming down Nicodemus' cheeks, drenching his long white beard. Gabriel pressed on through the storm, head down, one hand shielding his face from the downpour, the other leading Nicodemus. After they reached the cave, they huddled inside and looked out, protected first from the driving rain and then from the pounding hail.

By the time the storm ended, night had fallen. Gabriel reached into his bag for a dry tunic, put it on, and helped Nicodemus change into another robe. Meanwhile the sky was clearing and the moon had begun to rise. Gabriel spread out his mat, withdrew bread and cheese from the bag, and offered it to Nicodemus, who appeared exhausted.

"It has been a long journey," Gabriel said. "You must rest, rabbi."

"I am too old for these travels, my son. I would not have come this far except to see Jesus."

"I'm eager to meet him because some of his teachings perplex me."

Nicodemus took the bread and cheese. "When I first met him, I was also perplexed."

"I keep wondering how his teachings can make a difference to me personally." As Gabriel spoke the words, he hoped that Nicodemus would answer a deeper question: *How can I ever trust again after such a crushing betrayal?*

Nicodemus glanced up at the night sky, now clear of clouds, and then turned to fix his gaze on his friend. "Jesus tells us that if we want to be his disciples, we must be willing to suffer and die for him. This teaching sounds difficult because we want our lives to be easier, not harder. But the teaching contains a hidden truth: The more skilled we become at accepting our pain, the more we find its deeper meaning. We grow toward acceptance when we examine our suffering and ask what it has to teach us. We often suffer because of unfulfilled desires, which leave us feeling like victims. They then increase our anger, lust, and envy."

Nicodemus paused and leaned closer to Gabriel. "To break this cycle, we must learn to be happy with who we are and what we have. You longed for Judith to become your wife, and when she ran away, you felt rejected, betrayed, enraged. Your attachment to her is what is causing your pain. If you can let go of her and surrender your desire to God, you will find the beginning of freedom. Desire will not have the same power over you because your emptiness is filled from within."

Gabriel frowned. "I have always followed the law. Are you saying that's not good enough?"

Nicodemus held up a hand. "I am not saying it—Jesus is. He is an observant Jew like you and me, but his message goes deeper than religion. My conversation with him shocked me. He said that religion can actually keep us from God. When the law and rituals become our focus, we miss the love that can give us new life. Jesus invites us to find this love in what he calls the 'kingdom of God.' In the kingdom we find peace with God, others, and ourselves."

Gabriel raised an eyebrow. "How does this relate to me specifically?"

Understanding spread across Nicodemus' wrinkled face. "I have learned that falling in love is about the soul. Our yearning for another person is part of our lifelong yearning for God. You cannot heal heartbreak externally but only from within, at a deeper level."

"How is that possible?" Gabriel asked, unable to hide his despair.

Nicodemus gave him a reassuring smile. "You must understand that when a relationship dies, part of you dies with it. You must allow yourself to mourn the death, while keeping the love and goodness that you experienced in the relationship alive. In this way you can be born anew. With God nothing is ever lost, so every experience, even the most painful ones, can mold our souls for eternity. People who do not understand this get lost in their suffering because they see it as meaningless."

Gabriel got up and began to pace. "Well, isn't it meaningless?" He jabbed the air with a fist, the pain in his heart as intense as ever.

Nicodemus remained calm. "No, it is not. We are children of light, created in God's image with an eternal purpose to fulfill. Dying through our heartbreak and being born anew give us the spiritual awareness that Jesus has." He stood and gently squeezed Gabriel's shoulder. "When we embrace the light and love that he brings—and are embraced by them—we find the healing we need."

Gabriel closed his eyes, reflecting on what Nicodemus had said. "I don't understand everything you've told me, but I feel better for listening."

Nicodemus patted his shoulder. "Jesus' teachings apply directly to you. Judith and Dismas hurt you deeply. But forgiveness is the way to healing."

"Forgiveness! After what Judith and Dismas did? I could never forgive them!"

"Perhaps you are confusing forgiving with excusing," Nicodemus said. "You cannot excuse Judith and Dismas; their actions were not only wrong but also unjust and cruel. Forgiveness doesn't ask you to pretend that the wrong never happened. It invites you to let go of your pain and turn it over to God. Jesus places forgiveness at the heart of love. You don't forgive for the other person's sake but for your own. Forgiving is the only way to heal hurt and hate."

Gabriel clenched his hands into fists. "I'm too angry to even consider it!"

Nicodemus turned away for a moment, then turned back to him. "Haven't Judith and Dismas hurt you enough?" He spoke firmly. "Don't let them ruin the rest of your life."

Gabriel felt the cold settle around his heart and he set his jaw. "I can't talk myself into forgiving them. They should be stoned or sold into slavery."

Nicodemus reached out to touch his arm. "If you really love Judith, how can you wish her harm? True love wants what is best for another person. When we acknowledge our sins, we forgive out of our need for forgiveness."

Gabriel was breathing heavily, torn between wanting revenge and admitting that Nicodemus might be right. He put the food away, sat down on his mat and stared at the old man. "I wouldn't be here if it weren't for your reports about Jesus. I hope that meeting him will give me the serenity I see in you."

Nicodemus smiled. Gabriel handed him a blanket and took one for himself. After lying down and pulling the blanket to his chin, he gazed out at the stars. He wondered where Dismas and Judith were. Perhaps they were wandering in the desert, lost. Perhaps bandits had robbed them and left them for dead. But why should he care? He wanted them to pay for what they had done. To feel the rejection and loss he had felt. Dismas and Judith should be caught and punished. Gabriel felt the hairs on the back of his neck bristle.

The images of Judith and Dismas became clearer in his mind, and he admitted he *did* care. Both of them occupied revered places in his heart: Judith was the only woman he had ever loved, and Dismas was his only brother. Nicodemus' words came back to him: "We do not forgive for the other person's sake but for our own. Forgiving is the only way to heal hurt and hate."

Gabriel had heard Nicodemus relate Jesus' teachings about forgiveness but could not see how the words directly applied to him. Even the thought of forgiveness seemed to be a betrayal of the justice he needed to seek against Dismas. But as he lay there admiring the glittering stars and clinging to the blanket for warmth, he wondered if Nicodemus were right.

He felt a hand on his shoulder. "You are at a crossroads, my son," Nicodemus said. "One path leads to hate and destruction, the other to reconciliation and healing. I encourage you to take the latter. It is the only way to become complete, as God is complete."

Gabriel lay awake thinking about this goal, unsure he could ever achieve it. He hoped the Galilean rabbi could show him how.

When Gabriel and Nicodemus arrived at Simon ben Ephraim's house at noon the next day, they found it crowded with guests. About thirty men and women were gathered around a table in the courtyard, some sitting, some standing. Gabriel could tell by the guests' clothing that some were wealthy, others poor. Near the entrance, children were playing beside the fountain. When several of Jesus' disciples recognized Nicodemus, they came over and embraced him joyfully.

He introduced Gabriel to the heavyset Matthew and to the bearded brothers, James and John, as well as to several women disciples of Jesus. One of these, a striking, fine-boned woman named Mary Magdalene, carried herself with such dignity that she made an unforgettable impression on Gabriel. Nicodemus took him aside and whispered, "She is Jesus' special friend." Gabriel marveled at Mary Magdalene's slender but regal bearing, her exquisitely molded features, delicately contoured lips, and smooth olive skin stretched taut on high, elegant cheekbones.

He thought it was strange that few of the guests were eating the meal, which consisted of roast lamb, lentils, beans, salad, and bread. Only when he listened to the young man who was discussing the law of Moses did he understand. His words mesmerized the members of his audience, who were asking him why his teachings had offended the Pharisees.

So this is Jesus of Nazareth.

Gabriel felt disappointed by the man's appearance. After hearing Nicodemus describe how the controversial rabbi had affected him, Gabriel was expecting someone with a striking face and commanding build—someone larger than life. But his first impression was of a rather odd-looking man, broad-shouldered but gangly, sharp-featured with long, thin arms.

But when he focused on the man's eyes, with their mysterious and determined gaze, and heard the authority in his voice, Gabriel understood Nicodemus' devotion. Jesus' eyes locked on Gabriel's briefly, and the look penetrated to his heart.

Jesus was lamenting how religion without love harms people. "When the law becomes an idol," he said, "it no longer serves its intended purpose: to teach love for God and neighbor. My concern with the Pharisees is that they judge who is acceptable and who is not. Outcasts get mocked and shunned. They see themselves as unclean and wallow in self-hatred."

Gabriel edged closer, feeling the hot press of the crowd.

Jesus moved his fathomless eyes from face to face. "I have come not to condemn, but to heal and save," he said. Then he continued in an urgent voice, "Come to me, all you who are weary and are carrying heavy burdens, and I will give you rest. Take my yoke upon you and learn from me; for I am gentle and humble in heart, and you will find rest for your souls."

Gabriel's throat tightened as he yearned to have his burden lifted. A woman sitting near Jesus began to weep and turned slightly in Gabriel's direction. The swell of her breasts above the low-cut neckline of her blue tunic drew Gabriel's admiration. Her kohl-ringed eyes shone with the sparkle of black diamonds. Her raven hair, as lustrous as polished jade, reached below her shoulders, a telling sign of her shameful trade.

She purposely let her tears fall on Jesus' feet and then she tilted her head so that her hair brushed against the wet spots. After a bit she massaged his feet and slowly bathed and dried them. During this most intimate of gestures, Jesus continued speaking of love as being the fulfillment of the law.

Gabriel looked away, unable to watch what struck him as blatant hypocrisy. *How can this man let a prostitute caress him in front of Mary, the woman he supposedly loves?* Gabriel's rage turned his eyes blurry. It appeared that Jesus was doing to Mary Magdalene what Dismas and Judith had done to him. Gabriel bit his tongue to keep from crying out.

As Jesus spoke, the woman took ointment from the alabaster jar she was carrying and began to anoint and kiss his feet. Gabriel noticed Mary Magdalene frowning. He understood her pain, so similar to his own. She was obviously in love with Jesus, but did he even care? Gabriel watched as Mary diverted her eyes, crimson-faced, lips quivering. Then, brushing away a few silent tears, she stood and fled the courtyard.

As the prostitute continued to anoint and kiss Jesus' feet, other guests covered their mouths in disbelief or shook their heads in disgust. All this time Jesus appeared calm. Gabriel shook his head and backed away, unable to understand why a rabbi would allow this shameful behavior. A few of the women left with their children. Gabriel wanted to yell at Jesus, to demand to know why he would callously offend so many of his friends.

The Galilean is making a mockery of Nicodemus' praise of him. Gabriel considered leaving, for he now saw not a compassionate healer but a self-serving impostor. *Would a true rabbi condone a prostitute's scandalous behavior?*

Gabriel started out, but a stir in the room stopped him. The guests were murmuring, their eyes turned toward Simon ben Ephraim. The round-faced host in the elegant purple robe pursed his lips and shook his head. He pointed at the woman and began to condemn her, but Jesus interrupted him with a story about two debtors, one who owed a lot, the other a little. Neither could pay, but their creditor was a generous man and canceled both debts. Jesus stared directly at Simon and asked, "Which of them will love him more?"

"I suppose the one for whom he canceled the larger debt," Simon said.

"You have judged rightly." Jesus gestured toward the woman and said to Simon, "Do you see this woman? I entered your house; you gave me no water for my feet, but she has bathed my feet with her tears and dried them with her hair. You gave me no kiss, but from the time I came in she has not stopped kissing my feet. You did not anoint my head with oil, but she has anointed my feet. Therefore, I tell you, her sins, which were many, have been forgiven; hence she has shown great love. But the one to whom little is forgiven, loves little." Then he said to the woman, "Your sins are forgiven."

At these words Gabriel's chest tightened and his stomach began to spin. The other guests were whispering, "Who is this who even forgives sins?" Stunned by what he had heard, Gabriel turned and left the courtyard.

In the front of the house Gabriel saw four women talking to Mary Magdalene. Two were holding on to her arms, trying to convince her not to leave. "But I must," she told them, tearing her arms away. "How can I trust a man who shames me? I must go to my relatives in Jerusalem."

She started down the dusty street, which was surrounded by one-story homes. Gabriel ran to catch up. "Mary, please wait. I must talk with you." He pulled up beside her. She ignored him and kept walking in the direction of Nain's south gate. Breathing heavily, he said, "You must not travel through Samaria alone. Bandits roam the passes."

She shot him an angry glance. "I can protect myself."

He glimpsed her stormy dark eyes, the color of the sky at twilight, and wondered if she felt about Jesus the way he did about Judith. "I, too, was shocked at what that woman did to Jesus. I'm trying to understand why he let her anoint him."

Mary Magdalene spoke impatiently. "What is there to understand? No respectable man allows a prostitute to kiss his feet." She paused, shook her head and then started walking again. "He told me that he loved me. If this is what he thinks love is, I want no part of it."

Gabriel strained to keep up. "What are you saying?"

"What do you call it when a man shares his heart with you, and tells you that he loves you, and then allows a prostitute to anoint him in public? I call it betrayal." Her last words dissolved into muffled sobs.

Gabriel reached out to touch her hand, but she glared and pulled away. He raised his voice. "I, too, have known betrayal. My betrothed ran away with my brother." She turned and met his gaze as he went on. "I came here looking for solace, but like you, I found disappointment. If you wait until I bring Nicodemus, we'll accompany you through Samaria."

"No, I can't wait." Her eyes bore into his, glinting with resolve. "If you really know how betrayal feels, you will understand." Mary began to run and yelled over her shoulder, "I must go to Jerusalem and forget that I ever knew Jesus."

Gabriel realized what he must do—he could not let her travel alone. He turned to run back for Nicodemus. When he reached the people standing outside the house, he found Nicodemus holding a scroll and talking with some of the women. The Pharisee was defending Jesus, saying, "He came to teach us that true religion is not about following the law or being good; it's about loving God and one another. That's why he allowed the prostitute to anoint him. He was acting out one of his parables." Nicodemus saw Gabriel and waved. "I'm glad you didn't leave without me," he said, moving toward him. "Jesus wanted to speak with me before I left." Nicodemus kept his voice low and held up the scroll. "He gave me this for Mary Magdalene."

"What is it?"

"A letter that he wrote her. He said that he addressed it to Mary, but that the letter contains a message for all people. She ran out before he could give it to her. He wants me to tell Mary that he knows she is angry, but that once she reads the letter, she will understand everything."

"We must go now and quickly," Gabriel said, nudging him. "Mary Magdalene has already left, and we must not let her travel alone. Besides, we have important matters to discuss with her."

"More important than you realize," Nicodemus said, putting the scroll in his bag.

Gabriel urged him forward. "After what happened here, I was confused. Now I'm also intrigued."

Nicodemus picked up the bag and put his free arm around Gabriel as they began to walk. "There's much that you do not understand about Jesus, my son. He offered that sinful woman grace—our free and complete acceptance by God. We can't earn God's love. Our best deeds can't make us worthy of it, nor can our worst deeds deprive us of this love. Grace means that God totally accepts us, no matter what we do or fail to do. Jesus has come to lavish this miraculous gift on us, to offer us forgiveness, and to lead us to life abundant and eternal. What better way to demonstrate grace than to show compassion to a prostitute?"

Gabriel hurried the older man along. "But look at the price he paid. He offended many of his friends—even the woman he claims to love."

Nicodemus strained to keep pace. "Gabriel, you do not understand how radical Jesus is. He cares little about social or religious expectations, only about doing God's will. He may even offend people to make a point. We're all like the sinful woman: in need of grace to heal us of guilt, shame, and despair. If we aren't healed, we doubt our worth. We may even fall into self-hatred, as prostitutes do. Only by appealing to God's unfailing acceptance can we regain belief in ourselves. Wasn't it worth offending a few people to demonstrate the power of grace?"

Gabriel didn't answer but walked on in silence, intent on catching up with Mary Magdalene. He held Nicodemus' arm and pulled him along, reflecting on his words, which reminded him of their earlier conversations about forgiveness. He asked himself, *Is Judith an adulteress who deserves to be stoned or sold into slavery? Or is she a wounded woman who, like the prostitute, needs love?* Beads of sweat formed on his forehead as his heartbeat quickened. Remembering the anguish on Mary Magdalene's face, Gabriel had to question Jesus' methods. Yes, he had taught a lesson about forgiveness, but the woman he loved was suffering as a result. Couldn't he have found a better way?

Sweat began to flow down Gabriel's face. He raised an arm and wiped his forehead with his tunic. His head ached as he struggled with what to believe about Jesus. Could he trust this unpredictable rabbi? Would Jesus let him down?

Perhaps Nicodemus was right: Jesus had shown extraordinary grace to the prostitute to demonstrate God's love. Or perhaps Mary Magdalene was right: Jesus had betrayed her. Gabriel must settle the matter for himself. To help him do that, he had to catch up to Mary Magdalene. Each step became more urgent than the last.

CHAPTER SIX

THE END OF LONELINESS LIES NOT IN CLEVER TECHNIQUES FOR FINDING AND KEEPING LOVE, BUT RATHER IN GAINING INSIGHT INTO THE ESSENCE OF LOVE ITSELF—AND INTO HOW ONE'S HEART CAN BECOME NEW.

THE INSIGHT AND THE NEWNESS ARE AS CLOSELY RELATED AS SALT AND THE SEA. BUT THE NATURAL MIND DOES NOT UNDERSTAND THIS; IT IS SHROUDED IN ILLUSION.

ONLY BY ACKNOWLEDGING THE DARKNESS CAN WE TAKE THE FIRST STEP TOWARD THE LIGHT. GOD'S OWN HEART, IN WHICH THE ESSENCE OF LOVE RESIDES, INVITES US HOME. THE BRIEFEST GLIMPSE OF THIS ESSENCE PROVIDES INSPIRATION FOR THE JOURNEY.

UNLIMITED GROWTH LIES AHEAD, TURNING IGNORANCE INTO DEEP KNOWING.

THE SOURCE OF OUR GREATEST POWER.

—**Brother Gregory Andreou's Journal**

Bethlehem
Monday, April 1

"WE MUST DO THIS QUICKLY. THE ABBOT WILL BE COMING SOON." Brother Gregory Andreou's hazel eyes darted in all directions as he pulled Karim Musalaha into his modest room at the Holy Angels Monastery. Karim had been hiding at the monastery south of Bethlehem for nearly a month, still haunted by the attack at Qumran. Brother Gregory's urgent tone reminded him of his attacker's demanding voice, injecting cold terror into Karim's veins. He still wondered where the man had come from and why he was so desperate to get the scroll. After such a vicious attack, Karim needed to know whether the scroll was worth fighting for. Only a language scholar like Brother Gregory could tell him, but Karim had to leave in an hour. It was time to see the translation—even though it wasn't completely finished.

When Karim first took the scroll to Brother Gregory, the Greek Orthodox monk and scholar had informed him that, under the law, it belonged to the State of Israel. But Karim had persuaded him to begin translating it. After fending off the attack, Karim felt that he at least deserved to know what the writing said. Because of Brother Gregory's good standing with the Government Antiquities Agency, he went along. Brother Gregory planned to finish the translation and then take it to the GAA along with the scroll, revealing what Karim had found.

Karim's lungs heaved as he ducked into the dormitory-like apartment and watched the portly, white-bearded monk close and bolt the door. Brother Gregory's appearance was a sharp contrast to Karim's athletic build, dark hair and eyes, and above-average height. He envied the monk's full white eyebrows because his would never look as distinguished. A quarter of his right brow had been missing since it was scraped on the cement during a fight years ago.

He closed his eyes and promised himself that no matter what Brother Gregory told him, he would never return to Nablus or serve in his father's militia. Instead he would follow through on his plan to join the peace movement. In an hour he would leave for the protests against the Israeli separation barrier in the West Bank village of Bil'in, near Ramallah. But not without learning the truth about the scroll.

"Come over here," Brother Gregory said, taking Karim's arm. The monk led him to his desk, above which hung icons of Jesus and the Virgin Mary. "What I have to tell you must be kept secret." The spry elderly monk bowed and then latched onto Karim's hands and squeezed. "I've translated most of the scroll, as you asked." Brother Gregory's lips trembled slightly. "And now I must honor you as a messenger of God."

Karim stepped back and shook his head. "Why would you say such a thing? I'm a Muslim. I honor the Prophet Muhammad—may peace be upon him—as Allah's messenger."

Brother Gregory tightened his grip on Karim's hands. "Once you read the translation, you will understand." The monk scooped up some papers from his desk. "Here's a copy of what I have translated so far. It's in English, the language I use for most of my projects. These words are sacred. They affected me so powerfully"—he fell silent, as though struggling to continue—"I started a journal of my responses."

He sat on the bed and motioned for Karim to take the desk chair. "The words are from a letter that Jesus of Nazareth wrote Mary Magdalene. I photographed the scroll and then deposited it in a vault at the Bank of Bethlehem. Using the photos, I have translated all but the last section of the scroll." Once again firmly in control of his emotions, he held up the stapled pages. "This is a copy of my work."

Karim felt as if the desert wind were blowing through his heart. Brother Gregory was a scholar and a man of God—he wouldn't lie. But how could his words be true? "A letter from Jesus? That's impossible!"

The monk shook his head. "Hard to believe, yes, but not impossible.

Hundreds of ancient manuscripts or fragments of them have been found in the caves of Qumran. This one is the most priceless of all. We know that Jesus was educated because he read in the synagogue in Nazareth. He also wrote. We see him do so in the story of the woman taken in adultery, in the Gospel of John."

"So you believe that the letter is authentic?"

Brother Gregory clutched his heart. "The voice I hear sounds like that of Jesus Christ in the New Testament. Just as important, the letter reflects his teachings, while offering further explanations. Perhaps Jesus wrote a letter in the hope that it would be discovered by future generations."

Karim raised his eyebrows. "As a Muslim, I call Jesus 'Isa'—may peace be upon him—and honor him as a prophet. But my allegiance is to the Prophet Muhammad—may peace be upon him. My destiny lies with *him*."

The monk gave Karim the stapled pages. "Sit here and read this. Along with the letter from Jesus, there are entries written by a Judean woman named Judith of Jerusalem. I have more work to do on this diary, but even the unfinished translation may show you a destiny you have yet to discover." The monk got up and slipped into the courtyard that lay outside the door.

As Karim read the translation, he became lost in its words. It explained the deepest meaning of love by revealing the true nature of Jesus' relationship with Mary Magdalene. In the diary excerpts written by Judith of Jerusalem, she described meeting both of them, and how they helped her find healing for her broken heart.

Karim was struck by how the relationship between Jesus and Mary Magdalene differed from the portrayals of it that he had encountered at Birzeit University. In traditional church teaching, Jesus and Mary had only a platonic relationship. At the other extreme were theories that suggested they were married and even had a child. The revelation contained in the letter presented a very different possibility. A possibility that described love as he had never before heard it explained.

The letter said that peace would come to the world when the fullness of this love triumphed in the human heart. In this promise Karim recognized the teaching of the Qur'an: "On those who have faith and do good will the Most Gracious One bestow love" (19:96). But the letter proclaimed Jesus, not Muhammad, as the prophet of peace, and that Karim could never accept.

Yet as he read, the words seemed to glow from within, as if bathed in celestial light. He squinted against the glow and blinked until his eyes adjusted. The light flowed through his body and created an ecstatic sensation that swept a mysterious tremor through him. The experience continued and was heightened as he read that wherever love reigns, it bears witness to the truth of God. The letter explained the full extent of love's meaning—its power to transform hearts, create joy and abundance, and overcome evil.

When Karim finished reading, he felt an extreme sensitivity, a peculiar new awareness of everything around him, encompassing every nerve ending in his body. He set the pages on his lap and sat quietly, disturbed by the experience.

Soon he heard Brother Gregory return from the courtyard. Karim faced the monk with an expression of wonder. "Never have I read such a powerful letter, but as a Muslim, I could never tell the world about it. This is a Christian document."

The monk waved a hand dismissively. "The letter's message is meant for all people, not just Christians. Eventually we must take the scroll to the Government Antiquities Agency, but as the one who discovered it, you must decide what to do next."

Karim felt as if he had been scorched by the desert sun. How could he, a Muslim, tell the world of these teachings of Jesus? "To share these teachings would be blasphemy to Muhammad. Nor will I convert to Christianity."

Brother Gregory sat down next to him. "The letter says that love defines true religion. Any religion that doesn't produce kindness, justice, and compassion is false. Hating, hoarding, or killing in the name of God is blasphemy. In this age of terrorists, the world needs a prophet of love. I know your great writing skills. You could be that prophet."

Karim stiffened. To accept this challenge would disrupt his life. He wanted to use his writing skills to rally support for the cause of a Palestinian homeland. No one should have to live with the poverty and oppression he had known. The creation of a secure and prosperous Palestinian state offered a way out. But it should not be founded through military means. Senseless killing betrayed true Islam.

Perhaps the letter from Jesus could strengthen the languishing Palestinian peace movement. But he still believed he was not the one to share the letter. An invisible hand clawed his conscience. "As a Muslim, I cannot be allied with Christianity. I know the jihadists well. They would kill me if I were the one to bring this letter to light."

Brother Gregory placed his hands on Karim's shoulders. "Who needs the letter more than those who would kill a person for following his conscience? The letter is for people of every religion and no religion at all. It speaks of the fullness of love, and how that fullness can create a peaceful revolution in our hearts and in the world. Those who embrace love's new advent will find true happiness and learn to live in peace."

Karim stood and began to pace the cement floor. "You are asking me to do the impossible. Where would I even—"

A knock on the door cut him off. "I'm expecting the abbot," Brother Gregory said, grabbing the copy of the translation from Karim. "I don't want him to see this." He hid the translation in his desk before opening the door.

A large man with salt-and-pepper hair and a full beard walked in, concern glinting in his intense brown eyes. Karim recognized the abbot of the monastery, the rotund Father Erasmus Zeno.

"We had a suspicious visitor," Abbot Zeno said, laboring to catch his breath. "He was looking for Brother Gregory Andreou."

"Who was he?" Brother Gregory offered the abbot a chair.

Abbot Zeno shook his head and continued standing. "He wouldn't give his name, but he said that he's an archaeologist and a professor."

"I should leave," Karim said.

Brother Gregory motioned for him to stay and turned to Abbot Zeno. "Why did you find this man suspicious?"

"Because he asked too many questions. He wanted to know if a Brother Gregory Andreou lived here, and if you translated ancient texts. Finally he asked whether you were currently working on one."

"What did you tell him?"

"I asked if he knew you personally. When he said no, I invited him to leave his contact information with me to give you, but he insisted that he speak to you right away. When I said that was impossible, he became agitated."

A shiver of fear rippled through Karim, causing his breath to shorten. Why would an archaeologist snoop around and make inquiries about Brother Gregory's translations? "What did this man look like?"

"Average height," Abbot Zeno said. "Fair-haired, had strong arms and shoulders. He wore wire-rimmed glasses."

The abbot's description matched that of the man who had attacked Karim at Qumran. His blood turned to ice. If this man were an archaeologist, he had motives for wanting the ancient scroll—money and fame. Some might even kill for such rewards.

Karim tried to calm his thoughts with reason. He told himself that the archaeologist's visit was probably a coincidence. That the man probably wasn't the one who had attacked him at Qumran. That this archaeologist came to the monastery only because of Brother Gregory's reputation as a translator.

On the other hand, perhaps this visitor had tracked him here. Perhaps he suspected that Brother Gregory was translating a priceless scroll—the one found at Qumran. If the archaeologist had made these connections, he would be back. The chances of his recognizing Karim were high. As high as the chances of the archaeologist's carrying a weapon more lethal than a trowel. In light of these possibilities, Karim could not be too careful.

Abbot Zeno took a step toward the door, jarring Karim out of his thoughts. Then the abbot came back and squeezed Brother Gregory's arm. "This visitor made me curious about what you are working on. You seem preoccupied lately. Are you keeping some of your activities from me? If you are engaged in a secret project, I should know about it."

Karim watched as the blood drained from Brother Gregory's face, but the monk kept his composure as he said, "I have had the privilege of translating numerous ancient manuscripts. I work on these whenever the opportunity arises—"

"You haven't answered my question," the abbot said, interrupting. "Are you working on a project that you are keeping secret?"

Brother Gregory stared at him without blinking. "I have translated texts from Qumran in the past. I have been given the privilege of translating another one, but I don't know how this archaeologist would know about it."

Karim saw the abbot's gaze flash to the laptop computer that sat on the desk and then back to Brother Gregory. The abbot studied the monk silently for a moment and then said, "If he comes back, you will have to decide how to handle him."

"I agree that he sounds suspicious," Brother Gregory said. "I've never met him, and if he's so demanding, I would rather not."

"I must go," Abbot Zeno said, turning toward the door. Karim noticed the abbot's eyes darting to the laptop again as he said, "I hope to see you soon, Brother Gregory. I sometimes think you are more hermit than monk. With all the writing you do, I fear you are trying to become as prolific as our great Orthodox saint, John Chrysostom."

After Abbot Zeno had left and closed the door, Karim stood and grabbed Brother Gregory's shoulder. "Why did you admit that you're translating a scroll from Qumran? You may have raised the abbot's suspicions."

"He knows of my previous work on Qumran texts, so he shouldn't think anything of it."

Karim shook his head, his lips compressing into a thin line. "The archaeologist fits the description of the man who attacked me at Qumran. He's ruthless, and he may be searching for the scroll by tracking down possible translators. Keep your guard up."

Brother Gregory's eyes bore into Karim's. "Perhaps we should go to the police or the Government Antiquities Agency."

"You know I can't do that. The Palestinian police answer to my father's militia—he would find me for sure. If we went to the Israelis, they would confiscate the scroll and we would never see it again. I need more time to decide what to do."

"And I need time to finish the translation." Brother Gregory went to the desk, retrieved the copy he had made for Karim and held it out to him. "I suggest you keep this unfinished translation with you and read it often. I hope that you'll eventually find the courage to share its insights. In the meantime, I'll keep working."

Karim hesitated, his arms frozen at his sides. He agreed that the letter contained shocking revelations and powerful wisdom, but he couldn't be sure it was authentic, and he was determined not to get involved with a hoax. He considered not accepting the translation. Perhaps he should flee Bethlehem and never return. Go to Ramallah or even Hebron. Forget the scroll. Start a new life.

But he was curious about the letter and the secret it contained. A secret so provocative that he couldn't get it out of his thoughts. Perhaps the letter had become his destiny in a way that was impossible to shun or deny. As he considered what to do, warmth suffused his body. He felt as if the letter were calling to him without giving him the option of saying no.

He took the translation and folded and stuffed it into his pocket. "*As-salaam alaikum,*" he said to Brother Gregory. "Peace be upon you."

CHAPTER SEVEN

JUDITH TRIED TO SWALLOW BUT FOUND HER THROAT TIGHT, AS IF HER TONGUE HAD SWOLLEN AND THEN FROZEN IN HER MOUTH. She stared down, not wanting any of the other sixteen women at Qumran to notice the tears stinging her eyes. She was helping them set out dinner for the thirty-eight men; the rich, wheat-scented aroma of the freshly baked barley loaves had reminded her of home. *How I long for its security and comforts,* she thought as she laid out the loaves and goat cheese.

After three weeks with the Zealots at the Dead Sea, her wedding night with Dismas seemed as far away as Reuben's brief, magical childhood. Both times were like spring in her memory, blossoming and warmed by a golden sun. The morning after they exchanged their vows, she and Dismas had made love in the pink-orange dawn, their passion heightened by its risky and forbidden nature. Each time Dismas had come to her, he filled a bit more of her loneliness with his strength and the promise of justice and freedom. They told stories, drank wine, and laughed with the carefree joy that she had known only with Reuben.

She and Dismas had spent the morning in each other's arms, eating grapes and figs as he shared his plans for the future. He promised that after they defeated the Romans, he would build her an enviable home far from Jerusalem—in Tiberias, perhaps, on the Sea of Galilee. They would have a large family, supported by the skilled stonecutting of Dismas and his sons.

As Judith listened she became certain that life with him would never be boring, not like the lives of many girls stuck in empty arranged marriages. She had clung to him on the twelve-mile ride to Qumran, more secure and hopeful than she had ever remembered. When they finally rode into camp, the Zealots had cheered and welcomed them. She had felt so close to him, so sure that a noble destiny had brought them together, so committed to following that destiny with him.

But how quickly everything changed. The memory of making love to Dismas in the Judean Desert mocked her now. He and several other men had just returned from Jerusalem, where they had gone to find out when the next Roman convoy would leave for Herod's palace at Masada so that they could attack it. Dismas appeared exhausted when she handed him a bowl of lentil soup, unable to muster even a meager smile for her.

Exhaustion was her constant companion, along with loneliness. Amid the daily ordeal of cooking, forging swords and daggers, and bandaging wounds, passion seemed as far away as the glistening stars over the fathomless depths. She was afraid of losing Dismas but hated his growing indifference to her. In an effort to win back his affection, she had baked the barley loaves especially for him. But he appeared preoccupied and rebuffed her when she asked about the expedition.

"I just want to be left alone." He took a barley loaf and bit into it. Then he shook his head disgustedly. "This bread is hard enough to break a man's teeth."

After dinner the married Zealots went to their tents with their wives, while the unmarried men slept in the caves or around the fire. When

Judith and Dismas were alone in their tent, he wanted to make love. "After what you said about the bread, how can you ask this of me?" Judith changed into a nightshirt and lay down on the straw mat they used as a bed. "But if you must, you can come to me quickly."

Dismas blew out the torch, removed his sandals, and lay his muscular frame next to her. "I risk my life for your freedom every day. Showing a little interest in me is the least you can do."

Judith spoke cautiously but with conviction. "I need you to speak tenderly to me. If only I knew you cared . . . if only I felt that you cherished me, I would want you more often."

Dismas sat up in sullen silence, put on his sandals and left. She lay still, staring into the darkness, wondering where she had gone wrong and whether he would come back. He was all she had. What would she do without him? When he finally did come back, she was nearly asleep, but she gave in to him out of guilt, dutifully returning his kisses and caresses, trying to rekindle the ashen coals of their dying love.

As she received him, she wondered how he could enjoy an act that only increased her loneliness. After he had satisfied himself and fallen asleep, she rolled away, feeling more like an abused slave than a treasured wife. The truth confronted her in the darkness: She needed more from a man than passion or courage or even strength. She needed closeness and companionship, an intimate sharing of souls. Was Dismas capable of these?

The next afternoon Judith helped the other women light the fire to cook dinner. That morning the men had returned to Jerusalem to attack the Roman supply convoy that they had scouted the previous day. They would be back soon—if the Romans hadn't killed them. She stepped away from the fire and gazed at the lush blue of the Dead Sea, its scattered ripples sparkling in the late afternoon sun. Her eyes swept the towering cliffs that rose like fierce monsters above the spreading waters. The dullness of the cliffs' colors—beiges, greens, and browns—reflected her exhaustion. Even on a hot day, the terrain, like her spirits, was cold and lifeless. She would have felt estranged and abandoned anywhere, but this wilderness of jagged rock formations and dark caves intensified her anguish.

She wondered if she would ever have a home again, or read, or bathe in fresh water, or see her parents and sisters. Relentless questions arose from her fears: Did she really love this man who was always on a raid or planning one? Did he love her? Perhaps she should tell him about her homesickness and ask him to take her back to Jerusalem. But even if Dismas agreed to take her, she would have to face her family and his. How could she go back and risk being stoned? Then again, how could she stay here without losing her mind? Afraid to face the dreadful answers, she fixed her gaze on a hawk riding the upward thermals. The majestic bird abruptly swooped down on a rodent scurrying along a cliff. A final question stabbed at her: Did she believe in the Zealot way of violence?

As she put a large pot of porridge on the fire, she heard hoofbeats. The Zealots rode into camp with Barabbas, red of beard and brawny, galloping in the lead. As they approached, she saw that Dismas and the stocky Gestas ben Yaakov were carrying wounded men on their horses. Gestas dismounted, sweat dripping from his bearlike features, which were swollen from sunburn. "Now the Romans know they're in a fight," he said, steadying the wounded man on the horse. Soldiers had pursued them, but the Zealots had fought valiantly, inflicting as many casualties as they had suffered.

Along with the barrel-chested Amos ben Perez and his sturdy wife, Hanna, Judith helped get the nearly unconscious man off Gestas' horse. They carried the man to a blanket near the fire and laid him on it. The second wounded man was in better condition. Favoring a bloody shoulder, his white teeth clenched and his handsome, well-proportioned features twisted into a grimace. He steadied himself and dismounted with Dismas' help. As he stumbled toward the second blanket by the fire, Judith recognized the man as the firm-jawed Judas Iscariot.

Slightly taller than medium height, Judas had a thick beard and wide-set eyes the color of pine bark. Originally from Kerioth in Judea, he had been assisting the Zealots in Jerusalem, but they sent him to Qumran with a message for Barabbas. Having arrived a week earlier, he quickly became known for his fervent orations around the campfire, describing a glorious future for the Jews after they crushed the Romans.

Judas Iscariot made Judith suspicious. How could she trust an untested man who portrayed himself as such a visionary? His fast-talking had even won him Barabbas' confidence. *It doesn't surprise me that Judas got injured,* Judith thought. *He probably acted foolishly while trying to prove himself in battle.*

She turned back to the first injured man, who was seriously hurt. Stout and round-faced, he lay on the ground trembling and moaning. "A Roman soldier sliced into his neck with a sword," Dismas said. She saw the deep gash and winced as she recognized Eleazar Avaran. His face was ghastly pale and swollen; blood blanketed his body. She cleaned the wound with water, and then with a mixture of oil and wine. Finally she wrapped it tightly with bandages to stop the bleeding.

It was too late. Eleazar cried to God for mercy, retched hoarsely and then became still. He could not be saved. Eleazar was the first man Judith had seen die. She stared at his motionless body, transfixed in horror, her linen dress speckled with his blood. Dismas, who was at Eleazar's side, paid no attention to Judith. Rather than comfort her, he rose, cursed, and raised a fist against the Romans. "Eleazar, I will avenge your death. As God lives, your sacrifice will not be in vain!"

Dismas and several others carried the body outside the camp and buried it. Judith steadied herself until her labored breathing calmed; then she attended to Judas Iscariot's wound, which ran from the top of his right shoulder to the middle of his bicep. As she cleaned and bandaged the wound, he remained expressionless, stoic, as if the injury were an everyday occurrence.

When Judith finished, she picked up the basin of water, now red, and dumped it on the ground. She wondered if the earth itself demanded the blood of those who used violence to subdue it. When the men returned from burying Eleazar, Dismas made no attempt to console her. "Death is the price of freedom," he said. "May shame be upon me if I fail to avenge the Romans' treachery."

Judith glanced at the setting sun and wondered how she could live if he turned against her. As she, Hanna, and two middle-aged women named Naomi and Leah stirred the porridge and scooped it into bowls, Barabbas commended the men's bravery. "Dismas is right. We *must* avenge Eleazar's death." He stared hard at Judas. "But we cannot risk losing another man. Tomorrow you must stay in camp and rest."

Judith and the other women ate with the hungry men, their conversation focused on the uprising they were planning for Passover in Jerusalem. Barabbas reported that he had been assured that weapons were flowing into the holy city from the Zealot strongholds at Mount Gamla and Mount Arbel in Galilee. Their compatriots were forging swords and daggers at those secure sites and smuggling the arms into Jerusalem by night. The Zealots hiding in the massive underground quarry called Zedekiah's Cave, near the Temple, and in several other secret tunnels below the city received and distributed the weapons.

Judith heard the frustration in Barabbas' voice when he spoke of the Roman army. He felt that the Zealots should have inflicted more damage by now. A frown creased Barabbas' sharp, distinctive features as he said, "We must rally thousands of men to our cause. With hundreds of thousands of Jews in Jerusalem at Passover, we have the numbers to overwhelm the Romans. We must strike the garrison at the Antonia Fortress and drive Pilate and his forces out. Then we'll set fire to Herod's palace! He and his entire family of half-Jew impostors will be forced to flee—if they do not die first. Just as God delivered our ancestors from the Egyptians, so will he liberate us from the Romans!"

Judith listened intently as the men formulated their strategy. The production of weapons would continue in the east-west canyons on Mount Gamla, northeast of the Sea of Galilee, and in the Canyon of the Pigeons, located in the vertical cliffs of Mount Arbel on the sea's western shore. In preparation for the Passover revolt, the Zealots would sabotage Roman roads and waterworks; they would steal horses and raid Roman military installations; and they would assassinate Jewish traitors, such as tax collectors and the treasonous priests called Sadducees. No Zealot would pay taxes or use Roman coins with Caesar's image on them. This was idolatry! The Zealots would only touch the coins that they had forced Pontius Pilate to design—the coins emblazoned with palm branches instead of the emperor's image, for these coins had come to symbolize the Zealot resistance.

Barabbas stood, eyes glinting as he raised a forefinger toward heaven and said, "This will be the most triumphant Passover since the time of Moses. At the first blast of the ram's horn, we will lead our people to victory!"

As Judith listened she grew increasingly alarmed. How could a disorganized band of freedom fighters defeat the mighty Roman army? She feared that many Zealots would die and knew that some of their deaths would be slow and agonizing, for they would be carried out by Rome's cruelest form of revenge: crucifixion.

CHAPTER EIGHT

MARY MAGDALENE DIDN'T CARE IF SHE DIED BEFORE SHE GOT TO JERUSALEM. When she left Nain, she headed south, in the general direction of the city, heart racing, head throbbing. Jesus had done nothing to stop the prostitute's intimacy with him; the memory assaulted Mary. How *could* he? She was the one Jesus loved!

Her rage burned hotter with each cautious step on the uneven stones. So did her regrets. She had hoped that Jesus could save Israel from the Zealots' madness. How could she abandon the prophet of peace? Was she giving up on Israel's future? As she trudged the narrow path that led toward Samaria and then to Jerusalem, the heat of the day was making her hotter still. She paused and held a wineskin of water to her parched lips. With each swallow, she tried to drown her fears about the Zealot resistance. Having grown up in Magdala, in the shadow of the Zealot encampments on Mount Arbel, she knew how the resistance operated, and she feared that its violence would create a catastrophe for the Jews. Jesus offered a way out. He challenged people to trust God and love one another, even their enemies. Could she really leave him? Could she turn her back on Israel's best hope for survival?

After a last sip of water, she returned the wineskin to her bag and thought again of the conversations she had shared with Jesus. They were so personal, so sincere, so full of promise. Now the memory of those conversations tore at her heart. Hadn't the conversations proven that he not only loved her but was also *in love* with her? Hadn't her words shown how much she loved him? Why then did he speak publicly to a prostitute? Why did he allow this shameful woman to anoint his feet with her tears and dry them with her hair?

Torn between wanting to support Jesus' message of peace and needing to protect her heart, she felt unable to move forward through the barren landscape. Its scattered patches of sand, granite boulders, and haphazardly strewn stones appeared threatening. It was not too late to return. Perhaps she should. As the young man Gabriel ben Zebulun had told her, a woman traveling alone risked her life, especially in Samaria, with its robber-infested mountain passes.

She tried to swallow, but her mouth was too dry. No, she couldn't go back. The Zealots' madness no longer mattered, nor did the dangers of Samaria. All that mattered was the ache in her heart. *Jesus can call me jealous or petty, but I must go. I must find a new life.* Breaking into a run, she kept running until her lungs burned and sweat poured down her face. Still she did not stop.

Only when she came to a pass through a tree-studded hillside did she slow down to a brisk walk. Wary of robbers, she glanced often at the tall boulders that lined the narrow road. She saw no sign of robbers and tried to ease her concern by envisioning the kindly faces of her uncle Elkanah and her aunt Rachel, who lived in Jerusalem. She prayed that they would take her in. Two years earlier, after her husband, Jonathan, divorced her, they had offered to do so.

Jonathan had cursed her barrenness and put her out on the street. Her aunt and uncle were all that had stood between her and prostitution, so she had traveled this route before. As she forced her tired legs to keep moving, the events of that terrible time came back to her, and she couldn't stop thinking about the encounter that had changed her life.

After arriving in Jerusalem, she had gone to the Temple to offer a sacrifice and pray for strength. In the outer court a broad-shouldered rabbi with a strong voice was teaching. His features appeared peculiarly angular to Mary, his nose thin and pointed, his left eye lower than the right. He was tall and gangly, yet despite his odd appearance he was holding a large crowd spellbound with his eloquence. He ended his sermon by saying, "If you continue in my word, you are truly my disciples; and you will know the truth, and the truth will make you free."

Captivated, Mary had waited for the crowd to leave before speaking to him about how she earnestly desired this freedom. When she revealed her barrenness and how her husband had beaten and divorced her, the rabbi said, "This man was not worthy of you." Then the rabbi named the seven demons that were tormenting her—grief, terror, shame, rage, loneliness, desperation, and despair.

She remembered how he had stepped back, gently touched her forehead and said, "If you believe in me, your faith will make you well." His hand became so hot she feared her skin would catch fire. His voice echoed in her mind, the sound of rushing water, driving the demons out so that a deep peace came over her.

She had never made it to Uncle Elkanah and Aunt Rachel's home. Rather, she joined the other women who were following this rabbi called Jesus—Mary, his mother; Susanna; Joanna; Martha; and two other Marys. Along with his male companions, she became one of his disciples. That first encounter seemed long ago now because she felt desperate again, her dream of finding a man to protect and care for her shattered.

Again only her aunt and uncle could save her from a life of shame and destitution.

After Mary made it through the pass, she breathed a sigh of relief that no robbers had accosted her. On the right side of the road she noticed a weed-strewn olive grove, which she entered. Having walked for several hours, she was ravenous and dug into her bag for the unleavened bread, olives, and slices of lamb that she had taken from Simon ben Ephraim's feast. As she began to eat, she sat down and leaned against an old gnarled olive tree. She was struck by how much she still loved Jesus, but perplexed about what to do with her feelings. Dark clouds of sadness swept over her and she began to weep quietly. Fatigued from her arduous journey, she closed her eyes.

As she was about to doze off, the sound of breaking twigs jolted her awake. She glanced up, horrified. Two average-size men were approaching, clubs in hand. Springing up, she tried to flee, but one of the intruders, a curly-haired man with close-set, sinister-looking eyes, caught her by the arm and spun her around. "If you resist, it'll be worse." He tightened his grip while his potbellied partner seized her other arm. They held her fast, but her legs were free, so she kicked the second man in the stomach, evoking a grunt from him.

Screaming, she kicked again, this time aiming for the first man. When she missed, he slapped and then choked her. "You can't get away, so why not enjoy it?"

Gasping, she fought to free her arms but couldn't. The men were lifting up her skirt. She thought of Jesus and the gathering at Simon ben Ephraim's house and how stupid she had been to leave, but then she had never imagined that this could happen. The first man threw her down and climbed on top, strangling her with both hands.

CHAPTER NINE

JUDITH STOOD IN THE AFTERNOON SUN AND EMBRACED DISMAS WITH MORE WARMTH THAN SHE FELT. He and four other men were leaving for Jerusalem to spy on the Antonia Fortress and offer sacrifices at the Temple. Judith hoped that Dismas wouldn't sense her reticence, and he didn't seem to, because he just smiled and mounted his horse along with Barabbas and the others. "I'm eager to pray at the Temple again," he said, adjusting his reins. "I only hope Caiaphas still allows it. I hear the Temple is more like a marketplace than a house of God these days."

Judith waved as Dismas galloped off, and as she stared at the plume of dust that the horses kicked up, she remembered Eleazar Avaran and wondered, *What if Dismas were the next to die?* She knew it could happen, if not on this mission, then on the next; if not in the Judean Desert, then in the battle for Jerusalem.

The dust settled and she continued to stare. Did she secretly wish that Dismas wouldn't come back? Feeling ashamed even to acknowledge the question, she continued to hear it whisper from some dark place within her, and she realized why: Dismas might as well be dead to her. She no longer knew him. He cared about little else than overthrowing the Romans. Although she still met his needs—as wife, lover, and even nurse—he met few of hers, and she doubted he could change.

No wonder she longed for home and fantasized about throwing herself on her father's mercy and admitting what a terrible mistake she had made. The image of her mother embracing and welcoming her back played continually in her mind. If Dismas didn't return, she would go to Jerusalem, beg her parents' forgiveness, and start a new life.

Desperate to silence these relentless yearnings, she walked back toward the campfire, her mind struggling for memories of better days with Dismas. She thought of the first time he had kissed her in the Herodian gardens, how he had captivated her with his idealism, his passion for justice, his vow to avenge her brother's murder. The memory seemed distant now, but she couldn't deny that she had loved him. What they had shared together—and all that he had taught her—no one could take away. And yet she couldn't recapture that time, not after his coldness, not after her days of drudgery and her nights of loneliness.

The other women had cleaned up after their meal and gone off with the remaining men to make weapons. Only Judas Iscariot was still there, lying by the fire. Propped up on his good elbow, he looked rested and healthier than she expected.

As she approached, Judas nodded, acknowledging her presence. She could see dried blood on the cloth bandage she had applied the night before. "That bandage needs changing," she said, going to him and beginning to unwrap it. The blood had fused the cloth to Judas' skin, and he grimaced as she removed it. She fetched her medical supplies from the storage tent and knelt to clean the wound with a mixture of wine, oil, and water.

As she worked, Judas caught her eye and said, "It was worth getting stabbed to have you nurse me."

She went on cleaning the wound, ignoring the comment, but Judas reached over and laid a hand on hers. "I've noticed how Dismas ignores you. A fine woman like you deserves a man who truly cherishes her."

Judith stepped back, withdrawing her hand, alarm sizzling through her. For a moment she was unable to speak, but finally she regained her composure and said, "I'm here to help you, Judas, and that is *all* I intend to do."

Judas smiled and stretched out his wounded arm. "Then I'll be your best patient ever. I'm not in a rush, so you need not be either."

Judith tried to remain angry, but found Judas' gesture curiously disarming and couldn't keep a straight face. As soon as Judas noticed her smile, he sat up and playfully shook a finger at her. "I can tell when a woman likes me, Judith. Why resist? Make it easier for both of us."

Judith froze. Judas Iscariot was handsome, and his orations held her spellbound, his words colorful, his tone as smooth as a Jerusalem spice seller's. But his tendency toward self-promotion made her question his motives, and she considered his attempts to curry favor with Barabbas devious. She couldn't trust a man who needed approval so badly.

Judas pushed himself to his knees, his face inches from hers, and slipped his good arm around her neck. Pulling her toward him, he kissed her. He reeked of smoke from the fire, but the hotter fire was in his lips, trembling with risk and desire. She tried to pull away, but the more she fought to break free, the tighter he held her.

The kiss was a violation of her decency. How dare he impose himself on her! Pulling back, she shoved hard and pushed him away. "You had no right to do that."

He lost his balance and fell on his left side, favoring the wounded shoulder and protecting it. "Not a right, an obligation. I can't stand to see a beautiful woman suffer. The loneliness in your eyes compelled me to kiss you."

His condescending tone enraged her; it was that of an older man patronizing a naïve girl. A girl he assumed he could seduce at will. Since Dismas wasn't there to defend her, she had to defend herself, and so she slapped Judas squarely across the face. He let out a howl and fell backward. Walking away, she knew she had to expose Judas Iscariot for the scoundrel he was. He would be sorry he had ever touched her.

CHAPTER TEN

AS GABRIEL APPROACHED THE PASS THROUGH THE HILLSIDE, HE FEARED WHAT MIGHT LURK IN THE SHADOWS. After leaving Nain, he and Nicodemus had passed through other dangerous places—narrow ridges above high cliffs, deep crevices in dry streambeds, but this pass was different: It definitely could be a hiding place for robbers. Gabriel paused to consider what to do. Should he run ahead to determine whether the road was safe? Or should he stay with Nicodemus and risk endangering them both?

He glanced at the low-lying sun, its brilliance beginning to fade from burnished yellow to muted gold. It would be dark in less than an hour, and he wanted to catch up with Mary Magdalene by nightfall. He turned to Nicodemus, who was struggling to keep up. "I think I should go on by myself," he said. "I'm leery of this pass, and I want to make sure it's safe before helping you through it."

"You go ahead, my son. I will be fine."

Gabriel broke into a run, scanning the hills on both sides of the road as he approached the pass. The craggy rocks above, studded with bushy shrubs and scrawny pines, reminded him of the slope of the Hill of Moreh outside of Nain. He and Nicodemus had edged along the slope's challenging incline until the path flattened out and cut through hillsides and an occasional lush vineyard or field golden with grain. This was the first dangerous pass they had encountered; moving into it sent a shiver through him.

He hoped that Mary Magdalene had stopped early to avoid traveling at night. This was his best chance to find her—and find her he must. Only she and Nicodemus could help him settle who Jesus was and whether he could trust him. Nicodemus' words about love and grace had given him consolation, but if Jesus had betrayed Mary, then Gabriel wanted to hear no more.

He picked up his pace through the pass until he was running, legs thrusting, arms pumping. When he made it to the other side, he noticed an olive grove about fifty yards ahead. His heart leapt. He wondered if Mary might have stopped there for the night. The olive trees were so large that he couldn't tell if anyone was among them. But as he drew closer, he saw movement in the shadows. A sharp pain stabbed his heart. Could it be Mary? He ran faster still.

The scene came into focus. Now he could see that it was not one person but several, and two of them were attacking the other. *God help me for wishing bad fortune on another, but may it not be Mary Magdalene.* When Gabriel reached the thicket, he confronted his worst nightmare. Mary was on the ground, fighting off two attackers. *Oh God, no!* He dove headlong and slammed a shoulder into the man on top of her, sending the man reeling. The other man wrapped an arm around Gabriel's neck, trying to punch him with his free hand. But Gabriel bent low and flipped the man over his shoulder.

The first man recovered and charged, fists clenched, but Gabriel pivoted, sidestepped and drew the dagger from inside his tunic. Crouching low, he brandished it at the men. When they saw the length of the dagger and the confidence with which he handled it, they fled toward the pass. Gabriel chased them until they disappeared over the hillside. Then he returned to Mary Magdalene. He saw her shadow behind a thick olive tree, where she had gone to fix her clothes.

His lungs were heaving. "Are you all right?" He reached up to wipe the sweat from his face; his arm felt so numb he could barely manage the gesture. His neck ached and his mouth tasted sour. The memory of the vicious men's hard-as-stone expressions sent a shiver through him.

"Yes—I am unhurt." Mary's words sounded strained, as if she were swallowing after each one. He could hear her coughing and catching her breath. She stepped from behind the tree, straightening her disheveled hair and wiping dirt from her face. "You saved my life. How can I ever thank you?" She hugged him as tightly as a little girl seeking the security of her father's arms.

Gabriel remembered that he had left Nicodemus alone: What if the same men attacked his friend? Grabbing Mary's hand, he said, "We must go back for Nicodemus." They ran toward the pass. Halfway through it, he saw a stooped figure shuffling toward them. Mary also saw him and broke free to run toward him.

Gabriel scanned the rocks above the pass. When he saw no sign of the attackers, he sped up and reached Nicodemus as Mary was greeting him.

Nicodemus embraced her. "I am so relieved to see you, my daughter."

She stepped back and brushed a strand of hair from her eyes. "I am alive because of Gabriel. I owe him my—"

Gabriel waved off her thanks. "What matters is that we stay together now. And you, friend, should not have attempted to go through the pass alone." He led both his charges back toward the olive grove. "We'll camp here tonight." He glanced at Mary. "In the morning, you can travel with us."

"Please don't scold me," she said as they reached the grove. "I left Simon's house for a good reason." She directed them toward her belongings and pointed to some lamb, bread, and cheese on a napkin beside a knotted olive tree. "Would you like some food?"

Gabriel spread out blankets for the three of them. He then took enough food for himself and Nicodemus, and shared it with the old man. But Gabriel didn't feel hungry. Instead of eating, he sat down and rubbed his arms, trying to restore feeling to them. As he glanced at Mary, he thought of Judith, and he feared that the deepest numbness lay in his heart, too broken to heal.

Mary Magdalene had also lost all interest in food. Leaning back against the olive tree, she stared at the road and prayed that her attackers would not return. Her former husband had never tried to rape her, but the attack brought back memories of his abuse. She put the memories out of her mind by rummaging beneath the tree for dry weeds and branches with which to start a fire.

When Gabriel saw her and began to help, she remembered his earlier warning and understood how foolish she had been to travel. Lightheaded and wobbly, she tried to stop her hands from shaking but couldn't. Images of the men's scowling faces and the memory of their hands on her body wouldn't leave her. How revolting they were! And how utterly different from Jesus. During her conversations with him, she felt as if she were entering another world, a world of blessed memories and inspired dreams. By contrast, the world she had just been rescued from was one of terror and anguish. Disgusted, she took the weeds and broken branches that she had gathered and threw them on the ground across from where Nicodemus was sitting.

She needed to explain to him and Gabriel why she had decided to leave Jesus and run away. Sitting down next to Nicodemus, she caught Gabriel's eye as he was hauling over larger branches for the fire. "If you knew how deeply Jesus and that woman humiliated me, you would understand why I ran away," she said. "I couldn't stay with a man who encourages such shameful behavior."

"Nor could I," Gabriel said, arranging the wood.

Nicodemus put down his food and spoke sternly. "If you understood who Jesus really is, you might have stayed and been spared the attack you suffered."

Mary bristled at his reprimand but remained composed. "I know that Jesus is a powerful teacher and healer."

"I believe that he is more—I believe that he is the Messiah, Mary." Nicodemus' gaze hardened as he lowered his voice. "I became convinced of this during a nighttime conversation I had with him. He claimed to be the Son of God, who has come to save us."

Mary peered at him, her eyes large as she took in the full importance of what he had said. If Jesus was the Messiah, how could he love an ordinary woman like her? She had heard others proclaim him the anointed one of God, especially after the healings he had performed, but he always downplayed the idea and told his disciples not to repeat it. Such caution made sense to her since she didn't think Jesus fierce enough to be the kind of messiah the Jews wanted—a warrior who would free them from the Romans. His message of peace contradicted the Zealots' call to arms. Her parents, like many Jews in the towns around the Sea of Galilee, had quietly supported these freedom fighters, but after following Jesus, she no longer could.

She also couldn't believe he was divine because she had seen him sweat in the sun and shiver in the cold. Nicodemus' claims suddenly struck her as ridiculous. "Jesus is a loving man and a great teacher and healer," she said. "But he is not God. Nor could he be the Messiah, because he couldn't be a warrior-king as David was, and that's what our people expect."

"I had hoped that he would save us from war," Gabriel said, stepping back from the fire he had started. "I thought he was popular enough to turn the people against the Zealots." Gabriel sat next to Mary. "But the Messiah will be righteous, and Jesus isn't. After what we saw at Simon ben Ephraim's house, I think he only cares about himself. Besides, how can he stop the Zealots now? They're planning for war. Even my brother has joined them."

Mary heard the hurt in Gabriel's voice and saw the pain etched on his face and wondered what had happened. *Why would his brother's joining the Zealots hurt him so? Was theirs a troubled history?*

Nicodemus interrupted her thoughts. "If you two knew more about Jesus, you would change your minds about him. He loved that prostitute purely. He's a spiritual messiah. His message has nothing to do with lust, let alone war."

With the sun going down, Mary held out her hands to warm them by the fire, its smoke as gray as the dusk, its sooty smell inescapable. "How could a messiah who preaches grace and peace be our liberator?"

Nicodemus moved closer to the fire and said, "Jesus is the messiah we need, not the messiah we want. He brings us the grace that heals us from within. We cannot make peace if we're at war with ourselves. Sometimes we cause our own heartbreak because we live outside of God's will; other times, our hearts break through no fault of our own. When we are despairing, we fear that we'll never know happiness again. But by grace, either the circumstances change or we learn to adjust to them so that we recover our sense of hope, even joy. When we receive God's grace, healing takes root inside us. We begin to become whole, as Jesus is. Then we use peaceful means to secure the justice we deserve."

Mary turned away, not wanting to hear the words, but Gabriel squeezed her shoulder in understanding. "I know how deep your pain must go," he said. "When my brother joined the Zealots, he ran away with my betrothed. My heart is still heavy, and I fear I may never completely recover."

Mary glanced down and admired the hands that had rescued her. Swallowing against the tightness in her throat, she resisted the urge to embrace him because she feared that holding him would make her cry. And if she started she might never stop.

Nicodemus stared earnestly at Gabriel and said, "Jesus has more to say to you, my son." Nicodemus then met Mary's gaze. "And to you, my daughter." He reached into his bag, withdrew the scroll and held it out to her. "This is a letter that Jesus wrote you some time ago. He wanted to give it to you himself, but you left before he could."

Mary waved the scroll away and stared into the night. "If you care about this letter, you will keep it safe because I might throw it into the fire."

Nicodemus frowned. "Why would you say such a thing, my daughter?"

"Because if Jesus really cared about me, he would not have humiliated me in public. Nor would he have let me leave Simon's house. Forgive me, but I am too hurt to read this letter. I may never want to read it."

Nicodemus unfurled the scroll slightly. "But you will miss a message of great importance. Jesus told me that he addressed the letter to you, but that he intends its message for all people."

Mary gave another wave of a hand. "Then you read it. I don't care if I *ever* do." As Mary watched Nicodemus return the scroll to his bag, a gust of wind whipped through the grove and a hawk flew out of a nearby tree. The hawk's rustling wings and plaintive cawing startled Mary, as if mocking her hurt.

Nicodemus gently placed a hand on Mary's shoulder. "You fled Simon's house because you thought you had lost the love of your life, but maybe that loss can be used to help you grow." Nicodemus eyed Gabriel with understanding. "Your loss also goes deep, and what I have told Mary is just as true for you." He took Gabriel's hand and then reached for Mary's. "You have both been hurt, but now when you find true love, you will appreciate it more. Spiritual wisdom helps us to understand the deeper meaning of our wounds and losses. God is working, even through the worst tragedies, in the service of love and goodness. If we believe this, then our losses won't devastate us and we'll eventually recover. To desire only one outcome is to set ourselves up for heartbreak. It's better to seek God's love in the present moment and to let the future unfold as it will."

Mary appreciated these wise words, yet the fissure in her heart continued to lengthen, intensifying her pain. She feared that she might never heal from losing the special closeness she had shared with Jesus. Also, Nicodemus' claims troubled her. If Jesus was the Son of God, should people worship him? Wouldn't that break the laws against idolatry? She remembered that once, when Jesus was leaving on a journey, a man had knelt before him and asked, "Good teacher, what must I do to inherit eternal life?"

Jesus had acted irritated, as if offended by the question, and answered, "Why do you call me good? No one is good but God alone." On another occasion, after he had restored the speech of a mute man, a woman exclaimed to Jesus, "Blessed is the womb that bore you and the breasts that nursed you."

But he flatly rejected her praise and said, "Blessed rather are those who hear the word of God and obey it."

Mary pondered Nicodemus' shocking statements as she laid out her blanket in the deepening twilight. Worshipping Jesus seemed dangerous to her. He continually emphasized *doing* the word of God: living righteously, caring for the poor, upholding justice, loving your enemies. If people shunned these hard commands and instead idolized the giver of them, wouldn't they be sabotaging their own quest for the light? Jesus always pointed people to God, earnestly desiring their spiritual growth while remaining humble.

Further, she knew how human Jesus was—his desires weren't different from those of every man. After the incident with the prostitute, didn't his disciples see that? Mary expected them to be as scandalized as she was. Before she could confront Nicodemus with these concerns, she spied a traveler entering the olive grove and alerted Gabriel and Nicodemus. They stood, alarm written on their faces. The traveler moved slowly to the fire and said in Aramaic, "Hello, Mary. I have come to take you back."

She got up and peered into the man's welcoming eyes, dark as a starless night. The eyes studied her cautiously, their outer corners turned slightly upward, their gaze directed out from a pleasant face, striking for its contrast between delicate, almost feminine features and a heavy black beard. The face belonged to a disciple of Jesus' named John. She spoke crossly, "I won't go back."

Reaching out for her hand, he said, "You must. Jesus sent me to tell you how much he needs you."

Gabriel stepped between them. "Please don't pressure her. She must decide for herself."

Palms outward, Mary held up her hands and backed away. "I couldn't return, even if I wanted to. I can no longer be a disciple of Jesus."

John frowned. "If you had truly given him your heart, you wouldn't have run away."

Anger glinted in Mary's eyes. "You know nothing about my heart. How dare you suggest that!"

Nicodemus prevented John from responding by inviting everyone to sit down. When Mary had reluctantly conceded and they were all seated in front of the fire, Nicodemus said, "Perhaps you should give Jesus the chance to explain himself, Mary. Why would he have sent John if he didn't have deep feelings for you?"

"Please don't give up on him, Mary," John pleaded. "Jesus wants you to know how much he cares about you." Lowering his voice, he continued, "He has become increasingly concerned about the Zealots' reckless tactics. He needs everyone who believes in his message of peace to help him spread it. Thankfully, after he healed a man with a shriveled hand, his popularity is growing. People are coming to him not only from Judea but even from the regions across the Jordan and around Tyre and Sidon."

Mary could feel the blood draining from her cheeks. She thought of her aunt and uncle in Jerusalem. What a relief it would be to go and live with them. She could forget about men and avoid the pain of loving one. But what about her feelings for Jesus? He had hurt her, but if she left for good, would she ever get over him?

The fire drew her in as she pondered what to do. Would returning to Jesus lead to happiness or greater pain? She had never loved a man as she loved him, but the power of her feelings terrified her. What would she do if he didn't return them? Her breathing quickened and her pulse began to race.

And what about the Zealots? Like Jesus, she worried that they would bring the wrath of the Romans on the entire nation. To help him win the hearts of the masses could prevent a bloodbath. She also yearned to know who Jesus really was. The claim that he was some kind of a god seemed outrageous, yet Nicodemus had made her curious, and she couldn't deny that despite her hurt, she needed to decide the matter for herself. If she went to live with her aunt and uncle, she could never do that.

The tension in her chest was unbearable. It only began to ease as she said to Gabriel and Nicodemus, her voice choked with emotion, "I can never thank you enough for saving my life and offering to let me travel with you to Jerusalem. But I do need to go back and hear Jesus' explanation. I owe him that much—and myself too."

Nicodemus withdrew the scroll from his bag and held it out to her. "You should take this with you."

"No, I want Jesus to explain himself to me in person, not through a letter." Mary pointed at Nicodemus' bag. "Please keep the scroll somewhere safe. Someday I may be ready to read it."

Gabriel stood and intertwined his fingers with hers, and she felt the depth of his understanding. He had suffered at the hands of his betrothed and his brother, and Mary sensed that he still had feelings for those who had hurt him, as she had feelings for Jesus.

She gave his hands a gentle squeeze as Gabriel said, "I don't know what to think of Jesus anymore, Mary. But if he can offer us a way out of the Zealots' madness, I hope you can help him. Otherwise the Romans will destroy our nation."

"After hearing how your brother and your betrothed betrayed you, I'm more opposed to the Zealots than ever." Her rising emotion made it difficult for her to speak. "God has brought us together for a reason. You saved my life, and I hope to repay your kindness someday." She turned to Nicodemus and smiled her thanks.

Then Mary reached out to John, glad he had come for her. "In the morning I will go with you to find Jesus."

CHAPTER ELEVEN

CHAPTER ELEVEN

CELIBACY EXPRESSES AN IMPORTANT TRUTH ABOUT LOVE. BEFORE WE CAN BE HAPPY WITH ANOTHER PERSON, WE MUST LEARN TO BE HAPPY ALONE.

AT ITS BEST, CELIBACY IS A SPIRITUAL DISCIPLINE THAT TEACHES US HOW TO BE INTIMATE WITH OURSELVES. THIS INTIMACY RESTORES THE STATE OF LOVE, JOY, PEACE, AND FREEDOM INTO WHICH WE WERE BORN.

IN THIS STATE OF ABUNDANCE, LOVE FLOWS FROM THE UNION OF THE MASCULINE AND THE FEMININE WITHIN, MEETING OUR NEED FOR INTIMACY IN A WAY THAT NO HUMAN BEING CAN. UNTIL THIS UNION IS FORGED, WE WILL FEEL LONELY AND ALIENATED WHETHER SINGLE OR MARRIED.

IN MATTERS OF THE HEART, NO ONE CAN GIVE US WHAT WE DON'T ALREADY POSSESS.

FROM THIS SOURCE OF ALL NOBILITY, COURAGE, AND JOY, SOULS THAT SURRENDER TO THE LIGHT OF LOVE ARE INSPIRED AND TRANSFORMED. BEGINNING THIS VERY MOMENT.

—**Brother Gregory Andreou's Journal**

Village of Bil'in
Monday, April 1

THE TEAR-GAS CANISTER BARELY MISSED THE ENRAGED PALESTINIAN TEENAGER. Karim Musalaha snatched it up and hurled it toward the stony hillside, eyes burning, lungs heaving. The gangly boy had thrown a rock at the Israeli soldiers who patrolled the razor-wire separation wall outside Bil'in, twelve kilometers west of Ramallah. Up to this point, the demonstration against the wall had been peaceful. Now, among the several hundred demonstrators, more than thirty youths were throwing rocks.

Karim's skin turned clammy. The Holy Angels Monastery seemed far away, as did Brother Gregory's gentle ways. But only by protesting could he oppose the extremism of both the Palestinian Patriotic Alliance and the Israeli occupation. He forced himself forward and waded into the thick of the protesters. "Stop this violence! It will never bring peace."

The protesters ignored his shouts and kept cursing and throwing rocks. The cluster of soldiers stood in front of the electrified fence, about a hundred meters away, huddled behind tall rolls of barbed wire. The soldiers stepped around the wire and began advancing on the crowd, rifles drawn.

"Stop throwing rocks before someone gets hurt!" Karim's throat burned from yelling, but the shouts were futile. He could barely hear his own voice above the jeering, chanting, and clapping of the demonstrators. He looked to both sides and saw that some of them had stopped. An attractive young woman was running from youth to youth, waving her arms and imploring as many of the rock-throwers as possible to cease.

Most pushed her aside to continue their furious assault.

The bottom fell out of Karim's stomach as the soldiers started marching down the dusty slope. The protesters dodged in all directions, some of them continuing to hurl rocks. A burning sensation filled his chest as the first shots rang out. He and many others threw themselves to the ground as rubber-coated bullets whizzed above their heads. The protesters who kept running weren't so lucky. One went down and then another as the bullets found their marks. All the while clouds of tear gas plumed in the air. Friends of the protesters who'd been hit picked them up and carried them toward town.

Karim ran after them, coughing and wiping away tears, terrified of being arrested and jailed. All at once his left thigh erupted in pain as a rubber-coated bullet struck his leg. The impact drove him forward. His tennis shoe landed sideways on a stone, twisting his left ankle. Pain shot up his leg. He fell on the gravelly limestone and grabbed his ankle, writhing in agony. Dust caked his lips and face as he lay on the sun-baked earth. He felt a hand on his shoulder and heard a woman speaking Hebrew. Turning, he saw the same slender, dark-haired woman who had tried to stop the rock throwing. He motioned that he didn't understand.

"Is anything broken?" This time she spoke English, grabbing his arm and pulling him up. "Hurry! We must get out of here."

"I don't think anything is broken. If I can get back to my motorbike, I'll be okay. It's at the bottom of this hill." Karim half coughed, half choked the words in English, as she wrapped an arm around his neck and began to run.

She pointed toward Bil'in, a kilometer away. "You're in no condition to ride a motorbike. My Jeep is also parked at the bottom of the hill. I'll drive you to safety."

His leg and ankle throbbed as he hobbled ahead, leaning on her for support, gagging on the acrid stench of tear gas. Shorter than him and stronger than he expected, she continued to drag him forward as bullets whizzed over their heads. "I'll be okay," he said, balancing on his right leg. "If you stay with me, you'll get shot."

She supported him and forged ahead. "If I don't, the soldiers will arrest or beat you. Or worse."

Karim leaned on her shoulder and limped down the dusty, rock-strewn slope. Each touch with his left foot shot darts of pain into his ankle and up his leg. He caught a glimpse of his motorbike, parked at the end of a line of several cars. She pointed to one of them, a Jeep Cherokee with Israeli plates. "My name's Rachel and that's my Jeep."

He saw that about half of the fleeing protesters had already run as far as the Jeep. Out of range of the soldiers, they were now walking past the line of cars toward Bil'in. The rest of the protesters were clustered around him and Rachel, or spread between them and the line of parked cars, running from the soldiers.

Then Karim saw something that caught his breath—an old black Mercedes. It was approaching the line of cars from the direction of Bil'in. Abdul Fattah, his father's most trusted lieutenant, drove an old black Mercedes. Karim quickened his pace, forcing himself to breathe even as spasms seized his leg. He was fifty meters from the motorbike and the Jeep; the Mercedes was an equal distance beyond them. Karim's only hope of getting to the Jeep lay with the protesters who were in the road, slowing the Mercedes' progress.

He ducked and trudged forward, supported by Rachel. At twenty-five meters, he glanced up and saw that the Mercedes had stopped, surrounded by the crowd. Karim's lungs heaved and his heart pounded as he kept moving, head down. After ten more meters, he looked up and saw that the Mercedes was still at a standstill. Abdul Fattah was weaving through the crowd, talking to the protesters as he went. Karim shielded his face with his free hand. When he and Rachel reached his motorbike, he unlocked the carrying case and grabbed his backpack from inside. "You were right. I can't ride the bike. I have no choice but to leave it."

Rachel led him to the passenger side of her Jeep. "Get in." She opened the door and helped him.

Through the windshield he could see the distinctive features of Abdul Fattah—his forehead protruding slightly over close-set eyes, his nose somewhat flat, giving his face a concave appearance. Now Abdul was forty meters away. As the protesters cleared the road, Abdul headed to the Mercedes.

Karim reclined his seat, lay back, and covered his face with his hands. "Can we hurry, please?"

Rachel ran around the front of the Jeep and leapt in behind the wheel. Honking to clear the road, she drove the Jeep forward.

Sand flowing through his veins, Karim asked, "The Mercedes?"

"We're passing it."

Karim's heart was pounding. He turned away from the window, keeping his face covered.

The Jeep slowed.

Had a protester blocked the way? Was Abdul about to discover him?

"The protesters were in the road, but they're moving now," Rachel said, speeding up. "The man in the Mercedes must be looking for someone. He keeps talking to people."

As the Jeep headed toward Bil'in, Karim glimpsed utility poles and wires whizzing by. After a few minutes he propped himself up and saw clusters of shops and businesses. Eventually Rachel took a sharp right, pulled over, and stopped.

"Shouldn't we keep going?" Karim asked, his voice more shrill than he intended. "The soldiers will find us."

"No one will see us in this alley." She got out and retrieved something from the backseat. Then she came around and opened his door, holding up a first-aid kit.

"Why are you helping me?" Karim forced the words out through a grimace. "You could go to jail."

"Making peace means helping the protesters . . . on *both* sides."

"I wish more Israelis saw it that way."

She slipped off his left shoe and sock. "They think peace activists are unpatriotic." She examined his ankle and glanced up in concern. "You have a bad sprain. How's your leg?"

"It's sore where the bullet struck me." He heard a door slam in the distance and rolled onto his right side. Could Abdul have followed them?

She ducked and fell silent, glancing around nervously. When no one appeared, she surveyed the alley with fearful eyes. "I should not be talking to you." She listened for danger.

He peered at her without trying to hide his surprise. "Why are you taking the risk?"

"Because my brother probably gave the order for the soldiers to fire."

"Your brother? How can that be?"

"He's Commander Ezra Sharett, an officer who serves in both Bil'in and Jerusalem. I want to make up for the pain he's causing people."

Karim stared at her, speechless. What she had said seemed too far-fetched to believe, yet she had no reason to lie. "How do I know I can trust you?"

"You have no choice."

She was right. If she left him, he couldn't limp out of the alley alone. If he tried, he might encounter Abdul. Karim was stuck. At the same time, a Palestinian town was an unsafe place for an unaccompanied Jewish woman, so she needed him too. He wondered how she and her brother had arrived at opposing views of the Arab-Israeli conflict. Then he thought of his father and remembered how deeply the conflict had divided them.

She withdrew a chemical ice pack from the first-aid kit, smacked it against the car door, and nestled it on his ankle. He grimaced when he felt the cold. "You're pretty good with that ice pack. Do you have another for my thigh?"

She grabbed a second ice pack, activated it and handed it to him. "I'm a doctor. I just started my residency at Hadassah-Ein Kerem Hospital in Jerusalem." She slid the ice pack onto the welt on his thigh caused by the bullet.

The more this spunky woman spoke, the more she neutralized Karim's suspicions of Jews. Instead of distrusting her, he found himself wanting to know her, in spite of the alarms sounding in his head. He tried to look away, but her almond-shaped brown eyes, flawless olive complexion, and finely chiseled profile held him spellbound. She was beautiful. A relationship with an Israeli Jew could never work for a Palestinian Muslim, but something inside him defied the warning. He extended a hand, knowing that he dare not use his real name. "My name is Karim Muznah, from Bethlehem."

She hesitated a moment, before using her free hand to shake his. "I'm Rachel Sharett, from West Jerusalem."

He shifted his weight to ease the sting of the ice packs. "You're a doctor and an activist? How did that come about?"

She appeared caught off guard by his questions. After an uncomfortable silence, she said, "My father was killed by a suicide bomber on a bus. I'll never forget the date. It happened on March 23, a year ago. At first I wanted revenge like my brother—he reenlisted in the army and became friends with Itzak Kaufman, a Zionist professor with a national following. But I saw how bitter hate made him, and the killing on both sides seemed so endless and futile. I decided that working for peace was the only way out."

Her mention of suicide bombings sent horror coursing through Karim. A year earlier his brother Saed had blown up a bus in West Jerusalem—on March 23.

"I'm very sorry about your father." It was all he could manage to say. The Israelis were oppressors, and the Palestinians resorted to violence to resist them. He yearned to end the occupation as badly as Saed had, but not by taking innocent lives. Still, he doubted that the difference between Saed and him would matter to Rachel Sharett. If she knew the truth, she would dump him from the Jeep and drive away in revulsion. No matter how much danger she'd be in.

She fixed her gaze on him, her eyes glassy. "It has been more than a year, but the loss, well. . . ." Her voice quivered. "Ezra takes out his rage on the Palestinians. If he saw me at the demonstration, he will take it out on me later, as usual. He doesn't understand how I could be as committed to the two-state solution as he is to crushing Palestinian terrorists." She began to wrap the ice pack onto his ankle with an Ace bandage. "What drew you to the peace movement?"

Karim brought the back of his seat up—anything to stifle his raging feelings about his own family conflict and his fear that Abdul Fattah would catch him and return him to his father. "My mother died in childbirth at the A-Ram checkpoint. I grew up hating the occupation."

She stopped wrapping his ankle. "I am so sorry. . . . A-Ram is a tough checkpoint. The only good thing about it is the little girl that protesters have painted on the separation wall."

"I've seen her too. She's being carried over the wall by a cluster of balloons. We have a name for her in Arabic—*Rajiya*. It means 'hopeful.'" He wiped beads of sweat from his upper lip. "I worry that time is running out. The only hope is for people on both sides to live the teachings of their religions."

She finished wrapping his ankle and stared at him, her expression stern. "If you really believe that, you'll join the March for Peace in Jerusalem in two-and-a-half weeks. I'm a founder of one of the organizing groups, the Abrahamic Peace Initiative. We want to mobilize thousands of demonstrators from many countries to surround the holy sites and pray for peace. We hope the media attention in Israel and the United States, as well as in Europe and the Arab states, will create a groundswell of momentum for the two-state solution. I've been invited to speak at a publicity rally in Jerusalem on Monday."

He pointed at his leg. "I won't be joining any demonstrations for a while."

She stood. "I can understand how you feel. It's risky. But time is running out, and if the two-state solution isn't implemented soon, it will be too late."

Before she finished speaking, Karim noticed two Israeli soldiers approaching from about fifty meters away. He pointed at them.

Rachel shot a glance at the soldiers. "Keep your head down until I say otherwise." Slamming the door, she ran around the front of the car and leapt into the driver's seat. She started the engine, and the car lurched forward, gravel spinning under the wheels.

Karim gripped the dashboard as the Jeep made a U-turn. "Where are we going?"

"To my apartment in Jerusalem. It's the only place where you'll be safe while you recover."

A cry of protest rose in his throat. A Palestinian man and a Jewish woman could never be safe together. Especially in Jerusalem. If caught there without a permit, he'd be arrested and jailed. He wanted to scream, *No! Jerusalem is too dangerous—I can't go there!* But instead he swallowed the protest. For reasons he didn't fully understand, he was willing to take the risk in order to be with Rachel Sharett.

CHAPTER TWELVE

WE ARE WOUNDED. THIS IS AN INESCAPABLE FACT OF LIFE. WE BEGIN TO HEAL THE SLASHES ON OUR HEARTS BY ACKNOWLEDGING AND ACCEPTING THEM. WHEN WE GIVE THE WOUNDS TO GOD, THE BLEEDING GRADUALLY STOPS.

IF IT RETURNS, SURRENDER MORE DEEPLY. IN THESE DEPTHS, HOPE RISES OUT OF DESPAIR. INSTEAD OF HURTING OTHERS WITH OUR PAIN, WE WILL START TO HEAL THEM WITH OUR NEWFOUND HEALTH.

—**Brother Gregory Andreou's Journal**

West Jerusalem
Tuesday, April 2

RACHEL SHARETT'S BEWILDERED EXPRESSION CAUGHT KARIM OFF GUARD. He limped into the kitchen of her cramped apartment, freshly dressed after a shower. The long tunic and loose-fitting pants of his navy-colored *shalwar kamiz* usually offered him comfort and security. But when he saw what she held in her hands, he felt naked, as if her penetrating stare could read his thoughts and see inside his fears. "Where did you get that?" he asked.

"In front of the couch."

The conviction in her voice reminded him of her tone at Bil'in. The memory of getting shot at the demonstration tightened his stomach into a knot. Without her help, he could have been arrested, more seriously injured or even killed. Instead she had sneaked him into West Jerusalem in the back of her Jeep and offered him her apartment off Ben Yehuda Street as a place to recover. A nap on her couch followed by a shower had soothed his throbbing wounds and washed the dust and gassy odor off his body. But Rachel's questioning eyes set his stomach churning again.

She sat at the small kitchen table within arm's reach of the stove and sink. "You must have dropped these pages when you lay down for your nap."

Karim stared in disbelief at the translation of the letter from Jesus of Nazareth to Mary Magdalene. The tiny room began to close in around him. As thankful as he was for the chance to rest at Rachel's apartment, he needed to get out of West Jerusalem. No Palestinian was safe here. "A friend gave me this letter." He took the translation from her, folded it into a square, and stuffed it into the pocket of his collarless *shalwar.*

Rachel's eyes followed his hand. "Is this some kind of prank? Could Jesus of Nazareth have written this letter? And what do you make of the entries by the woman named Judith of Jerusalem?"

Karim shrugged. "The antiquities business is full of hoaxes. Then again, it has given the world ancient treasures."

Rachel stood and moved closer to him. "Have you read the New Testament?"

"Yes, at Birzeit University."

"So have I." She tapped her foot nervously on the tile floor. "This letter contains phrases found in the Gospels and explains them in fascinating ways."

He stepped back, caught off guard by Rachel's revelations. "Did you read all of the pages?"

"I didn't intend to. Then I saw who had supposedly written the letter and I became intrigued. As a Jew, I of course have mixed feelings about Jesus of Nazareth. His followers have caused my people great suffering, yet he, too, was Jewish, and I have always admired him as a teacher." Rachel bit her lip. "I kept reading because the letter's insights about love . . . I don't know. They were just so powerful, and Judith's story, even though it's incomplete, well . . ." She lowered her eyes as if embarrassed to be speaking of love to him, a stranger in her home. "If the letter and the diary are authentic, they're priceless. I kept wondering where you got the translation and where the original is."

Karim met her gaze only for a moment, nervous about saying too much, especially to an Israeli. But she grasped his arm, her eyes searching his. "I can understand your reluctance to tell me more," she said, "but now that I know your secret, don't you see that I have an interest in protecting the letter too?"

The hum of her refrigerator and the honks of the car horns outside competed with Karim's jumbled thoughts. "I've just met you, and we're from different worlds. I'm not sure what to make of the letter, let alone how to discuss it with an . . . an Israeli."

Karim tried to look away, but Rachel kept her eyes trained on his. "I would like to meet your friend. You have nothing to fear by introducing me to him. If the letter is a fake, it's worthless and no one will care about it. But if the original is genuine, it's perhaps the most valuable artifact ever found. It would be worth untold millions—and the letter's revelation of love could be used to create peace. Maybe it's just what we need."

Karim felt the blood drain from his cheeks. He hadn't intended to tell anyone—and certainly not an Israeli—about the translation, let alone the original scroll. Had Jesus really written the letter? Or was it written by an impostor? As a Muslim, Karim had been reluctant to explore the question further. This Jewish woman was showing no such reluctance. But could he trust her? "I—"

The doorbell rang, cutting him off.

Rachel got up and spoke into the intercom on the kitchen wall. "Who is it?"

"It's Ezra. It's important."

She glanced at Karim with terror in her eyes. "It's my brother." After buzzing Ezra through the downstairs door, she grabbed Karim's arm and said, "Come quickly. You must hide." She led him into her bedroom and checked the closet. Seeing that it was full, she motioned toward the bed, but when she looked under it, she said, "The space is too narrow. You'll have to squeeze into the closet. Be careful where you step."

He parted the clothes and saw two shoe shelves at the bottom, stacked one on top of the other. Since the shelves spanned the width of the closet, he had no choice but to stand on them. He climbed in and closed the door as Rachel ran from the room. When the shelves bowed under his weight, he relieved the stress by grabbing the bar on which the clothes hung.

Darkness engulfed him. Suspended precariously, he was barely able to breathe. When he heard Rachel greet her brother, he realized that she had left the bedroom door open.

"Were you in Bil'in today?" Ezra's tone smoldered with accusation. "One of my soldiers said he saw you."

"Why would I deny it?" Rachel spoke with confidence. "I will keep protesting the separation barrier until it is dismantled."

Karim cocked an ear toward the door, straining to hear.

Ezra went on, "Will you also throw rocks at my soldiers? You know that we have orders to protect ourselves. And worse yet, I hear that you helped a Palestinian who'd been shot. Is that true?"

"I am a doctor." Rachel's tone struck Karim as assertive but controlled.

She continued firmly but without yelling. "It is my duty to help the injured. There was no need for your soldiers to fire on us."

"The reason was the rock-throwing," Ezra said, raising his voice. "We refuse to stand for that. The soldier said you took the Palestinian in your Jeep. True again?"

"I am an Israeli citizen." Rachel sounded defiant. "I will associate with whomever I choose."

Karim remained motionless in the darkness, nearly suffocating among the clothes, amazed at how Rachel was defending her rescue of him. He clung to the bar, his palms slippery with sweat, his throat dry as desert sand.

Ezra began to yell. "Don't you understand how sensitive this is, Rachel? You are not just any woman! You are the sister of a commander in the Israel Defense Forces. Your actions reflect on me. Where did you take the Palestinian?"

A loud crack prevented Karim from hearing Rachel's answer. He fell to the floor, pulling the bar down and burying himself under a pile of clothes. Nausea rose in his throat as he realized what had happened: The braces that held the bar had given way, and his weight had caused the shoe shelves to snap. He lay still, buried under the clothes, praying without hope that Ezra and Rachel hadn't heard the crash.

Footsteps clamored into the bedroom and soon the closet door opened. He attempted to stay hidden, but to no avail. Commander Ezra Sharett, in uniform, pulled the clothes off him, his penetrating dark eyes flashing beneath a thick head of straight black hair. Ezra seized him and hoisted him to his feet. "Your only hope of staying out of jail is to surrender peacefully."

After Karim climbed out of the closet, Ezra grabbed him by the shoulders and pinned him against the wall. "Do you have a permit to be in Jerusalem?" Ezra's piercing gaze cut through Karim.

"This is my friend Karim Muznah. I invited him here!" Rachel latched on to her brother's arm, trying to pull him away.

When Karim didn't answer, Ezra let him go, shook off his sister, and withdrew a cell phone from his pocket, all the while keeping his eyes on Karim.

He began to punch in numbers, but before the call went through, Rachel reached for the phone and interrupted him. "You have no right to barge in and attack my friend."

Ezra narrowed his eyes at her. "I am enforcing the law, not breaking it. This Palestinian is here illegally and should be arrested."

"None of this would have happened if your soldiers hadn't fired on the protesters."

Ezra flicked his hand dismissively. "When protesters harass soldiers, they have no choice." He yanked the phone away, finished punching in the numbers and pressed the receiver to his ear.

Rachel grabbed his arm and tried to dislodge the phone. "I'm the one who brought him here illegally. If you arrest him, you'll have to arrest me too!"

Ezra turned to keep her from wrenching the phone away a second time. "Don't be ridiculous."

Rachel stopped interfering and stepped back. "All right, go ahead and make the call. When the police arrive, I'll turn myself in."

Karim watched her lips press together into a thin, determined line.

"But be ready to pay the price. Word will spread that Commander Ezra Sharett's sister harbors fugitive Palestinians. You can forget about future promotions. Your hopes for military glory will be over."

Ezra abruptly closed the phone and shoved it into his pocket. Turning to Karim, he said, "You've caused enough trouble for one day. I should have you arrested, but for my sister's sake I'll let you return to the West Bank." He jabbed a finger into Karim's chest. "But I'm warning you—stay away from her. If I ever catch you in Jerusalem again, I'll have you shot on sight. Do you understand?"

"Every word."

Ezra gave Rachel a withering glare and then stormed out of the apartment, slamming the door behind him.

She took Karim's arm and led him from the bedroom to the living room. "I apologize for my brother's behavior. His zealotry has propelled him through the ranks of the IDF, but his wife divorced him in the process and he alienated his two kids. Please believe me—when I brought you here, I never expected Ezra to make a scene."

"I appreciate your kindness, in spite of your brother's threats."

She pointed at the worn tan couch. "You need more rest, and it's too late to drive you to Bethlehem. I suggest that you sleep here and I'll take you wherever you want to go in the morning."

Karim hesitated, staring at the couch and then glancing out the window behind it at the darkening sky, his leg and ankle throbbing. He couldn't allow her to drive him to the Holy Angels Monastery. If she dropped him there, she would become suspicious and ask uncomfortable questions—questions that might expose where he was really from, who his father and brother were. Those questions would end the possibility of a deeper relationship with her.

When he was slow to respond, she said, "I risked my life for you in Bil'in, and I broke the law to bring you here. Isn't that enough to win your trust?"

Her question stirred his conscience. He owed her his life, but he couldn't let her drive him to the monastery—regardless of how much gratitude he felt or how attractive he found her. "You have already done so much for me. I can't ask you to do more."

Her dark eyes turned fiery. "Do you distrust me because I am a woman or because I am a Jew?"

He slumped into the couch, his bones feeling as though they were crushing to dust. He groped for an explanation to indicate that he appreciated her kindness and wanted to continue their relationship, but one that would prevent her from driving him to the monastery. He decided to ask Brother Gregory to pick him up at a safe location in East Jerusalem. Rachel wanted to meet the man who had translated the letter. This was Karim's chance. He could avoid questions about where he was from, and he could also get Brother Gregory's advice on how to handle this woman who knew about the Jesus letter.

He took a quick breath. "I'm ready for you to meet the friend I mentioned, tomorrow in East Jerusalem. He's a Christian and understands the letter better than I do."

"I have a lot of questions about the letter and about Judith of Jerusalem's diary." Rachel shifted her weight nervously. "There's something about her and about what she did that's familiar to me."

Her words filled Karim with a mixture of emotions, from compassion to understanding to intense shame that his family was the cause of her loss. And yet his people had suffered losses too.

"Let's hope it's not too late for Israelis and Palestinians to find a better way," she said. Then she said goodnight and excused herself.

After Rachel left Karim in the living room, he used his cell phone to call Brother Gregory. Karim knew what he must show her in the morning. . . . Thankfully Brother Gregory agreed to meet them and to keep Karim's family background confidential.

As he lay on the couch and stared into the darkness, he thought about Rachel's words and tried to believe that peace was still possible. Treachery on both sides had destroyed it in the past. He hoped it wasn't too late for forgiveness and trust to create a new future. Staring into the darkness, he imagined Rachel's lovely face staring back. Tomorrow he would show her where that new future had already arrived.

CHAPTER THIRTEEN

AS HE ENTERED THE GREAT COURT OF THE TEMPLE, DISMAS DIDN'T KNOW HOW HE WOULD DO IT, BUT HE KNEW IT HAD TO BE DONE. No matter the cost to him. His skin felt clammy as the shouting of the money changers and the clanging of coins into metal bowls rang in his ears. *Caiaphas has turned the Temple into a crude marketplace. It must be cleansed and he must die.* Trembling with rage, Dismas entered the area known as the Colonnades with Barabbas and Gestas, Mattathias ben Gaddi and Simeon of Bethany.

With Passover a month away, the Temple was not yet full, but Dismas marveled at the sea of people flowing through the Court, their sweat glistening in the morning sun. He cringed at the dung-steeped odor of the cows, goats, and sheep. This was his first visit to the Temple since Caiaphas had moved the marketplace to the Great Court from the Mount of Olives. He lowered his head and took small breaths through his mouth to guard against the stench.

The feverish money changing and bartering swirled around him chaotically. Repulsed but mesmerized, he watched a moment longer as the other men went ahead. He pondered how to convince the Zealots to cleanse the Temple and kill Caiaphas before attacking the Romans. If he opposed Barabbas' plan to storm the Antonia Fortress, and insisted on cleansing the Temple first, he would have to force Judith to take sides, and she had already turned cold toward him.

He could lose her.

A wave of panic swept over him. Closing his eyes, he had to fight against the image of Judith's lovely face that appeared in his mind—the eyes that glowed with inner fire, the petite nose, and the finely sculpted lips. In spite of her demands for more time and attention, he still loved her. But if forced to choose between keeping her happy and doing God's will, he must choose the latter.

He took a breath and shuddered. Judith was young and didn't fully understand the sacrifices of a Zealot, nor did she completely meet his needs. He hoped that this would change, that they would rekindle their earlier passion. But he would not betray the Zealot cause to do so. His hands balled into fists as he hurried to catch up with the others.

A short, bald man, balancing a dove on each hand, approached him. "My birds are pure, without spot or blemish, as the law requires. How many would you like, sir?"

Dismas pushed him aside; they had come to Jerusalem to determine the strength of Pilate's troops and to pray for the triumph of the Passover revolt, not to buy doves. The Lord had protected them the previous night as they spied on the Antonia Fortress. Dismas would not insult him now with such paltry offerings.

He caught up with his comrades at a curly-haired money changer's table, and along with them, exchanged his unclean Roman coins for the half-shekels approved for Temple use. Having to pay the added tax galled him, so he decided to risk mentioning his assassination plan to Barabbas.

Dismas turned away from the table, pulled him aside and whispered, "Caiaphas has turned this holy place into a den of thieves, and he profits from the corruption. We must stop this before we attack the Antonia."

Barabbas squeezed Dismas' arm and kept his voice low. "The corruption isn't the main problem. The Romans put Caiaphas in power, and nothing will change until we drive them out."

Disappointed by Barabbas' response, Dismas remained silent as he followed the others to purchase a goat and a calf for sacrifice. He told himself that Barabbas didn't understand the urgency of the matter. Since Caiaphas had banished the Sanhedrin to the Mount of Olives, he was accountable to no one—and free to do the bidding of Judea's brutal and profane governor, Pontius Pilate. Caiaphas even allowed Pilate to store the high priest's vestments in the Antonia Fortress. During the sacred festivals, Israel's spiritual leader donned his robes in the citadel of the pagans! Dismas approached the animal stalls, knowing what the Zealots must do. To ensure God's blessing on the Passover revolt, they *must* purify the Temple first.

Barabbas and Gestas were now bartering with the merchants for the purchase of the goat and the calf. When they had agreed on a price, Barabbas held out a hand to each Zealot. Dismas contributed his money toward the cost and then followed the others into the Court of the Israelites, with Barabbas and Gestas carrying the animals.

As Dismas hurried past hundreds of bustling pilgrims, doubts heavier than the oxen being wrestled toward the altar assailed him. Why not go along with Barabbas? The Temple would be purified soon enough. Was the timing of it worth causing strife among the Zealots? Maybe he didn't care. Maybe Judith was all he needed. But then he wrung his hands as he considered a harder question: Would Judith support him against Barabbas? Or would she use the conflict as an excuse to leave him?

He eyed Barabbas from behind and noticed passersby admiring the Zealot leader's towering height and powerful arms and chest. As Barabbas handed the calf to the priests for slaughter and Gestas did the same with the goat, Dismas listened to the Levite choir and breathed in the scent of incense and roasting meat.

None of it consoled him—not even the sight of the towering altar or the majestic tapestry that covered the door of the Holy of Holies. He joined the congregation in the sanctuary and, along with them, raised his arms toward the heavens. *Oh, God, what am I to do?* he prayed silently. *Should I hold my tongue and go into battle without your blessing? Or should I speak up and risk alienating the other Zealots and Judith?* He closed his eyes and blocked out every sound and smell. *I have sacrificed everything to serve you. Be gracious and give me a sign. Help me to do your will, and may your holy cause succeed.*

Dismas remained silent and listened for any hint of response, but as the moments passed, nothing happened. The disappointment took his breath away. Standing at the holy altar, he felt as estranged from God as from his brother Gabriel. Then he opened his eyes.

There stood Caiaphas, on the top stair behind the altar, his eyes the color of burnished almonds, his shiny white hair flowing to his shoulders. He wore the high priest's linen vestments of gold, scarlet, and blue. Rotund from eating the best sacrifices of beef and lamb and from drinking rich Cypriot wine, Caiaphas oozed arrogance and privilege. The self-satisfied expression on his pear-shaped face turned Dismas' stomach.

This man had corrupted the Temple. Now Dismas felt God's presence in his soul. He heard no words, no specific command, but felt a spine-tingling presence ripple from his feet to his head. He glanced at the other

Zealots and affirmed what he must do. No matter who opposed him, no matter what he risked losing, he *must* raise his voice against Barabbas' plan. The revolt must begin at the Temple. If it didn't, he would threaten to quit the Zealots, even if it meant leaving Judith.

Dismas glanced at the late-afternoon sky, the scorching sun low on the horizon, and decided that he must first build support for his alternative plan before confronting Barabbas. An opportunity arose as the men began the steep descent to the Dead Sea. They dismounted their horses and walked, with Barabbas and Gestas in the lead. Dismas stayed behind with the hefty Simeon of Bethany and the slender, bowlegged Mattathias ben Gaddi.

He thought of Judith's brother Reuben and of Eleazar dying by a Roman sword, his arms flailing in a futile attempt to protect himself. For their sakes he needed to convince the Zealots to accept his plan. He tightened his grip on the reins of his horse as he spoke to Mattathias. "Our spying reinforced my respect for Roman power, and I'm worried. No matter how many men we enlist, we can't match the arms and skill of the Roman legions."

Mattathias bristled. "We've always known that we will suffer losses, but they're necessary. Each death is a victory of heroism over cowardice and brings our freedom closer. The Romans must be badgered at every turn, made to fear our attacks. We can't worry about how many of us die."

Dismas frowned and hardened his tone. "But we're facing the greatest army in the world. They could slaughter—"

Simeon didn't let him finish. "God will fight with us, and with his help the Romans will be finished. The Lord will free us from them, as he freed Moses and his people from the Egyptians."

Dismas stopped and wrapped the reins around his wrist in order to grab Mattathias and Simeon by the arms. "How do we know God is with us? The problem in Jerusalem is not just the Roman presence. It's also the Temple. We have allowed Caiaphas to desecrate it by turning its courts into a marketplace. Before any revolt can succeed, the Temple must be purified and Caiaphas must be killed. Otherwise God will not bless us with victory."

Simeon raised an eyebrow. "The Romans have police who patrol the Temple at all times. Anyone who causes trouble gets arrested immediately."

Mattathias nodded his agreement. "Your plan is as risky as Barabbas', Dismas. Anyone who tries to drive out the money changers will be stopped, and the Temple police will kill anyone who attempts to assassinate Caiaphas."

Dismas started walking again. "I've considered the risks, but we have no choice: Only by purifying the Temple can we be sure of God's blessing."

After walking for a time in silence, Simeon said, "Even if you're right, Dismas, it won't be easy to change Barabbas' mind. He's a determined man."

Dismas kept his voice low, glancing first at Simeon and then at Mattathias. "That's why I need your support. My reasoning is sound; Barabbas' is not. He thinks we can win our freedom through military means alone. But the deeper problems are religious and moral. If you will back me, I'll raise the matter with him, and together we can convince him to alter his plan."

Simeon glanced at Mattathias, and then both men paused, stepping away from Dismas to talk privately. When they were finished, Simeon turned to Dismas and said, "We wouldn't be here if we weren't willing to die for our freedom. Whether we fight first at the Antonia or at the

Temple makes no difference to us. What does matter is unity within our ranks. Barabbas is our leader, and we must follow him. To permit division would cause chaos—we all would die. Only if you can convince Barabbas to cleanse the Temple first will we go along with you. If you can't, we will remain with him."

When Simeon finished speaking, he nudged Mattathias, and the two of them quickened their pace, leaving Dismas to walk alone. He pondered the risk he planned to take, and it staggered him. Barabbas might accuse him of disloyalty—or become angry and have him whipped, even banished. Dismas felt his stomach clench as the Dead Sea came into view. As the incline steepened, he dug his sandals into the stones on the path and kept the horse tightly reined.

No matter what the outcome, he must present his plan to Barabbas. To attack the Antonia without first winning God's blessing would be suicidal. He had no choice but to speak. As he led his horse into the corral on the outskirts of the camp, he caught a whiff of smoke from the fire. Haunted by Simeon's words, he replaced the wooden beam that served as a gate and started into camp, rehearsing the speech he would give. He would have only one chance to make his case.

And he dared not fail.

CHAPTER FOURTEEN

THE COMMOTION ON THE BROAD PLATEAU BROUGHT JUDITH RUNNING FROM THE HILLSIDE BEHIND THE CAMP. She saw Naomi and Leah, the wives of Simeon and Mattathias, embracing their husbands, while Barabbas and Gestas were drinking water amid a swarm of Zealots welcoming them home. Where was Dismas? Her palms began to sweat as she searched for him. A vision of his death flickered across her mind. She imagined him lying in the desert, a Roman sword impaled in his stomach, agony frozen on his bloodstained face. She had wondered if she would miss him if he didn't return. Now she knew the answer: yes. In the commotion, no one noticed her. Her feet felt rooted to the ground. A second passed. Two. Three. An eternity. Then Mattathias caught a glimpse of her and motioned toward the corral. "Dismas fell behind, but he's all right. He's putting his horse away."

Judith gripped her heart in gratitude and headed toward the corral. Haunted by Judas Iscariot's crudeness, she needed Dismas to be her protector. When she saw his muscular frame moving toward her, silhouetted against the setting sun, she ran and fell into his arms. He held her tightly, evoking a memory of when he had first embraced her in the Herodian gardens. Then she stiffened. "There's something I must tell you," she said, stepping back and taking Dismas' hand. "I want you to know what happened while you were gone."

He gave a concerned frown. "What are you talking about?"

She met Dismas' gaze, her stomach tightening. "I am talking about Judas Iscariot. As I was changing his bandages, he grabbed and kissed me. He said that he wanted me to leave you and run away with him. I slapped him hard and demanded an apology, but he refused. I cannot express how humiliated I feel."

Dismas looked as if he'd been cut in two. Without a word he turned and stormed back to camp. She followed close behind and arrived breathless on the marl plateau. There she saw Judas by the fire, listening to Barabbas and Gestas tell the others, both men and women, about their spying. She paused as Dismas burst into the group, pointed at Judas, and said, "You, sir, have no honor!" Lunging at him, Dismas knocked Judas to the ground and began to choke him.

Judith gasped as Judas resisted with his good arm, but Dismas held on. Judas' face turned red; he coughed and twisted desperately so that Dismas lost his balance and tumbled over. A shudder of terror ran through Judith. She felt the urge to help Dismas but dared not as he and Judas stood staring at each other, enraged. Barabbas, Gestas, and Simeon leapt between them and held them apart.

Barabbas glared at Dismas. "Why did you attack a fellow Zealot?"

Dismas was panting, trying to catch his breath. His eyes searched the group and locked on Judith's. He gestured toward her. "While I was away, Judas kissed my wife. He treated Judith as a whore! If she hadn't resisted, he would have stolen her from me."

Barabbas spoke sharply. "How do you answer these charges, Judas?"

"This man's wife *is* a whore."

Judith cringed to hear the words, and then anger crept up her spine. She began to protest, but Judas interrupted.

"Judith cared little for changing my bandages; she only wanted to lie with me, and when I rebuked her, she said I would regret it." Judas straightened his tunic and caught his breath. "How can an honest man defend himself against such a conniving woman?"

Judith felt every eye staring at her.

"What do you have to say?" Barabbas asked.

Judith made no attempt to restrain herself. "I say that Judas Iscariot is a liar!"

Barabbas narrowed his eyes at Judas. "It is your word against hers."

"Yes," Judas said with a slight grin, "and who would believe a woman?"

Dismas lunged at him again, but again the other men intervened and kept the two apart.

Judith's heart was thumping, every muscle in her body tensed. Her eyes were riveted on Judas.

Barabbas grabbed Dismas and Judas by the arms. "I won't tolerate dissension in my camp. You're good fighters, and our movement needs both of you." He released Judas and turned to Dismas. "I will talk with *you* in private." Then he said to Judas, "I'm sending you to Mount Arbel in Galilee to forge weapons for the revolt."

"Forge weapons!" Judas sounded shocked. "That's not fair. I've helped you plan the revolt. You need me to carry it through."

Judith saw a flash of anger in Barabbas' tawny eyes. "You *think* we need you. That's because you consider yourself more valuable than you are."

After Judas had stormed off, the others retired to their tents, and Barabbas took Dismas for a walk, leaving Judith by the fire. She feared that Barabbas would also banish Dismas. That would be unjust. Judas had lied. *How could he act so treacherously and then accuse me of being a whore?* Hearing Judas call her one was like getting attacked in a dark alley. She had given herself only to Dismas, and then not until after she knew she loved him and had married him. Judith felt a twisting in her stomach and pressed her hands there to quiet it. Speeding her pace, she circled the dying flames, as if to ward off the encroaching darkness.

When Dismas finally returned, she stopped and embraced him. "Are you all right?"

He took her arm and led her toward their tent. "I'm fine, but Judas' accusations raised questions about you in Barabbas' mind. I assured him that he can trust you, but he expects you to prove it by your actions."

Judith nearly choked on the sulfurous Dead Sea air—the odor reminded her of rotten eggs. She clenched her teeth as hot shame flooded her cheeks. How could she have gotten herself into such a mess? Her mistake wasn't telling Dismas about what Judas had done; rather, it was not realizing that Judas would lie and call her a whore, and that he would have everyone in camp questioning her morals. She appreciated that Dismas had defended her, but she knew he had done it as much for himself as for her, as a vindication of his manhood. He was good at fighting, but not at listening or taking a real interest in her concerns and feelings.

As they wove a path through the tents that were scattered across the broad plateau, Dismas said nothing. On this moonlit night, the desert's indifferent silence echoed with the injustice of it all. How could she regain her reputation? It would happen only if Judas admitted he had lied and publicly apologized. But with him banished, that could not happen. She thought of the steep hillsides beyond, as creviced as an old man's sun-ravaged skin, and wondered how she had ended up in this desolate place. Her arms and chest felt heavy, as if she were buried in sand and couldn't dig out. Her thoughts swirled from the loneliness of the camp to Eleazar's death to Judas' lies.

Maybe she should never have joined the Zealots. As much as she wanted to drive out the Romans, she needed more reason to live than to fight a war. Just because Dismas had defended her against Judas didn't mean that she wanted to stay with him. For her entire life she had lived by the Torah and maintained her honor. Now her reputation was ruined, first by eloping with Dismas and then by making herself vulnerable to a scoundrel like Judas. She should never have changed his bandages alone.

If the Zealots thought she was a whore, she might as well go home. There, too, of course, she would be called one! But her father was influential. Perhaps he could save her from being stoned. After facing her shame, she could again live in safety.

Dismas laid a hand on her shoulder, which seemed to her more threat than comfort, but not wanting to make him suspicious, she didn't pull away. She had decided to go home. It was the only way to begin a new life. She had always admired Dismas' strength and his ability to protect her and provide for her. But these weren't enough. Life was more than cooking and forging weapons and bandaging wounds. She needed a man with whom she could truly share her life, her thoughts and dreams. Even when Dismas was with her, he showed little interest in her except as a sexual object. Rather than heal her loneliness, being with him increased it.

As she and Dismas entered their tent, she considered how to leave. Her best chance was to steal a horse and ride for Jerusalem. Home was only twelve miles away. She donned her nightshirt and lay down. When Dismas joined her on the straw mat, she turned and stared into the dark. The odor of his dried sweat overpowered her. The tent felt smaller than ever, as if constricting her with each heavy breath he took. Tomorrow she would fill a wineskin with water and hide it in a corner of the tent, along with some honey-dried locusts for the horse, and some lentils, figs, and olives for her. Then at night, as Dismas fell asleep, she would flee for home with only the clothes on her back.

CHAPTER FIFTEEN

WHEN MARY MAGDALENE SAW JESUS FROM A DISTANCE, SHE FROZE, HER FEET SEEMINGLY STUCK IN THE HOT, GRAINY SOIL. He was with his disciples outside Bethsaida, along the Sea of Galilee. They were setting up camp when she and John emerged undetected from a cluster of date palms. John ran ahead and didn't notice that she had stopped.

She drew a breath and glanced at the late-afternoon sun, low and ornament-like in the cloudless sky. A breeze was beginning to blow in off the sea. The fishy smell of the moist air, so familiar to her from her childhood in Magdala, would usually have comforted her but not now. Not as she pondered risking her heart again.

Jesus was hammering the stakes of a tent. Watching him, she fought back the old feeling of being out of control. Of losing herself to him. He laughed, and the memories poured in—the quiet moments together, the depth of their conversations. She dug her fingernails into her palms as she remembered leaving him and getting attacked in the olive grove.

Her mouth went dry, her knees weak. If Gabriel ben Zebulun hadn't come when he did, she could have been killed. She gazed at the sails of the fishing boats gliding effortlessly toward shore, and thought of how much she owed Gabriel; he had risked his life to save her. How could she ever repay him?

Jesus spoke to his disciples, asking them to get dinner ready, and the sound of his voice sent a tremor through her. He may have humiliated her at Simon's house, but she realized that she still loved him. And the best way to repay Gabriel's kindness was to help Jesus stop the Zealots' violence.

"Hurry, Mary!" John's voice broke into her thoughts. He had stopped to glance back at her. As he approached, he reached for her hand. "Are you all right?"

Mary stared at him, speechless. She wanted to say yes but couldn't. Not yet. Not until she knew where she stood with Jesus. Did he love her? Would he apologize? She could stay with him only if they began anew—and only if she settled John's claim about him. Could Jesus really be the Messiah? Before she could truly be all right, she needed to know.

She reached for John, linked her arm in his, and descended the soft slope that led to the camp. They walked past bushy green mimosa trees, across a landscape dotted with jasmine and oleander. Joanna saw them coming and rushed to hug her, followed by Susanna and the sisters Martha and Mary. Rejoicing, they guided her toward the grassy area where several tents had been pitched around a pile of firewood.

Jesus was setting up a fourth tent with Philip and Matthew. Mary Magdalene glanced at him and resisted running to confess how much she had missed him. When his eyes met hers, he smiled, stopped his work, and walked over to embrace her. "I'm so glad you're back." He turned to the others and told them to finish preparing the camp. "Mary and I need to talk. . . . We will return in time for dinner."

Jesus led her down the sandy trail toward the beach. He said nothing until they were far from the others. Then he stopped and took both of her hands in his. "I missed you, Mary."

Disarmed by the sincerity in his eyes, she considered discussing some unthreatening subject—how he had been, the weather—to avoid the tension between them. Turning away she admired the sea, its colors ranging from sapphire blue to jade green. All at once she realized that she had to risk being honest with him. She would either lose him or establish a new bond, truer than before. Lightheaded, her temples pounding, she faced him. "I had to leave. When the prostitute anointed you at Simon's house, I felt humiliated. How could you allow such a thing?"

He was silent for a moment, and then he peered into her eyes and said, "I'm sorry that I didn't give you the letter sooner. If you had read it before we went to Simon's house, you would have understood."

"I still haven't read the letter."

"What? Didn't Nicodemus take it to you?"

Mary watched a lone beetle scurry across the sand. "Yes, but I was too angry to read it."

"I spent hours writing that letter."

"I spent many more supporting your work."

Jesus raised an eyebrow and shook his head. "I know you have, and I considered giving it all up for you, but . . . well, I prayed about it . . . all night . . . on more than one occasion. In the end, I couldn't abandon my calling. The letter reveals what came of my prayers. I wrote it to help others who may struggle with love and attraction, as I did . . . and to honor your influence on me. Because of the struggle, I came to know God in a much fuller way, and it would be a betrayal of this knowledge not to share it."

She touched his hand. "I told Nicodemus to keep the letter. Someday I may be ready to read it but not yet."

He drew a long, slow breath. "You have loved me as no one else has. Don't you see? Your love has made me sensitive to the needs of *all* women, even prostitutes. Please do not resent either them or me. Rather, give thanks for the love that sees good in all people, and for your part in awakening that love in me."

Mary stepped back and glared at him. "How can I be thankful that you cared more for another woman than for me?"

He said nothing until she calmed down. Then he began to walk again and led her to the water. The wind had picked up. Clouds were rolling in and whitecaps were beginning to form atop the water. "I am so sorry, Mary," he said, rubbing the sand with his foot. "I didn't mean to hurt you; I was trying to help that poor woman." He paused and glanced at Mary, his large, wide-set eyes moist. "And I will always believe that you taught me the true meaning of love. I tried to describe this love in the letter, hoping that the explanation might be consoling to you and helpful to others as well."

Mary frowned and measured her words. "But when you spoke publicly to a prostitute, you cheapened your love for me."

"That woman was burdened with shame. I wanted to help her recover her worth, and to teach everyone how valuable even the worst sinner is."

Mary walked a few steps down the beach, her back toward him, and studied the distant fishing boats, pondering his words. He was affirming what Nicodemus ben Gorion had said—that Jesus had offered a radical example of love by accepting the tears and kisses of a prostitute. It still sounded like an excuse. She moved back and faced him. "But I thought that you loved only me, that we would eventually marry. I feel betrayed." She swallowed hard before continuing. "Now I realize how stupid I was." Without thinking, she said, "When I ran away, two men attacked me in Samaria."

Jesus narrowed his eyes. His face reddened. Storms of turmoil rose in his expression. "Oh, Mary!" He took her in his arms and gently stroked her cheek.

She rested her head on his chest and felt his frantic breathing, which was oddly comforting. When it finally slowed, she said, "Nicodemus' friend, Gabriel ben Zebulun, saved me. If it weren't for Gabriel's bravery, I would have been raped and possibly killed." Eager to forget the traumatic memories, she continued with what was really on her mind. "I came back because I still love you."

He began to weep. "Your suffering is my fault. How can you ever forgive me?"

Mary felt her cheeks grow hot. "I'm trying to get over what happened. I'm beginning to understand, but it's still taking me time." She paused and lowered her voice. "I owe Gabriel my life. Now I want to spread your message of healing and peace. Gabriel's betrothed and his brother ran off to join the Zealots. You may be the only one who can stop them."

Jesus wiped away his tears and grasped her hands. "The best way to stop the Zealots is to win them over to love. In order to do this, there must be a spiritual awakening in the land."

A shudder ran through Mary, as if the force of the waves pounding the beach had entered her body. She had heard Jesus speak of love and healing many times, and she would never forget how he had healed her. But now he was speaking with deeper conviction, and this distressed her because it was leading him away from her. "If you love me, why must you let me go?"

Sadness etched his face. "I should never have allowed myself to become too close to you, Mary. I explained in the letter that the love I feel for you should lead to marriage, but I cannot marry you. I must give myself completely to preaching the kingdom of God. The destiny of our nation is at stake, for if the Zealots start a war with the Romans, thousands will die. And there's even more at stake than this—more than you could ever imagine."

Mary felt her jaw begin to shake. Her arms and hands trembled too. He had said the words that she feared most, and she fought to steady herself. "But I want you to continue preaching." A wave slapped her feet, and she backed away. "Why can't you love your work *and* me? I will always support your dreams."

He glanced at the darkening sky and then at her. "My dreams bring great danger to those around me. There was another miracle, the healing of a man with a withered hand. Rumors have spread that I am the Messiah. If the Romans hear this, they will want to kill me. It would not be safe for a wife and a child."

She kept her voice low and spoke deliberately. "True love is also a miracle. If you turn your back on it, you may never find it again."

Jesus regarded her tenderly. "You will always be special to me, Mary, and I will always love you. But the closer you get to me, the greater your heartbreak will be if my enemies kill me." Drawing a long, slow breath, he said, "I should have realized these things earlier, but my feelings clouded my judgment. Now I know that I cannot continue to see you in private; the others resent it, and knowing how we feel about each other, it would not be wise for either of us."

She threw up her hands. "Why did I come back?"

"Because you feel the same for me as I do for you." He never took his eyes from hers. "I believe that we can have an even richer future, but not as lovers or as husband and wife."

Mary reached to embrace him, wanting to hold onto him, to bring him back. When she spoke, she felt the words clotting in her throat. "I need more from you than friendship."

He accepted her embrace and then stepped away. "It would be easy for us to give in to passion, but I am inviting you to do something harder. We must resist the passion in order to serve something higher. In this way we will both become more than we thought we could be."

"And how are we to do this?"

"We must manage our feelings from within and give them fully to God."

She began to pace to lessen the impact of his words. "What you are asking is not hard—it is impossible."

Jesus thought for a moment and then spoke. "With God all things are possible. Struggling with my feelings for you has taught me this. As I examined myself, I found more love than I ever imagined, and I learned that I must give that love to all women, all *people*, not just one. That is why I allowed the prostitute to shed tears on my feet. Without my struggle, I would never have grown strong enough to do that. You also must struggle. Otherwise you will always be vulnerable to unhealthy men like your former husband."

Mary said nothing but stared at the parched earth, evading Jesus' eyes. How dare he talk of struggle! Did he really know what struggle was? If he could let her go, then he clearly had never felt for her what she felt for him; losing him was like an amputation, a bloody severing of a limb that would never grow back. *What he says may be true, but he can never talk me out of loving him.* "Perhaps some day I will find the love of which you speak."

"It is already yours, Mary. Look within yourself, and you will find it."

It really is over, she thought. Part of her wished that she hadn't returned; another part was glad that she knew the truth. What should she do now? Could she rejoin the disciples as if nothing had happened? She knew she had no choice. Even if she couldn't marry Jesus, she still believed that he was the only one who could mediate between the Romans and the Zealots. She owed it to Gabriel and to herself to stay and help. Moreover, she wondered what the miracles meant. Could John be right about him? Whatever the answer, she decided that things would be different now. When they finally started back to camp, she thought, *If he wants only a distant relationship, that is what he'll get.*

CHAPTER SIXTEEN

AFTER A LONG DAY OF COOKING AND FORGING WEAPONS, JUDITH LAY IN THE TENT BESIDE DISMAS, waiting for his breathing to deepen so she could flee Qumran for Jerusalem. Staring into the darkness, she was haunted by the memory of Judas Iscariot's treachery and unwelcome advances. The consequence of eloping with Dismas was that men like Judas perceived her as immoral and felt free to insult and humiliate her. Tears pooled in her eyes.

What did it matter that Barabbas had sent Judas to Mount Arbel? Without a public apology from him, the banishment couldn't repair her damaged reputation. There was only one way for her to find hope for her life: admit her mistakes and throw herself on the mercy of those she had hurt—her parents, Gabriel's parents, and, most of all, Gabriel himself.

But did she have the courage to run away? A chill sprinted down her spine at the thought of stealing a horse and riding into the night and the desert. She blinked to help her eyes adjust to the dark. Dismas grunted and rolled onto his back. Perhaps she should stay with him. What if the horse galloped and threw her? Or she could get raped by bandits or captured by soldiers. Even if she made it home, would her father turn her away or have her stoned?

She took another breath and fought the urge to weep. Gabriel came to mind, and she pondered how different life would have been with him. Only his forgiveness would shine light into the darkness that engulfed her heart.

When Dismas' heavy breathing signaled that he was deep into sleep, she drew back the blanket and crawled out from under it, her stomach heaving into her throat. After tying on her sandals she groped for the wineskin of water and the food that she had hidden in the back corner. When she located the bundle, she secured it and the wineskin to her waist with a belt of rope.

Dismas rolled over. Afraid he was waking, she became still and prepared to explain that she was up because she couldn't sleep. Only when he quieted did she breathe easier and crawl toward the entrance. She wished Dismas and the Zealots well, and hoped their revolt would succeed, but she could no longer sacrifice her happiness for it.

A brilliant moon and a host of glittering stars brightened the windless night as she peeked out the tent flap. No one was stirring among the nearly twenty tents on the plateau. She crawled west, leopardlike, along the baseline of one tent after another, pausing at the front of each and peering in all directions. The lowest point in Judea was as quiet as the desert at dawn. The sentry would be circling the camp and keeping watch; she had to sneak past him. If she made the slightest sound, her plan would be ruined. Knowing it would be safest to flee when he was on the other side of the plateau, she waited for him to pass.

After several tense minutes, she heard footsteps, their gravelly crunch a rude intrusion into the night's haunting stillness. She peeked around the side of a tent and saw that it was the guard, as she expected. The sentry this night was the burly Simeon of Bethany, his gait steady, his robust arms swinging, his gaze moving from side to side.

He passed within twenty feet of her. Holding her breath and waiting until she could no longer hear footsteps, she eventually broke into the clearing that surrounded the camp. The corral was located outside this area, a tenth of a mile to the west. After passing through the open area, she hid behind a large boulder at the head of the trail until she was sure that no one was following her. Drawn by the scent of hay and manure, she came to the corral, which was wedged into a three-sided canyon of cliffs with a fence of wooden beams for the fourth side. All five horses had been stolen from the Romans. When a tawny stallion noticed her, it began to nicker and trot in circles.

Afraid that the sentry would hear the commotion, she moved quickly and picked up the rope that would serve as a bridle. After entering the corral, she replaced the beams and dug the honey-dried locusts out of the bundle. The sleek, charcoal-colored horse that she and Dismas had ridden from Jerusalem kept circling, bucking and snorting and braying. She put a finger to her lips. "*Shh!*" The horse wouldn't calm down. She made a kissing sound and edged toward the animal, holding out the locusts. The horse reared up and clawed the air, braying loudly, but then caught a whiff of the honey and quieted. She breathed easier when the horse ambled over and began to eat from her palm.

While the horse was preoccupied, she slipped the bridle on him and used the locusts to coax him toward the gate. The horse resisted at first and started to rear up, but she pulled the rope taut and guided him out of the corral. After she had replaced the beams, she seized the horse's mane, kicked her right leg up and mounted. The horse began to buck, but she held on.

Just then she saw Simeon of Bethany running toward the corral.

"Get off that horse!" His yelling and frantic waving spooked the animal. The horse kicked wildly, threw her to the ground, and reared up over her. She could have been trampled had Simeon not grabbed the rope and taken control. He pulled the horse away and returned it to the corral.

When he stormed back to her, out of breath, he yanked her up by an arm. "You foolish woman! All the horses could've escaped, and you could've been killed." He glared at her and tightened his grip. "I'm taking you to Barabbas."

"Please, Simeon, no. I'm in enough trouble with him already." She tried to remain composed but felt her voice breaking. "Won't you please take me to Dismas instead? Can't we just forget this ever happened?"

Simeon pushed her ahead on the trail, and then caught up. "You're nothing but a thief, and if Judas is right, a whore too. What would Dismas want with you now?"

She tried to run, but Simeon was too fast. She had wanted to flee from Dismas, but now she would do anything, if only he would take her back.

CHAPTER SEVENTEEN

LOVE OFTEN DOES ITS WORK QUIETLY, ESCAPING THE NOTICE OF INATTENTIVE SOULS.
BUT IT IS ALWAYS WORKING.

ALWAYS.

THE MORE WE SEE LIFE THROUGH SPIRITUAL EYES, THE MORE AWARE WE BECOME OF LOVE'S UNHERALDED ACTS OF KINDNESS, GENEROSITY, HEROISM.

THESE ACTS OFTEN OCCUR IN UNEXPECTED PLACES, AMONG UNLIKELY PEOPLE.

NEVER LOSE THE CAPACITY TO BE SURPRISED BY LOVE.
THESE SURPRISES INSPIRE TRUE HOPE AND LASTING JOY.

—**Brother Gregory Andreou's Journal**

East Jerusalem
Wednesday, April 3

WHEN DOES A MAN KNOW HE'S FALLING IN LOVE? The question gnawed at Karim as he got off the elevator with Rachel and Brother Gregory. As they entered the pediatric cancer ward of Augusta Victoria Hospital, Karim noticed the apricot turtleneck that accentuated Rachel's attractive figure, and how her lustrous auburn hair fell lazily on her shoulders. He also observed how she charmed Brother Gregory. She had an engaging way of asking about his life as a monk, laughing with him, and sharing her story of becoming a medical resident and peace activist.

Under ordinary circumstances, riding in an elevator with a woman would have meant little, but something about Rachel Sharett continued to fascinate Karim. He hated feeling out of control—he felt as if he had been stricken with a fatal disease. As he led Rachel and Brother Gregory onto the ward, he knew of no cure for this fledgling feeling he had for her. She exuded such beauty and vitality that she brightened the faces of the sick children being wheeled around by nurses and parents.

This ward was the one place where, as a journalism student, he had witnessed harmony between Palestinians and Israelis. He had done a story about the children and doctors of this ward, and he particularly remembered the activities in the community room. Rachel Sharett had helped him in Bil'in and at her apartment. Now he wanted to show her a place where Israelis and Palestinians treated one another as equals and friends.

What he didn't expect was trouble. It began when he recognized a couple he had known in Nablus—Ahmed and Jamilia Marzouqa, who were at the bedside of their son Emad. As he tiptoed past Emad's door and waved for Rachel and Brother Gregory to keep up, he prayed that the couple hadn't seen him.

He remembered when the Marzouqas' four-year-old son had contracted leukemia and when the family first received financial help from the Palestinian Patriotic Alliance. This couple was so indebted to his father that they would like nothing better than to help Sadiq find his wayward son. Karim feared that if they saw him, they would call his father, who would alert Abdul Fattah to his whereabouts. If Abdul had tracked him to East Jerusalem, he could be nearby.

Seeing the Marzouqa family had caught Karim off guard, but as he led Rachel and Brother Gregory down the broad corridor, he realized it shouldn't have. Augusta Victoria was the only hospital with a cancer ward for Palestinian children. Here he could easily encounter patients from Nablus or from any city in the West Bank.

Karim moved right so that a teenage girl pushing an IV pole could get by. Since they stepped onto the elevator, Rachel and Brother Gregory had done nothing but talk about the letter. The monk had not said anything about the original scroll, where Karim had found it, or where it was now. Instead he had emphasized the truths contained in the letter—how they brought the fullness of historic Christian teachings to light.

As Karim dodged a bald-headed boy who was driving his wheelchair erratically, he heard Rachel say, "The letter's revelation that Jesus struggled with his feelings for Mary Magdalene bothered me. If he was the Son of God, as Christians believe, wasn't he above romantic temptation?"

Brother Gregory said, "According to orthodox church teachings, Jesus is fully divine *and* fully human. Some Christians deny the second part—at least in practice. By doing so they fall into a heresy called docetism—the idea that Jesus didn't really have a body, that he only appeared to." Karim listened closely as Brother Gregory went on, "The letter corrects this. It reveals that Jesus was as human as you or I. He experienced every feeling that we have, including sexual feelings, yet without sin. Christians who emphasize the divinity of Jesus may find this hard to imagine, but affirming his full humanity gives me more reverence for him, not less."

Karim stopped them near the bustling nurses' station as Rachel spoke with excitement. "If what Judith of Jerusalem writes is true—that Judas betrayed Jesus to Pilate before he went to the Sanhedrin—then her witness could help bring Jews and Christians together." Then she frowned. "Still, as a Jew, I believe that Jesus was human, not divine."

After seeing the Marzouqa family, Karim wanted to hurry Rachel through the program in the community room and then leave as quickly as possible. He led her and Brother Gregory toward the end of the hallway, where children and their parents were gathering. "As a Muslim I also do not believe that Jesus was the Son of God," he said. "Only Allah is divine."

"I acknowledge the differences among our religions," Brother Gregory said. "But the letter challenges us to find common ground. It can illumine the depths of Judaism, Christianity, *and* Islam. Jesus is a teacher to us all, and the letter is truly prophetic in that it contains a powerful message that is as relevant today as when he wrote it."

Karim stopped outside a child's room. He peered in and saw a woman, her head covered with a yellow hijab, sitting at the bedside of a small, jaundiced boy. A tall doctor wearing a yarmulke was speaking to them. Karim moved and let Rachel peer in. "This is what I wanted you to see," he said. "There are sick children all over this ward. Most of them are Palestinian, but the doctors are both Palestinian and Israeli. The only enemy here is disease."

When they reached the community room, Karim held the door for a nurse with a little girl, perhaps five or six years old, in her arms. The girl's head was bald, except for a few strands of long black hair on the sides. Her eyes were sunken, ringed with dark circles and perched above a gaunt face. Why did Allah allow such suffering? Sometimes Karim cried out the question with tears, but no answer came. When Rachel saw the girl, she shook her head sadly. Karim took her hand and moved inside the room.

The children sat in folding chairs or wheelchairs. Karim and Rachel followed Brother Gregory to the back, where they stood with a few doctors and nurses to watch the ebullient activities director lead the children in songs. The director, a short, attractive woman with curly chestnut hair, held a microphone and followed the music coming from a portable CD player.

Karim recognized several of the songs from his childhood and felt a pang of longing for his mother and her love of peace. He couldn't think about his brief, happy time with her without tearing up, so he joined in the singing, as did the adults who knew Arabic. After each chorus, the director translated the song into English and invited everyone to sing. The blending of Palestinian and Israeli accents sent chills up and down Karim's spine as they sang,

"When will there be peace on earth?
Peace that will last, for the children's sake?
Oh, when will we be free from hate and fear?
The day must come when love, like the sun, shines in our hearts."

One of the Israeli doctors suggested "The Song of Peace," which had become popular in his country after Prime Minister Yitzhak Rabin was assassinated. When the activities director played the CD, Karim could hear Rachel's voice soar above the others,

"Let the sun rise, and give the morning light
The purest prayer will not bring back
He whose candle was snuffed out and was buried in the dust. . . .
So sing only a song for peace
Do not whisper a prayer
Better sing a song for peace
With a great shout."

With the hopeful lyrics echoing in his ears, Karim noticed a stocky man in a gold shirt peek in the door. The man surveyed the group and then locked his eyes on Karim's. As soon as their eyes met, Karim recognized Ahmed Marzouqa. As Ahmed turned and walked away, Karim signaled

Rachel and Brother Gregory that he was ready to leave. Fortunately the group was breaking up. When he reached the corridor, he watched as Ahmed hurried to his son's room, a cell phone pressed to his ear.

Karim feared that the call was to Sadiq Musalaha and waited for Ahmed to disappear before heading for the elevator. He motioned for Rachel and Brother Gregory to follow, trying not to appear rushed. They caught up outside the doors as Karim pressed the down button. He glared at the light that tracked the elevator's ascent, silently cursing its slowness.

Rachel and Brother Gregory were still talking about the gathering in the community room. "I think we just experienced what Jesus wrote about in the letter," Brother Gregory said. "The love he describes unites people across all barriers."

Karim pressed the down button several times as Rachel, oblivious to his plight, said, "Unfortunately, it's easier to sing about peace than to live it."

"Agreed," Brother Gregory said. "The music brought us together, as did seeing the unity of the Israeli and Palestinian doctors and nurses. But religion often does the opposite. Rather than unite us to fight evil and suffering, it may fuel the fires of hatred and injustice. This trend has afflicted humanity through the ages."

The elevator bell rang as the door whooshed open. Karim breathed a sigh of thanks as they entered—doubly so because the elevator was empty.

"Why is so much evil done in the name of God?" Rachel asked, her brow furrowed as the elevator descended to the lobby. Her voice sounded as if it had steel in it. "The influence that a radical Zionist named Itzak Kaufman has on my brother breaks my heart."

Brother Gregory cleared his throat, his eyes flashing. "Religion can inspire great evil, but also great good. This hospital is a mission of Lutheran Christians to heal the sick. We must not give up on religion because it has been misused. We must seek greater understanding for questions such as why the stories about Isaac and Ishmael in Judaism and Islam are different. The Jesus letter affirms that the Creator of us all is merciful, loving, and just. The only way we can know and please God is to embody these qualities ourselves."

Karim shifted his weight from one leg to the other, hot with stress. The ride seemed endless. Were they descending to the earth's core? In an effort to stop thinking about Abdul Fattah possibly being in East Jerusalem and coming after him, he said, "The jihadists will never become merciful, loving, or just. They think they please God by killing infidels in his name."

Brother Gregory gave him a determined glance. "To make peace we must win the war of ideas, and that's where the Jesus letter can help."

"The jihadists will mock the letter," Karim said over the hum of the elevator. "It is not Islamic and it advocates peace for all."

Brother Gregory cocked his head in a studious pose. "Why not take a more hopeful view? Jihadists long to drink from the spring of inner intimacy that Jesus describes in the letter, but they don't realize it. If they knew the depths of love, they wouldn't promise suicide bombers seventy-two virgins in paradise. They would teach them to find the fullness of God's love within. Jesus promises that this love will win in the end. Then peace will come at last."

Finally the elevator stopped moving. Karim waded through the people waiting to get on, cautiously scanning each face. He warned himself not to do anything rash. He didn't know if Ahmed Marzouqa had reached his father—or had even called him. If he had, it would take time for his father to contact Abdul Fattah and for Abdul to find him. Karim rehearsed his plan to walk Rachel to her Jeep and say good-bye without raising questions.

She and Brother Gregory caught up to him, still discussing the letter. "I don't understand," Rachel said. "All three of our religions teach that

Adam and Eve lived in paradise but then lost it. You're talking about getting paradise back. But how? Because, let's face it, the West Bank and Gaza are hell on earth."

Karim held the front door. As Brother Gregory passed through, he said, "We all believe in one God, whom we call by different names, and our three religions trace their roots to Abraham. We are members of the same family—brothers and sisters. We should treat one another fairly and share this land and its holy sites."

Karim surveyed the rows of cars in the parking lot. He knew that Abdul Fattah drove an older-model black Mercedes. He saw several in the lot. Thankfully, none were occupied. Rachel had parked in the far corner. As Karim led her toward the Jeep, Rachel said, "Every attempt to make peace in this land has failed. I'm committed to this work, but I worry that time is running out."

Brother Gregory said, "If the letter *is* real, perhaps a new opportunity is within our grasp. Jews, Christians, and Muslims revere their scriptures but don't emphasize the shared teachings they contain. Maybe the discovery of the letter is God's way of inspiring this search for common ground."

Rachel stopped as if struck by a new thought and grabbed Karim and Brother Gregory each by an arm. "We've got to prove it's genuine. The original can be tested to determine its age, but unless we can prove that the revelations about Jesus and Mary Magdalene are true, we'll have no evidence that the letter is authentic. Its value will remain in doubt." She stopped and turned to Karim. "Let me help with the research. Please."

Karim placed his left hand on hers. Could he trust her? As he gazed into her depthless eyes, as dark as black satin, he thought he saw character and integrity and compassion. If Rachel were Palestinian, he would have no problem trusting her. But she was Israeli. He left her question unanswered as he turned toward the Jeep, glancing nervously at the entrance to the lot.

She pulled him back so that he faced her again. "Please, Karim. Let me help."

This time he caught a glimpse of longing in her eyes. A longing he had seen before but couldn't place. As he held her gaze, he did remember. He had seen this same longing in his father's eyes, a longing for his wife who had died in childbirth. A longing for the mother whom Karim still wept for—the mother who had remained hopeful until the end like *Rajiya,* painted on the wall at A-Ram. He drew a quick breath, wondering if Rachel had seen longing in his eyes and decided to help him in Bil'in because of it.

Here in this unremarkable place, a parking lot, he finally knew he could trust her—and fully confide in her about the letter. "Yes, Rachel, I accept your help," he said, embracing her before he led her to her Jeep. He hesitated as she opened the door and got in. "When will I see you again?" he asked, regretting having to let her go.

She wrote her cell phone number on a slip of paper and gave it to him. "I have some ideas about how to start researching the letter. Give me a call. Okay?"

"Soon," he said, "and thank you again for all you did."

As she said good-bye and drove out of the parking lot, Karim caught a glimpse of a car entering. A black Mercedes. He quickly followed Brother Gregory to his Ford Escort. "We need to leave now," Karim said, ducking into the passenger seat and reclining it. "Abdul Fattah may be in that Mercedes."

As Brother Gregory took a right out of the parking lot, Karim heard the screech of tires behind them. He kept his head down as the resourceful monk began to weave in and out of traffic. Karim said a brief prayer. Whether they would make it the eight kilometers to Holy Angels Monastery was in Brother Gregory's white-knuckled hands.

CHAPTER EIGHTEEN

THE MOMENT GABRIEL SAW NICODEMUS BEN GORION'S FACE, HE KNEW SOMETHING WAS WRONG. The wise old Pharisee had entered the marketplace in Jerusalem and was weaving through the crowd. Gabriel moved toward him, guiding his four-wheel pushcart, half full of Passover supplies for his market, around the bustling shoppers. He hadn't seen Nicodemus' brow so furrowed since they found Mary Magdalene in Samaria.

Moving toward him, Gabriel dodged a man carrying a sack of grain and thought of Mary, wondering how she had fared when she returned to Jesus. The memory of Mary's heartbreak made him think of Judith's and his own. It had been more than a month since Judith and Dismas eloped, but Gabriel's grief was as raw as the beef in the market's butcher shops. He saw the displays of fine silks and imagined how lovely Judith would have looked in her wedding dress. The jewelry reminded him of the ring he would never place on her finger.

He passed two women balancing baskets of vegetables on their heads and gripped the pushcart tighter. He had sought to forget Judith but failed. Nor could he forgive. Each time he tried, his hurt got in the way. The piercing stings of the pain kept him awake at night and distracted him during the day.

He steered the cart around some children playing in the street and again raised his hand to wave at Nicodemus. Never had he seen his friend's eyes so anxious or his jaw so tense. Gabriel yelled to get Nicodemus' attention, but his voice got lost amid the haggling of customers and merchants, the shrieks of the children, the pleas of the beggars.

Finally he caught the old man's eye and Nicodemus rushed over and took Gabriel's arm. He led him into an alley beside a bakeshop, its fresh bread emitting a rich yeasty scent. "Something awful has happened," the Pharisee said, his voice trembling. "Pilate had his soldiers kill four Galileans and mix their blood with the sacrifices in the Temple." Nicodemus' deep-set eyes were wet, his round cheeks flushed. "I fear what might happen because of this outrage."

Gabriel drew a hand to his mouth to stifle a cry. The baking bread no longer smelled inviting but offensive. He stared at the worn stones of the alley, which was only wide enough for an oxcart, and struggled to contain his rage. "Why would Pilate provoke our people like this? He knows that we have rioted over less."

Nicodemus grabbed Gabriel's arms and stared into his eyes. "The priests say that Pilate suspected the Galileans of planning a revolt. He won't tolerate even the hint of insurrection."

Gabriel held Nicodemus' gaze. "How did the Sanhedrin respond?"

Nicodemus gave a frustrated shrug. "Caiaphas protested, but he dared not say much; the Romans might close the Temple for good. I'm outraged by what happened, but I am also worried about Jesus. He, too, is Galilean and popular with the masses. If Pilate suspects him of helping the Zealots, he may try to kill him."

Gabriel had planned to have a meal with Nicodemus, but he was no longer hungry. He, too, was thinking about Jesus and drew a cleansing breath. "We need Jesus' message of peace, but it will only succeed if he lives morally and preaches with power and passion."

The old man shot him a wary glance. "As heinous as Pilate's actions were, they're further evidence of the truth of Jesus' gospel." Nicodemus kept his voice at a whisper. "Jesus warns of the darkness in each of us. It makes us do dreadful things. The only way to contain this dark side is to increase our awareness of it, and to work tirelessly to bring it into the light. Few people do this. Most of us condemn the sins of others without examining our own. My fellow Pharisees are especially good at this. Pilate has sinned, but before we condemn him, we must acknowledge the evil in our own hearts."

Gabriel glared at him. "I could never do what Pilate did."

Nicodemus gave a weary sigh. "Perhaps not, but we all have our weaknesses and hatreds. Our discontent comes from the disowned part of ourselves. If we deny our darkness or remain unaware of it, we will blame it on others or act it out in harmful ways. The result increases our pain and makes us vulnerable to actions that betray our souls. This is the way to terrible suffering. In order to find healing, we must befriend our darkness and let the light illuminate more and more of it. This is the way to true enlightenment."

Gabriel reached for Nicodemus' hand. "I don't feel like eating. Please come with me as I finish shopping; then we can walk home together."

Gabriel led him from the alley into the open market, pushing his cart across the uneven stones through the noisy crowd. In the next block they came to a produce stand. There he and Nicodemus loaded the cart with apples, grapes, figs, walnuts, and bitter herbs. As Gabriel was paying the merchant, he noticed that a group of people had gathered in front.

Nearly thirty men were standing in rows in a tight semicircle. As Gabriel edged his way to the front, he saw two bearded men in soiled animal skins. Both were rugged, with athletic builds and dirty faces. One was tall, with a wide forehead and large ears. The other was of medium height, with pockmarked skin and several missing teeth. They held crude daggers, and the taller man waved his as he addressed the group in a low voice.

Gabriel quickly grasped who these men were and what they were doing. The tall one said in Aramaic, "This time Pilate has gone too far. How long will we allow the Romans to kill our men and mock our religion? My friend and I are Galileans. We're helping the great Barabbas to organize a revolt, and we need every able-bodied man to fight with us. On the first day of Passover we'll strike at the heart of Roman military power and oppression—the Antonia Fortress. Pilate will pay for his blasphemy. This time we will fight him to the death!"

A murmur swept through the group. Gabriel felt his stomach drop as if he had stepped off a cliff. Rage burned hot in his throat. These Galileans were the kind of men his brother had joined. They had corrupted Dismas. If Gabriel didn't speak against them, they could lead many gullible Jews to their deaths. He steadied himself and stepped to the front of the group. The noontime sun was glaringly hot. The air, redolent with odors from the cooking and the baking and the milling shoppers, smelled sour. He glanced around; no Roman soldiers were nearby.

Gabriel waved a hand and addressed the crowd. "You've heard these men speak. Now listen to me. We're all outraged by what Pilate did, but helping these men will lead to disaster. We may outnumber the Romans, but they have superior armor and swords and training. If we attack them, they'll slaughter us."

The tall man shoved Gabriel aside and spoke forcefully. "Don't listen to this coward. We have more weapons than he thinks. Hundreds of us have been training in the mountains of Galilee. We're disciplined, strong, and brave."

Hearing himself called a coward poured fury through Gabriel's veins. He clenched his fingers into tight fists and felt a surge of energy rise from his feet into his legs and back. He wouldn't let these foreigners mislead his countrymen. He pushed the tall man. "You've said enough." Gabriel's voice was loud and defiant. "I know of the Zealot plan to take over our nation. You don't care how many of us die."

Both Galileans tried to push Gabriel aside, but he lunged at them, head down, legs driving. Several men from the crowd joined in, and a melee erupted. In the confusion, the taller Galilean approached Gabriel from behind. He wrapped an arm around Gabriel's neck and threw him to the ground in a quick spinning motion. When his head hit the stone pavement, light exploded in his brain.

And then everything went dark.

CHAPTER NINETEEN

JUDAS ISCARIOT PUT DOWN HIS HAMMER. His lungs were heaving, his temples pounding. This happened whenever he thought of Barabbas and Judith. He was so enraged that he could barely see. Enraged at Barabbas for sending him away. Enraged at Judith for rejecting his advances and telling her husband.

The clanking of dozens of blacksmiths' hammers echoed throughout the Zealot camp on Mount Arbel. Judas grimaced and went back to pounding the hot strip of metal that he was shaping into a sword. He had to swallow his pride to do such menial work, but at least forging swords and daggers was better than making slingshots or bows and arrows. It was physical and would keep him strong. More importantly, he was supporting the resistance, the success of which depended on the weapons made on Mount Arbel and Mount Gamla.

He drew a breath of smoky, acrid air and asked himself, *How could a trusted advisor to the great Barabbas fall so low?* The question haunted him like a nightmare. Yet Judas was determined to earn the respect of the more than one hundred sweating, bare-chested men in the camp. He hammered each sword and dagger smooth and filed the edges sharp.

Although his muscles ached at night, especially beneath the scar on his wounded arm, he was getting used to this work and to these steep cliffs northwest of the Sea of Galilee. Fish were plentiful here, and he enjoyed gazing out on the Plain of Gennesaret on peaceful, cloudless afternoons like this one. Unfortunately, not all days were as placid. The mountainous terrain made Roman attacks rare, but they sometimes happened. If soldiers tried to scale the cliffs, the Zealots killed or drove them away by rolling enormous boulders down on them.

Judas kept hammering, venting his rage at Judith and Dismas. How had he allowed a naïve young girl to shame him? And why had he not prevailed against her hotheaded husband? He now admitted that he had misjudged them both. Judith was not as naïve as he thought, nor was Dismas as gullible.

Knowing that he had brought his exile on himself deepened the regret. What had he expected? Judith had appeared lonely, but after all, she *was* a Zealot's wife, passionate about following the law. And she was more committed to her marriage than he had guessed. He wished that he had realized this earlier, and that Dismas had controlled his temper. Judas felt fortunate that the incident had happened at Qumran instead of in Jerusalem: He could have been stoned.

How wrong he had been! Now, banished from the inner circle of Zealot leaders, his future appeared bleak. He had lost everything and needed to prove himself again. If he failed to regain Barabbas' trust, he would have to return home to Kerioth in Judea a defeated man.

That was out of the question. He dipped the rough shaft of metal into a vat of water and then set the metal on the large stone that served as an anvil. When he saw that the shaft was straight, he took a file and began to sharpen the edges. Working with the metal triggered memories of his boyhood in Kerioth, where he had grown up the son of a silversmith.

His negotiating ability had made him good at the business side of the trade, and he often met customers in their homes. One of them, the voluptuous wife of a wealthy tax collector, had seduced him when he was seventeen. He stopped his filing and admired the gold ring on his finger. She had given him the ring, and he had worn it ever since. The memory of what happened seized his mind. Her name was Helena. She was an Egyptian who had converted to Judaism when she married. Her skin was the color of coffee and carried the scent of almond blossoms. She had initiated him into the mysteries of sexual pleasure; since then he had always wanted more. Other women had followed, but no matter how many obliged him, there could never be enough.

Had it not been for the Romans, he would still be in Kerioth. The outrageous Roman taxes had put his father out of business and left the family in poverty. Judas bit his lip and returned to his filing. What he missed most were the raven-haired Judean women, but he had a plan to enjoy their company again—this time not as a humble silversmith but as a conquering warrior. In order to accomplish this, he had to succeed where another Judas—Judas the Galilean, the *Sicarii* visionary who had led a revolt in Sepphoris at the time of the census—had failed.

A clanging bell interrupted his thoughts. He threw down the file and glanced around. A young, fleet-footed sentry ran through the camp. "The Romans are coming!" The sentry swore and yelled in all directions. "To the cliffs! To the cliffs!" The men near Judas stopped their work and picked up their swords, slingshots, bows, and arrows.

The clanging grew louder, resounding up and down the mountain. Judas hurried to the nearest ledge, about thirty feet away. At least twenty men were swarming around the towering boulders perched there. To send a boulder crashing down would take three men pushing in tandem. Judas stared out toward the Plain of Gennesaret and saw a dark mass in the distance, moving toward the mountain. *Let them come,* he thought, his stomach grinding. *We'll slaughter them if they try.*

A husky voice was barking orders. Judas turned and saw Simon the Canaanite, the sturdy, round-faced leader of the camp, directing the men to their positions.

Simon went from boulder to boulder. "Don't push until I give the order!" When he approached Judas and the three men near him, he stopped and peered out. "Get ready."

Judas followed his gaze. A huge mob was drawing closer, but the people were not in formation and marching like soldiers. He shook his head, puzzled.

Simon clapped his hands. "They're almost here!"

The closer the massive crowd came, the more Judas doubted that it was made up of soldiers. He glared at Simon. "That crowd is unarmed."

Simon pushed him aside. "How do you know that? They could be concealing their weapons." He faced the men. "Hands on the stones!"

The men did as Simon commanded, standing behind the boulders, knees bent, hands pressed against the stones, waiting. Judas stepped around them and found a spot where he could see clearly. As the mass of people moved closer, he was certain they were unarmed. He ran back to confront Simon. "If we roll these boulders down, we'll kill innocent people."

Simon put a hand up, trying to silence him. "We can't take chances. We must defend ourselves."

Judas began to shove the men toward the ledge. "Don't listen to him!" He went from boulder to boulder. "See for yourselves."

Nine of the men stepped forward and peered out. Almost in unison they began to laugh, and one of them, gap-toothed and pudgy, asked sarcastically, "For this they sounded the alarm?"

Judas moved closer and saw the cause of the laughter—a crowd of at least five thousand on the plain below. Many of the people appeared able-bodied, but some were blind and feeling their way; others walked with canes or crutches; still others carried the lame on straw mats; and groups of lepers were ringing their bells on the fringes of the gathering.

Simon came forward and stared. He cupped a hand over his eyes to shield them from the afternoon sun; then he shrugged, red-faced as he waved the men away from the boulders. "Well, you can never be too prepared," Simon said, smiling. "Let's find out who these people are."

Most of the men went back to their forging, but Judas joined the four who followed Simon down the mountain.

The enormous crowd staggered Judas Iscariot. No one seemed to be in charge until a tall, white-robed man in front held up his arms. Those who were carrying the sick and the lame rushed forward, as did the blind and the lepers. Donkeys brayed; sheep scattered; the crowd grew quiet. All eyes were on the white-robed man.

Judging from their homespun tunics and mantles, these people were farmers, shepherds, fishermen, merchants, tradesmen. Only a few wore the white linen tunics of the wealthy. Many of the men, women, and children appeared poor, their bodies thin, their clothes ragged. *Who are these people?* Judas wondered. *Why are they here?*

Curious, he left the other Zealots and made his way into the crowd, where he was staggered by the odor of sweat and dung. As he pushed his way to the front, he noticed that the eyes of the teacher were focused on some distant horizon. Judas paused beside a skinny teenage boy with a sunburned face. "Who is this man, and where are these people from?" he asked.

The boy stepped back and raised an eyebrow. "Where have *you* been, mister? Everyone knows he is Jesus, the prophet from Nazareth. We believe that he's the Messiah. He fed us beside the sea, and we've followed him here."

Judas strained to see the people rushing forward. The man called Jesus closed his eyes and stood perfectly still, waiting. The blind, sick, and lame formed a line and began to approach him one by one. Jesus laid his hands on each person and prayed. When he looked up, he said in Aramaic, "Be well," or "Receive thy sight," or "Rise and walk." His voice was melodic, a rich, enchanting sound that carried well and echoed faintly off the cliffs.

The lame walked. The blind saw. The deaf heard. The lepers were healed.

With each miracle, Judas felt a peculiar warmth flow through his body. It penetrated his heart, and a fist-size stone lodged in his throat. He blinked back tears. Shaking his head, he stared down and folded his arms on his chest, trying to stifle these strange new feelings, but they remained. Only when the healings ended did Judas relax and swallow easier.

Then Jesus began to address the entire gathering. He did not raise his voice, yet it carried so that everyone heard. "Very truly, I tell you, the one who believes in me will also do the works that I do and, in fact, will do greater works than these." Judas shook his head in disbelief. *Greater works than these?* Searching for the other Zealots, he saw no one. He kept listening. Jesus was going on about the law. About how he had come not to abolish it but to fulfill it.

Judas stared straight ahead, so captivated that he could barely breathe. The man spoke with conviction; the power of his words held the crowd spellbound. *Where does this power come from?* Judas wondered.

Jesus continued, "Blessed are you who are poor, for yours is the kingdom of God."

He calls the poor blessed! Judas remembered his father losing his business, the family not having enough to eat. He also remembered the rich in Kerioth—the disgusting tax collectors who worked for the Romans; the moneylenders who charged exorbitant interest; the shopkeepers who inflated prices. Injustice caused poverty; this prophet called Jesus understood that as the Zealots did. He also understood that the poor deserved better. Was he organizing his own revolt?

Jesus went on, "Blessed are you who are hungry now, for you will be filled. Blessed are you who weep now, for you will laugh."

The words set Judas' heart racing. Barabbas' vision of the future included the Zealots driving out the Romans and returning Israel to the true worship of God—there would be feasting and rejoicing in the land. Jesus of Nazareth's vision sounded similar. He, too, was calling for an insurrection—in the very region from which the legendary Judas the Galilean had come.

Could this man really be the Messiah? Judas wondered. A tremor swept through him as if the ground had shaken. He closed his eyes, but rather than see darkness, he saw brilliant light. People were talking around him, but he heard nothing. Opening his eyes, he shuddered, his body burning from head to foot. A few moments later he could hear again, and it seemed as if a voice were saying, "'This is the Messiah. Follow him."

Someone nudged Judas. He turned and saw Simon the Canaanite and Tobias Naphtali, another of the Zealots, thin-faced, with close-set eyes. "This preacher sounds like one of ours," Simon said, keeping his voice low.

"Even Barabbas doesn't give as much hope to the poor," Judas said. "This man may be more than a preacher. He could rally the masses to our cause."

A surprised expression appeared on Simon's rather homely face. "You mean you think he's a Zealot?"

Judas kept staring at the preacher and whispered, "He might even be greater than Barabbas."

Simon the Canaanite pointed toward Mount Arbel. "The others who came with us didn't think so. They said they don't trust these traveling healers and went back to forging weapons. Only Tobias was intrigued enough to stay."

Judas returned his attention to Jesus of Nazareth, who was saying, "Blessed are the peacemakers, for they will be called children of God. I say to you, love your enemies, do good to those who hate you, bless those who curse you, pray for those who abuse you." Judas shifted his weight uncomfortably, sure that he could never pray for an enemy. Jesus kept talking. "If anyone strikes you on the cheek, offer the other also; and from anyone who takes away your coat do not withhold even your shirt. Give to everyone who begs from you; and if anyone takes away your goods, do not ask for them again. Do to others as you would have them do to you."

Judas frowned. *How can anyone make peace with an enemy?* He heard the distant clanking of the Zealots hammering on Mount Arbel and thought, *Peace only comes when the enemy is defeated.*

Simon turned to go. "This preacher is no Zealot," he said.

Judas grabbed Simon's arm. "Wait. You heard him promise that the poor will be fed and all tears will be dried. He may be an even greater leader than Barabbas." Judas started toward Jesus. "I'm not leaving until I learn more about this man."

Judas Iscariot wove through the crowd, dodging fishermen, shepherds, and farmers who were returning home with their families. *I must know if this man is the Messiah.* He quickened his pace. *If he is, he will lead us to true victory and lasting peace.*

Jesus was standing about thirty feet away. Halfway to him, Judas glanced back and saw Simon the Canaanite and Tobias Naphtali close behind. He moved ahead until he came to a group of about twenty women and men sitting on the grass. Judas slipped to the ground and joined them. A few moments later someone jostled him; he turned to see Simon and Tobias. "We decided that you're right—we came to hear more," Simon said as he and Tobias sat down. "No Galilean has been this popular since Judas of Gamla."

There were baskets of bread and fish on the grass in front of the group. Jesus picked up the baskets, blessed them, and began to pass them around. When he saw Judas Iscariot, Simon the Canaanite, and Tobias Naphtali, he offered them the bread and fish. Famished, Judas took some of each and began to eat.

"What is your name?" Jesus asked.

"I am Judas Iscariot, from Kerioth in Judea." He pointed to the other two men. "These are my friends Simon the Canaanite and Tobias Naphtali."

Jesus put down the baskets. "You are a long way from home."

"Yes, but for good reason." Judas hesitated a moment. "We're working to free our people."

Jesus sat down, a serious expression on his angular features. "So am I." He gestured toward the group. "These are my disciples. I invite you and your friends to join us. You will learn the true meaning of peace and freedom."

Judas' breathing became labored as he noticed a strikingly elegant woman with dark eyes and high cheekbones. She was slender, with long, silken hair the color of cinnamon and a radiant smile that shone with warmth and a touch of mystery. He was immediately attracted to her and as he listened to Jesus, he began to plan how he might meet her.

Jesus spoke with greater confidence than Judas had ever heard, even from Barabbas. The Galilean's eyes bore into him, reaching deep into his soul and making him feel embarrassed by his lust for the woman. Judas pondered whether to tell him about the uprising. Finally he decided only to make a general statement and said, "My friends and I are working with the great Barabbas to drive out the Romans."

Jesus did not alter his expression. "Until our hearts are pure, winning wars will not make us free."

Judas finished eating and set the basket aside. "But you promised freedom for the poor and the oppressed. That's what Barabbas promises. Are you the one who is to bring us this freedom, or are we to wait for another?"

Jesus spread his hands. "Consider what you have seen and heard: The blind receive their sight, the lame walk, the lepers are cleansed, the deaf hear, the poor have good news brought to them. And blessed is anyone who takes no offense at me."

Judas moved away, shocked. The man was hinting that he was the Messiah. Judas' head throbbed. He tried to swallow but could not, nor could he stop his eyes from burning. Had he found the Messiah? Should he follow him? What about the uprising? If the Galilean were lying, Judas would be left with nothing. On the other hand, Barabbas had no miraculous powers and was pinning his hopes on a disorganized band of fighters. If Jesus were the Messiah, he would surely lead the Jews to victory—and give his supporters prominent positions in the new government.

Why should I care about Barabbas? Judas asked himself. *He exiled me. Fighting with the Messiah would be sweet revenge! And who knows what the rewards could be?*

Jesus instructed his disciples to prepare to leave. Judas wiped sweat from his upper lip as he stood with Simon the Canaanite and Tobias Naphtali, watching as everyone gathered their belongings. A heavyset man with a thick black beard came over. "My name is Matthew," he said. "I was a tax collector until I joined Jesus and found peace. He speaks the truth."

Simon the Canaanite confronted Jesus. "You allow tax collectors to follow you?"

"Matthew now seeks justice for those he once cheated." Jesus eyed Simon compassionately. "I can tell that you are a bitter man. If you follow me, love will change you too."

Judas seized Simon and Tobias by the arms and led them away from the group. When they were out of earshot, he said, "I've never seen anyone heal as the Galilean did. We've been waiting for the Messiah so long; maybe he has finally come."

Tobias pulled his arm away. "Would the Messiah associate with tax collectors?"

Simon raised a hand dismissively. "This tax collector no longer works for the Romans—he's following a man who speaks of freedom. I say we stay with the Galilean and convince him to join our movement."

Judas shifted his gaze from Simon to Tobias. "I agree. Simon and I will stay with the Galilean. Tobias, you go back and tell the Zealots that we've found a strong ally for our cause."

Concern swept across Tobias' youthful face, but he nodded and hurried back to the Zealots. Judas turned and saw that Jesus and his disciples were leaving. He and Simon ran to catch up. When they came alongside Matthew, Judas asked about the striking woman he had noticed earlier.

"Her name is Mary Magdalene," Matthew said without looking at him. "She is Jesus' special friend."

Judas thanked him and vowed to meet her at the first opportunity.

CHAPTER TWENTY

A WAVE OF TERROR WASHED OVER JUDITH AS SHE AWAITED HER TRIAL. She had attempted to steal a horse, and Barabbas had ordered the entire camp to join in deciding her fate. With dinner over, she was helping the women clean up, her cheeks burning at the thought of appearing before the thirty-eight men and sixteen women. The assembly would have influence, but Barabbas would render the final verdict.

Which could mean her death.

With the trial set to begin in half an hour, Judith scrubbed a large iron pot, choking from fear and the briny odor. She picked up the tall ceramic jar that held the seawater for washing dishes, poured some water into the pot and cleaned out the crusted lentils with a homespun towel. When she finished, she brushed a wisp of hair out of her eyes and glanced at the gray-blue twilight sky. The evening was hot and stifling, with no wind blowing off the sea, and the sulfur stench hung heavily in the air.

Several men across the plateau were adding wood to the fire and talking among themselves. The women were beginning to congregate and greet one another. Suspicious that they were talking about her, she started to rehearse her defense but worried that no one would understand her actions.

True, it was wrong to steal a horse, but what else could she have done? As she pondered the question, she noticed a one-armed scorpion on the ground heading for the shelter of a cratered rock. The scorpion was weaving from side to side and convulsing in spastic gyrations whenever it hit a pebble. Her life seemed equally pathetic, except that her path was strewn with enormous stones, not small pebbles. Loneliness and shame had become as oppressive to her as the sheer cliffs of Qumran. That was why she had risked stealing the horse.

If she told her story, some of the women would have to empathize. Those by the fire appeared as forlorn as she did, their tunics ragged and soiled, their hair in need of washing, their faces showing the tension they felt. Didn't they also get tired of living like outlaws? Didn't they also feel lonely and estranged from their husbands? They must but couldn't admit it—even to themselves.

She was one of them—a woman living in unbearable conditions and totally dependent on a man. She prayed that some of the women would sense her emptiness and relate it to their own. Then perhaps they would speak up and convince Barabbas to be merciful.

Hanna, the sturdy, plain-faced wife of Amos ben Perez, approached with another pot. She set it down and said, "You know how scarce horses are and how they're prized by the men. How could you dare try to steal one?"

Judith just kept scrubbing and remembered how Simeon of Bethany had dragged her to Barabbas' tent in the middle of the night; how Barabbas had stared stonily at her through sleepy eyes, his bushy hair disheveled. Finally he spoke. "What demons got into you, woman?" After scolding her profusely, he said, "You have risked the welfare of the camp for your own selfish ends, and you must pay for your recklessness."

Barabbas had ordered Simeon to take her back to Dismas, who then stomped around their tent in rage and disbelief. "You were so concerned about your own reputation, but what about mine? You'll make me a laughingstock!" He pulled his hair with both hands. "You're younger and more naïve than I ever imagined."

Pleading for mercy, Judith had finally calmed down Dismas. Now she owed him her life. He could have sent her into the desert to starve.

Her face reddened as she looked up at Hanna. "I was so angry at Judas . . . and terribly lonely. I felt I had to leave."

Hanna raised an eyebrow and turned to walk away. "Are you less lonely now?"

Judith poured water into the pot and stared after her. She wasn't less lonely but hopefully wiser. As she finished washing the pot, the irony struck her: She had wanted to shame Judas Iscariot in front of everyone. Now she was being shamed. Her eyes filled with tears as she thought of how foolish she'd been. As Simeon of Bethany had said, the horses could have escaped, and the resistance might never have recovered. She would tell her side of the incident with Judas and dispel the lies and gossip, but she would not involve Dismas by admitting her loneliness.

Barabbas blew the ram's horn, so she left the pots, walked over to the fire and sat cross-legged on the ground. It took a few minutes for everyone to gather, but when they were all seated in a large circle, Barabbas said, "You know why we are here. A very serious charge has been brought against Judith, wife of Dismas ben Zebulun. Dismas is a courageous warrior, respected by all, so we must treat his wife fairly. I first call on Simeon of Bethany to explain what happened."

Simeon stood and described how he had apprehended Judith. "She was determined to flee—I saw it in her eyes," he said, sweeping the entire assembly with his gaze. "Her deceit endangered us all. The horses could have escaped, and we would have become easy prey for the Romans."

When Simeon had finished, Barabbas said, "I was tempted to send Judith away. I thought that if she wanted to leave, I would allow it. But I'm not a cruel man, and I decided to bring her before the entire camp. Now Dismas will speak in her defense."

Dismas glanced at Judith and then stood and faced the assembly. "Judith left her home and family for our cause. She has tended wounds and forged weapons and prepared meals. No one can doubt her devotion—she has worked as hard as anyone in the dust and the heat." Dismas paused, his mouth hardening into a tight line. "But she's also quite young, and some of you women, especially, can understand how lonely she must feel to be away from home. I plead with you to show her mercy." He caught Judith's eye, his nostrils flaring. "She has assured me that she'll never do anything so foolish again."

The spare, firm-jawed Mattathias ben Gaddi raised a hand and Barabbas called on him. Mattathias stood and drew a breath, glancing skyward as he composed his thoughts. His eyes turned fiery as he began to speak. "Let's get to the heart of the matter. We have a horse thief among us! She may be young. She may be the wife of a respected fighter. But she committed a heinous crime. To have one horse stolen would have been a great loss, but if all the horses had been set free, we would be facing disaster."

Mattathias surveyed the group. "We can never again trust Dismas' wife. If we allow her to go unpunished, she may try to run away again, and others may be emboldened to do the same by our leniency. I, too, am not a cruel man, but I am a practical one." Mattathias narrowed his eyes and glared at Judith. "As I see it, we have only two choices: Banish this woman to the desert or throw her off a cliff into the sea."

An uncomfortable silence settled over the camp, broken only by an occasional fizzle or pop from the fire. Judith sat and stared into the flames. Despite the stifling air, she suddenly felt cold. So cold that she had to flex every muscle to keep from shivering. Not meeting anyone's gaze for fear that the condemning stares would shatter her heart, she wondered why no one understood the stress she'd been under. Had no one acted in a way that they later regretted? Yes, she had done wrong, but not wrong enough to be driven into the desert or dashed on the rocks.

Miriam, the slender wife of the fierce fighter Uriah of Jericho, broke the silence. "I am haunted by Judith's actions. At first I couldn't believe that any woman could be so foolish. Now I feel that Judith has shamed all the women in camp. Our husbands wonder if they can trust us or if we might also try to steal a horse and flee. I agree with Mattathias. This woman must be purged from our ranks. Banishment or death is the only way to restore order and trust among us."

Judith stole a glimpse at Miriam's eyes, which were the color of a well shaft at midnight. She expected to see them brimming with rage and hate. Instead she saw fear, and it struck her how related hate and fear are, and how they combine to incite vengeance and make mercy impossible.

Amos ben Perez, thick-chested and balding, began to speak. "I must say a word on behalf of Judith," he said. "I was there when she bandaged Judas Iscariot, and I saw her try to save Eleazar Avaran's life. This woman has bravely served our cause. She has made a terrible mistake, but she's not wholly to blame." He paused and shot an indignant glance at Simeon of Bethany. "I'm appalled that the sentry let her get as far as the corral. This incident is partly his fault."

Simeon leapt up, jutted out his rounded chin, and placed both hands on his hefty waist. He glared at Amos and said, "How can you possibly blame me for this woman's thievery? I risked my life to stop her."

Barabbas waved a hand and ordered both men to sit down. "This trial is not about either of you," he said. "It's about Judith of Jerusalem." Barabbas called for order and invited anyone else to speak. When no one rose, he said, "You have all had the chance to share in this judgment." He turned toward Judith. "Now, young woman, what do you have to say in your defense?"

Judith knew that she must convince the assembly to give her another chance or she would be banished or killed. She stood and spoke in a steady, measured voice. "I came to Qumran with the best intentions. Like you, I yearn to drive the Romans from our land. But when Judas Iscariot lied and called me a whore, I felt humiliated and enraged." Judith's heart was beating in her throat. She glanced into the darkness and felt its murky oppression seep into her bones. "When he didn't apologize, it was more than I could take." Without thinking, she found herself speaking of Dismas and their relationship. "Dismas . . . Dismas is a good man, but the warfare has changed him. I felt lonely as well as humiliated, and I longed for home. I know how wrong it was to steal the horse. I only pray that you will try to understand and show me God's mercy."

When she had sat down, Barabbas remained quiet for a moment and then he said, "The camp has heard from all parties, and everyone has had the chance to speak. What say you about Judith's punishment?"

The meeting erupted in shouting.

"Throw her off a cliff!"

"Show her mercy!"

"Drive her into the desert!"

"Give her another chance!"

The shouts set off a chorus of murmurs, which Barabbas quelled by saying, "Since there's division among us, as commander, I will render the final judgment. Our camp is low on supplies, and Judith has shown herself to be a fearless thief. I order Dismas to go to Jerusalem to steal for our cause, and I propose that Judith go with him. They must rob the homes of the rich who live near Herod's palace. We will meet them later, in Zedekiah's Cave beneath the city, and enjoy the spoils." He looked first at Judith and then at Dismas. "I'm giving you the chance to restore our trust. Your fate is in your hands."

Dismas raised an eyebrow, a sober expression on his evenly molded features. "This will not be easy, but a woman will arouse fewer suspicions than another man."

Barabbas raised his arms and declared the meeting over. As everyone was leaving, Judith approached Dismas and fell into his arms. "I am so sorry for all I've put you through," she said, laying her head on his chest. Mattathias was the last to walk away and they were finally alone. "I must be honest—I'm not sure I can stay with you, let alone help you rob houses."

Dismas backed away and sat down, his loneliness showing as he stared up at her. "I'm sorry that you are unhappy. I have not been much of a husband to you."

Kneeling beside him, she struggled to keep her voice steady. "No, you haven't. War, not me, is what you live for. Before Judas Iscariot forced himself on me, I was planning to ask you to take me home."

Dismas reached out to touch her arm. "I need you more than ever. If you'll give me another chance, I promise to change."

Judith hadn't expected such an honest response. "Would you really try?"

"Yes," he said, taking her hand in his, "because I still love you, and I believe that you love me." He gave her a roguish grin. "Now we have the chance to steal for the resistance. We'll make a good team. Barabbas mentioned the rich Jews who live near Herod's palace. I know one of them—a Pharisee named Nicodemus ben Gorion, an old friend of my father's. He has purchased incense and spices from our market for many years. He's wealthy and his family worships in the Temple on the Sabbath, so he won't be home. I'll make you a promise: When we get to Jerusalem, if you still want to leave, you can return to your family. But if you decide you love me, you can help with the robbery and recommit to the Zealot cause."

As the fire died down, Judith knew that she couldn't stay at Qumran: Judas' lies and the shame of her failed thievery made the already heavy burden of her loneliness impossible to carry. To buy time she decided to go with Dismas. "All right, I'm willing to help with the robberies in Jerusalem."

Dismas pulled her close, and she didn't resist. Nestled gently against his chest, she felt the warmth of his body and the rhythm of his heart. She peered up into his large brown eyes, as earnest as when they had first met. He kissed her tenderly and laid a hand on her breast. As the last embers of the fire went dark, a sharp yearning for love—real love—seized her. But she wondered if she would ever find it with Dismas.

CHAPTER TWENTY-ONE

SOONER OR LATER ALMOST EVERYONE FALLS IN LOVE. RECOGNIZE THE CONDITION FOR WHAT IT IS—A FORM OF TEMPORARY INSANITY. WE REMAIN MORTAL BUT EXPERIENCE LIFE IN HEAVEN.

OR HELL.

WE BECOME OBSESSED WITH ANOTHER PERSON. OUR SLEEP GETS DISTURBED; WE LOSE OUR APPETITE; WE CAN'T CONCENTRATE.

THESE SYMPTOMS INDICATE THAT WE HAVE SURRENDERED PART OF OUR SOUL TO THIS PERSON. WE HAVE GIVEN HIM OR HER THE POWER TO HEAL AND FULFILL US.

OR TO DESTROY US.

OUR SALVATION LIES IN TAKING BACK THE POWER WE HAVE SURRENDERED. AS THE POWER ORIGINATED IN OUR SOULS, SO MUST WE RETURN THERE AND ESTABLISH DEEPER INTIMACY WITH GOD AND WITH OURSELVES. THE SOONER WE BEGIN THIS WORK, AND THE MORE COMPLETELY WE GIVE OURSELVES TO IT, THE GREATER WILL BE OUR CHANCES FOR SURVIVAL AND GROWTH, NOT DEVASTATION AND DESPAIR.

—**Brother Gregory Andreou's Journal**

Jerusalem
Thursday, April 4

IF KARIM MUSALAHA HAD KNOWN WHAT AWAITED HIM AT JERUSALEM INTERNATIONAL UNIVERSITY, HE WOULDN'T HAVE COME. Being on campus reminded him of Birzeit University in Ramallah, fifteen kilometers away. Although Birzeit didn't have JIU's modern sculptures, meandering stone walkways, and mix of old and new buildings, it had the same energetic, inquisitive students.

He missed them.

Missed what they had learned together.

What they had taught him.

Birzeit had shown him how different he was from his father and the PPA. So different that he couldn't stay. Karim suspected that a phone call from Ahmed Marzouqa had sent Abdul Fattah to Augusta Victoria Hospital to bring him back. Fortunately, Brother Gregory had lost Abdul in Jerusalem traffic and returned Karim safely to the monastery.

A wave of foreboding settled over him. He couldn't have imagined where his life would lead him after dropping out. Nor could he have guessed that he would find an ancient scroll, meet a beautiful Israeli peace activist, and begin a quest for the truth about the relationship between Jesus Christ and Mary Magdalene.

Now he couldn't turn back.

He was walking between Rachel Sharett and Professor Deborah Stottlemeyer, a distinguished scholar of the New Testament and early Christian origins. He and Rachel had met with the professor briefly in her cluttered office to seek an expert opinion on Jesus' relationship with his leading woman disciple. Professor Stottlemeyer had invited them to continue the conversation over lunch in the student center.

Karim kept his gaze trained on the walkway's large stone rectangles so that Rachel wouldn't see the turmoil in his eyes. His developing interest in her gnawed at him like hunger pangs during Ramadan. The interest had begun as a subtle attraction, a spontaneous stirring of the heart that came and went. But as they walked the campus prior to their meeting with the professor, the stirring had deepened in a way that caught him by surprise. As they crossed the quadrangle, surrounded by old stone buildings as well as contemporary glass and steel designs, she told him more about her father. He had worked at this university, not as a member of the faculty or administration, but as a custodian. "My acceptance to medical school fulfilled his dream of a better life for me," she said. "I only wish he could have lived to see me graduate."

Karim had wrapped an arm around her as they walked in silence, and then she asked about his mother. When he spoke of her dying too young to share in his educational achievements, Rachel had met his gaze with teary eyes and said, "If we don't help to heal this land, who will?" In that moment he felt a shift occur in his heart, moving him from attraction to something deeper—something he wasn't sure he was ready to embrace. He didn't want to love an Israeli woman but found himself drawn to her. Since that earlier conversation, the struggle had been exhausting him; he needed to think about something else.

Turning to Professor Stottlemeyer, Karim asked, "Is it possible that Jesus had anything more than a friendship with Mary Magdalene?"

Professor Stottlemeyer adjusted her horn-rimmed glasses and ran a hand through her short red hair. "Like most scholars, I've wrestled with this question. The New Testament suggests that Jesus and Mary Magdalene were very close. According to the Gospel of Luke, he cast seven demons out of her. She stayed with him at the cross and led the other women to the tomb on Easter morning. In the Gospel of John, the risen Jesus even appears to her individually and calls her by name."

Karim missed some of the professor's answer because he was thinking about Rachel and her obvious love for her father. He understood, because he'd had the same deep love for his mother, who suffered for opposing his father's militant Islam. Rachel's voice startled Karim out of his reverie when she said to the professor, "Where do novelists and filmmakers get the idea that Jesus and Mary Magdalene were lovers or even husband and wife?"

The slightly overweight professor chuckled. "Speculation. In the sixth century, Pope Gregory the Great said that Mary Magdalene was the 'sinful woman' in Luke's Gospel who anointed Jesus and wiped his feet with her hair. Gregory got this idea by conflating Luke's version of the story with a similar story in John's Gospel, where the 'sinful woman' is called 'Mary.' But the word 'Magdalene' isn't in the text. The novel and film *The Last Temptation of Christ* show Jesus being tempted to have sex with this woman, but no credible New Testament scholar believes that Pope Gregory was right. Mary Magdalene wasn't a prostitute. She and the 'sinful woman' who anointed Jesus are two different people."

Karim kept walking in spite of the odd sensation inside of him—excited queasiness mixed with withering dread. He had felt the queasiness at Birzeit when dating Mira Ansari, but she was Palestinian. The short-lived romance had never filled him with dread.

He thought of the Jesus letter and remembered something that Brother Gregory had told him. "What about the idea that Jesus and Mary Magdalene were married and had a child?"

"That idea is wildly speculative," Professor Stottlemeyer said, dodging a student who had her nose in a book. "Writers who promote it look outside the New Testament for evidence, but not much exists. They draw on what are called the 'Gnostic Gospels' for support."

Rachel stopped, causing Karim and the professor to do likewise. "What do you mean by 'Gnostic'?"

"The Greek word *gnosis* means knowledge," Professor Stottlemeyer said. "Members of Gnostic groups believed that spiritual enlightenment required secret knowledge. Many Gnostic Gospels were discovered in Nag Hammadi, Egypt, in 1945. Mary Magdalene appears in some of them. She's also the only woman who has a Gospel named for her. The Gospel of Mary was discovered in 1896 and purchased in Cairo. But in none of these sources is she called the wife of Jesus."

"So if there's no evidence, why does the idea persist?" Karim asked.

Professor Stottlemeyer turned serious. "Perhaps because of the human yearning for the divine feminine. If Jesus was the Son of God and Mary Magdalene was his wife, then she, too, becomes a divine figure."

The professor started to walk again and climbed the few stairs that led onto the plaza in front of the student center. "Some of these authors use the Gnostic Gospel of Philip as evidence. Philip describes Mary Magdalene as the 'companion' of Jesus but not his wife. The verse says that he kissed her often, but the manuscript is damaged, so we don't know *where* or *how* he kissed her."

The professor's words stopped Karim cold. It struck him that the popularity of some American novels and films about Jesus and Mary Magdalene stemmed in part from their focus on forbidden love. He couldn't imagine the esteemed prophet Jesus doing anything forbidden. But for Karim the subject was more than a theme—it held ramifications for him. Jewish tradition forbade Rachel to marry outside her religion. If she defied her family and became involved with a Muslim, Ezra and her mother would hold a mock funeral and declare her dead.

Karim's father would treat him similarly if he were to marry a Jewish woman. His relationship with Rachel seemed doomed from the outset. And yet he couldn't deny the stirrings of his heart. He calmed himself by thinking about Jesus' radical vision of love as set forth in his powerful letter. If the letter were genuine, it not only disproved the theory that Jesus and Mary Magdalene were married but also made the idea appear quaint and outdated.

Karim had slowed, and when he looked ahead, he saw Rachel motioning for him to catch up. He hurried toward the two women. As he got to the glass doors that led into the student center, Karim asked the professor, "Have you ever heard of a letter that Jesus wrote?"

She laughed dismissively. "Heavens no."

Karim pushed the door open for her. "Is there any reason he couldn't have written one?"

"If you're asking whether Jesus could read and write, the answer is yes. In the Gospel of Luke he reads during a synagogue service, and in John, he writes in the sand when defending an adulterous woman." She paused thoughtfully before going on. "His ability to quote scripture suggests that he studied with the rabbis; some scholars even speculate that he learned from the cynic philosophers in Sepphoris, near Nazareth. But as far as we know, he never wrote any letters."

"But it's not impossible that he did?" Karim followed the two women into the crowded dining room in the student center.

Professor Stottlemeyer shrugged. "Theoretically, no. But if Jesus had written a letter and the manuscript survived, believe me, we would know about it. The manuscript would be priceless—perhaps humanity's greatest treasure—and if the writings of the New Testament have changed the world, I can't imagine the impact that such a letter would have." She set her briefcase down to stake her claim on one of the few available tables. "Let's get our food and then we can chat some more."

As the professor headed for the salad bar in the food service area, Karim led Rachel toward the grill. He wove a path through rows of rectangular tables, most of them with clusters of students gathered around. An occupant at one of the tables toward the center of the room caught his eye—a middle-aged man sitting with four or five students. Thinking that the man's profile looked familiar, Karim stopped Rachel and moved closer to get a better view.

With his tweed jacket and tan slacks, the man appeared to be dressed as the stereotypical professor, but what raised Karim's curiosity was the man's sandy hair and wire-rimmed glasses. When a blonde-haired girl stood to leave his table, the man extended a hand to say good-bye. In that moment Karim recognized him. He turned his back and carefully directed Rachel where to look. "Do you see that man? He's the one who attacked me at Qumran."

"Are you certain?" Rachel asked.

Karim didn't answer but kept his back turned to the man, waited for the blonde student to pass, and then fell in step beside her. "Excuse me," he said. "Could you tell me the name of the man who was at your table?"

The athletic-looking girl barely altered her pace. "Professor Robert Kenyon. He teaches archaeology."

Rachel caught up to Karim. "Who is he and how can you be sure he's the right man?"

"He's an archaeologist named Kenyon. When a man attacks you with a trowel, you don't forget his face." Karim took her arm and turned his face away from Kenyon as he steered Rachel toward the salad bar. "We can't stay for lunch. We have to tell the professor that something came up."

They intercepted Professor Stottlemeyer as she walked toward the table where she had left her briefcase. Karim began his explanation but someone interrupted, yelling, "Stop that man! He's a thief!" He turned and saw Robert Kenyon running toward him from the center of the room. A hefty security guard in a navy blue uniform heard the commotion and started toward Karim.

Karim grabbed Rachel's hand as Kenyon stumbled into a food cart, sending the dishes crashing, slowing him down. Karim and Rachel sprinted onto the plaza. They planned to swing around and head for her

Jeep in the visitors' lot, near the front entrance, on the other side of the student center. But with the guard radioing for help and pursuing them with Kenyon, they saw that they wouldn't make it and decided to hide. Beyond the plaza lay three brick buildings. Karim squeezed Rachel's hand and ran for the one on the left.

After sprinting down the path and entering the building, he nudged Rachel to the right, up the stairs. Several students were coming down, talking and laughing. Karim and Rachel took the stairs two at a time to pass them and ran down the corridor on the second floor, classes in session on either side. Halfway up the corridor they came to three doors, two opposite the other, marked with the names of professors.

The last door on the right was open a crack. Karim heard footsteps on the stairs as he pulled Rachel inside the small office. He closed and locked the door. The air smelled of warm candle wax. Karim scanned the cubicle-like office and saw a half-burned candle on the tidy wooden desktop. The candle was in a brass holder beside an open Bible.

Rachel squeezed his arm. "I know that professor back there, the one in the classroom on the left."

Karim had glanced at the two professors in the classrooms across from each other. The one on the left wore the black beard and suit of an orthodox Jew. "Who is he?"

"His name is Itzak Kaufman. I've mentioned him to you before."

"Your brother's friend?"

"Yes. He's the outspoken Zionist who teaches political science."

"Did he see you?"

"I don't think so."

Karim pressed an ear to the door and heard shuffling outside.

A commanding voice said, "I'll search the rest of the building. You check this floor."

Karim pulled away and pressed a finger to his lips. Light streamed from the window behind the desk. Rachel leaned into him, her dark eyes glinting with fear. Someone was searching door to door, rapping on each one. He remained still as she pressed her cheek against his chest. He felt her breath through his threadbare *shalwar*, her body trembling slightly. It took all of his willpower to resist kissing her, but he didn't move.

Then someone banged on the door. The rattling calmed his desire. When the banging stopped, he heard the commotion of the classrooms emptying. Rachel let go and pulled him toward the desk as she wiped sweat from her cheeks. That's when he saw it—the small rectangular wooden nameplate with "Dr. Itzak Kaufman, Professor of Political Science" engraved on brass. He pointed to the nameplate as Rachel read it, her lips tightening into a thin line.

"We can't let Kaufman find us here," she said, her voice barely audible.

Just then Karim's cell phone vibrated in his pocket. He withdrew it and read a text message from Brother Gregory: "Come quickly. Finished translating Judith's diary. A stunning revelation." He held out the open phone so that Rachel could read the text.

She glanced at it quickly and said in a low voice, "Let's run for it. If Kaufman catches us here, he'll tell my brother."

Karim pressed an ear against the door. When he heard nothing, he cracked the door and peeked out. No security guard, no Kenyon. A group of students stood near the end of the hall to the left. He stepped out and Rachel followed. "We can't go through the student center," he said. "We must pass alongside it and weave around the adjacent buildings to reach the parking lot."

When she nodded, he led her down the hall, knowing that they would have to pass through the students. He hoped that Kaufman wouldn't see them. To Karim's relief, the professor wasn't in his classroom. But when Karim stepped into the stairwell, Kaufman was on his way into the hall, cup of tea in hand. The professor stopped abruptly when he saw Rachel, his strong features lighting up in recognition and surprise. "Rachel Sharett, what are you doing here?"

"Hello, Professor Kaufman," she said, her voice steady. "I'm here doing some research."

"And who is your friend?" Professor Kaufman asked.

"We're in a hurry right now," she said, continuing to move along. "Sorry. We'll chat sometime very soon. Sorry," she called again over her shoulder.

Karim kept pace with her as they rushed down the stairs. He planned to lead her outside, but when he glanced through the narrow window in the door, he saw a second security guard, athletically trim, headed toward the building, walkie-talkie pressed to his ear. Karim grabbed Rachel's hand and ran down the stairs to the basement.

The first door on the right was open—the boiler room. He slipped inside and turned on the light, a single bulb hanging from a long wire. The large room had an industrial-size furnace in the middle, two high windows in back, and ladders, mops, and brooms stacked along one wall. The boiler was off, the room quiet. Drawing Rachel in, Karim closed and locked the metal door and turned off the light. Then he led her to the back, behind the boiler. "We'll have to stay here until dark," he said. "Then we can run to the Jeep without being seen."

Leaning against the cement wall, she nodded and whispered, "You'd better text Brother Gregory and tell him we'll be late."

Karim tapped out the message and then turned toward Rachel. "I'm so sorry to have put you in this situation. I had no way of knowing that the man who tried to take the scroll from me was a professor or that he taught at JIU."

"It's not your fault. At least we now know his motivation. I suspect that he was on a dig at Qumran and had a permit to excavate that cave. He's not only jealous that you found the scroll and he didn't, but he also thinks you're a thief."

Karim frowned. "Did you see his eyes? I think he's crazy."

"We have to get out of here before he finds us," she said, her eyes filled with worry.

He reached for her hands. When he touched her fingers, she didn't pull away. He remembered how her cheek had felt against his chest in Kaufman's office, her breath warm and soothing. This could be his last chance to learn if she would return his feelings. "In the professor's office, when you held me, I felt . . ."

"Shh!" She put her finger to his lips, and then interlocked her other fingers with his. "I was scared—scared because we were being chased, and scared that you might be feeling something that could cause us both trouble. But then I held you and the fear went away."

In the pale light from the windows, he saw her pulse beating at the base of her neck. "I know that loving you is impossible . . . but I can't help what I feel." He reached up and ran a hand through her hair. "If we're caught, we could lose everything. All we have is this moment." He leaned toward her and felt her lips meet his, full and soft and moist.

The kiss, as refreshing as cool water in the desert, felt so right. He found her buttery scent intoxicating. As he wrapped his arms around her and she did the same, he was transported to that distant, magical place that gives birth to dreams. He surrendered completely and forgot where he was. A darkening boiler room became an ocean of calm, inviting him into its mysterious depths. He felt her heart beating and knew he would return forever changed.

When the kiss ended, he scoured his mind for something to say, but no words came. He prayed that Allah would help him, and he hoped that Rachel was praying too, because they would need divine intervention to make this unlikely relationship work. He eased his head back but continued to hold her. "Do you think what Jesus wrote to Mary Magdalene is true?"

"What part do you mean?"

"The part about the male and the female within. He said that their spiritual union holds the secret of love."

She ran a finger across his cheek as if needing physical proof that this moment was real. "Maybe this is our chance to find out. Everything is against us—religion, politics, history, our families. It would take something miraculous to make this relationship last."

"But isn't that what we have in the letter—a miracle?" He found her hand again and held it along with her eyes, in which he saw a reflection of all the love, pain, and hope for the future that he held locked behind his own. "Maybe if we don't expect the other person to be responsible for meeting our needs, as the letter says, we'll find the purest love. Maybe that's why we've been brought together—to show that this kind of love can triumph even in this tortured land."

Karim's cell phone vibrated again. He wished he could ignore it and make this moment last forever, but he knew it would have to end sometime. Reluctantly he withdrew the phone and read another text message from Brother Gregory: "We must test Judith's revelation now. If true, the letter is genuine. Come quickly."

When he showed the message on the lighted screen to Rachel, she asked, "What does he mean that we must test her revelation?'"

Karim shook his head. "Hopefully we'll find out soon." As Karim returned the phone to his pocket, he noticed the darkness outside the small windows high on the wall. He led Rachel to the door and listened. When he heard no sound, he kissed her one last time, wishing it could last an eternity. Then he whispered, "We've got to sneak out. It's our only hope."

He opened the door and saw that the corridor was deserted. Grabbing her hand, he headed in the direction of the parking lot.

CHAPTER TWENTY-TWO

GABRIEL OPENED HIS EYES AND TRIED TO MOVE, BUT COULDN'T. The whitewashed stone ceiling above him appeared familiar, but his mind was hazy, and he couldn't remember where he had seen the rough, pitted surface. The brilliant light of midmorning was flooding the room, and he heard the clumping of donkeys' hooves outside the window, mingling with the voices of merchants and the laughter of children.

The light hurt his eyes. *Where am I?* He blinked to moisten the burning dryness. His head throbbed as he remembered the two Galileans in the marketplace, and how they had slammed him on the stone pavement. The haze clouding his mind made him feel as if he'd been asleep for days. He tried to move his arms, but they wouldn't respond, nor would his legs. And the back of his head ached. The pain was agonizing, but as he remembered the ache in his heart, the hurt felt mild in comparison.

How could you, Judith? The question echoed in his mind, as unanswered as his prayers for relief. Perhaps she considered Dismas more handsome than he—or smarter or braver or stronger. If so, Gabriel had no power to change her mind. He had lived with comparisons to Dismas all his life, and he found the competition between them grueling. His brother *was* better at some things, such as working with his hands. Making this concession gave Gabriel a degree of peace, but competing for Judith brought the turmoil back. Her choice of Dismas had left Gabriel's spirit more paralyzed than his body.

He drew a breath, thankful to be alive; then he tried to sit up and this time his muscles worked. Dust motes danced in the sunlight streaming through the window. A clothing chest, a desk, and a stool made of pine sat across from him in the room, which smelled faintly of sickness. He blinked again and recognized where he was—his bedroom in his parents' home in Jerusalem. Touching his head, he felt bandages and recognized the smell as coming from ointments and dried blood.

The two Galilean men came to mind again—the revolt they were planning, the fire in their eyes. He swung his legs over the edge of the bed and knew he must go to Galilee to convince Jesus of Nazareth to increase his efforts for peace. With the support of the masses, Jesus was the only one who could stop the revolt and the terror it would cause. Even more, Gabriel had to warn Jesus to stay away from Jerusalem because Pilate had become suspicious of all Galileans, and the city would be dangerous for Galilee's most outspoken prophet.

Gabriel tried to stand but became lightheaded and fell backward. The bed's wooden legs scraped the stone floor and made a screeching noise. As he propped himself up in bed, a rotund woman and two older men rushed into the room. He recognized his mother and father and Nicodemus ben Gorion.

"Thank God you're back with us," his mother said, kissing him on the cheek. "Nicodemus brought you home and has been keeping vigil with us since yesterday. You could have been killed. Sometimes I think you're as reckless as Dismas."

Gabriel opened his eyes further and tried to speak. "I must go to Galilee." He was grateful to hear his voice come out clear and true. "The men who hurt me must be stopped."

"Don't think about that now," his stern-faced father said, gripping Gabriel's legs. "Just try to rest. Passover is coming, and you'll be needed at the market."

"Passover will be a time of slaughter if the Galileans have their way." Gabriel tried to lift a leg to get up, but his father restrained him. "Please, Father, I must go. Dismas and Judith may be involved in the revolt." He pushed against his father's hands, but couldn't move.

Nicodemus, who was standing beside the baldheaded Zebulun at the foot of the bed, spoke to him. "May I speak with your son in private, please?"

"You may not leave until you're well," Zebulun said, taking his wife's hand to lead her from the room. "No matter what Nicodemus tells you."

"I agree with your father, my son," Nicodemus said when they were alone. "It would be unwise for you to go to Galilee until you are better. Your fighting in the marketplace speaks of your need for greater maturity. As I told you earlier, you must look within before you condemn Judith and Dismas or the Galileans."

Gabriel hardened his stare. He had a right to be angry and to fight if he wanted to. Furious, he said, "Those Galileans are supporting the men who corrupted Judith and Dismas. Of course I fought them."

Disappointment showed in Nicodemus' large round eyes. "You have not yet understood the teachings of Jesus, my son. Their wisdom explains why Judith and Dismas betrayed you. They didn't set out to do it. They were led astray by their emotions. If you understood the power of their attraction, you might still be angry, but you would also feel compassion for them."

Nicodemus paused and went to get the stool sitting beneath the window. When he had settled himself beside the bed, he continued. "Judith and Dismas were unaware of the pain that's driving them, and they made harmful choices based on ignorance. Your violence shows that you also don't know yourself intimately, nor do you understand what brings happiness. If you want to be healed, you must not condemn others without acknowledging your own wounds and faults. As you do this, you grow in the inner knowledge that produces freedom."

Gabriel swallowed hard to stop himself from raising his voice. "You should save those words for Judith and Dismas."

Nicodemus laid a hand on the bed and kept his voice low. "I read the letter that Jesus wrote to Mary Magdalene, and I discovered many truths that Judith and Dismas need, but so do you and I. When sex is forbidden, its power to beguile the heart increases, because it comes from our dark, unknown self—a self filled with hidden feelings and sinister desires. Judith and Dismas became lost in the darkness, but they will soon learn that no couple can happily live there."

Gabriel was struck by Nicodemus' statement and leaned forward to hear more. "Why didn't you tell me about this darkness before?"

"Because you weren't ready. The letter discusses sexual matters in a way that most people never understand. It tells of Jesus' struggles in his relationship with Mary Magdalene, and how he came to an enlightened understanding of sex. Now he wants to bring all of us to this enlightenment."

Gabriel's stomach tensed at the mention of Mary Magdalene. He remembered not only Mary's striking beauty but also the emptiness in her eyes—the same emptiness that he saw when he looked at himself in the mirror. He searched Nicodemus' face for understanding and kept his voice low. "Why didn't you tell me that you knew these things about Jesus and Mary Magdalene?"

Nicodemus hesitated a moment and then said, "Because I am still learning the letter's teachings myself, and I can only speak from my incomplete knowledge." Diverting his eyes from Gabriel's, he went on, "The heartbreak that Jesus endured because of his feelings for Mary Magdalene led him to examine his life. He yearned for her as passionately as any man ever yearned for a woman, but he spent hours praying about his feelings and developed an abiding respect for how sexual attraction flows from people's souls and how it shapes them. Through his anguish, he arrived at the true purpose of his life, which is to preach the kingdom of God. In order to accept this dangerous mission, he decided that he must remain unmarried. Through his own turmoil and heartbreak, he developed a keen compassion for people's suffering."

Gabriel felt regret gnawing at his conscience. He had condemned Jesus without considering his struggle as a man—a struggle similar to Gabriel's—to give up an impossible love. "I need to go to Jesus to find out if he's as wise as you think."

Nicodemus put a hand on Gabriel's arm. "Please hear me out. In his letter to Mary Magdalene, Jesus reflected on the sexual wounds that have shaped our people's history. For example, in Abraham's family, the fierce rivalry between his wife, Sarah, and her maidservant, Hagar, caused heartbreak for all three, and for their sons Isaac and Ishmael. Jealousies erupted in Jacob's family when he had sons by four women, his wives Leah and Rachel and their servants Zilpah and Bilhah. Jacob's son Judah had sex with his daughter-in-law Tamar, who bore him twins. Boaz was the son of Salmon and Rahab, the harlot of Jericho. And most notoriously, King David committed adultery with Bathsheba and then had her husband killed on the battlefield. Don't you see, Gabriel? Jesus shows compassion and understanding to sexual sinners such as the prostitute at Simon's house because he knew this painful history. He wrote the letter to show the way to healing."

Gabriel stared at Nicodemus, wide-eyed. "If what you're saying is true, it casts a different light on how Jesus treated Mary Magdalene."

"Yes, but there's more to it than that." Nicodemus raised a finger as a teacher making a point would. "The letter acknowledges that sexual attraction can overwhelm us all. When it strikes, our lives feel out of control. We can think of little else, can hardly eat or sleep. Isn't this the way you felt about Judith?"

Gabriel recalled studying Hebrew with Judith under their demanding teacher, Josiah ben Zakkai. The wiry and fun-loving Josiah took the class of five to the Garden of Gethsemane and had them read from the Torah. Gabriel often stumbled on words and asked for help, but Judith read Bible stories and texts of the law perfectly. Listening to her, surrounded by the spring grass, budding olive trees, and flocks of sparrows soaring skyward, he heard more than a young girl's voice. It was as if a voice other than Judith's invited him to adventure, to discovery and joy. He often heard it in Judith's presence, especially when she was with the neighborhood children. She played tag and hide-and-seek with them and word games that kept them giggling for hours. How could Gabriel not have loved her? Everyone did, and he was overjoyed when his father had arranged the match. He brought his gaze back to Nicodemus and frowned. "What good are the letter's teachings to me? Judith has made her choice, and I must live with it."

Nicodemus gazed slowly out the window, his voice sounding wistful as he said, "The letter says that when we fall in love, we are unaware of why we are attracted to the other person. We believe it's because she is beautiful or intelligent, or because we are interested in the same things. But really what we see in the other person is some lost or disowned part of ourselves, or she reminds us of a past lover or one of our parents or someone who cared for us as children."

Nicodemus moved to the foot of the bed. "Gabriel, when we see a person as more than human, we become disillusioned quickly. No mortal can embody godlike qualities for long. Eventually the person begins to appear ordinary—or worse. And we can end up angry and despairing because we believe we chose the wrong person, someone we realize we don't even like, let alone love."

Gabriel felt a chill spiral through him at Nicodemus' words. The wise Pharisee could be describing Gabriel's experience with Judith, and he wished that he had heard these teachings earlier. He wiped sweat from his forehead and asked, "Is all of this in the letter that Jesus wrote Mary Magdalene?"

Nicodemus gave him a wide smile. "And much more. Jesus provides guidance for living in harmony and peace. He reveals how to bring the unknown side of ourselves into the light of understanding. When we do this, we can choose our mates wisely because we are more aware of the illusions of falling in love. We consider the person's character, depth, and maturity; the values and interests we share; and whether we are really compatible. In order to find true love, we must accept the darkness in ourselves and in our mates. Then, when we get hurt by these people, we can empathize with the wounds that caused the hurtful behavior, and we can *choose* to love in spite of the maddening habits of our mates."

Gabriel let out a sigh. "So our ability to love comes from both our light *and* our darkness?"

Nicodemus' face brightened as he gave an affirming nod. "The letter emphasizes that true holiness brings the light and the darkness together, and I know from applying this wisdom to my own struggles with marriage that it can give a couple new life. Relating to one another becomes an opportunity for growth, for learning to love as God loves. You see, if we are not aware of our darkness, we will deny it or act it out unknowingly, as Judith and Dismas did, and we will cause great anguish. Really loving is so much harder than falling in love. It involves caring for a person even when the initial attraction has faded. For this we need the light."

Gabriel didn't move his eyes from Nicodemus'. "After what you've told me, I'm more determined than ever to find Jesus." He began to get up.

"Not until you are well," Nicodemus said, gently holding him back.

Gabriel pushed against Nicodemus' arms. "I must go *now*."

"You heard what your father said."

"I don't care." Gabriel tried to throw him aside, but couldn't. "I must go! Jesus is the only one who can stop the Zealots from destroying our country, and if I don't warn him about Pilate's rage, he could walk into a trap in Jerusalem." He eyed the old Pharisee. "Now get out of my way!"

Nicodemus held him tightly. "I will see that he gets the warning; there is still time. For now you must rest. Besides, I have more to tell you about the letter."

Gabriel stared at him, stone-faced. Was the wise old Pharisee right that there was time? Would Nicodemus warn Jesus as he promised? Gabriel couldn't take the chance. He would go himself in case Jesus refused to listen to reason, as was often his way. But perhaps Nicodemus was right. He should wait a few days to be sure he was well enough to travel. While recovering he could hear the rest of what Nicodemus had to say. His promise might be a ploy to keep him in bed, but he had to admit that the Pharisee had captured his interest.

"All right," Gabriel said. "I'll stay in Jerusalem to rest, but no matter what you do, I must find Jesus before he enters the city and speak to him personally."

Nicodemus embraced him and got up to leave. "If you're better by the Sabbath, come to my home after the morning sacrifices. It's quiet there, and we can talk without interruption. Then, if you're strong enough, you can go to Jesus. In the meantime, I will send a carrier with your message."

Gabriel fingered his bandages, wishing he could remove them. He thought about what the Galileans had done to him and about the revolt they were planning. If Pilate got wind of the uprising, his reprisal would be swift and fierce. Gabriel quivered. He would warn Jesus, even if it meant risking his life.

CHAPTER TWENTY-THREE

THE WHITE MARBLE OF NICODEMUS BEN GORION'S HOME FELT COOL AGAINST JUDITH'S TREMBLING HANDS. She and Dismas were there to rob it, having arrived two days earlier and hidden out with resistance fighters in Zedekiah's Cave, the sprawling underground quarry in northwestern Jerusalem that was named for the last king of Judah. Now it was time to break into this spacious three-level house with wide terraces, expansive roofs, and glorious views of the Temple. On this Sabbath morning, most people were at worship and the streets were deserted as expected. But Nicodemus and his family would return soon, so she and Dismas had to act fast.

As she followed him toward the back of the house, she knew that this could be her last chance to leave. A week earlier, she had been desperate enough to steal a horse. Now, because Dismas had saved her from banishment, possibly even death, everything was different. On the ride from Qumran to Jerusalem, the memory of her young brother Reuben getting run over by a chariot had played across her mind. Her craving for justice and her gratitude to Dismas had kept her with him.

Remembering his promise to be a better husband, she nevertheless worried that his good intentions were only words. His first priority had to be to win back Barabbas' trust, not to build a life with her. If she robbed this house, she would be breaking the law and become even more tied to Dismas. She stopped and let him walk ahead. This was her chance to go home and apologize to all the people she had hurt. Perhaps they would forgive her and she could rebuild her life.

Dismas turned around and saw her standing there. He waved a hand impatiently and mouthed the words, "Come on."

By stealing for the Zealots she would contribute to their cause. She might also regain the respect of those who had believed Judas' lies. On the other hand, stealing was wrong, and she was preparing to steal from a rich Pharisee; the consequences of getting caught would be worse than standing trial before Barabbas.

She had no choice but to rob the home. Her face grew hot and her palms sweaty thinking about it. She ran to Dismas. Memories of the night they had eloped came back to her: how close she had felt to him beneath the stars; the desert wet with dew; the night silent except for the crackle of the fire and the distant cry of a hawk. He took her hand and strode faster, carrying a long rope and a large homespun bag. "It's time to steal a rich man blind," he said with a grin as he tossed the noosed end of the rope onto the roof.

Judith watched as he attempted to lasso a corner or a ledge, but he kept missing. Her chest ached from her heart's pounding. "Hurry, Dismas," she whispered. "The Temple service will get out soon." The noose finally caught on a corner of the roof, and he tossed her the bag and began to climb. He straddled the rope and ascended hand over hand, his sandaled feet fighting to gain traction on the dusty limestone. Halfway to the top, he slipped, his body slamming against the wall and then dangling as he struggled to gain a foothold. His heavy grunts and gasps made her wonder if he would make it, but he redoubled his efforts, and in spite of several missteps and moments of swaying wildly, he finally hoisted himself onto the roof. She ran toward the side door off the alley, and in a matter of minutes, he was unlocking and opening the door from within.

Judith followed him inside, and they rushed through the courtyard, past linen-cushioned divans, well-designed gardens, and a cavernous bathing pool. The floral mosaics and colorful frescoes in the main room were enhanced by the hibiscus-like scent of fine perfume. He shook his head in disgust. "These rich men have profited from the Romans. Now it's our turn."

Dismas eyed a purple curtain beside the dining room. Heading toward it, he waved for Judith to follow. Behind the curtain lay a small chamber that housed elegant clay tableware, pale green Roman glass vessels, gold and silverware, and pottery inlaid with sapphires. He opened the homespun bag and began to fill it.

At the far end Judith discovered the folded robes and phylacteries of a Pharisee. The name *Nicodemus ben Gorion* was inscribed on several parchments. On a shelf lay what looked like an ornately carved jewelry box, long and deep. Setting the box on top of the polished silverware caused a ringing that sent an echo of guilt through her.

Watching as Dismas hurried to fill the bag, she shuddered to have sunk so low—robbing a rich man like a common thief. The thought paralyzed her, and she stood fused to the polished stone floor as the guilt caused her eyes to water.

Voices.

The expression on Dismas' face said that he had heard them too. He pulled the curtain closed and then pressed his index finger to his lips. They both stood silent and still, trapped in the storage chamber.

The voices drew closer, and she identified the voice of an older man, whom she assumed was Nicodemus ben Gorion, as he invited a companion to sit and drink wine. "It's quiet here and we can talk about the letter," Nicodemus said.

"What you told me about the darkness within has helped me to understand why Judith and Dismas betrayed me," Gabriel said, pain lacing his words.

Judith gasped.

"What was that?" Nicodemus asked and then became quiet as though listening for another sound. After a few moments, he said, "Must have been the wind."

Judith stared at Dismas, her mouth agape with the realization that Gabriel was Nicodemus' guest and was seeking counsel from his father's friend about his broken heart. Dismas scowled at the sound of his brother's voice. She watched as beads of sweat dotted his forehead.

Gabriel went on, "After what you told me about the rabbi Jesus of Nazareth's letter to Mary Magdalene, I understand his compassion for the harlot at Simon ben Ephraim's house. I know Jesus didn't mean to hurt Mary."

Confronted by how deeply she had hurt Gabriel, Judith brought a hand to her mouth, sickened by how she had betrayed him. Tempted to cry out, she remained silent by biting her lip till she drew blood. She wondered who this rabbi named Jesus of Nazareth was.

"The letter contains more radical ideas," Nicodemus said. "Forgiving Judith and Dismas will help to release your pain, but it cannot make you well. For that, you must become more whole. And that is accomplished when you embrace the female within you."

"The female?" Gabriel said, agitated. "There's no female in me!"

Hearing Gabriel now, Judith remembered his fun-loving nature as a child, and how people were drawn to him, how impressed they were by his intelligence and his natural gift for business. The guilt hit her again, taking her breath away like a punch in the stomach.

Nicodemus cleared his throat and said, "In the letter Jesus describes the oneness of the male and the female by referring to the creation story in the Torah. The story explains that God created the first human being both male *and* female, in God's image."

"I thought the first human being was a man called Adam, and that God created the first woman from his rib," Gabriel said.

"That's one reading of the story," Nicodemus replied from his place on the other side of the curtain. "But the Hebrew word *tsela,* which is often translated 'rib,' more often means 'side.' The letter emphasizes the wonderful meanings associated with this second reading. 'Adam' is not necessarily a man's name; it literally means 'red earth.' Perhaps the first human was both male *and* female, as the Torah implies. This reading pictures God putting the first human to sleep and dividing it into two separate beings, a man and a woman. Adam and Eve originally shared a common side. They were created equal, a perfect union of male and female."

Judith felt tension grow within her as she listened. A sharp throbbing began as she realized that Nicodemus' telling of the creation story mirrored her own experience. Falling in love with Dismas felt like a homecoming, a return to a joy that she had known long ago but then lost. When she made love to him in the desert, the joy had become complete. But when there was conflict between them, she felt lost again. The feeling had continued until the present and she had not known a moment of peace, except on those rare occasions when Dismas listened to her long enough to lure her into sex.

The smirk on Dismas' hard, unexpressive face made her feel estranged from him. She had betrayed Gabriel and now she was trapped in an empty marriage that felt as suffocating and inescapable as the storage chamber in which they were standing. It took all her resolve to keep from sobbing out loud, for she suddenly felt overwhelmed with guilt.

Nicodemus went on, "With the woman's creation, Adam became alienated from her spiritual essence that had resided within him, and he began to ache for her, body and soul. Her voice woke him from his deep sleep, and from then on, he yearned to hear her whisper his name. The woman felt the same yearning. The letter quotes the Torah: 'This is why a man leaves his father and mother and joins himself to his wife, and they become one flesh.'"

Judith could hear Gabriel's labored breathing. He began to speak but then stopped, his voice cracking. Finally he managed to say, "But what does all of this have to do with how Judith broke my heart?"

Judith stared at the floor, avoiding Dismas' gaze as tears burned her eyes and a tight knot formed in her throat. The tears fell onto her soiled tunic, leaving spots that appeared dark and lasting. Keeping her head low, she prayed that the wise Pharisee's reply would ease her grief.

Nicodemus said, "Eve once lived within Adam, and he within her, but she became an earthly being when God separated her from Adam's side. Eve was female, but her soul remembered its original oneness with Adam, and their painful separation could only be healed through a physical reunion. They accomplished this by celebrating their nakedness in the sexual ecstasy of paradise. Adam and Eve were naked and unashamed because they remembered being both male and female. Only when they disobeyed God did the man begin to see himself as exclusively male and the woman as exclusively female. They became aware of the separation that left them scarred in body and fractured in soul. Their pain reminded them that their sexual opposite, which was once part of their very essence, now existed outside of them. Thus the man and the woman were left suffering in body and estranged in spirit. They became ashamed because they were with a person of the opposite sex, and they covered up their nakedness. Finally, when God banished them from the Garden, he placed cherubim at the entrance, along with a flaming sword, to prevent them from returning. Ever since, sex has given men and women a taste of Eden."

Tears filled Judith's eyes so she couldn't see Dismas, and she bit down on the cloth of her tunic to keep from crying out. *What have I done?* The thought kept echoing in her mind, each repetition more devastating than the last. The only relief and comfort she found was in Nicodemus' words. She wondered what Gabriel was thinking, and whether he would accept or challenge the letter's teachings. Once again she wondered how Nicodemus had come to possess this letter. He said that the rabbi Jesus had written to a woman named Mary Magdalene. Who was she, and why didn't she have the letter?

Finally Gabriel said, "I've never heard the story of Adam and Eve explained this way." His voice sounded hoarse and strained, burdened with sorrow. "To accept the letter's teaching would mean changing my view of myself. It would mean seeing myself as both male and female. How do I do that?"

Nicodemus didn't answer immediately, but eventually he said, "You can only do this through deep reflection and a growing awareness of your true nature. We are all like Adam and Eve outside the Garden. Sexual attraction feels euphoric because it returns us to when man and woman were one. Lovers find in each other the bond they have lost between the male and the female in themselves. They also see *through* each other to the image of God in their partner. This makes the woman appear as a goddess and the man a god."

"Is this what you meant when you told me that I didn't understand sexual attraction?" Gabriel asked.

Judith stole a glance at Dismas. He appeared to be listening as intently as she was to Nicodemus. "The woman in the man and the man in the woman are the unseen partners in the attraction. Healthy people know this and use it to their benefit, in both their courting and married lives. Unfortunately, it is difficult to live in this healthy way because it takes continual vigilance and discipline. The pain in the marriages and families of Abraham, Isaac, Jacob, and David illustrate this point, as well as many others. Dismas and Judith are like these people who, in their ignorance, brought suffering upon themselves. Thankfully Jesus has recovered God's image as male and female, and he can show us the way to healing."

Gabriel struggled to keep his voice steady. "I want to see Jesus again. But now I will see him with new eyes."

Nicodemus said, "If you want to recover from the blow that Judith dealt you, you must find the feminine image of God in yourself. That is how a man gains access to the treasures in his soul as Jesus has. He is like the first human being before the separation of Adam and Eve. He is the new Adam, a perfectly whole man, with deep intimacy between the male and the female in his soul. The deeper you go into this intimacy within yourself, the more capable of love you will become. I know this because, after reading the letter, I have been going deeper myself, and I have never been happier in my life and marriage."

As Nicodemus was speaking, Judith heard other voices. A woman called from the courtyard, imploring him to come quickly. "Hadassah is near death and wants to see you!" Judith assumed that the voice belonged to Nicodemus' wife, since he and Gabriel left immediately.

After they were gone, Dismas quietly stole out into the dining room, Judith following. As they went up to the third-floor roof, Judith couldn't forget Gabriel's anguish. But neither could she forget the part Nicodemus had played. His words still whispered in her mind, puzzling and comforting.

Dismas handed her the bag, secured the rope to the ledge and shimmied down it. Judith threw him the bag and then started down the rope. As she neared the ground, she heard someone yell, "Thieves! Stop, thieves!" Judith jumped the final three feet and ran with Dismas, reminded of the night they had eloped. *How I wish I had never left home.* She strained to keep up with her husband, sprinting for Zedekiah's Cave and the tunnels beneath the city.

CHAPTER TWENTY-FOUR

THE GREATEST FIGHT OF JUDAS ISCARIOT'S LIFE BEGAN ON A GRASSY TERRACE IN CAESAREA PHILIPPI. He was with Jesus of Nazareth and his inner circle of followers on the west side of the city. Simon the Canaanite handed him a wineskin of water, and as Judas drank, he caught a glimpse of Mary Magdalene wiping her face with a towel. Intrigued by her eyes, which peeked over the towel, he admired her lustrous hair, her full lips and breasts, and found himself wanting her—a hot wanting, and frantic.

The bottom dropped out of Judas' stomach. His thoughts spun as he helped the others clear away the small stones scattered on the terrace, which sat above an ancient Roman road. There were both men and women among the followers: the brothers Simon Peter and Andrew; Thomas and Matthew the tax collector; John and his brother James; Philip and Bartholomew; Thaddaeus and James, the son of Alphaeus; Mary Magdalene and Joanna; Martha and her sister Mary;

Susanna and Mary, the wife of Clopas. As Judas tossed the stones aside, he glimpsed the cloudless sky and thought of Qumran.

And how Judith had slapped him.

Emboldened by his past successes with women, he had forced himself on her—and paid dearly.

When they finished clearing away the stones, Judas sat down, removed his sandals and angrily ground his teeth as he remembered Dismas attacking him and Barabbas exiling him to Mount Arbel. He doubted he would make the same mistake with Mary Magdalene. Mary wasn't another man's wife, as Judith had been, and though Mary was Jesus' special friend, the Galilean kept his distance from her. Judas was aware of the resemblance between the two women, although Mary Magdalene—the most beautiful woman he had ever seen—was older and more mature than Judith.

To calm himself, he drew a breath of the crisp early spring air. How could he be thinking of Mary like this when Jesus had shown him nothing but kindness? A fertile valley of marbled green lay below the road, but he didn't really see its richness, let alone the whites and yellows of the budding trees and flowers. In his mind he saw only the fantasy of Mary's nakedness, the image of them together in bed, with their bodies surrendered to each other.

Simon the Canaanite nudged him. Judas glanced up and saw Jesus, a concerned expression on his sun-weathered face, approaching.

"You both look weary," Jesus said, kneeling beside them.

Judas reached for his sandals, avoiding Jesus' gaze. "You give us the refreshment we need, rabbi."

Jesus laid a hand on Judas' shoulder, causing him to look up. "Have you really been refreshed, Judas? Or are you saying what you think I want to hear?"

Judas' cheeks grew hot as he felt Jesus staring right through him. Judas played with the thong of his sandal. "Rabbi, I always find your words refreshing, as do the masses. They believe that you're the one who can free our nation."

Jesus stood and smiled. "I pray that you will find the freedom I offer, Judas." As Jesus moved on to talk with the other disciples, Judas watched him from behind. He told himself not to be jealous of Jesus' relationship with Mary and his power over people, but the urge only got stronger, and he had to look away.

Judas' blistered feet were sore from the two-day journey from the Sea of Galilee, so he pulled them close and poured water over them, trying at the same time to wash the fantasies from his mind. He had never met a man as gentle and compassionate as Jesus. How could he even think of stealing Mary Magdalene from him? The water cooled his feet and soothed his blisters. He didn't want to hurt Jesus, but his fantasies were like demons that possessed his mind, devouring his sanity and leaving him in torment.

The demons had struck early. After meeting the Galilean on the Plain of Gennesaret and joining his disciples, Judas had become accustomed to the moaning of the sick, the chiming bells of the lepers, the thudding crutches of the lame. As their suffering turned to joy because of their healings, he was as awestruck as anyone. But when he noticed how attentive Mary Magdalene was to Jesus, Judas craved the attention for himself and began scheming to get it.

He withdrew a towel from the travel bag that the women had given him. The other disciples were talking among themselves as they spread their belongings on the grass. He began to dry his feet and pondered how to win the acclaim of the masses and the power that came with it—the power to attract a woman of radiant beauty.

Mount Hermon rose majestically in the distance, its heights bathed in muted shades of amber and gray. He listened for the tumble of the headwaters of the Jordan nearby, but instead he heard some of the men discussing what Jesus had done while teaching beside the Sea of Galilee.

Matthew, his dark eyes flashing, said, "I will never deny what I saw."

The stout, broad-shouldered Thomas shook his head defiantly. "What you *think* you saw."

Judas noticed Jesus moving toward the men and followed him as the women also gathered around.

Simon Peter, large and tanned like his brother, with piercing eyes and a beard the color of mahogany, said, "Anyone who can feed all those people with just a few loaves and fish is more than a man."

Judas watched as Jesus slowly measured each face. "Who do people say that I am?" he asked. Everyone stared at him, surprised by the question.

Thomas darted his eyes around the group and said, "Some say you are John the Baptist."

Matthew gestured with an expressive hand. "Others say you are Elijah."

"Still others say you are Jeremiah or one of the prophets," Andrew said.

Judas saw fire in Jesus' eyes as he locked them on Peter's. "But who do you say that I am?"

Peter became quiet for a moment and then answered boldly, "You are the Christ, the Son of the living God."

Shocked by Peter's words, Judas wanted to ask what they meant, but before he could speak, Jesus said, "Blessed are you, Simon, son of Jonah! For flesh and blood has not revealed this to you, but my Father in heaven." Judas moved closer, as did the other men and women, and Jesus lowered his voice. "But you must not tell anyone who I am, for my time has not yet come."

The disciples whispered about the healings and how they related to the claim that Jesus was the Messiah, but Judas barely heard them. He was too consumed by the storm raging within himself. A chill swept through him as his respect for Jesus clashed with his jealousy of him. The

Galilean had something he wanted—Mary Magdalene—and it didn't matter that Judas had come to love him. He *had* to have her.

Judas' knees became weak as violent images flooded his mind. He imagined strangling Jesus, or attacking him with a knife, or drowning him in the Jordan. With the Galilean gone, Judas could become the admired and powerful one. He imagined himself on the throne in Jerusalem, wearing a king's robes, giving orders to the servants, eating extravagant meals, and, most of all, enjoying the favors of Mary Magdalene, his dazzling wife.

Where did these images come from? Judas didn't know, nor could he break their hold on his mind. Horrified, he backed away from the others and walked aimlessly among the scattered belongings on the ground. Then he glanced back at Jesus and saw Mary Magdalene standing beside him. Judas tried to look away, but the sight of her held him, and his fantasies became so vivid that he could think of nothing else. Staring at her as he toyed with the ring that Helena had given him so many years ago, he knew he had to have the pleasures of his fantasies.

Mary Magdalene blushed when she noticed Judas Iscariot staring at her as he approached the circle of disciples. She diverted her eyes as her heartbeat quickened. Then she glanced at Jesus and the beating slowed, replaced by a numbness that spread out from her heart. Although she was standing beside him, she felt as far away as the windswept shores of Magdala. To have Jesus say that he loved her but couldn't marry her was devastating. Didn't he know that love and marriage belonged together? That a man shouldn't profess one without offering the other?

She fought to control the anger that had been brewing since they talked at the Sea of Galilee. What could she do? Three weeks earlier she had fled for her aunt and uncle's home. Now she couldn't leave. Caesarea Philippi was farther from Jerusalem than Nain had been, and after being attacked on the road, she would never again travel alone.

Besides, she wanted to stay. Jesus had the support of the masses, and he was the only one who could bring peace to their troubled land. But she needed more than friendship from a man. She thirsted for love like a parched desert thirsts for rain.

Should she meet Judas' gaze as he joined the circle, even though she still loved Jesus? How could she be interested in anyone else? The shadows were falling on Mount Hermon in the distance as she pondered the question. Judas, along with his friend Simon the Canaanite, whom Jesus had nicknamed "the Zealot," had joined them two weeks earlier on the Plain of Gennesaret. She barely knew Judas, yet his attention intrigued her. Did she just want to become better acquainted with him? Or did she hope that his flirting would make Jesus jealous?

The latter motivation rang true. Making Jesus jealous might make his heart grow fonder. Then he might reconsider and decide to marry her after all.

She hesitated, vowing not to let her interest in Judas go too far. A ribbon of sweat began to form on her back. A voice inside was warning her to be careful, that she was taking a risk, but what else could she do?

She met Judas' gaze.

He smiled, and for a moment she measured him cautiously. Then she smiled back. Embarrassed, she looked away but secretly welcomed his approach as the gathering broke up.

"Your smile caught my eye," Judas said, holding out a hand and keeping his voice low. "It is most beautiful."

Seeing the warmth in his confident dark eyes, she said, "You are too kind, sir."

Judas gave her a sheepish grin. "I'm not kind, just observant and honest." He drew her hand close and studied it. "Why would such a striking woman not be wearing a wedding ring?" He gently stroked the hand before letting it go. "You must be a discerning woman who hasn't met the right man."

Mary felt blood rush into her neck and cheeks as she changed the subject. "You and your friend are new to our group. What brought you to Jesus?"

"We saw the multitudes come to him and watched as he healed them and spoke of liberation."

Enchanted by Judas' smooth, evenly cadenced voice, she couldn't turn away as he spoke and his eyes held hers. He appeared oddly familiar, as if he were an old friend, and she felt no need for caution. "Jesus *is* a liberator," she said. "He proclaims justice for the poor and promises that God's reign will come soon."

Judas' casual manner suddenly turned formal, and urgency laced his speech. "If Jesus is the Messiah, he will free our people. As he said, it's best to keep this a secret now. If the Romans knew that the Messiah was among us, they would try to kill him. Even the pagans know that they cannot stand against the anointed one of God."

Mary stepped back, surprised by the confidence with which Judas spoke. She admired Jesus, but she found it hard to believe that the man was the Messiah. Before she could ask Judas to explain further, Jesus gathered the group around him and announced that he was taking Peter, James, and John to Mount Hermon to pray after supper. He expected the rest of them to set up camp and share the good news about the kingdom of God in Caesarea Philippi.

With the sunset painting the sky pink and orange, the men sat down and the women began to pass around bread, cheese, figs, and olives. Mary helped but avoided Judas. When she finished and joined the others on the grass, she glanced at him and felt a shiver of excitement. Her thoughts racing, she was relieved to hear Jesus' calming voice. But her relief turned to alarm when he said, "When I return, I must go to Jerusalem to cleanse the Temple. I will endure great suffering, and be rejected by the elders, the chief priests, and the scribes." He paused as a hush fell over the group. "Then I will be killed, and after three days rise again."

Mary covered her mouth in shock and terror. How could he be saying this? The people needed him more than ever. If he thought his life would be threatened in Jerusalem, he must not go. She was ready to tell him this when she noticed Peter's sun-bronzed face going pale. He stood, straightened his large body to its full height, and glared at Jesus. "God forbid it, Lord! This must never happen to you."

Mary was glad that Peter had expressed what she felt, but she became alarmed when Jesus stopped eating and met Peter's gaze. "Get behind me, Satan!" he told him. "You are a stumbling block for me; for you are setting your mind not on the divine but on the human." Jesus surveyed the entire group. "If any want to become my followers, let them deny themselves and take up their cross and follow me. For those who want to save their lives will lose them, and those who lose their lives for my sake will find them. For what will it profit them if they gain the whole world but forfeit their lives? Or what will they give in return for their lives?"

In response to Jesus' words, the group grew somber as they continued eating in silence. Mary crossed her arms to keep from shaking. Tears clouded her vision. If suffering awaited Jesus in Jerusalem, why did he insist on going there? Was he incapable of choosing happiness over hardship? He could have married her and lived peacefully in Galilee. Instead he wanted to go to Jerusalem and provoke a confrontation with the religious and political authorities that he couldn't possibly win.

Her hand trembled as she ran it through her hair. Why was Jesus so reckless? Didn't he realize what he was giving up? Her head was pounding. The back of her neck felt hot. If he wanted to destroy himself, she couldn't stop him. It was his choice. But she refused to destroy herself with him. Judas was ready to fill the void. Perhaps if Jesus saw them together, he would become jealous and want her again.

The other women were taking their mats and blankets and going up the hill, where they would sleep apart from the men. The air was warm and the sky clear, so they didn't need tents. She picked up her bag and began to follow them. Then she felt someone squeeze her hand. She turned and saw Judas. He smiled and whispered, "I'll come for you later. There's something I must show you."

She hesitated, unsettled by the smoldering passion she saw in his eyes. She must not let him know why she would go with him. If he found out, he could become enraged, and she would lose both men—and her sanity as well. She squeezed his hand and hurried to catch up with the other women.

Judas Iscariot slipped into the group of disciples and prayed that none of them had noticed he was gone. He drew several quick breaths to slow his heart, but it kept beating out of control. He hoped that no one would ask him questions or make him speak because he couldn't. It was as if Mary Magdalene had entered his body. Her naked image danced behind his eyes. He could smell her lemony scent, feel her soft skin, hear her gentle voice. His blood ran hot and wild, as if he had been dead and was miraculously raised to life.

Thankfully the others knew nothing of what he was feeling. They were distracted by Peter, James, and John leaving with Jesus. The four of them were starting up the dusty road below the terrace that led northeast toward Mount Hermon in the distance. As they disappeared from sight, Judas heard Andrew say, "The rabbi is determined to go to Jerusalem. I hope that my brother and James and John will persuade him to stay. If Jesus wants to live, Jerusalem is the last place he should go."

Judas edged forward, eager to hear the response to Andrew's comment, and pondered how to take advantage of Jesus' plan to cleanse the Temple.

The slender Nathanael held up a hand. "Let's tell the rabbi that we won't go with him."

Thomas made no attempt to hide his irritation. "What good would that do? He's stubborn enough to go without us."

Hearing the disciples' conversation gave Judas an idea. He would convince them that he had a plan for protecting Jesus, but the plan would actually endanger him. He stepped forward and eyed the eight men. "If Jesus is determined to go to Jerusalem, then we must keep him from harm. I have friends there who are rebel fighters. I'll go to the city and hire some of them to protect him."

Matthew shot him a suspicious glance. "And why would we trust you to do this?"

Judas didn't answer immediately, continuing to formulate his plan. He knew that the resistance fighters would be hiding in Zedekiah's Cave; before leaving for Qumran he had hid there himself. He would go and tell them that Jesus was coming and bringing the crowds with him. If the Zealots waited to attack the Romans until Jesus was in the city, Pilate would think the Galilean was one of them and kill him with the rebels. It was the perfect scheme for Judas: He could present himself as Jesus' protector while arranging to get rid of him.

He drew a breath and spoke confidently. "I can't prove that I'm worthy of your trust, but I'm willing to travel to Jerusalem alone. It's a dangerous journey, and I could leave and go back to Mount Arbel, but instead I'm offering to help."

The lean, stubble-bearded Philip glared at Matthew. "We don't have the luxury of questioning Judas. We have no plan of our own, and we can't let Jesus go to Jerusalem unprotected. Unless someone has a better idea, I say we give Judas money and send him on his way."

Judas felt his stomach flutter. His plan was going better than he expected. The disciples were so concerned about the dangers in Jerusalem that they weren't even suspicious of him.

Philip walked over and stood in front of Matthew. "We need to act before Peter, James, and John return—they might disapprove." Philip held out his hand. "You've been carrying the moneybag, Matthew. I suggest we give enough to Judas so the Zealots will know he has sufficient funds to hire them."

Matthew wrapped his arms around the leather bag and held it to his chest. "This is a risky plan." He shook an accusing finger at Judas. "If we give this man money, we may never see him again."

Judas feared that the conversation was turning against him and knew he must do something dramatic to win their trust. He took off the ring that Helena had given him. "Here, take this. It's my most valuable possession. I would rather die than lose it."

Nathanael approached and accepted the ring before turning to the others. "I agree with Philip. We have no alternative but to accept Judas' offer. If he wants to see his ring again, he'll meet us in Jericho before we go to Jerusalem." Nathanael went to Matthew and handed him the ring. Only then did Matthew reluctantly give him the moneybag. "We're relying on you, Judas," Nathanael said as he handed him the bag.

Judas tucked the moneybag inside his tunic. "I'll prove myself worthy of your trust." As he spoke the words, the image of a naked Mary Magdalene pulsated in his mind, her soft lips held up to kiss him. He would lead Jesus into a trap from which he couldn't escape, and once the Galilean was gone, Judas would have Mary Magdalene. He held the moneybag against his breast and contemplated his great luck.

Mary Magdalene couldn't sleep. As she gazed into the heavens, the moon and stars appeared farther away than she remembered. Hearing Jesus predict his suffering and death, she felt as if the air had been forced out of her lungs. She was being suffocated by fear and confusion.

All she wanted was to share her life with the man she loved, but that dream had just about slipped away, and now she wondered what to do about Judas. Why was she eager to have Judas come for her? Was she attracted to him but afraid to admit it? It was too much to ponder. All she could do was proceed with her plan and hope it was not too late to save Jesus.

The other women were asleep; she didn't want to wake them, so she lay perfectly still. When she felt someone shaking her arm, she sat up and peered into the seductively appealing face of Judas Iscariot. "Come with me," he said, gently pulling her arm. "There's something I want to show you, and we don't have much time."

Mary glanced at the full moon, its distant glow bathing the camp in soft light. "Come with you where?"

"Please, don't make any noise or wake anyone. Just follow me."

Afraid of getting caught with a man at night, she hesitated, but in Judas' glistening eyes she saw an earnestness and intensity that intrigued her. She couldn't say no. After slipping her sandals on, she followed him down the sloping terrace toward the sound of water rushing in the distance. Her eyes gradually adjusted, and she could see that Judas was leading her toward a rugged hillside. As they approached it, she saw a wide cavity at its base, abrupt and deep and full of water. Judas pointed and said, "From these springs the mighty Jordan begins to flow."

"Why did you bring me here?" she asked.

"Because I saw desire in your eyes—the same desire I feel for you."

Mary's knees felt weak; her stomach became queasy. Judas smiled, and she turned away, but he reached for her chin and coaxed it back toward him. "I had to bring you here, Mary. I wanted you to see the headwaters of the Jordan in the moonlight. This river belongs to our people, as does Jerusalem. I'm leaving tomorrow to go there. If Jesus is the Messiah, he'll take the city back from the Romans, but without protection he'll certainly be killed. I spoke to the others and offered to travel ahead and arrange for the Zealots to guard him. Afterward I'll wait in Jericho and go up to Jerusalem with Jesus." He stepped back and studied her. "Most of all, I wanted to see your beauty reflected in the water."

Flattered, she couldn't help smiling. When her lips parted, Judas leaned forward and kissed her, slowly, deeply. She felt the hardened muscles of his chest and caught a whiff of his cinnamon-like scent. She had forgotten what a sweet pleasure kisses were, how warm and tangy and full of delight. At the same time she thought, *What am I doing? Judas is leaving for Jerusalem, and now Jesus has predicted his own death.*

She should withdraw from Judas and run back to camp, but the power of her feelings surprised her. She hadn't expected to want Judas, and wondered if the feelings were real, or if she wanted him only because she couldn't have Jesus. She felt as if the roar of the Jordan had penetrated her body and lodged in her heart, its rapids treacherous.

The sound reminded her of a storm approaching on the Sea of Galilee, and suddenly she was a girl again, running barefoot on the beach in Magdala, the sand wet beneath her feet, the wind strong against her face, the waves pounding in her ears. It seemed that she had forever to live, and each day would be happier than the last. It was as if she had never been married, never divorced, never disappointed in love. Only this moment was real.

Desperate to make it last, she leaned into Judas' embrace. His arms felt warm around her, his caresses gentle, and she tasted the sweetness of his lips. As she surrendered to the kiss in the pale moonlight, with the headwaters of the Jordan roaring in her ears, she forgot about Jesus.

Only Judas mattered.

CHAPTER TWENTY-FIVE

MATTERS OF THE HEART DEFY EASY ANSWERS. AMID THE UPHEAVALS OF ATTRACTION OR THE STRUGGLES OF RELATING TO A PARTNER, ONE MAY WONDER WHETHER ANY ANSWERS EXIST.

THEY DO.

BUT FINDING THEM REQUIRES ONGOING INNER WORK. THIS IS THE WORK OF EXPLORING FAMILY HISTORIES, UNDERSTANDING WOUNDS FROM PREVIOUS RELATIONSHIPS, EMBRACING ONE'S UNIQUENESS AS A MAN OR A WOMAN. MOST OF ALL, IT'S THE WORK OF SEEKING GOD'S GRACE WHEN COPING STRATEGIES FAIL.

AND FINDING THIS GRACE SUFFICIENT.

—**Brother Gregory Andreou's Journal**

Holy Angels Monastery
Thursday, April 4

KARIM MUSALAHA SUSPECTED THAT SOMETHING WAS WRONG AS HE KEPT KNOCKING ON BROTHER GREGORY'S UNANSWERED DOOR. Glancing at Rachel, her face barely visible in the darkness, Karim felt his marrow harden to stone at the thought of harm coming to

Brother Gregory. Karim stopped knocking and shot Rachel a frantic look. He wished that they had left the university an hour earlier when he had texted Brother Gregory. But it had been too light to flee the boiler room without getting caught. By waiting until dark, they had crept through the university's maze of buildings and walkways and made it back to the Jeep without being seen. Now he feared that Kenyon had beaten them to the monastery and harmed Brother Gregory.

Karim moved a few steps to his left, grabbed the wooden window frame, and pulled himself up to get a better look. All he saw through the glass was thick darkness. "He can't take this long to answer a door."

"Let's go find someone with a key," Rachel said.

Karim rapped once more and waited a moment. Hearing no response, he and Rachel started up the walkway in front of the monks' apartments. He thought of Robert Kenyon. Of whether seeing Karim at the university had prompted him to come looking for Brother Gregory's latest translation. Karim considered calling the police but decided he couldn't risk revealing his identity. The PPA was strong in Bethlehem; word of his whereabouts would reach his father. Besides, without physical evidence that an upstanding professor had attacked him, the police wouldn't believe his story. His heart pounded in his throat. No matter what happened, he had to find out what Judith of Jerusalem had written in her diary.

After they had passed several apartments, Rachel said, "About what happened in the boiler room . . . The kiss took me by surprise."

"Me too."

"I've never kissed a Palestinian before."

"Nor I an Israeli. It was wonderful."

Rachel latched on to his arm. "It's all so new and, honestly, dangerous. You heard Ezra's warning. Now Brother Gregory has turned up missing." She pulled to a stop. "I'm scared."

He put an arm around her. "If we think about the dangers, our relationship and our search for the truth about the Jesus letter will be over. We can't change our parents or our religions or the history of this land. All we can do is trust what's in our hearts and accomplish what we can for peace."

She ran a hand along his cheek and studied him as he held her gaze. They stood like that for a second longer, and then, as though they both knew they needed to be careful, they hurried down the walkway.

Karim led her to the abbot's apartment. Finding it dark, he knocked and waited. When a light finally came on, Abbot Zeno answered. "It is after nine. What are you doing here at this hour?" He turned his gaze toward Rachel. "And why have you brought a woman to the monastery?"

"This is my friend Rachel Sharett," Karim said. "I can tell you about her later, but right now we're concerned about Brother Gregory. We have been knocking on his door, but he doesn't answer."

Abbot Zeno stroked his thick salt-and-pepper beard. "Perhaps he went to bed early. He is getting older and losing his hearing."

Karim shook his head impatiently. "I knocked long and hard. If he were home, he would have heard me."

The abbot disappeared into his apartment and returned with a set of keys. "You have me worried. We must make sure that our dear brother is all right."

Karim and Rachel followed the abbot back to Brother Gregory's apartment. The abbot appeared calm, but Karim's thoughts spun a dreadful scenario. Thieves could have broken in. He imagined finding Brother Gregory beaten or even dead.

When they reached the apartment, the abbot fumbled with his keys before unlocking the door. Karim sensed danger; it was too quiet. When the door was finally opened, Karim slipped inside first and then froze. Books and papers were strewn everywhere. The desk was on its side, and the swivel chair was upside down on the floor, which was splattered with blood. Karim did a quick check of the one-room cinderblock apartment.

No Brother Gregory.

No laptop computer.

Just then a balding, middle-aged man in a brown robe rushed in. "I heard a commotion. When I arrived, I found Brother Gregory unconscious," he said breathlessly. "I woke him up. He's resting in my apartment."

"Please take us to him," Karim said.

As they headed up the walkway, Abbot Zeno introduced the man as Brother Theodore. "How did you get into Brother Gregory's apartment?" the abbot asked.

"The door was open," Brother Theodore said, leading them back to his apartment. "After Brother Gregory regained consciousness, I called your number, but you didn't answer, so I brought him here and locked his door and mine. I was afraid the burglar would return."

When Karim saw Brother Gregory lying on the bed, he hurried to his side, as did Rachel. The monk was resting his head on ice cubes wrapped in a blood-soaked towel and laid on a pillow. Rachel felt Brother Gregory's carotid artery for a pulse. "His heartbeat is normal, but I still think we should take him to the hospital."

"No, you won't. I'll be fine." Brother Gregory tried to sound strong, but his voice was trembling.

"I think you should follow the doctor's orders," Karim said. Then, turning sober, he asked, "Who did this to you?"

Brother Gregory grimaced, rolling his head on the pillow. "I don't know." He reached up and rubbed his temples. After nearly a minute he said, "The last thing I remember was returning to my apartment and settling down to work. Someone must have hit me from behind. He must have been hiding in the bathroom."

"How could he have gotten in?" Karim asked.

"I don't know," Brother Gregory said. "When I got home, there were no signs of a forced entry." He paused, his expression darkening. "The intruder must have had a key—or maybe he knew someone with a key. He obviously attacked me from behind so that I couldn't identify him."

Abbot Zeno laid a gentle hand on Brother Gregory's leg. "I can assure you that there will be a thorough investigation. For now, you just need to rest."

Brother Gregory's pleasant features twisted into dismay. "The laptop—where is it?"

"Gone. Along with everything on your desk," Karim said.

Rachel shook a finger at Brother Gregory. "Let's just get you to the hospital. You can deal with the missing laptop later."

Brother Gregory waved dismissively. "I'll be fine with some aspirin. You're the only doctor I need."

"This doctor says you're going to the hospital. You could have a concussion." She got up, reaching for her keys. "I'll back the Jeep up to the door. Karim and these gentlemen will help you into it."

Brother Gregory propped himself up on an elbow. "No, really, I'll be fine."

After Karim heard the Jeep pull up, he took hold of the monk's arm to help him stand. Brother Gregory protested again and Karim said, "You heard the doctor. You're going to the hospital—that's an order."

Brother Theodore took the other arm, and the two of them supported him to the Jeep, which Rachel had positioned near the door. Karim and Brother Theodore maneuvered him into the front seat. Getting into the back, Karim handed Brother Gregory the ice wrapped in the towel as the abbot closed the doors and backed away with Brother Theodore.

"The closest hospital is in Beit Jala, just west of Bethlehem." Rachel drove out of the parking lot and turned north on Manger Street. "Keep the ice on your head until we get there."

Brother Gregory reclined his seat. "If I need stitches, I want you as my doctor."

"If I had a cut, I would too," Karim said. "But if I needed someone to protect my home, I wouldn't choose you."

Brother Gregory gave a strained laugh. "I don't blame you. If the thief stole everything on my desk, he has more than my laptop. He also has my copy of the translation, the photographs of the writings, and the flash drive on which I save my work."

Karim leaned forward as the Jeep wound through the outskirts of Bethlehem toward downtown. "That means the thief has everything except the original scroll. When he discovers what the scroll contains, there's no telling what he will do to get it." As Karim finished his sentence, he felt the Jeep speed up. The road was nearly abandoned at that hour, but now Karim noticed headlights—high beams—close behind them.

Rachel gave the Jeep more gas. "That car seemed to come out of nowhere. He's riding my bumper, and whenever I speed up, he does the same."

"Robert Kenyon may have hid at the monastery and saw us leave," Karim said, speaking loudly and then explaining to Brother Gregory what had happened at the university. At the same time he thought that Abdul Fattah might be trailing them. Abdul, who would force him to return to Nablus. Abdul, who could reveal to Rachel who Karim's brother had been.

Cold terror spread through Karim as he stole a glance out the rear window, but all he could see was a fog of white light, nothing of a black Mercedes nor a gray Impala. He finished explaining about Kenyon and then said to Brother Gregory, "The man who attacked me at Qumran is probably the archaeologist who came looking for you at the monastery."

Tires squealed as Rachel took a curve at high speed, the other car continuing to tailgate. "I'll try to lose him in Bethlehem," she said, slowing a bit as they approached the Alexander Hotel on the right. Before they reached it, she executed a hairpin left turn and the Jeep fishtailed up a narrow cobblestone side street.

Karim slammed against the door and jerked himself upright. He looked back as the other car spun into the turn, still unable to identify its make. Then he nervously glanced at Rachel, her sculpted profile silhouetted in the headlights, her gaze riveted on the winding street. She had said she was scared, but he saw only grit and determination in her eyes. As in Bil'in, his life was in her hands, as was Brother Gregory's.

His back muscles tightened as he gulped in air. She was an Israeli, but, Allah help him, he loved her. Holding and kissing her had brought him home to some lost part of himself. He hoped that he had done the same for her, and that together they had begun to reclaim the dreams that terrorists had stolen from them. If only they could make it to the hospital. . .

Brother Gregory threw the ice on the floor and spoke. "In case I don't get out of this, I must tell you what I found in the diary."

Rachel steered the Jeep up an alley, heading toward Manger Square. Several pedestrians leaped out of the way, pinning themselves against the brick apartment houses that lined each side. Karim pulled himself closer to hear Brother Gregory over the roar of the engines. "Tell us quickly."

Brother Gregory craned his neck to face Karim and raised his voice above the grinding engine. "Judith of Jerusalem wrote that Judas Iscariot was in love with Mary Magdalene. He felt that he was in a competition with Jesus for her—and losing. According to Judith, Judas betrayed Jesus for reasons not recorded in the Bible." Brother Gregory's voice became strained and trembled when the car bumped the Jeep from behind. "Judas didn't betray Jesus just for money. He didn't do it just because he was disillusioned with him. He did it out of jealousy."

The Jeep hit a garbage can, sending it crashing. "Rachel, be careful!" Karim's heart was racing because of the danger but also because of Brother Gregory's shocking statement. "How can you be sure that both Jesus and Judas were in love with Mary Magdalene?"

"We can't prove it from any existing sources," Brother Gregory said, raising his voice to be heard above Rachel's honking. "Neither the canonical nor the Gnostic Gospels say anything about Judas' jealousy. But Judith claims there is a source that does—another ancient text."

Brother Gregory paused to emphasize each word. "Judas Iscariot left a note for Mary Magdalene explaining why he committed suicide. Mary told Judith that she buried the note in the largest cave in Gethsemane. Mary even revealed the spot—the northeast corner."

"What did Judas write?" Rachel asked, braking around a corner.

Brother Gregory grabbed the dashboard. "Judith only says that Mary Magdalene spoke of it with wrenching sobs."

"So in order to learn the truth, we must find Judas' note to Mary." Karim raised his voice above the screech of tires. "How ironic. The betrayer now holds the key to whether the Jesus letter and Judith's diary are authentic. If we can find Judas' note, we can solve the mystery."

Brother Gregory stared straight ahead. "You had better hurry, because whoever stole my laptop will be searching for the note in the Cave of Gethsemane."

As Rachel turned right at the Church of the Nativity, the car behind them moved up closer and tried to force them off the road. The Jeep spun sideways with a squeal of tires, and Karim got a glimpse of the car chasing them—a gray Impala. "That's Kenyon behind us." His voice rose above the squeaks and rattles of the Jeep as it straightened and lurched forward.

Then he heard a siren.

Rachel kept going straight as the Impala disappeared down an alley.

"The police must have scared Kenyon off," Rachel said, slowing down and stopping. Soon the flashing lights of the cruiser approached. "Don't say a word unless I ask you to."

With Karim's limited knowledge of Hebrew, he couldn't understand what Rachel said to the sturdy Israeli policeman. She gestured frantically toward Brother Gregory and pointed at the cut on his head. For a brief heart-stopping moment the clean-shaven officer stared at Karim. Rachel held up the monk's blood-stained towel and said something that Karim couldn't understand—except for the name *Ezra Sharett*. The officer hesitated as though considering what to do. Then he gave Karim one last look, nodded, and hurried back to his car.

After the officer turned on his lights and siren, Rachel followed him away from the Church of the Nativity and wound back onto Manger Street. As the cruiser led them to the hospital, Karim had never been more relieved.

CHAPTER TWENTY-SIX

JUDITH COULD NOT GET GABRIEL'S VOICE OUT OF HER MIND. As she bathed by torchlight in Zedekiah's Cave, she kept thinking about his conversation with Nicodemus ben Gorion that she had overheard. The murky water in the underground cistern felt like ice. She splashed at its surface, hoping the noise would distract her thoughts, but Gabriel's voice kept gnawing at her conscience. After three days in Jerusalem spent with the Zealots in the cave, she was feeling worse. She longed more and more for home, and home was nearby. . . .

But now she was not only an adulteress but also a thief. If caught, she would be stoned for certain. She had no choice but to stay with Dismas.

She inhaled the cave's musty air and stared at its blackened limestone walls, struggling to understand how she had ended up in this place. Minutes passed. *No woman could have resisted Dismas,* she told herself. Passion had possessed her and was bent on destroying her.

As she washed, she tried to rinse away both the dirt from her skin and the guilt of having betrayed Gabriel. Her face felt clean but not her conscience. She dipped her head underwater and shook it back and forth, trying to erase the memory of her betrayal. The sloshing in her ears, as loud as the sound of ocean waves, couldn't drown out her regrets. Lightheaded from being underwater, she pushed to the surface, gasping for air. Someone was shouting.

Dismas.

She hadn't heard him approach the cistern, but there he stood, torch in hand, calling her name.

"Are you all right?" he asked as she struggled to catch her breath.

Judith turned to face him. "I'm fine, but I would like to be alone."

"Haven't you been in there long enough?" Frustration glinted in his eyes. "Barabbas has come to Jerusalem and will eat with us tonight. I want you to join us."

"All right," she said, knowing that she had no choice. "Just give me a few minutes."

Dismas nodded and left. She leaned back in the water and kicked at the rough stone of the cistern. *I would leave if I had somewhere to go!* She climbed out of the water and reached for the tunic that served as a makeshift towel. As she dried herself, memories of how she had become involved with Dismas played in her mind.

Her father had hired him to expand the courtyard of their home. She recalled that her conversations with Dismas had remained casual until she complimented his work and predicted that he would excel in his trade. To her surprise, he threw down a large stone and said, "No Jew can go far as long as the Romans rule Judea." When she remarked that she also resented the Romans, his demeanor had changed, as if an equilibrium shift had occurred, banishing his inhibitions. That night Judith had tossed and turned for hours, unable to get Dismas out of her mind.

The next day she asked him to meet her at the Herodian gardens at dusk. She told him how the Romans had murdered Reuben; the story darkened Dismas' expression as he railed against them: against their unjust taxes, their idolatry and blasphemy, their oppression of the Jews, their arrogance and brutality. Then he sat down and took her in his arms. She went on about how her father had blamed her for Reuben's death. How he had arranged her marriage quickly after the funeral. How he had turned a deaf ear to her objections. When she finished, Dismas pressed a finger to her lips and said, "Please, do not go on; it will only cause you more pain."

Judith mused about how much they had talked, and the more they had talked the more she felt that only Dismas understood her. She had tried to forget him but couldn't. Now, as she began to dress, she cursed her weakness, her stupidity. She had just put on her sandals when Dismas arrived, ready to take her to dinner with Barabbas and the other Zealots. As they began to walk back to camp, the way lit by the torch he carried, she asked, "Are we never going to talk about Gabriel?"

"Never." He stared straight ahead. "For all the help my family gives our cause, they may as well be Romans. Especially Gabriel, the coward."

More than thirty Zealots were sitting around a blazing fire. Judith noticed that Dismas had set out the treasures they had stolen—the pottery, the Roman glass vessels, the gold and silverware and the jewelry box. He had not opened the box. "I saved this for you," he said, handing it to her. "After all your help, you deserve the most valuable treasure."

Judith stared at the wooden box, wracked by guilt, but because everyone was watching, she bit back her discomfort and reluctantly took the box. When she set it on the ground and opened it, she drew back in surprise. The box contained a papyrus scroll. She concealed it behind the lid and unfurled a bit of it. Obviously a long letter, it began, "A message from Jesus of Nazareth to Mary of Magdala, and to all people in every age. . . ." She gasped and unrolled the letter farther. It was written by a steady hand in a distinctive script. This was the letter that Nicodemus ben Gorion had spoken of! She rolled it up quickly, not wanting Dismas to know.

"Is there nothing else in the box?" he asked.

Her hands shaking, she checked the box again. "No, it's empty."

When he looked away, she quickly returned the scroll to the box and closed the lid. *I will read the letter but not until I'm alone,* she thought, setting the box among the other stolen items. To divert attention from it, she admired the silverware until Barabbas invited everyone to have lentil stew.

CHAPTER TWENTY-SEVEN

THE FIRE SUDDENLY FELT SO HOT THAT DISMAS FEARED GETTING BURNED. He stood and moved away, allowing the other Zealots to fill their bowls, his stomach unsettled by the thought of food. Judith's questions about Gabriel were haunting him, as was the conversation he had overheard in Nicodemus ben Gorion's home. As Dismas watched Judith fill her bowl, he realized that she had come at a price: He felt sympathy for Gabriel and guilt for having stolen Judith. Only as he studied her finely molded profile and the lines of character in her face was the guilt replaced by pride. Attaining such a lovely and spirited wife was worth any sacrifice.

Dismas only wished that there were peace. He dreamed of building a home in the country with her and the strong sons—and perhaps a daughter or two—whom she would give him. His family would prosper as he expanded his stonecutting business and passed the trade on to his sons. It was a dream of freedom and security. As Barabbas rose to speak, Dismas wondered if the dream would ever come true.

A large-chested man with legs as sturdy as pillars, Barabbas stood near the fire, its flames silhouetting his powerful frame against the gnarled stone of the cave. His deep voice echoed off the walls. "The time of our victory is nearly at hand. Next week thousands of Jewish patriots will gather in Jerusalem. On Passover we'll rally our people and assault the Roman army at the Antonia Fortress. Our numbers will overwhelm Pilate's soldiers, and we'll drive them from our city!"

At first Barabbas' proclamation was greeted with silence. The men stared nervously at one another, knowing that their leader was asking for loyalty unto death. Finally Gestas raised a fist and shouted, "Victory to the God of Israel!" As if given the cue they needed, the rest of the Zealots let out a cry in unison, "Victory to our God!"

Although Dismas joined the shout, he had reservations about Barabbas' plan. The Antonia Fortress stood next to the Temple and overlooked it. Pilate's army had horses, armor, and the finest swords; the Zealots' horses were few, their swords crudely made, and their clubs and daggers would not fare well in open warfare. He worried that the Zealots would act rashly and get slaughtered. Their founder, Judas the Galilean, had met that fate nearly three decades earlier, when the Romans crushed him and his band of rebels at the time of the census.

Dismas steeled his will as he stood up and cleared his throat. "Your plan is too risky, Barabbas. We should purify the Temple first. Our priority should be to assassinate Caiaphas and his corrupt Sadducee supporters. The cleansing of the Temple will inspire our people! We can't attack the Romans until we're sure the masses are with us."

"And how can we carry out the cleansing?" Barabbas asked.

Every eye was focused on Dismas. "I suggest that we enter the Temple courts with our daggers hidden beneath our cloaks, so we can take our enemies by surprise."

Gestas pointed an accusing finger at him. "I say we stick with

Barabbas' plan. A surprise attack on the Antonia is our best chance for victory."

Another cry went up from the men. Dismas wasn't sure if they believed in Barabbas' plan or just wanted to support their leader. They continued to murmur among themselves and Dismas listened hard and overheard several denouncing the leader's plan. He hoped that they would be brave enough to stand with him against a flawed strategy. He had to bring Barabbas to his senses before the flaw proved fatal for all of them.

Judas Iscariot felt his stomach tighten as he rejoined the Zealots in Zedekiah's Cave. From the rear of the group, he could observe Barabbas, Dismas, and Judith, but was hidden from their view. He swallowed hard as he listened to the discussion swirling around him. After two days of hiding, he knew it was time to speak but hesitated. He had only one chance to set his trap for Jesus of Nazareth—a trap that could also get him the revenge on Barabbas and Dismas that he'd longed for since that day he kissed Judith.

Judas gnawed his lip and rehearsed his speech as he admired Judith from twenty feet away. She looked older than he remembered. The brightness had left her eyes. Her shoulder-length chestnut hair, once thick and lustrous, was tangled and dull. Anxiety clouded her pleasant features, and her complexion appeared sallow, as if she were recovering from an illness.

Yet he still found Judith attractive, her breasts full, her waist trim, her profile lovely. He admired her finely tapered fingers—the fingers that had once so gently changed his bandages. He had yearned for those fingers to caress the sensitive parts of his body as many women had, for her arms to receive him, and her lips to return his kisses.

The memories of her slapping his cheek and of Dismas attacking him sent the heat in his cheeks sizzling into his neck and chest. The time for revenge had come. Now Dismas was at his mercy, and Dismas' proposal that the Zealots cleanse the Temple before attacking the Antonia was playing right into Judas' hands. He grinned at his good fortune. If all went as planned, Dismas and Barabbas, not to mention Jesus of Nazareth, would be killed by the Romans.

A wave of sadness washed over Judas as he remembered the children coming to Jesus along the Sea of Galilee. The disciples had been annoyed and wanted to send them away, but Jesus hugged the little ones and said that they reminded him of the kingdom of heaven. Judas had never known a kinder man.

This man had accepted him as a disciple. This man had spent time trying to help him understand the true meaning of freedom, and had once listened late into the night as Judas told him of his boyhood in Kerioth. Yet none of that mattered now—not with the love of Mary Magdalene at stake. Judas craved her as a drowning man craves air. The mere thought of Mary sent him into a crazed panic, and he tried to put away the thought of Jesus dying. He felt short of breath; his blood ran hot. Only if he won her love would he ever truly be free.

Judas drew a breath and rehearsed his speech one more time. Those who argued that attempting to cleanse the Temple was dangerous were right. But he would exploit the danger for all it was worth. To do so he needed to convince the Zealots that their chances of success were greater if they coordinated their efforts with those of Jesus of Nazareth.

He had to make sure that Jesus, Dismas, and Barabbas were at the Temple at the same time. And that the Roman soldiers were waiting for them. Judas smiled as he pictured himself stepping in and using his leadership abilities. He would become a hero to the masses. He would win concessions from Pilate, depose Herod, and force Caiaphas to do his bidding. The people would herald *him* as Messiah! They would crown *him* king! He was ready to speak.

Dismas stared into the thick darkness of Zedekiah's Cave. The debate over his proposal was spiraling out of control, with factions quickly forming. The tall, robust Elisha ben Jonas stood over him, glaring down. "Who are you to challenge Barabbas, Dismas? He has organized the revolt and risked everything for its success. If you think you have better ideas, keep them to yourself!"

When the Zealots cheered, Dismas was sure that the majority were against him. Many of them were proclaiming that they would support Barabbas to the death. But in the midst of the clamor, a handsome, dark-haired man in back stood and asked for calm.

Dismas recognized him immediately—Judas Iscariot.

What could he possibly have to say? The last time he saw Judas, they had fought. Dismas tightened his hands into fists as he remembered the anguish that Judas had caused him with Judith. He was ready to shout that no one should listen to Judas, but Barabbas interrupted. "Seize that man. He's not supposed to be here."

Judas bounded away from the group and into the large open area next to it. But Simeon of Bethany and Mattathias ben Gaddi caught him and held him by the arms. They restrained him as Barabbas approached. Dismas moved close, eager to see Judas punished.

"You're supposed to be at Mount Arbel making weapons," Barabbas said. "Who gave you permission to come to Jerusalem?"

Judas struggled to break free. "I don't need permission to work for the success of the revolt, and my work has paid off. If these men will let me go, I'll tell you how."

Dismas stepped closer to the two men standing nose to nose.

"Why should I not order them to throw you into the hands of the Romans?" Barabbas grabbed the front of Judas' neck. "They'll let you go if you promise not to run. If you break the promise, the punishment will be severe."

Judas squirmed and grimaced, but Dismas felt no sympathy for him. "I have . . . no reason . . . to run," Judas said, choking. "I came here . . . to do business." Barabbas let him go and nodded at Simeon and Mattathias. They released him.

Judas reached inside his tunic and withdrew a leather moneybag. He held it up and said, "I've been making weapons, but I've also been making money for our cause." He loosened the drawstring of the bag, withdrew a handful of coins, and gave them to Barabbas. "*Now* do you believe that I'm sincere and can be trusted?"

The question echoed off the walls of the cave and rang in Dismas' ears. When the Zealots saw the money, they surrounded Judas.

"What do you want from us?" Dismas asked, expecting Judas to denounce his suggestion that they cleanse the Temple before attacking the Antonia.

Instead Judas threw out his chest and said, "I have heard both plans, and I agree with Dismas. The Romans have superiority over us. If we're going to win, we must have God on our side. The only way to ensure God's blessing is to restore the purity of the Temple."

Dismas drew back in surprise. Judas Iscariot was the last man he expected to support him. Dismas wiped sweat from his forehead, suspicious of Judas' motives, and pondered how to respond. He would rather that Barabbas had beaten Judas for leaving Mount Arbel. But Dismas needed all the support he could get. Unless the Temple was cleansed before the uprising began, they could all die. "Let's hear Judas out," he said.

Judith grabbed Dismas' arm and pulled him back. "No! This man cannot be trusted."

Barabbas held up a hand and pressed a finger to his lips. "You're not in charge here. I am. And I give Judas permission to speak."

Dismas held Judith as he watched Judas put the moneybag inside his tunic. Then Judas said, "I've met the rabbi called Jesus of Nazareth. Large crowds flock to hear him, and I know that he too plans to cleanse the Temple. I propose that we use him and his popularity to our advantage. If we strike the Temple when he does, he'll look like a Zealot. The crowds that revere him will help with the cleansing and then join our revolt. We need the support of Jesus and his followers in order for the revolt to succeed." Judas surveyed the assembly with a determined stare. "The Galilean is now on his way to the city. He plans to arrive six days before Passover. As soon as I learn when he will cleanse the Temple, I'll get word to you and you can join him."

Dismas noticed the lanky, fiery-eyed Mattathias ben Gaddi whispering to Simeon of Bethany and Mishael the Just, both oversized men respected as fighters. Mattathias stepped forward to speak. "We think Dismas and Judas are right. Purifying the Temple must be our priority. Unless we rid the holy site of pagan influence, how can we expect God to give us victory over the Romans? Why not use this Jesus of Nazareth to our advantage? We share a common goal and his followers will swell our ranks. If this plan will ever work, it has to be at Passover. We will fight for our God and he will protect us in battle!"

Dismas was thankful to hear this support, but he was aghast when Judith broke free and said, "I beg you all to listen to me. Judas Iscariot is a liar and a fraud. Cleanse the Temple if you must, but don't make any deals with this treacherous man!"

Dismas shot Judith a disapproving glance, but she looked away as Barabbas waved a dismissive hand, returned to the fire, and sat down.

He motioned for the others to join him. "Let me consider Judas' proposal," Barabbas said, crossing his arms on his chest. An eerie quiet settled over the cave; Dismas heard only the faint gurgling of an underground spring in the distance. He squeezed Judith's hand, but she pulled away and tucked the jewelry box under her arm as if protecting it with her life. Struck by how lovely she appeared against the backdrop of the severe rock formations, Dismas feared he was losing her. He needed to make the cleansing of the Temple succeed. If she saw him as strong and successful, she would realize how much she needed him.

Finally Barabbas rose and spoke thoughtfully. "I have decided with Dismas and Judas and Mattathias: We do need God's blessing to defeat the Romans. We will coordinate our efforts with those of Jesus of Nazareth. Judas can inform us when Jesus will be at the Temple; then we'll join the Nazarene in driving out the money changers. We will also kill Caiaphas and his supporters before we rally the people and attack the Antonia Fortress."

The group listened in reverent silence as Barabbas' fervor built. "For his corruption Caiaphas must die, and Pilate must suffer for bringing idolatrous shields into our city. He will never again steal money from the Temple to build his aqueducts. Never again will we pay Roman taxes or tolerate Roman meddling in our religion. By the blood of Judas the Galilean, we will not fail. May God's vengeance flow through us to defeat our enemies!"

As Barabbas spoke, the Zealots roared their approval. They chanted Barabbas' name and hugged one another jubilantly, raising their swords and daggers and cursing Caiaphas and the Roman blasphemers. Dismas joined in, his heart racing excitedly, his voice strained from shouting. But when he turned toward Judith, he saw only disgust on her face.

"You have made a pact with treachery," she said.

"We had no choice. We needed Judas to convince Barabbas to accept a better plan." Dismas placed a hand on her shoulder. "Please don't worry. Judas would lose too much if he betrayed us."

She pushed him away. "You know what could happen. If we lose, we could all get—"

He pressed a finger to her lips, interrupting.

She picked up a torch. "I'm going to bed."

Not wanting to cause a scene, Dismas waved a hand and said goodnight.

As she left, he noticed Gestas by the fire, staring aimlessly at the wall of the cave. Dismas walked over. "Why aren't you joining in?"

"Because there will be death at the Temple." Gestas stood and eyed him contemptuously. "And it will be your fault!"

"You have no right—"

Gestas cut him off. "Barabbas is eager for battle, and you encouraged him. At least his plan made sense; yours distracts us from fighting the Romans and will get us arrested—if we're not killed first." Gestas grabbed him by the tunic. "The plan was better before you changed it." Gestas shoved him and walked away. "The failure and the death will be on your head!"

CHAPTER TWENTY-EIGHT

JUDITH BIT BACK A SOB AS SHE PRESSED THE JEWELRY BOX TO HER BREAST AND TRUDGED THROUGH THE DARKNESS. The deeper darkness lay within her, an abyss of shame and guilt as formless as the void before the world's creation. She had fallen into the abyss when she heard Gabriel describe how she and Dismas had devastated him. When she stole from the kind Pharisee who was trying to help Gabriel, the fall had accelerated, cutting her off from all light, all warmth.

Her foot slipped on the moist limestone. She paused to regain her balance and cursed under her breath. How could she be in this position? Judas Iscariot, whom she hated more than she hated the Romans, could now determine her future. The cleansing of the Temple had become more important than she ever imagined, and she was carrying a letter written by the rabbi Jesus of Nazareth, whose assistance could mean success or failure.

If the cleansing succeeded, the masses would join the revolt; the Zealots would have their best chance of defeating the Romans; and perhaps she could begin a new life in a free Jerusalem. If the cleansing failed, the Zealots would be arrested or killed, and the revolt would end before it began. In that case, all her efforts would be for naught, and she would be alone.

Quickening her pace, she shook her head in disgust. Why had Dismas and Barabbas trusted Judas Iscariot? He was a liar who cared only about himself. She had hoped never to see him again. Now he was back, with more power over her than ever. Oh, why had she robbed the house? As an adulteress and now as a thief, she had nowhere to go—unless she could return the jewelry box and the letter to Nicodemus ben Gorion. Perhaps he would help her. . . .

But before putting any plan into effect, she had to read the letter, she decided. She knew it contained timeless wisdom, but would this wisdom have meaning for her? She needed to know. Relieved to be in her refuge, the ledge on which she and Dismas slept, she opened the box and began to read the scroll by the light of the torch:

A message from Jesus of Nazareth to Mary of Magdala, and to all people in every age: Grace to you and peace from him who was and who is and who is to come. Let anyone with ears to hear listen.

This letter contains news of the greatest of all loves. I want its truths to become your own, especially in times of confusion, trouble, or sorrow. Great tribulation must occur in order to bring the letter's message to distant times and places, and to all who need it. Honest seekers of God will understand its truths. Beware of those who try to refute or ridicule the letter, and keep your faith pure by heeding my promise: Ask, and it will be given you; seek, and you will find; knock, and the door will be opened to you. . . .

As Judith read, her eyes felt riveted to the papyrus. The ideas in the letter were new, yet they sounded strangely familiar, as if she were remembering them, not hearing them for the first time. The rabbi Jesus discussed how the love between a man and a woman related to the greatest of all loves—the love of God. This love was the source of all goodness and blessing. It expanded with each human birth and embraced every person.

Judith opened the scroll farther. Her heart grew warm as she read that God loved her as only she needed to be loved. The letter said that no one had ever been loved this way before or would be again. Putting down the scroll, she stood up. Did this mean that God accepted her completely? Forever? She crossed her arms and stared out into the night. A voice whispered in her heart, "Yes, you are accepted forever! Never doubt your acceptance, even when you do not feel loved." Although she had never heard the voice before, she had known its sound forever.

She drew a deep breath and read on until she came to Jesus' teachings about guilt and forgiveness. He emphasized that at times everybody needs to be forgiven, from others and from God. In a story about a father and the younger of his two sons, Jesus described the joy that forgiveness brings. Her eyes blurred with tears as she read that the son had demanded his inheritance and then squandered it in a distant land. Had she not done worse? When the son returned home, his father did not send him away. Instead he embraced him, put a robe around the young man's shoulders and a ring on his finger, and then threw a lavish party in his honor. Her hands trembled and the tears flowed as she wondered if her father would do the same.

The letter stated that God is like the forgiving father and like a woman searching for her lost coin. Again Judith heard the voice. "You can trust God's love. Never can you lose it. Never will it abandon you. There is joy among the angels of God over one sinner who repents."

Her entire body grew warm as her eyes moved from line to line. The letter stressed the importance of receiving forgiveness from the person you hurt. Judith fought to calm her shaking hands. Jesus said that you must go to that person and acknowledge your fault. If you are forgiven, you will be freed from your guilt; if you are not forgiven, you must still forgive yourself and trust that God does the same.

She thought of Gabriel, of how she yearned to throw herself on his mercy and beg his forgiveness. Of how she would never have the chance. The back of her mouth felt raw from trying to swallow against the ache in her throat. As she set down the scroll and dried her tears on her tunic, she heard the voice say, "Make amends as best you can. Do not dwell on your hurtful actions. If you do, you give them the power to destroy your soul."

She picked up the scroll and read on for a time, but then she stopped, troubled. As a faithful Jew, Judith had always found God by following the law. To join the Zealots—to help them drive the Romans from the land—was the supreme act of obedience. But the letter challenged this notion. Jesus wrote about a kingdom greater than one under Roman power—the kingdom of God. He claimed to have brought this kingdom's presence to the earth, but its fullness would arrive in the future. Receiving the kingdom would bring peace of heart and promote peace on earth. The kingdom's coming would end poverty, war, and suffering. Jesus Christ would reign over a new earth, in which all people knew the security of justice in the fullness of peace.

Judith heard the Zealots cheering in the distance and wondered what further inspiration Barabbas had given them. She waited until the cheering faded, and then she read faster, eager to finish before Dismas came.

She gasped when the letter described the union of male and female in the kingdom of God—the same union that existed in the Garden of Eden before Adam and Eve sinned. This teaching was new to her, and she found it shocking. The letter also stated that the male images of God would be balanced by female images. As in the scriptures, God would be pictured not only as a father but also as a woman giving birth, a nursing mother, a midwife or a mother eagle or bear. The letter emphasized that human beings could not find peace, either within themselves or among themselves, until a balance between the male and the female was achieved.

Judith touched her forehead. Now the conversation that she had overheard made sense. As Nicodemus had told Gabriel, to become whole, a man must find the female image of God within, and a woman, the male. She had tried to find the male image through Dismas, giving up her own sense of self to please him, but he had bitterly disappointed her, and if the letter were true, his violence would destroy them both. Worse, it would destroy everyone, Jew and Roman alike, for only love had the capacity to heal.

Judith broke out in a sweat as she pondered the implications of this teaching. Jesus' values turned the Zealots' values upside down. The Zealots believed in peace through conquest; Jesus promised peace through inner rebirth. According to him, love was supreme, even love for one's enemies. But how could any human achieve such an impossible standard? Only by being born of the Spirit, the letter said. This new birth revealed the true reason people were born. By losing their lives to God, they gained them back, fuller and richer than before.

The letter's wisdom was an offer of happiness. The material world rewarded the wealthy, powerful, and beautiful with its pleasures. The letter showed the way out of this folly. It promised a whole new life to those who opened their hearts to Jesus and were born anew in spirit. Compelled by these insights, Judith sensed that he was speaking to her.

Tears clouded her vision, making it impossible to read farther. She heard Dismas approaching. She set down the letter and dried her tears. More than anything, she wanted the love that Jesus described, even if she lost everything else. Without this love, nothing else mattered. As the letter had instructed, she began to pray that the Lord would fill her heart with his love.

"What are you doing?"

Dismas stood above her, the torchlight accentuating the fatigue on his dark, brooding features. Resolved to leave him unless he forsook violence and his dealings with Judas Iscariot, she had to give him one last chance. After rolling up the scroll, she handed it to him. "I have been reading a letter from the rabbi Jesus of Nazareth. I want you to read it too."

Dismas frowned and reluctantly took the scroll. "Ordinarily I wouldn't care what any rabbi says, but this man's reputation has spread far and wide."

Judith remained silent as Dismas read. Watching his dark eyes scan the papyrus, she prayed that he, too, would open his heart to the letter's message.

Dismas had not read far when he smirked and began to quote the letter in a mocking voice. "'Love your enemies; do good to those who hate you; bless those who curse you; pray for those who abuse you.' What foolishness!" He went on sarcastically, "'If anyone strikes you on the cheek, offer the other also; and from anyone who takes away your coat do not withhold even your shirt. Give to everyone who begs from you; and if anyone takes away your goods, do not ask for them again. Do to others as you would have them do to you.'" He tossed the scroll on the blanket-covered stone. "This Jesus of Nazareth speaks nonsense! Love and forgiveness are for the weak. Only a fool would follow such a man."

She picked up the scroll and protected it against her chest. "Is that really what you think? Then why did you agree to Judas' plan?"

"Of course it's what I think. Our enemies don't need love." He withdrew his dagger from its sheaf and held it up. "They need this! I only agreed to the plan because Jesus can help us cleanse the Temple."

"If violence is all you believe in, I cannot stay with you."

"Don't be naïve, Judith. The world doesn't work by love. The only way to get respect is to fight—to the death, if necessary. First we'll cleanse the Temple, and then we'll attack the Antonia. After we rid the holy place of impurities, God will help us drive the Romans from our land. Our victory will prove my point. If you leave me, you're the worst fool of all!"

"I know how set in your ways you are, but I can't live like this." She placed the letter inside the box, picked up her bag, and moved away from Dismas, the box under her arm. The letter didn't belong to her, and it contained the most powerful message she had ever heard. Her future would depend on what she did with it. Somehow she had to get the letter back to Nicodemus ben Gorion. She didn't know where she would go, but she knew she needed to leave, even if it meant that she would die. *It is the only way that my spirit will live.*

CHAPTER TWENTY-NINE

THE SIGHT OF SOLDIERS ON JERICHO'S MAIN STREET TURNED JUDAS ISCARIOT'S BLOOD TO WATER. He had come twenty-three miles from Jerusalem to rejoin Jesus and his disciples. They had dined the night before with a wealthy tax collector called Zacchaeus and were now ready to travel up to the holy city. The trap for Jesus was set. Judas couldn't let anything ruin it, not even a confrontation with the Romans, whom he feared saw the Galilean as a troublemaker.

He slipped a hand inside the belt of his tunic and felt the dagger concealed there. Assured that the weapon was ready if he needed it, he withdrew his hand as he surveyed the gathering crowd and then glanced at the disciples. The fishermen among them appeared brawny, but in light of Jesus' teachings about loving one's enemies, Judas feared that the only disciple who would fight with him was Simon the Zealot.

As the early sun was turning the morning golden, Judas kept his eyes on the approaching soldiers, prepared for anything. Fortunately, there were only two of them, and the crowd had grown to nearly thirty. Dressed in full regalia, the soldiers were riding white stallions past the bushy sycamore trees and lush date palms that dotted the dusty, shop-lined road. Judas vowed not to let the soldiers block Jesus' path to Jerusalem. If the Galilean stayed away from the city, he could remain safe. Only if he died would Mary Magdalene be free to love another man. Jesus had to go to Jerusalem.

The thought of having Mary to himself made Judas lightheaded and he drew a deep breath to calm down. He was so desperate for her love that he would do anything—even monstrous evil—to win it. This made him feel powerful.

And full of lust.

Yesterday their conversations had been casual but friendly, leading Judas to believe that Mary wanted him. The memory of their kisses in Caesarea Philippi was constantly on his mind, fueling his desire for more. The kisses had been so enthralling that he didn't dare imagine the ecstasy of making love to her. The mere thought caused his bones to ache.

Standing up to the soldiers would be an opportunity to impress Mary. His future with her might depend on how he handled them. He stole a glance at her as she walked beside the Galilean, the crowd swirling around him. The soldiers were drawing near, their armor flashing in the sun. Judas shielded his eyes as they stopped their horses and climbed down, blocking the road. The lanky younger soldier held both sets of reins while the older one, a thickset man with fiery eyes, said, "None of you will be allowed to go farther until we've searched you."

Judas stepped forward. "Why? We've done no wrong."

The thickset soldier stood firm. "You Jews are nothing but trouble. Our job is to find the enemies of Rome and stop any rebellion before it starts."

Judas saw Mary Magdalene move back as the disciples and Jesus crowded around. John presented himself to the soldier, followed by his brother James. "I have nothing to hide," John said. "Search me if you must." The thickset soldier ordered the brothers to stand still, arms at their sides, while he patted them down.

He found nothing and moved on to Judas. The soldier made him hold his arms out at the shoulders and began to search him. Judas could feel his face turning red, the veins in his neck throbbing, but he remained still until the soldier's hand approached his waist. A moment before the soldier got there, Judas darted a hand inside his tunic and withdrew the dagger.

He caught the soldier off guard and hit him backhanded across the face. The soldier recoiled; Judas pounced and began to choke the Roman with his left arm, holding the dagger to the man's throat with his right hand. Judas was about to slit the man's throat when Jesus cried out, "No, Judas! This man does not deserve to die. Put your dagger away and let him go."

Judas ignored him and pressed the dagger against the soldier's throat. He glared at the man's partner and said, "Throw down your sword or your friend will die." The younger man tossed his sword on the ground. Simon the Zealot retrieved it and also took the other soldier's sword. Judas let the thickset Roman go, grabbed a sword from Simon, and wielding it fiercely, said, "Both of you, take off your helmets, your armor, and your sandals."

Jesus stepped out of the group, his jaw set, and jabbed a finger at Judas. "You have disarmed these men. There is no reason to humiliate them."

Judas kept brandishing the sword, forcing the soldiers to strip down to their undergarments. "Now get on your knees," Judas said, pointing to the ground. "You Romans have no right to treat Jews as you do. All we want is to govern ourselves and live in peace." He turned to Jesus. "We have no choice but to deal severely with these men. Otherwise they will send reinforcements against us."

Jesus grabbed Judas' wrist and lowered the sword. "This is not the way to defeat an enemy. We defeat our enemies by making them friends."

Judas resisted for a moment and then decided that in order for his pact with the rebels to work, he could not alienate Jesus. He dropped the sword and left Simon the Zealot to guard the soldiers as he walked over to the two white stallions, slapped them on their hindquarters, and watched them gallop off. As the hooves pounded the ground, he couldn't yell loudly enough to stop James and John from picking up the helmets, armor, and sandals and returning them to the Romans.

Red-faced and breathing hard, Judas confronted the brothers. "What are you doing? We must teach these Romans to respect us. If they think we're weak, they'll never stop oppressing us."

Jesus said to him, "If you think that love is weak, you do not understand my teachings." Then he turned to the soldiers. "Go on your way and let us go on ours."

As Jesus began to leave, Judas hesitated, grimacing as John gave one of the swords to a portly man in the crowd. When Simon the Zealot did the same with the second sword, Judas rejoined the group, satisfied that the soldiers couldn't retaliate but disgruntled that he had not appeared stronger. Most of all, he was relieved that Jesus would continue toward Jerusalem.

Gabriel stepped out of the growing crowd, his heart pounding in his ears. He gave silent thanks that the rumors had been true, that Jesus of Nazareth was passing through Jericho on his way to Jerusalem. When Gabriel's head injury had healed and he had stocked his market for Passover, he came down to find the Galilean but hadn't expected to see a fight with the Romans. The potential for retaliation made his task even more urgent.

His insides were quivering as he approached Jesus' entourage of about twenty men and women. Having waited since dawn along Jericho's main street, Gabriel couldn't worry about the violence now and had to warn Jesus of the dangers in Jerusalem.

If Gabriel failed and Jesus died, the Jews would lose their best hope for peace. The Romans would crush the Zealots, and he might never see Judith again.

He noticed Mary Magdalene walking behind Jesus with several other women, their hands shielding their eyes from the morning sun. Gabriel slipped through and gently touched her arm. "Mary, do you remember me?"

When she saw him, a wide smile brightened her face. "How could I forget the man who saved my life? But what are you doing here, Gabriel?"

He pulled her aside as the others moved ahead. "It's a long story, and I don't have time to tell it, but I need your help, Mary. There are new dangers in Jerusalem. We must convince Jesus to stay away."

"His disciples have already tried, but he insists on going." Mary Magdalene's voice rose in frustration. "Since you have just come from the city, perhaps he'll listen to you." She took Gabriel's hand and hurried to catch up with the others.

The growing entourage was approaching Jericho's front gate, its rounded arch framing the hole in the massive stone wall that surrounded the city. As more people joined the crowd, Gabriel felt the surge of bodies and heard a chorus of expectant murmuring ring in his ears. He must act soon, or he would never stop the momentum toward Jerusalem.

He listened closely as Jesus said to his disciples, "You still do not understand what I have been teaching. Judas and Simon wanted power over those soldiers. It must not be so among you. Whoever wishes to become great must be your servant, and whoever wishes to be first among you shall be slave of all. For the Son of Man did not come to be served, but to serve, and to give his life as a ransom for many."

Jesus' words had a sobering effect, and the crowd passed through the enormous wooden gates in silence. Gabriel's thighs burned as the road began ascending to Jerusalem, but his concern for the rabbi burned even hotter—he needed to speak with him. As Gabriel rushed ahead, several beggars, dirty and in rags, converged on Jesus from beyond the gate, clamoring for alms. Gabriel covered his mouth to shut out the smell of their unwashed bodies. He could tell by their sunken eyes that the men were blind.

Jesus surprised him by pausing. One blind man, short, with a straggly beard, began to cry out, "Jesus, Son of David, have mercy on me!"

Gabriel didn't join those in the crowd who tried to shut the beggar up. He heard Jesus ask the man, "What is your name?"

"I am Bartimaeus, the son of Timaeus," the man said.

"What do you want of me?" Jesus asked.

Bartimaeus reached out both arms and spoke haltingly. "Rabbi, I want to see again."

Jesus took his hands and then gently touched his eyes. "Go your way; your faith has made you well."

Gabriel held still and watched Bartimaeus slowly open his eyes, shielding them with his hands and shaking his head, as if he were in pain. Bartimaeus turned away from the sun and blinked wildly. He bent low and felt the ground; then, without warning, he sprang up with all his might. "I can see! I can see!" he cried, leaping for joy.

Gabriel hurried toward him with several men, who examined Bartimaeus' eyes and asked what he saw. When Bartimaeus identified the sycamores, the date palms, the stone wall, and what the men were wearing, they hugged him, and Bartimaeus, too, joined the swelling crowd.

With the disciples and the women, Gabriel marveled at what Jesus had done. Could Nicodemus be right about this man? Was God unleashing extraordinary power and wisdom through the rabbi from Nazareth? If so, Gabriel had even more reason to keep him out of Jerusalem. If Jesus went there, his power and wisdom could be lost forever.

Gabriel stayed close as the Galilean said to his disciples, "By believing in me, you will receive eternal life. But if you want *abundant* life, you must abide in me and let my words abide in you, that your joy may be full."

Gabriel noticed the confusion on Mary Magdalene's face when she said to Jesus, "None of us truly understands your teachings, rabbi."

Jesus lifted an eyebrow. "Even a Pharisee named Nicodemus ben Gorion did not understand them, and he is a member of the Sanhedrin."

Gabriel knew this was his chance. "I'm a friend of Nicodemus'," he said, touching Jesus' arm. "I met you in Nain at the home of Simon ben Ephraim. I've come from Jerusalem with an urgent warning for you. Pilate suspected several Galileans of planning a revolt, and he killed them. I'm afraid the same will happen to you."

Jesus appeared unfazed. "I am aware of the dangers, but I believe it is God's will for me to go to Jerusalem."

Gabriel could see fervor and dedication in the Galilean's eyes. He remembered when he had first glimpsed those penetrating eyes and felt totally known and accepted. Feeling this way again, he gripped Jesus' arm. "You are needed in Galilee, rabbi. Only you can save our people from the murderous schemes of the Zealots." Gabriel reached for Jesus' other arm and became passionate. "Please don't go any farther. Pilate crucifies rebels to make examples of them, and I fear that he may see you as a threat." Gabriel shook both of Jesus' arms. "Sir, I beg you. If you care about your life, please go home!"

Gabriel felt a hand squeeze the back of his neck. He turned and saw the firm-jawed disciple who had humiliated the soldiers a few minutes earlier. The disciple glared at him. "Who are you? And why are you disturbing Jesus?"

Gabriel eyed the man with an unflinching stare. "I am Gabriel ben Zebulun, a merchant from Jerusalem. I have come to warn him of how dangerous the city has become."

The man's expression became noticeably agitated as he said to Jesus, "You go ahead. I will answer these concerns." As Jesus and the others continued walking, the man took Gabriel aside and said, "Do you have a brother called Dismas?"

Gabriel's eyebrows shot up in surprise. "How do you know this?"

"I worked with Dismas by the Dead Sea. I also know his wife, Judith."

Gabriel grabbed the sleeve of the man's tunic. "What is your name?"

"Judas Iscariot. I was once a Zealot, but now I am a follower of the Galilean."

Gabriel kept his voice even, so as not to arouse Judas' suspicions. "Is Judith alive?" He narrowed his eyes. "Do you know where she is?"

Judas' lips flattened into a thin line. "Yes, she's alive, and I will tell you where she and your brother are—but only if you promise not to deter Jesus from going up to Jerusalem."

Gabriel stepped back, his neck burning as his stomach tensed and his mind reeled. Finally he had met someone with information about Judith and Dismas. Now he could go after them and exact a just revenge. But as he considered how he might kill his brother or bring his betrothed before the Sanhedrin, he realized he could do neither.

The letter had explained why Judith and Dismas betrayed him. He knew now that they had not acted maliciously but out of ignorance, and this knowledge filled him more with pity than rage. Without the betrayal, he might never have discovered the image of God as both male and female. This discovery was giving him a deeper understanding of himself—an understanding that freed him.

No longer naïve about the power of sexual attraction, Gabriel was trying to forgive, as the letter counseled. His desire to find Judith and Dismas would eventually fade, he thought, unless Judith was in danger. His heart began to beat double-time. He measured Judas with searching eyes. "When you last saw Judith, was she all right?"

Judas gave him a shrewd smile. "It depends on what you mean by 'all right.'"

Gabriel sensed dishonesty in this man, as if he were hiding something behind his smooth talk and breezy swagger. Why would a man who seemed vain and hostile want to follow the prophet of peace? Gabriel wiped sweat from his brow with the back of a hand. He didn't have an answer, but this man was his only source of information about Judith. "Please tell me everything you know."

Judas avoided eye contact as he answered, "I saw Judith about a month ago. She was safe at the time, but quite unhappy."

Judas' darting eyes made Gabriel wonder if there were more to the story. Could he trust this man? Perhaps Judith was unhappy, perhaps not. Maybe Judas was playing on Gabriel's emotions so he would promise not to deter Jesus. If so, why was Judas so adamant that Jesus go to Jerusalem?

Gabriel pressed his hands together, struggling with his many thoughts. How could he let Jesus go where Pilate might kill him? On the other hand, how could he not, if he had the chance to find Judith? Gabriel glanced at the sun climbing higher in the morning sky. He interlocked his fingers and pushed them together and pulled them apart. His head ached as if it had been slammed to the pavement.

Judas was staring at him, waiting. "Why are you so interested in your brother's wife? Maybe you care about more than her safety—I can understand why. I, too, found Judith attractive."

Gabriel held Judas' gaze and ignored the remark. He had done all he could to turn Jesus back, he decided. Now he must know where Judith was. "All right," he told Judas. "I won't try to deter Jesus any longer."

Judas widened his smile. "The last I knew, Judith and Dismas were at Qumran near the Dead Sea, but they were planning to go to Jerusalem."

When Judas had finished speaking, he ran to catch up with the crowd. Gabriel followed, wondering where Judith and Dismas might be hiding in Jerusalem, and considering what to say if he found them.

Later that morning, when Jesus and his disciples stopped to rest at a spring beside the road, Mary Magdalene wandered downstream by herself. Still distraught over the confrontation with the soldiers, she tried to calm herself. She despised the Romans as much as any Jew, but she had no need to humiliate the soldiers as Judas had. Knowing him only as a charming, affectionate man, she had been presented with a side of him that she had never seen.

Splashing water on her face, she realized that her plan to make Jesus jealous had failed, and now she might be entangled with a violent man. A memory surfaced of her former husband coming home late one night. She had suspected that Jonathan had been with another woman, and when she confronted him with her suspicion, he had slapped her, knocking her down and causing her face to swell. Then he fell into bed in a drunken stupor. She ran a hand over her once-bruised cheekbone. *Why would Judas be any different?*

Gone was the sensitive man who had gently kissed her by the headwaters of the Jordan. He had been replaced by a warrior seething with rage, ready to maim and kill. *Will he turn violent when I tell him that I don't love him?* Rehearsing her words, she knew that she would not find peace until she spoke them to Judas and made a clean break with him.

Walking back toward the group, she began to search for Judas. There were more than thirty other travelers also drinking from the spring and filling their wineskins with water. Among them were numerous families, their donkeys and pushcarts stacked with fruits, grains, and vegetables for the sacrifices and celebrations of Passover.

Children were wading and splashing one another in the shallow area near the bank. Amid the chaos, Mary saw Judas at the water's edge eating dried figs. After she approached she lightly touched Judas' arm. He smiled up at her. She kept her voice low. "I must speak with you."

She moved farther down the spring, out of earshot of the others. Judas joined her as she was dipping her wineskin in the water. She spoke softly. "I am concerned about how you treated those soldiers in Jericho. I can't stop thinking about it."

Judas kept his distance. "Why should you be concerned? You saw that I am capable of defending myself. The way the soldiers demeaned us, we had no choice but to fight back."

"You did more than defend yourself. You tried to humiliate them."

Anger flared in Judas' eyes, but he kept his voice steady. "You should support, not condemn me. If Jesus hadn't interfered, I would have killed those soldiers."

Mary finished filling the wineskin and stood up. "So Jesus was wrong?"

Judas spoke quietly but could not disguise his belittling tone. "Of course he was wrong! If he were really the Messiah, he would be brave, not cowardly. In Jerusalem he'll have one last chance to prove himself. If he doesn't rally the masses to war, we'll know he's an impostor."

Mary stepped to one side, ready to leave. "If you are so skeptical about Jesus, why do you stay with him?"

Judas blocked her way, preventing her from going. "Because being with him means I get to be with you."

"Not any longer. I never should have let you kiss me, and I won't make that mistake again." As he reached for her, she brushed past him.

"If you choose Jesus over me, you will both be sorry," he called to her back.

CHAPTER THIRTY

THE ONLY WAY TO FIND LOVE IS BY LOVING. STAY CONNECTED TO PEOPLE. GET INVOLVED IN ACTIVITIES THAT FOSTER CONTACT WITH THEM.

NEVER BECOME TOO CYNICAL OR JADED TO BE AWAKENED TO, BY, AND FOR LOVE. THIS AWAKENING AND THE RELATIONSHIPS THAT GROW OUT OF IT BRING TRUE HAPPINESS.

EVEN WHEN SACRIFICES ARE REQUIRED.

RECOGNITION, SUCCESS, FINANCIAL GAIN, PHYSICAL BEAUTY: NONE OF THESE SATISFY WITHOUT LOVE. PRACTICE GIVING AND RECEIVING THIS GREATEST OF GIFTS, AND YOU WILL POSSESS EVERYTHING THAT REALLY MATTERS.

—**Brother Gregory Andreou's Journal**

Jerusalem
Friday, April 5

THE ANCIENT NICHE IN THE CAVE OF GETHSEMANE MADE A PERFECT HIDING PLACE FOR KARIM MUSALAHA AND RACHEL SHARETT. They slipped away from the last tour group of the day and squeezed into the squarish, tomblike enclosure. Located in the back of the sprawling cave's chapel area, the niche provided storage space for the monks who held services here.

As the tourists snapped pictures and talked among themselves, Karim reached for Rachel's hand and found her palm moist. The memory of her hands steering the Jeep through Bethlehem reminded him of how expertly she had kept them safe. After getting Brother Gregory treated at the hospital, she had driven them back to Holy Angels Monastery and then returned to her apartment. They had rested overnight and through the day until she picked him up at the monastery in the late afternoon.

"Where did that young couple go?"

A man's voice among the other tourists posed the question. Karim's throat went dry. His backpack chafed against his shoulder blades as he pressed against the wall, his knees bent and head bowed beneath the slanted, low-lying ceiling. Rachel had wedged herself in beside him, her head tucked below the uneven limestone. They could see into the main body of the cave because light flowed into it through a hole in the roof. But the niche they were sequestered in was dark; no one could see them without peering inside.

"The couple was here a minute ago," a woman's shrill voice said.

Karim heard footsteps moving toward them. Then abruptly the steps stopped.

"They must have already left," the man's voice said.

Karim quietly drew a breath, listening to the conversations. He remained still and thought through the plan that he had devised with Rachel and Brother Gregory. The monk would withdraw the scroll from the vault at the Bank of Bethlehem, take new photos of it, and begin a second translation. It wouldn't take him long since he could remember most of what he had already done. He would first translate the section in which Judith of Jerusalem spoke of Judas' note being buried here.

Meanwhile Karim and Rachel would photograph, measure, and sketch the spot that Mary had described, the northeast corner. With these materials in hand, they would approach a prominent museum or university to elicit support for an excavation.

Karim's cheeks grew hot. It was likely that the thief also saw the note as the missing piece of the puzzle—the piece that would reveal and confirm the secret of Jesus' relationship with Mary Magdalene. They could not let him beat them to it. At this thought, Karim noticed two women standing outside the niche. He and Rachel froze. If the women looked inside, he prepared to tell them that he and his friend were just exploring.

The women turned toward the niche.

Karim's stomach leaped into his throat.

Then an authoritative male voice said, "All right, everyone. Time to go."

Karim relaxed as the footsteps began to recede. He waited until the cave was completely quiet and then led Rachel out of the niche. "We have work to do." When they reached the northeast corner, he bowed reverently and then went behind the altar that had been erected for religious services. Bending down to examine the floor, he said, "This modern stone will make an excavation difficult. Brother Gregory says that the first-century surface is at least a meter down."

Rachel held the digital camera up and took pictures of the crypt-like area. "It makes sense that Mary Magdalene buried the note in Gethsemane, the place of Judas' betrayal."

Karim withdrew a small shovel from his backpack and stabbed at the floor. When he confirmed that the stone was too hard for digging, he put the shovel away and took out the tape measure. "If Judith's diary is accurate, when Judas realized that Mary Magdalene didn't love him, he began to lose his way. He reached his lowest point when he gave Jesus the kiss that betrayed him. It may also have been an act of revenge. Since Judas no longer shared Mary Magdalene's kisses, he betrayed the man she loved—with a kiss."

Rachel put the camera in the backpack. "I can't begin to imagine what he wrote to her before he hanged himself." Withdrawing a legal pad from the pack, Rachel began to sketch a diagram of the area behind the altar. "Do you think Mary hoped the note would be found someday?"

"She must have. Otherwise why wouldn't she have burned it?" Karim took some measurements. "Maybe she buried the note because it contained important information—information too personal to share while she was living. Or maybe she wanted to reveal the real Judas." He returned the tape measure to the backpack. "Even if we find the note," he said, leaving the altar area, "we may never know her reasons."

Rachel approached Karim in the center of the cave, put the pad into the backpack, and zipped up the bag. "We'd better go. The Sabbath will begin soon." She squeezed his hand.

Her touch sent a shiver through him. How lovely she looked, slender with a proud profile. She turned and glanced up at him, flashing eyes that conveyed undying optimism, vulnerability expressed on her arresting features. Thoughts of refugee camps and checkpoints and separation barriers faded into the background of Karim's mind. The early evening air carried a chill that smelled of springtime, fresh with possibility. The sun's last rays filtered through the hole in the roof, creating a luminous glow.

He leaned toward her, testing how she would respond. When she moved toward him, neck tilted back and eyes closed, he took her in his arms and kissed her gently. Her upper lip quivered, mirroring the rapid beating of his heart. He wished they were somewhere else—her apartment, a quiet room at the monastery. But he pushed those thoughts from his mind and said, "Forget that I'm Palestinian, that you're Israeli. Forget that I'm in Jerusalem illegally. Forget even why we came here." He drew her closer. "All that matters right now is that I love you."

Rachel studied him with tears in her eyes and said, "I knew you were special from the first time I met you. But I was afraid I would betray my family, my country. Now I know that the real betrayer was my heart." She seized him by the arms. "When I believe in something, I fight for it. That's why I went to medical school, why I joined the peace movement. I'm not afraid to fight for my right to love you."

He felt his throat tighten as he ran his fingers through her hair. "If I live for decades or die tomorrow, I will never forget you—never take your love for granted. If our love is real, all the barbed wire and electric fences in the land won't keep us apart." Seeing warmth in her glistening eyes, he kissed her again with soft, adventurous lips. His heart caught fire, erupting in a molten heat of passion. She returned every kiss and caress, their bodies as close as the line of the horizon, their souls bonded by the light that casts out all darkness and the warmth that dispels all cold.

Rachel caressed his forehead. "If the extremists on both sides could feel what we feel right now, they would lay down their arms."

Karim took her hands in his and kept his voice low. "The Jesus letter brought us together. If only it could do the same for other Muslims and Jews. . . ."

"That's why we must prove that it's genuine." She buried her face in his chest and he felt the warmth of her tears. Karim held her in silence, lost in the emotion of the moment. They had been standing that way for some time when suddenly he heard a noise.

Footsteps!

He scooped up the backpack, grabbed Rachel's hand and ran for the niche. Wedging himself in with Rachel, he hid beside her in the dark as the footsteps grew louder. He caught a glimpse of a large man entering the cave, using a walking stick.

A man too big to be Kenyon.

How could this be? Only Kenyon knew that Mary Magdalene had buried Judas' note here, because Kenyon had stolen Brother Gregory's laptop and the original translation. Who was the man in the cave?

The footsteps moved farther inside and stopped. Karim inched to the front of the niche, Rachel close behind, and peeked out. The intruder was observing the area behind the altar and snapping pictures. Then he began to poke the ground with his walking stick.

When the man turned, Karim recognized the double-chinned profile of Abbot Erasmus Zeno.

Stepping out of the niche, Karim waved for Rachel to follow him. They approached the altar without the abbot noticing.

"Did you lose something?" Karim said.

The abbot spun around, startled. "What are you doing here?"

"We wonder the same about you," Rachel said.

"I like this cave. I come here often."

Karim shook his head. "At dusk, after everyone has left? Not likely."

"Who appointed you my guardian? I can explore a cave anytime I like."

"You're exploring all right—for the note that Judas wrote Mary Magdalene." Karim stepped toward him, fighting to restrain his anger. "You led us to believe that Kenyon attacked Brother Gregory and stole his laptop. But it was you, wasn't it?"

"Be quiet!" The abbot's voice was hostile and threatening. "Who are *you* to question *me?*"

The words sent a stab of pain into Karim's chest. "Someone who thought you were a man of God."

Silence filled the cave.

"Why?" Rachel asked.

The abbot didn't answer, but stared down, his lips quivering. "I have worked so hard at the monastic life and never had any recognition. I was going to die and be forgotten. Then I saw the chance to be remembered as the man who discovered the Jesus letter. . . ."

"Would you jeopardize your position and betray your monastic vows for fame?" Rachel asked. "If you need recognition, then you haven't understood the letter."

The abbot's retort was brusque. "What would you know about the monastic life? I have given up every pleasure. What is wrong with wanting recognition for my hard work and sacrifice?"

"Through deceit?" Karim said. "Through violence? You sneaked into Brother Gregory's apartment and hid so that you could attack him from behind, didn't you? You almost killed him."

"I could have killed him but I didn't. And besides, you're here illegally, so there's nothing you can do about it." The abbot jutted out his chin in defiance.

"That's where you're wrong," Rachel said. "My brother, Ezra Sharett, is a commander in the Israel Defense Forces, and he's well-known among the police in Jerusalem. You can either return to the monastery and confess, or you can spend the next few years in prison thinking about what you've done."

For a moment Abbot Zeno appeared ready for a fight, but then he must have seen the futility in it because he looked away, his shoulders slumping in defeat.

Rachel took his arm and led him away from the altar. "You can begin to make amends by returning the laptop and everything else you stole."

The abbot jerked away. "Leave me alone. My life is ruined."

"You're mistaken," Karim said. "Your life has just begun, because one thing *all* our religions have in common is the chance to receive forgiveness and start over."

CHAPTER THIRTY-ONE

JUDITH STOOD BEFORE NICODEMUS BEN GORION'S DOOR, TERRIFIED THAT HE WOULD HAVE HER ARRESTED AS A THIEF. But he was her only hope. She had broken every rule of etiquette, not to mention the commandments against lying, stealing, and dishonoring her father and mother. What could she say to the people whom she had hurt if she went home? Perhaps someday she would find the courage to face them, but not yet. Not until her heart began to heal.

She had wandered Jerusalem's streets, the jewelry box tucked firmly beneath her cloak, and slept one night in a secluded alley. Now, after a second day with nowhere to go, she decided the time had come to return the box and the letter it contained. She could also warn Nicodemus about the Zealots' plans, and perhaps he could prevent the deaths of many people, including the rabbi called Jesus.

Night was falling and the light of the rising moon barely penetrated the gloomy darkness. She prayed that Nicodemus had not retired and would open the door himself. Through the window, she saw a lamp burning in the back of the house. She got up her courage and knocked. Her rapping might wake the neighbors, but she didn't care.

Someone stirred inside, and she heard footsteps approach. "Who's there?" a man's voice asked.

"You don't know me, but I must speak to the Pharisee named Nicodemus ben Gorion." Judith forced herself to sound bold. When the door opened a crack, she saw an older man with a long white beard. Dressed in a brown robe of woven camel hair, he peered suspiciously at her.

"I am Nicodemus," he said. "What do you want?" She lifted the jewelry box from under her cloak and held it out to him. An expression of amazement rippled across his broad, slightly wrinkled face. He opened the door and reached for the box. "Where did you get this?" he asked, taking the box and opening it. When Nicodemus saw the scroll inside, he sighed, closed the lid and invited her in. A plump woman with rosy cheeks was standing in the expansive courtyard, wearing a white robe and holding a candle. "This is my wife, Esther," he said, pointing toward the woman. "And what is your name?"

"My name is Judith of Jerusalem."

He stepped back, trying to hide his shock. "I know who you are."

Judith heard surprise in his voice and feared that it also contained rage. "Yes, you do, although we have never met." She glanced around and remembered the first time she had entered this man's house—as a thief. Overcome by shame, she felt as though the walls of the courtyard were closing in on her. Stifling the urge to scream or run away, she searched for the right words but knew there were none. "How I got your jewelry box is a long story." She paused, fidgeting nervously. "Unfortunately, it's a story of deceit. I know you are a kind man. I have come to throw myself on your mercy."

Nicodemus shifted his weight, staring at her dirt-smudged face and disheveled clothes. After a moment's hesitation, he led her into the house, into the dining room, its tasteful wall hangings a sharp contrast to her ragged appearance. He offered her a seat at the long table. His wife brought in a blanket, draped it over Judith's shoulders and asked if she wanted a cup of water.

Judith, who hadn't had a drink for hours, said, "Yes, please."

Esther returned with two cups of water. She placed them on the table and lit a candle. Then she said goodnight and left the room.

Nicodemus sat down next to Judith and cleared his throat. "Very well. I'm listening."

She hesitated, her lips trembling. If she told the truth, would he yell at her? Throw her out of the house? Have her arrested? As these scenarios played in her mind, she felt short of breath, tempted to tell lies. Then she peered into Nicodemus' aged eyes and saw compassion. "My husband and I broke into your home and stole the box, along with some other items. No one was here when we entered, but you came back when we were still hidden."

Nicodemus appeared shocked. "How could you rob me right under my nose?"

Judith tensed as she recalled the deserted streets and the house as quiet as a tomb. "It was the Sabbath. You returned from the Temple with Gabriel. As you know, I was betrothed to him before I ran away with his brother. I heard every word you spoke, and when your wife called you to her sick friend's house, we fled." Judith paused and bit her lip. "It was because of how you counseled Gabriel, and because of the letter, that I decided to seek you out."

Nicodemus opened the box, removed the scroll and unrolled it. "Jesus warned that mysterious things would happen to the letter. He told me not to worry, but I did, of course."

Judith glanced at the storage chamber, aghast that she had crouched behind its purple curtain as a common thief. She fought the urge to cry and turned away. Condemned by her actions but helpless to change them, she grasped for any shred of hope. "It's because of Jesus that I am here. When I was hiding, I heard you explain to Gabriel what it means to be created in the image of God, and how Jesus saw that image as both male and female."

Nicodemus peered at her, eyes flashing. "I was trying to help Gabriel. After what you and Dismas did, he was in despair. The more I shared with him about the letter, the more hopeful he became."

She stared at the fine grain of the tabletop, blinking back tears, her hands shaking. "I'm glad you helped Gabriel. He's a good man and didn't deserve to be hurt," she said, her voice unsteady. "Now I'm the one who needs help. I eloped with Dismas to get justice for my brother, whom the Romans killed. Dismas is a Zealot, and I thought I loved him. Now I know it was all a terrible mistake."

Nicodemus sat perfectly still, listening, which only added to her nervousness. She tried to hide the tremor in her voice. "When I saw one of the Zealots die, I questioned their violent ways and wanted to leave, yet I had no option but to stay. I kept hoping that Dismas would change." She paused and summoned the courage to continue. "Not until I read the letter did I realize what a mess I had made. The letter gave me the strength to leave. Now I want to know more about this Jesus of Nazareth—and Mary Magdalene too. I came here hoping that you would teach me—and forgive me," she added, lowering her eyes.

Nicodemus reached for her hand. "It took great courage for you to come here. I can see that you are sincerely sorry, so yes, I do forgive you. But you need something more—God's forgiveness. When you receive that gift, you will learn to forgive yourself. The letter calls this process being 'born anew.' It begins when you surrender your heart to Jesus."

"I would like to meet him."

"I've received word that he is coming to the city to celebrate Passover. I will ask if you can join us. It would be good for you to meet some of the women who follow him, especially Mary Magdalene."

Judith wanted to speak, but the words wouldn't leave her throat. If she revealed the Zealots' plan, Nicodemus might misunderstand and see her as an enemy, a plotter of evil. Now that Nicodemus had forgiven her, could she risk alienating him again? What if he turned against her? No, she must do what was right and act to stop the violence. "Tell Jesus to stay away from the Temple! The Zealots are planning an attack there!"

Nicodemus turned pale. "So Gabriel was right about the danger. I tried to get a message to Jesus, but I see I've failed. Unfortunately, I only know where Jesus will celebrate Passover, not where he is staying now, so I have no way of getting another message to him. We must pray. Since there's nothing else we can do, I'll bring you some dinner and then you must get a good night's sleep. The women will know more in the morning."

Judith feared she would sleep little until Jesus was safe and she had received God's forgiveness. She had no choice but to wait and see what would happen. When Nicodemus brought her a dinner of bread, fish, and cheese, she ate ravenously. "One thing I have been wondering," she said. "Jesus wrote the letter to Mary Magdalene, so why did you have it?"

"I was supposed to deliver it to her," he said. "Mary doesn't know that you stole the letter, and I don't plan to tell her."

As Nicodemus led Judith to a small guestroom, she thought, *This Passover will be like no other.* He said goodnight, and she lay down and tried to sleep, but sleep would not come. Staring into the darkness, she couldn't control the racing of her mind.

To her surprise, she began to feel queasy. She sat up and took several deep breaths, thinking she had eaten too fast and hoping the feeling would pass. Instead it grew worse. Suddenly overtaken by nausea, she leaped out of bed and vomited. At first she blamed the stresses of the day or perhaps a sickness. Then she thought of her monthly period, usually so regular, and began to perspire.

No, it can't be!

CHAPTER THIRTY-TWO

AS MARY MAGDALENE PICKED HER WAY OVER THE ROCKS, JUDAS ISCARIOT'S WORDS RANG IN HER THOUGHTS: "If you choose Jesus over me, you will both be sorry." Beyond the rocks she could make out a narrow stream below a sloping hillside. The impact of the words nearly made her fall. Pausing to regain her balance, she stepped gingerly, bending low and moving from one stone to the next.

Earlier she had helped to set up camp along the road from Jericho to Jerusalem. In the morning Jesus and his entourage would enter the holy city; in preparation he had gone off to pray. This was her last chance to speak with him alone. She steadied herself and lurched forward as twilight began to fade toward darkness. *In Jerusalem, he will have no time for me. I must find him!*

She fixed her gaze on the rugged hillside and kept moving toward it. A spindly olive tree stood beside the stream. The tree's crooked branches reminded her of her own misshapen life, of why she must speak with Jesus. Her breathing was becoming labored, and she prayed that she would find him. *Why do I love him so?* He wasn't handsome like Judas. His features were quite angular, and his arms and legs too long for his body. Yet when she gazed into his eyes and listened to his wisdom, she felt a powerful oneness with him. *It must be because he has such depth and heart, qualities I've always cherished in a man.*

Mary came to the end of the rocks and glanced back. In the murky light she saw someone with a torch bounding toward her. Not wanting to be found, she sped up her pace, nearly leaping now from stone to stone, her eyes straining against the encroaching darkness. She thought she had left camp undetected. Now all she could hope was that this man would see her quickened pace and realize that she wanted no company. But when she looked back again, the man was almost running, gaining ground fast.

Now she ran too, trying to get away. Carelessly, she jumped from a large stone to a smaller one and her foot slipped, causing her to land on her side, scraping a hip and an elbow. Sprawled on the sharp-edged stone, she struggled to catch her breath. She could see that whoever was carrying the torch was muscular and slightly taller than medium height. When his face came into view, she recognized him and sighed.

It was Gabriel ben Zebulun.

He sounded breathless. "Mary, are you all right?" He held out a hand. "I woke and noticed you weren't in camp. I got worried and came searching."

She took his hand to pull herself up. If anyone would understand her need to speak with Jesus, it was Gabriel, but she felt hesitant to tell him her concern. "I'm glad it's you, Gabriel, and I appreciate your coming after me, but . . ." She trailed off and examined her elbow, relieved to find only a few scrapes. "I need to talk with Jesus alone."

Gabriel held the torch close and peered at her suspiciously. "Couldn't you wait for him to return to camp? What could be so urgent?"

Embarrassment rose in her cheeks. Gabriel had rescued her once before. Because of his kindness and strength, she felt comfortable confiding in him again. "You may be the only man I would admit this to, but I must tell Jesus about a problem I'm having with Judas Iscariot."

A frown creased Gabriel's forehead. "I spoke with Judas earlier today, and I don't trust him. I understand why you may have a problem with him."

"To be truthful, Judas frightens me," Mary said. "I did something foolish, Gabriel. I let myself get too close to him." She looked away, drew a breath to collect her thoughts and then went on. "After you found me in Samaria, I returned to Jesus, and when I confessed that I loved him, he said that he couldn't marry me because of his mission. I was lonely and befriended Judas, but now he wants more of me than I can give him. He's angry that I rejected him. I fear that he may be jealous of Jesus and take revenge on him."

Gabriel sat on a large boulder and motioned for her to do the same. When she was seated beside him, he said, "Judas claimed he knew where my brother and my betrothed were hiding. He agreed to tell me, but only if I promised not to deter Jesus from going to Jerusalem." Gabriel paused before he continued, "I finally gave my word, because I have no other way of finding Dismas and Judith."

Mary empathized as she listened and took in the vast night sky, which seemed to mock her smallness. The sighing of the nearby olive branches in the breeze sounded like a mournful chorus. She measured her words carefully but decided that she must speak. "Judith has betrayed you to your very soul, Gabriel. Why do you want to see her again?"

He shook his head with resignation. "I can't let go of her any more than you can let go of Jesus. She owes me an explanation. Perhaps if I get one, I can stop dwelling on the pain."

"If only it were that easy. Jesus tried to explain the incident with the prostitute to me, and it only made matters worse."

"But I think you would feel differently if you would read the letter he wrote you. Nicodemus shared its insights with me, and I found them very helpful."

Mary thought for a moment before speaking. "The letter is the farthest thing from my mind right now. When I told Judas that I didn't love him, he made what sounded like a threat. I must warn Jesus to be on guard. Judas calls himself a disciple, but I believe he could be the rabbi's worst enemy."

Gabriel held the torch out to her. "Take this, find the rabbi, and I'll look for Judas. He probably has little understanding of women. I know it won't be easy, but the truths in the letter have given me much to share with him."

Mary thanked Gabriel and took the torch, its oily scent wafting in the breeze. When he was gone, she continued down to the bank of the stream. She waded across, the shallow ripples barely covering her ankles, the water cold against her feet. Nothing moved on the stony hillside, but she found a trail and began to follow it. As she focused her gaze closer, she saw a lone figure sitting beneath an olive tree halfway up the gentle slope. It was a man, silhouetted against the fading light. As she drew closer, she could tell that his eyes were closed, his legs crossed beneath him, and his hands folded on his lap.

Jesus.

She hurried toward him. "Rabbi, I'm sorry to interrupt, but I must speak with you."

Jesus opened his eyes, startled. "Mary." He stood and embraced her, his strong arms firm yet gentle. When he stepped back and reached out for her, she took his hand and a tremor ran through her at his touch. "Come with me," he said.

Shivering slightly in the night breeze, she followed him down the hillside. "I must talk to you about Judas Iscariot."

He stopped, a knowing look in his eyes.

She hesitated, embarrassed to tell him what had happened; then she gathered her courage and said, "I . . . I grew too close to him." Then she rushed to add, "I quickly realized that it was a mistake and I told him so. Judas knows how I feel about you, and I fear what he may do to you out of jealousy."

Instead of becoming upset, Jesus' eyes filled with compassion. "Do not worry about me. My concern is for you."

Mary felt her heart leap, grateful for his understanding. "If you really care about me, you would let yourself love me, as I love you."

Jesus became very still. "I never rejected your love, Mary; I have received it as a treasured gift. But I am choosing not to express my love for you physically, and I am asking you to do the same, not because I don't love you, but because I must fulfill a different calling." He took her hands in his. "Be assured that loving you has changed me in ways I never could have imagined. I thought that I understood love, but you taught me how much I had to learn. We cannot marry, but I am a better man for having loved you."

His words made Mary feel as if she were dying inside. How could she get him to change his mind? If he didn't, how could she accept that they would never be married? The thought was too heavy to bear, so she gave a dismissive laugh. "You are the wisest man I have ever known—what could I teach you about love?"

The wind picked up, and Jesus didn't answer right away. Instead he took the torch and led her down to the dry riverbed, which cut into the hillside. She could hear the wind whistling softly, but she was protected from the chill by the canyon's high walls of dirt and stone.

Jesus stood a few feet away and said, "My yearning for you forced me to examine my desire. I thought I understood why men and women are so powerfully drawn to one another. As it is written, God ordained that they multiply and fill the earth." He moved closer but didn't touch her. "Now I know that our yearning is the same as Adam and Eve's—the yearning not only to multiply but also to restore our lost oneness. I needed to withdraw from you because I was beginning to expect more from you than a woman can give a man."

Knowing that they might never be one, she said, "Most men need a woman to feel complete. Is that so wrong?"

"No, of course not." His eyes flashed with an intensity that was fiery but controlled. "Marriage is a gift from God and should be honored and celebrated. In order for a marriage to fulfill God's will, the husband and wife must enter it in a healthy way. In my case, I was in danger of losing myself in you, and that wouldn't be good for either of us. Only when I began to meditate on the image of God as both male and female did I regain control of my feelings. I said no to my desire because I knew I couldn't marry you and remain true to my mission." He paused and drew a breath. "But I will always be grateful for your helping me to grow. I am humbled by the power of my longing for you and how tempted I was by it."

Fighting back tears, she wondered why he couldn't both love her and follow his ministry. "I still don't understand. Why would it be wrong to surrender to love?"

Jesus placed a comforting hand on her shoulder. "What you want from me, you must find within yourself, Mary. Sometimes the deepest, truest love is not consummated but savored as friendship. You will only understand this when you become fully unified and honor both the female and the male within. Then you will be happier than you have ever been, and you will be a strong woman."

Mary frowned and said in a trembling voice, "I would rather be weak and have you."

Jesus cupped her face in his hands. "Oh, Mary, please understand.

You don't need a man to give you an abundant life. You will find that life when you discover your inner abundance. Then, if you choose to love, you will marry a man who is truly good for you." He stepped back and took her hands in his. "I have a special mission for you, Mary. The male disciples want power over the women, but you must not give it to them. You must nurture your harmony within and proclaim the gospel out of that unity. Then you will be a powerful witness to God's love, and you will be revered by men as well as women. You must encourage the men to preach the gospel in a way that brings men and women together, because they do not yet understand unity, and they are afraid of it. Only those who find the depths of love become fearless."

Mary walked past him to the entrance of the gorge and listened to the word *fearless* echoing in her mind. The word contrasted sharply with the image she had of herself. Since childhood she had organized her life around finding a man to provide for and protect her. But Jesus was describing a woman who could manage these challenges herself, inviting her into a new way of seeing herself and the world. A swirl of wind whipped up some dust and blew it toward her. She covered her eyes with her hands. When the dust cleared, she said, "I don't know where I will find the strength you're talking about."

The wind began to die down and the night grew quiet. The glow from the torch played gently on Jesus' face as he said, "The Spirit of God is more powerful than you can imagine. This power lives within you. Surrender your heart in prayer, and the power will be yours."

Jesus' words challenged her to shift her focus away from him and onto an unknown part of herself. Perhaps her dream of love would come true but in an unexpected way. Sitting on a large boulder, she said, "I feel closest to God when I'm with you."

Jesus raised his hand as if to bless her. "I hope you will seek that closeness always, for it is the source of harmony and strength."

Mary wiped beads of sweat from her forehead as she thought about seeking inner strength and harmony. She couldn't deny that she needed them. If she had embraced her inner strength, she would have left Jonathan the first time he hit her. But she was terrified of being without a man so she had tolerated the abuse until Jonathan put her on the street. Her involvement with Judas Iscariot was even more dangerous. How could she have been so foolish as to get involved with this violent man? Standing, she acknowledged the answer. Her deep need had made her vulnerable to him, and by scheming to make Jesus jealous, she had put both herself and the rabbi at risk.

Jesus stepped toward her, and she took in the subtle radiance that shone in his eyes. Her breath grew short as she said, "It's hard for me to accept that we will never be together, but I know I must. You have grown, and I'm happy for you even though that growth has cost us our love." Suddenly she felt shy and small in his serene presence, a presence that modeled the person she hoped to become. In losing him, perhaps she could find herself. She rose up on her toes and kissed him on the cheek. "Only a great rabbi could have your insight into God and life. I shall become the fearless woman you want me to be."

Jesus took her in his arms. "No matter what happens, Mary, our hearts will always be together. And never stop making God your first desire, for in doing so, all good things will come to you."

His arms felt comforting, but now she understood him not as a potential husband or lover but as a wise friend who had helped her to understand herself. It finally made sense. With every breath she promised herself to seek the fullness of God's image. She stepped away, knowing that she was finally letting go of her desire for him.

Jesus peered in the direction of the stream and listened closely. "Someone is calling my name," he said, leading her over the dirt and stone of the dry riverbed's terraced sides.

As they hurried toward the stream, she recognized Peter's voice. When they neared the stream, she saw Peter, James, and John leading several of the other disciples toward them. Peter said, "Lord, where have you been? We were worried about you."

"I needed to speak with him before we enter Jerusalem," Mary said.

"And I needed to speak with her." The firmness of Jesus' voice turned every eye toward him. "Mary Magdalene understands me as no one else. I have explained my teachings to her, and she can show you the way to inner healing and to preaching the gospel with power."

Mary caught the shock and confusion on Peter's face, but before he could respond, Jesus began moving back toward camp.

"I have taught her about love," Jesus said. "If she teaches others, her wisdom will live for ages." Jesus slipped an arm through hers and began to lead the group toward the camp. "When she shares her insights, it will be impossible to ignore her."

As they walked, she felt awed by his confidence in her and prayed that she wouldn't disappoint him. He stared straight ahead as if focusing on some distant horizon that only he could see. Could he really be the Messiah? If so, she knew that what lay ahead in Jerusalem would determine his future—and the future of the nation. She prayed that Judas Iscariot wouldn't carry out his threat.

CHAPTER THIRTY-THREE

THIS WAS THE PERFECT OPPORTUNITY TO STEAL THE MONEY, JUDAS THOUGHT. With Mary Magdalene withdrawing from him, he hoped that having money would make him more desirable and finance his rise to power.

He pulled the flap of the tent closed, loosened the drawstring on the leather moneybag, and lay the coins on the grassy earth. Some of the disciples had gone to find Jesus; others were talking around the fire. He had to act quickly so that no one would miss him. This could be his last chance before they reached Jerusalem in the morning.

He grinned when he thought of how easy it had been to trick the other disciples. He had convinced them that his experience in the silver trade qualified him for the treasurer's job. And they were naïve enough to fall for it.

By the light of a torch stuck into the ground, he divided the denarii from the half shekels that would be used to pay the Temple tax. Organizing the coins in stacks of ten, he counted twenty-four denarii and twenty-two half shekels. Since Jesus and his disciples would stay with

Mary, Martha, and Lazarus in Bethany, their needs would be minimal. Ten denarii would be enough for food and other necessities. He could keep fourteen denarii along with the ten he had held back from paying the Zealots to protect Jesus.

He began to sort the coins, the tent stuffy with the odor of his sweat. Some of the coins he placed in the leather moneybag and others in his personal travel bag. He loved the feel of money. It was nearly as sweet to him as the feel of a woman's nakedness. But he had to admit that he craved Mary Magdalene's body more than money, and he was convinced that being rich and powerful would help him to attain it.

His head began to throb as he remembered how his plan to impress her had failed. How she had been frightened by his humiliating the soldiers. He hadn't anticipated the severity of her response. But no woman had ever resisted him for long. Mary Magdalene would be his; she just needed the right incentive.

Judas envisioned how she would finally surrender to him. Grief-stricken over the death of Jesus, she would realize that she needed a man, and with his newfound money, Judas would be the one to whom she would turn.

He removed from his travel bag the towel that the women had given him, and as he placed the coins in the bottom of the bag, he decided that he needed to go to Pilate to warn him of the threat that the outspoken Galilean posed. The best way to ensure Jesus' death was to depict him as an enemy of Rome. Caiaphas would be equally enraged by the Galilean's attempt to cleanse the Temple and would also want him dead. Perhaps the governor or the high priest would be willing to pay for information about where to find this troublemaker.

At the sound of footsteps Judas quickly returned the towel to his bag and pretended to be counting the remaining coins. Someone entered the tent.

Gabriel ben Zebulun.

Startled, Judas narrowed his eyes. "Why didn't you announce yourself? I thought you were a thief."

Gabriel held up his hands in a gesture of contrition. "I need to speak with you."

"We have already settled our business. What do you want?"

Gabriel shifted his weight, appearing uncomfortable. "I come as a friend of Mary Magdalene. She tells me that something she said upset you."

Judas kept pretending to count the money. The last thing he wanted was Dismas' little brother prying into his affairs. "Did you come here to spy on me?"

Gabriel knelt beside him. "No, I came because I'm concerned about you. My feelings for the woman called Judith of Jerusalem, who was with my brother at Qumran, were similar to yours for Mary Magdalene. I think I can help you."

The mention of Judith sent a shiver through Judas. Judith was the only woman besides Mary Magdalene who had rejected him, and he was still angry. Judas picked up a few of the denarii and stuffed them into the moneybag. "*You* are going to help *me*?" he said with disdain.

Gabriel raised the torch and held it closer to the coins. "Most men don't like admitting that they need help. But now that I am on the path to knowing what true happiness is I can tell when another man is hurting."

Judas scooped up the rest of the coins and threw them into the moneybag. They hit the bottom with a clank, as if to emphasize Judas' annoyance. Perhaps if he played on Gabriel's interest in Judith, Judas could get him to leave. "I didn't tell you everything I know about Judith and Dismas," Judas said, taking the torch from Gabriel and peering at him through the thick darkness. "They're probably hiding with the Zealots in Zedekiah's Cave in Jerusalem."

Gabriel drew back but decided not to let Judas change the subject.

"When they first ran away, I was crushed, but I have grown since then. It all began with the conversations I had with a Pharisee called Nicodemus ben Gorion."

When Gabriel explained what he had learned, Judas laughed and stood up. "I've listened to the Galilean's teachings. How can he possibly know about men and women and sex?" Judas opened the flap of the tent and stepped outside with the torch. As Gabriel followed, Judas headed toward the spring across the grassy floodplain. "Jesus could have Mary Magdalene as a wife or lover. Instead he ignores her."

Gabriel put a hand on Judas' shoulder to stop him. "Jesus could marry her, as you say, but he remains celibate to follow another calling. His wisdom powers his ministry of compassion, the same wisdom that can help you to heal after experiencing rejection."

Judas couldn't remember any man fixing him with a stare as intense as Gabriel's. In the light from the flickering torch, Judas saw fierce passion in the young man's eyes. The night was quiet and smelled faintly of weeds and grass. The moon and stars brightened the path to the spring. Judas pressed on. "I've been following Jesus for more than a month, and I've never heard him speak of this wisdom."

"That's because it's still a secret." Gabriel kept pace and spoke resolutely. "What we yearn to find through women exists inside us. In other words, the passion you feel for Mary Magdalene contains an illusion. You see her as the perfect woman, the fulfillment of your dreams, but she's only human, with flaws and annoying habits like anyone else."

Judas wondered how much Mary Magdalene had told this man. How did Gabriel know about the passion he felt for her? Part of him wanted to end this conversation, to lash out. Another part was fascinated by what Gabriel was saying. Fascination won. "So, what do you know about love that I don't?"

"I know that when a man marries a woman—no matter how

beautiful—he quickly discovers her faults and stops seeing her as divine. Whatever is attracting you to Mary Magdalene now may become an annoyance later." Gabriel moved closer to Judas and kept his voice low. "Sexual attraction is not just about the woman; it's about the forces inside you. What you see in Mary Magdalene is a reflection of the female image of God in your soul. You need to stop looking for this image in her and find it in yourself. This is the way to take back your power as a man and feel whole again."

Judas pushed Gabriel away and continued toward the spring, troubled by his words. What self-respecting man would talk of a female image of God? Judas shook his head. Didn't Gabriel know that God was male and so was a man's soul? He threw up a hand in frustration. "What you're saying is offensive to me."

Gabriel caught up. "When I first heard these teachings, I responded in the same way. Most men do. They struggle to find the wellspring of happiness, but it eludes them. That's why they place impossible expectations on women, and if a woman rejects them, they're devastated. Even if she gives herself to them, they become disillusioned and downcast over time, because no woman can fully satisfy a man's yearning for the inner female."

The more Judas heard of Gabriel's explanation of love, the less he understood it. With each step toward the spring, he was losing more patience with Gabriel. He quickened his pace. "If a woman doesn't satisfy you, you haven't found the right woman; that's all."

"The problem is often not with the woman; it's with the man's lack of awareness." When Gabriel reached the spring, he scooped some water into a hand, drank it and then continued. "Once a man embraces the feminine side of himself, he finds a great secret of happiness. This experience of deep communion frees him to really love. Now his love isn't based on the woman's appearance but on the completeness of the man's soul. It flows from his joy in being fully alive."

Judas splashed water on his face, brooding over these strange ideas. If Gabriel didn't recognize Mary Magdalene's incomparable beauty, he was blind. In the presence of such a goddess, what man cares how he feels inside? He only cares about making love to her. Gabriel's words were absurd. Judas grabbed him by the arm and spun him around. "You're talking nonsense." Judas' blood was flowing now. He shoved Gabriel. "You say you want to help me? Well I don't need your kind of help. My plan for our people and for Mary Magdalene is *my* secret of happiness."

Judas watched the expression of youthful enthusiasm on Gabriel's face fade to dark concern. Judas didn't care. Only a fool would say that a man has a feminine soul. The thought was ludicrous. How dare Gabriel insult him like this! Anger poured from Judas as he grabbed Gabriel by the throat. "Keep your stupid ideas to yourself!" Judas tightened his grip, choking him. "Do you understand me? Never speak of these ideas again!"

Gabriel dug his fingers into Judas' wrists, gasping for breath and straining to break his grip. Finally Gabriel managed to throw him off, but Judas ran at him and shoved him into the water. As Gabriel splashed to regain his footing, Judas walked away and spoke with angry intensity over a shoulder. "What I said to Mary Magdalene, I'll also say to you: If she chooses Jesus over me, they will both be sorry."

CHAPTER THIRTY-FOUR

LIKE EVERY TRUE ZEALOT, DISMAS LIVED TO KILL OR BE KILLED FOR HIS CAUSE. As he entered the Temple in Jerusalem, he was ready for either, but he prayed that the latter would not be his fate. The morning sunshine in the expansive courtyard, beyond which the Gentiles could not pass, seemed to be reaching out and inviting him into a new future. As he walked south, toward the long cloistered portico called the Royal Stoa, his heart yearned for that coming time of peace.

A time that could only be attained through armed rebellion.

He looked west, toward two stories of dignified colonnades, the marble pillars sheathed in gold. Several thousand pilgrims swarmed the Temple grounds; he had lost Barabbas and Gestas among them. Not wanting to raise suspicions, he dared not look back to see if Mattathias, Simeon, and the more than twenty other Zealots were following.

He headed for the money changers' tables within the southern cloister. Barabbas and Gestas had arranged with Judas Iscariot to begin the assault there, and to join forces with Jesus of Nazareth and his crowd of supporters. Together they would drive out the money changers, and when Caiaphas and his police intervened, the Zealots would assassinate them and flee.

Dismas stared straight ahead, hoping to spot Barabbas and Gestas in the crowd. The bleating and bellowing of tethered cattle, sheep, and goats rang in his ears, nearly drowning out the squawking of the caged doves and pigeons. Even at this early hour, the Temple reeked of burning meat, the result of the morning sacrifices known as the *tamid*. The burnished steel of the dagger concealed beneath his belt reassured Dismas with each step. Any doubts about the uprising at this time were dangerous. To question the righteousness of the cause—even for a moment—would be to sow the seeds of defeat. The Zealots would battle the Romans to the death. To think otherwise would be to consign oneself to slavery.

Yet as Dismas moved stealthily toward the money changers' booths, he wondered for a moment if he had made a mistake by not convincing Judith to stay with him. The memory of Zedekiah's Cave, of their painful parting, haunted him.

Now his mind turned to the letter from Jesus of Nazareth. *Concentrate,* Dismas told himself. The letter spoke of a love that could change lives, even the world. Jesus claimed that the Spirit of the Lord was upon him, because the Lord had anointed him to bring good news to the poor. Jesus believed that God had sent him to proclaim release to the captives and recovery of sight to the blind, to let the oppressed go free, and to proclaim the year of the Lord's favor.

Could this be true? Would the meek, not the powerful, inherit the earth? Did the kingdom of God belong to the merciful and the humble in spirit, not the mighty and the proud?

Jesus' teachings condemning violence haunted Dismas. He lived by the dagger and was willing to die by it. Could there be a better way? Had Jesus really come to save the world, as he claimed? And would his teachings on peacemaking, justice for the oppressed, and reconciliation between enemies bring this salvation sooner than the use of arms?

Enough, Dismas said to himself. *This letter is dangerous! Tempting me to let down my guard. To rely on something other than my own strength. I will not. A man must stand up for what is right and fight for it. Violently, if necessary!*

"Get your Temple coins here! Exchange your dirty Roman money for the purest Tyrian silver!" The cries of the money changers interrupted his thoughts.

"Don't settle for goats or pigeons! Buy an unblemished lamb here!" A stocky man shouted the words, pointing toward a large pen of bleating lambs. He fixed Dismas with an imploring gaze. "May I get you one, sir?"

Before Dismas could decline the offer, a wiry money changer with darting eyes accosted him. "Right this way, my friend!" The man gestured toward three large stone tables. They were piled high with coins and tended by busy vendors. "We will be glad to help you," the man said as the vendors served long lines of customers. "Our rates are the best in Jerusalem."

Dismas shook his head and backed away, offended by the barnyard stench and shrill chaos of the Temple's Great Court. Once a sacred space where Pharisees gathered to discuss and debate the law, the Court had been defiled. The marketplace atmosphere, the clanging of the bronze and silver coins into metal containers, the endless haggling of the merchants, the noise and dung of the animals . . . it was all an offense to God. Caiaphas allowed it. He was to blame!

I am ready to strike, but where are Barabbas and Gestas? Where are Judas Iscariot and Jesus of Nazareth? A muscle twitched in Dismas' neck. His breath became short as he stole a glance at the guards atop the Antonia Fortress. Dressed in full regalia, there were at least twenty of them. He felt like a gladiator on the eve of battle. So much could go wrong, and most of it was beyond his control. The Zealots would need to act with speed and precision or face the wrath of the Roman legions, and he knew what that meant. His mouth went dry, his knees ready to buckle. Swallowing hard to fight the terror that tightened his stomach into a fist, he knew he must not give in to it. He had to fight valiantly.

For his future.

For the future of the nation.

For the love and honor of Yahweh.

Dismas heard a ruckus near the entrance to the cloistered portico. A tall, lanky young man was standing nose to nose with several red-faced money changers. When Dismas approached, he watched as the young man swept a hand over a table, sending dozens of coins flying. The money changers cursed him and rushed to retrieve the coins.

This man must be Jesus of Nazareth. Dismas moved closer, while maintaining a safe distance. As much as he hated Judas Iscariot, he was grateful that Judas had supported the cleansing and got Jesus to the Temple. But where was the crowd? The Galilean had only a handful of friends with him. Dismas cursed under his breath. Judas had promised more than he could deliver. Between the Zealots and Jesus and his followers, there were only about thirty men, and they had never drilled as a unit. Dismas didn't know what kind of fighters these Galileans were or how they planned to proceed, but he couldn't worry about that now. By striking against the money changers, the Galilean had become an ally, and Dismas could see that he was brave and strong. Hopefully his friends were fierce fighters and would help the Zealots finish what he had begun.

When Dismas spotted Barabbas and Gestas approaching the Galilean, he put a hand on his dagger, ready to join the fray. Jesus untethered the cows and goats and opened the stalls of the lambs, creating a minor stampede. Two of the pigeon sellers tried to restrain him, but he threw them aside and opened several of their cages. "Police!" they yelled. "Help! Arrest this madman!"

Jesus ignored their protests, shoved the sellers aside and heaved over money changers' tables. One after another, he sent the tables tumbling to the stone pavement. As hundreds of coins clanged and pinged on the ground, he said, "It is written, 'My house shall be called a house of prayer,' but you are making it a den of robbers. Get out! Leave this sacred Court and never come back!"

Out of the corner of an eye, Dismas saw Barabbas and Gestas threatening several money changers with their daggers. The two Zealots then joined in knocking over the tables, one after another, creating panic and outrage up and down the money-changing plaza. "Get out, you thieves and robbers!" Barabbas shouted. "You have desecrated God's holy Temple!"

This was Dismas' agreed-upon cue. He charged forward and waved Mattathias, Simeon, and the others on. They cast the money changers aside, upended table after table, and freed animals from their cages and stalls. Soon Caiaphas came running, surrounded by the Temple police, their swords drawn. Dismas had prepared for this moment for years. Blood rushed to his head; his rage made him feel stronger than ten men.

Barabbas and Gestas first moved toward Caiaphas, with Dismas close behind. A hefty man with a bushy red beard cried out, "Jesus! Look! These men are armed!" When Jesus saw the daggers, he stopped turning over tables and began to back away, as did his friends. Dismas caught a glimpse of Judas Iscariot and waved a frantic hand. "Judas, where are you going? We need all of you and the Galilean to fight with us!"

Judas ignored him and turned to leave with the others, heading toward the eastern gate and the Mount of Olives. Dismas was furious. The surprise written on the faces of Jesus and his friends suggested that they hadn't expected the onslaught. What had Judas told them? That the cleansing would be peaceful? That the Zealots would turn over a few tables and flee? Or had he told them nothing at all? Perhaps Judas was using the situation for another purpose, for some personal benefit.

Dismas chided himself for trusting a man who was a proven liar. And hadn't he read in the letter that the Galilean opposed violence?

Now Dismas had to fight even harder. As he joined the melee, a poker-faced guard was stabbing at Barabbas with his sword. The thrust missed and left the guard off balance. Barabbas swung hard, drove his dagger into the guard's stomach, withdrew it quickly and tossed him aside. Outraged at the murder, several of the Temple police attacked Barabbas.

Dismas joined Gestas in defending him. Under assault, Dismas lunged at a guard, but the blow grazed the man's breastplate and twisted the dagger out of Dismas' hand. Now all he had were his fists. The police came at him; he stepped back. Without a weapon, he would not last long. Barabbas and Gestas fought valiantly, dagger against sword, as did the others. Dismas parried blow after blow but lost ground fast.

The money changers and merchants shouted for the Romans to stop the riot. Caiaphas' bodyguards encircled Barabbas, and he killed another of them, stabbing him in the throat. As the guard fell, more than a hundred soldiers swept down from the Antonia Fortress, and many of the Zealots fled. The dozen rebels who remained fought valiantly, but the soldiers used their javelins to push them back, gaining the advantage with superior weapons and numbers.

Two soldiers surprised Dismas from behind and wrestled him to the ground. They drove his face into the pavement and shackled his hands and feet. By this time Jesus was long gone, but as the blood clouded Dismas' vision, he wondered if the Galilean hadn't made the better choice. Perhaps violence does beget violence. When he stood up, Dismas saw that Barabbas and Gestas were receiving similar treatment. "You are all under arrest!" a brawny tribune yelled as Caiaphas looked on, smirking. As the soldiers led the Zealots away, Dismas heard the cries of the money changers: "Murderers! May they crucify you for your crimes!"

CHAPTER THIRTY-FIVE

CHAPTER THIRTY-FIVE

OUR CHANCES OF FINDING AND KEEPING LOVE IMPROVE AS WE GROW IN SPIRITUAL UNDERSTANDING. EXPERIENCING THE LOVE OF GOD INCREASES OUR CAPACITY TO LOVE OURSELVES.

ACCEPTANCE AND FORGIVENESS, PATIENCE AND COMPASSION, UNDERSTANDING AND SUPPORT—HOW CONSISTENTLY DO WE GIVE OURSELVES THESE GIFTS? ONLY AFTER WE HAVE RECEIVED THEM FROM GOD CAN WE BESTOW THEM ON OURSELVES.

IT ISN'T SELFISH TO DO SO.

IT'S AN ACT OF GENEROSITY.

LOVING OURSELVES AS GOD LOVES US IS THE FIRST STEP TOWARD LOVING ANOTHER HUMAN BEING.

—**Brother Gregory Andreou's Journal**

Jerusalem
Monday, April 8

OF ALL THE RISKS THAT KARIM MUSALAHA HAD TAKEN, ATTENDING A RECRUITMENT RALLY IN JERUSALEM FOR THE MARCH FOR PEACE WAS THE GREATEST. He joined the rally on the plaza between the Damascus Gate and the New Gate, haunted by Ezra Sharett's threat to have him shot on sight. A crowd of more than a thousand had gathered here, in front of the Old City wall, northwest of the Temple Mount. When Karim saw an Israeli police officer in the crowd, his vision blurred. He scanned the faces in search of other officers in blue berets. None patrolled near the stage on which an Israeli rock band was playing. But a female officer was mingling with participants who carried banners that read "Change the Future Now!" and "Join the March for Peace!" in Hebrew and Arabic.

Karim considered leaving but continued to pass out flyers. Anything for Rachel. She needed his help publicizing the international demonstration that would surround the sacred sites on Wednesday, April 17. She also wanted his support when she spoke at today's rally as a founding member of the Abrahamic Peace Initiative.

Karim pushed down the impatience rising in his chest. Every minute at the rally distracted him from solving the mystery of Jesus' relationship with Mary Magdalene and whether it involved Judas Iscariot. He was planning to rush back to the monastery as soon as the rally ended. He and Rachel had to solve the mystery and report the discovery of the Jesus letter to the Government Antiquities Agency. Otherwise Robert Kenyon could mount another threat and gain possession of the original scroll or translation. If that happened, Kenyon would claim credit for the discovery and use it for personal gain. Rachel had a different plan—to display the scroll at the march as a witness to the Galilean secret of peace.

If she and Karim could prove that the scroll was authentic, it could draw thousands to participate and become a symbol of religious unity. Thankfully Erasmus Zeno had returned Brother Gregory's laptop and other translation materials upon his ouster as abbot of the monastery. Now Brother Gregory was getting the scroll carbon-tested. Only if it truly could be dated to the time of Jesus could they begin to make the case for authenticity. Then they could find support for excavating the Cave of Gethsemane.

"Don't look so worried." Rachel nearly shouted to be heard above the wailing of electric guitars and the pounding of drums. She pulled Karim close and lowered her voice. "We have no choice but to be here. The march is this land's best hope for peace. It may also be its last."

Karim nodded in agreement and continued to pass out flyers as the music wound down. When the speeches began, Rachel gave him a wave and moved toward the stage. The gesture prompted the stirring in his heart that he felt in her presence. The stirring that had brought him to Jerusalem against his better judgment.

Like being buried in quicksand, the more he tried to dig himself out, the more entrapped he became. Finally he had surrendered. If it were wrong for a Palestinian to love an Israeli, he would plead guilty—but with no remorse. Why judge himself for what he couldn't control? He saw his love as neither wise nor foolish, neither rational nor irrational, neither right nor wrong.

It just was.

As a result of his powerful desire, an already dangerous situation had become even more so. Rachel had insisted on attending the rally, but he didn't want her to go alone. His attending with her was an opportunity for him to prove his love. So he avoided the Israeli police and waited for her to keep her promise to leave after she spoke.

An older man with a bushy gray beard finished his remarks as Karim moved toward the stage. Weaving through the crowd, he noticed a man to his left who had a prominent forehead and a flat-looking nose. Karim turned away, his mind reeling. Only one man had such distinctive features—Abdul Fattah. The possibility of Abdul's learning about the rally and coming here had occurred to Karim, but he had decided not to let his fear deter him from helping Rachel. Now he needed to avoid Abdul, make his way to the front, and leave with Rachel right after her speech.

Karim looked up as she approached the podium, her shoulder-length auburn hair blowing in the gentle breeze, her full-length linen dress accentuating her slender figure. She began with a brief introduction of herself and the Abrahamic Peace Initiative, the interfaith group she had helped to found. Then she lamented the suffering associated with the separation barrier and the checkpoints, the refugee camps and the settlements. And she decried the endless bloodletting and death that had been visited on both sides.

Her voice gained urgency. "In spite of this anguish, I believe that Israelis and Palestinians can have a bright future, living side by side in two sovereign states. It can be done! The Israelis and Egyptians were worse enemies than the Israelis and Palestinians, and yet we made peace with the Egyptians, and that peace has endured. In order for the two-state solution to work, people of conscience on both sides must become more visible and vocal than the extremists. We also need support from all other countries, because what happens here affects the entire world."

Karim paused as he neared the front. A tall, blond young man wearing a yarmulke nudged him. "She's a powerful speaker. Have you heard of her?"

Karim gave him a wry smile. "Not until she saved my life."

"You're kidding!"

"No, actually I'm not."

Karim returned his attention to Rachel as she continued. "We must recognize the common ground among our three religions as a fertile garden in which to grow lasting peace. We Jews speak of the messianic age; Christians look for the return of Christ; and Muslims await the advent of the Madhi. In this coming age, hostilities will end and all people will live in justice, harmony, and abundance. We may disagree about who will initiate this golden age; we may not know how or when it will come, but we all must believe in it."

Karim glanced around as applause rippled through the crowd. A cadre of photographers surged toward the stage snapping pictures. Newspaper reporters furiously scribbled notes, and television crews positioned their lights and rolled their cameras.

Rachel's voice rose in melodic cadences. "We don't need more religious doctrines. We need a spirituality of peace. If the world is not moving toward catastrophe but toward transformation, the ultimate victory belongs to love, not to evil."

Rachel's words lifted Karim's spirits, but a man's voice cried out from the crowd, startling him.

"Don't be naive! The ultimate victory belongs to the country with the strongest military and the best weapons."

Rachel pulled the microphone closer. "I know it's hard to believe that love will triumph, but without this belief, what hope do we have? Israel possesses more than two hundred nuclear weapons, and sooner or later the terrorists will acquire them too. The more weapons there are, the less secure we become. I say this not as one who has been immune from the suffering, but as one who has experienced it. My own father was killed by a suicide bomber."

Karim sensed reverence in the hush that fell over the crowd. The blond young man stared at him, his eyes wide.

Rachel drew a breath and went on. "I've learned that we only move beyond our anger, hate, and fear when we find healing within. Through this healing we discover love at its deepest level—the level of forgiveness. Then we're able to live nonviolently and seek interfaith understanding. We can share the land and its resources and work to end oppression and war. Have the courage to dream! Imagine a world free of terrorist bombings. Envision a world in which squalid neighborhoods and despair-ridden refugee camps are no more. It can happen, but only if forgiveness triumphs."

As the crowd applauded, Karim moved closer to the stage.

Rachel built to her conclusion. "I invite you to make hope real in this holy city on April 17th. The strength of our numbers will arouse the conscience of the world. You can help to ignite a revolution of justice and healing. If you march with us here, surrounding the Dome of the Rock, the Wailing Wall, and the Church of the Holy Sepulchre, you'll stir the conscience of the world. We will make a powerful statement about how our religions need to change to support lasting peace. We will say no to any interpretation of a holy book that justifies violence. We will say no to uses of religion that create injustice and oppression. We will say no to religion that divides and impoverishes people rather than unites and sustains them. The Israeli-Palestinian conflict is *the* moral issue of our time. If we can make peace, the future will hold great blessings for Jews, for Muslims—for all people. But if our generation fails at this task, the result will be catastrophic. The current one-state reality will be impossible to change, and the Arab world will never forget the injustice done to the Palestinians. That will mean a future of fear and insecurity not only for Israelis and Arabs but also for all nations with a stake in the conflict. Let's not let that happen! Let's come together! Let's make this march a resounding call for humane and ethical religion so that we may live in peace and that peace may live in us. May God's blessing and protection be with us all!"

Raucous applause echoed through the plaza as Karim went to the stairs at the back of the stage. When Rachel finally descended, he congratulated her, and as they stood talking, he sensed someone approaching. He turned to see Ezra, dressed in a white shirt and black pants, bearing down on them. "Why didn't you return my calls?" he said to Rachel.

"I've been busy."

Ezra turned to Karim. "Didn't I tell you to stay away? With the police presence here, you can't escape jail now."

Rachel stepped between them. "Ezra, no!"

"I told him never to come to Jerusalem again."

"Ezra, please. He's my friend."

Ezra labored to catch his breath. "You'll feel differently about your friend when I tell you who he really is."

"What—?" Rachel tried to ask a question, but Ezra cut her off.

"I did some research on *your friend* and learned his real name—Karim Musalaha, not Muznah. He's from Nablus, not Bethlehem." Ezra pointed a finger at Karim. "His father is Sadiq Musalaha—the political leader of the PPA, and his older brother was Saed Musalaha." Ezra held both of his fists in the air and shook them angrily. "Do you realize who Saed Musalaha was?" He raised his voice and emphasized each word. "He killed our father."

Rachel turned to face Karim. "How could this be? Please tell me he's lying."

Karim stared at the flat stones of the plaza, bile rising in his throat. "I wish I could."

Rachel's face became ashen. "Your brother killed my father? You knew about this but acted as if you didn't?" Her voice cracked. "You've been deceiving me from the very first."

The stones of the plaza seemed to shift beneath Karim's feet. He felt dizzy, his knees weak. "How could I have told you the truth? You would have hated me, refused to listen to anything I had to say."

Rachel shook her head with disgust. "And you said you loved me." Her voice dripped with disdain as she began to walk away.

Turning back, she said to Ezra, "Do what you need to do. I'll forget I ever met him."

Ezra grabbed Karim's arm and spun him around. That's when all motion was stopped by a voice.

"Let him go."

Karim turned to see Abdul Fattah staring at Ezra.

"Who are you?" Ezra said, his tone indignant.

"I am Sadiq Musalaha's chief lieutenant. I can't let you put his son in an Israeli prison. He would never get out alive, and that would have consequences with his father."

"Why should I care what his father thinks?"

"Because," Abdul said, "Sadiq Musalaha can unleash a dozen suicide bombers at will, and if his son were in Israeli custody, he would have the perfect excuse to do it."

As Ezra released him with a shove, Karim felt fortunate to be avoiding an Israeli prison. But as Abdul yanked him toward the Mercedes, Karim knew he was being led to a prison of another kind.

CHAPTER THIRTY-SIX

THE HOLLOW THUD OF THE DOOR SLAMMING BEHIND JUDITH SENT DREAD INTO HER BONES. It was the door to the courtyard of the home where Jesus of Nazareth would celebrate Passover, but the sound made her think of the door to a Roman prison cell shutting. Of how it would feel to be locked in a cell and become a victim of the same cruelty as her murdered brother. A spike of terror shot up her spine. A neighbor had seen her and Dismas flee Nicodemus' home. If she were arrested and charged with aiding the Zealots, she would suffer Reuben's fate, and no one could save her.

As Judith followed Nicodemus ben Gorion through the modest courtyard that led to the kitchen, her mind leapt from one terrifying scenario to another. Her stomach felt as if it would rise into her throat. The same sensation had awakened her before dawn, and she had vomited. Convinced that she was pregnant and afraid she would vomit again, she paused and took several deep breaths to quiet herself.

An image of Dismas' face on the night she had left, contorted with hurt and rage, flashed across her mind. She had departed on the eve of his greatest challenge, when he needed her most, and so she had betrayed him as surely as she had betrayed Gabriel. Perhaps neither brother could forgive her, but Nicodemus had. As a sign of his goodwill, he had promised not to tell Mary Magdalene that Judith stole the letter. Now that she was alone in the world, Nicodemus was her only hope. He had found peace through Jesus of Nazareth, and he believed that Jesus and his followers could help her do the same.

She wanted to accept the letter's promise of new life. But who could forgive the deep sins she had committed, when she couldn't forgive herself? Mary Magdalene had just cause to be angry with her. Jesus had addressed the letter to Mary—it was her property, and Judith had stolen it. Mary and her friends had more reason to report her to the Romans than to show her kindness. Judith put a hand on her stomach and rubbed gently to relieve the anxiety stirring inside. Rather than revive her, the springtime morning air mocked the winter of her heart, in which no flower bloomed and no bird sang.

She forced herself to catch up with Nicodemus. With nowhere else to go, she had no choice but to trust these women. She felt lightheaded as she entered the kitchen, which was strewn with large bowls and jars full of Passover ingredients. All five women looked up from their preparations for the seder that night. The familiarity of the women performing these tasks calmed her jittery nerves.

Judith dodged several children underfoot as she was introduced to Joanna, wife of Herod Antipas' steward, Chuza. Nicodemus shared how Joanna, once beset by unhappiness that wealth could not cure, had found joy in following Jesus. Judith also met Susanna, a widow whom Jesus had healed of grief, and Salome, the mother of the children, who lived nearby with her husband and family.

As Nicodemus introduced Jesus' mother, Mary, and finally Mary Magdalene, he said, "I brought Judith here because she wants to follow the rabbi. And she needs you to guide her." Judith admired Mary Magdalene's dark red hair, her smooth olive skin, and her elegant, high cheekbones. Nicodemus regarded the dignified woman thoughtfully and continued, "Judith needs a friend who has struggled with the same questions she has. You could be that friend, Mary. Please help her find the answers."

An inquisitive smile creased Mary's full, sensuous lips. "Any woman who wants to follow Jesus is already my friend."

Turning to leave, Nicodemus assured Judith that he would return that evening. Mary Magdalene handed her a knife and invited her to chop apples, dates, and walnuts for the charoseth, a symbol of the mortar that the Hebrew slaves used in laying bricks. Judith worked silently for a time, the aroma of matzo in the clay oven reminding her of the Passovers she had shared with her family. By eating the unleavened matzo, the Jews recalled how hurriedly their ancestors had had to flee their Egyptian oppressors.

All at once she yearned to go home, to help her mother rid the house of every trace of chametz, or leaven; to grate bitter herbs for the *maror*, eaten to share their ancestors' suffering; and to pour the four cups of wine, representing the promises of God, for each participant in the seder. Judith wondered if she could ever go home again.

"Jesus is becoming more controversial each day," Mary said. "And all those who follow him endanger their lives."

"I've been living with danger since I left my father's house. But mysterious events led me to Nicodemus, and to Jesus. The events involved a Zealot called—"

Dismas' name was on Judith's lips when a knock rattled the door and cut her off. The door opened, and three men walked in. Jesus' mother, a sturdy woman with thick auburn hair and a pleasant oval face, introduced the largest man. She called him Peter, and his brother, who looked like a younger version of him, Andrew. "These men fish for a living," she said.

"Not me!" The third man's close-set eyes flashed indignantly, his roundish features contorted in a grimace. He introduced himself as Matthew, a former tax collector.

Peter measured Judith suspiciously and then asked Mary Magdalene, "Is she a follower of the Way?"

"She is here as a seeker," Mary said, putting an arm around her.

Peter eyed Judith with contempt. "I don't trust her. Nicodemus told me that she aided the Zealots." He lowered his voice to nearly a whisper and spoke to Mary Magdalene. "Don't you realize that the Romans arrested the men who started the riot when Jesus was cleansing the Temple? They were Zealots leading a revolt. Pilate probably thinks Jesus was one of them." He pointed an accusing finger at Judith. "If the Romans catch her here, they'll arrest Jesus for sure—and us with him. This girl must leave, and we should warn Jesus to stay out of the city."

Joanna, a matronly woman who wore her grayish-brown hair pulled back, shook her head dismissively. "I wonder who you're really afraid for, Peter. Jesus or yourself?"

Mary Magdalene pleaded with everyone to calm down. "We cannot predict what is going to happen," she said. "But Jesus always welcomed everyone at his table, even outcasts. Judith has come to seek his grace like the rest of us. Who are we to throw her out?"

"You're being naïve, Mary," Peter said. "This girl is a danger to Jesus. If the Romans think he's a Zealot, they'll crucify him. If we get caught with him, the same will happen to us. She must go. Now!" He moved toward Judith.

Mary Magdalene stepped in front of her, arms outstretched. "Your words show how little you understand of Jesus' teachings, Peter. He's so alive in God that he doesn't fear death, and neither should we. It's when we are attached to this earthly life that we become afraid. Our higher purpose is to do God's will. This is the truth behind Jesus' serenity. We must be willing to love as radically as he does and not fear the consequences."

Peter threw up his hands. "We know that Jesus loved you differently from other women, but that doesn't give you the right to endanger the rest of us."

"This girl is not the only one who has sinned. There's darkness as well as light in all of us. But to overcome the dark, we must follow Jesus and seek the truth beyond ignorance. When we do this, we will no longer be the slaves of our bodies. Nor will we be deceived by the world's illusion of treasure. Jesus told me that the true treasure is our vision of God and God's reign. We find this treasure within ourselves. Since discovering it, I have been at peace."

Judith noticed Andrew crossing his arms on his chest and appearing uncomfortable. When Mary Magdalene finished, he said, "I never heard Jesus teach these things. How are we to believe them from a woman?"

"What's worse is that she says them to defend a Zealot!" Peter added.

Mary's expression darkened. "How can either of you call yourselves his disciples if you demean women? Jesus never does! He says that there is neither male nor female in heaven. Men have no special status before God; what matters is the quality of one's soul, male or female."

"If Jesus loves Mary, we must respect what she says," Matthew said. "We'll show we are true followers of his by living in love, which means letting the girl stay. Jesus' choice to come here tonight means he is willing to die for this ideal; we should be too. Let's go to Bethany to be with him at the home of Mary and Martha and Lazarus."

Mary Magdalene took Judith's hand and led her from the kitchen, up a long staircase and into a large room. The sun's brilliant rays streamed in through the room's open windows, which offered a view of Jerusalem's narrow, congested streets. A half-dozen long couches lined the room's walls; a low rectangular table stood in the middle. Mary and Judith began to move the couches around the table to prepare for the seder. As they lifted the first one, Mary said, "Jesus' teachings are a mystery to most people, sometimes even his disciples."

Judith helped her place the couch near the table. "After what I've been through, I need his love more than anything."

"I have been wondering what brought you here."

Judith told Mary about running away with Dismas ben Zebulun, her fiancé's brother, on her wedding day. "It was wrong, but it felt right at the time. When I finally came to my senses, I left. I don't know where Gabriel is, but I must find him and beg his forgiveness."

Mary Magdalene, eyes large as half shekels and face alight with wonder, said, "Gabriel ben Zebulun was your betrothed?"

"Yes, do you know him?"

Mary shook her head and took Judith's hands in hers. "Gabriel saved my life." Her voice was so full that her words were slurring. "He is the bravest and truest of men, and now he, too, has become a follower of Jesus."

Judith couldn't believe what she was hearing. She squeezed Mary's hands. "How could this possibly be true?"

"Gabriel heard about Jesus from Nicodemus. I met your betrothed at the home of a Pharisee called Simon, in Nain."

Judith drew a breath to keep from trembling. "How did Gabriel save your life?"

"I was attacked by two men on the road through Samaria, when Gabriel was returning to Jerusalem with Nicodemus. Later Gabriel came looking for Jesus to warn him that Pilate had murdered some Galileans. Like many of us, Gabriel believes that only Jesus can save us from the violence of the Zealots."

Judith wasn't surprised to hear of Gabriel's bravery. She had always known Gabriel as a man of character and resourcefulness. She tried to turn away, but Mary Magdalene pulled her close and embraced her. Judith pressed a cheek against Mary's neck and said, "If what you say is true, we both know what a rare man Gabriel is . . . and I . . . I betrayed him."

Mary Magdalene sat down on a couch. "Sooner or later passion wounds us all. I, too, have known its heartbreak."

Relief filtered through Judith as she continued to stand. She knew she would eventually have to confess to stealing the letter, and Mary's honesty gave her an opening to do so. But Judith hesitated, afraid of Mary's anger or, worse, her rejection. Judith stared at her, unable to move or speak. Part of her wanted to be honest; otherwise Mary would feel betrayed when she learned the truth. Another part of her was tempted to flee the room and find somewhere to hide. Only when Mary waved her over did Judith find her courage. Sitting on the couch, Judith said, "I know what you're referring to because I read the letter that Jesus wrote you."

Mary appeared shocked, as if hit by a blow. "What? How?"

Judith stared at the floor. "Dismas and I robbed Nicodemus' house in order to get money for the Zealots. The scroll was among the items we took. Reading the letter showed me the causes of my anguish. I returned it to Nicodemus and vowed to change my life."

Mary gave a sigh. "I haven't read the letter myself."

"You haven't?" Judith couldn't hide her surprise. "May I ask why?"

"Because Jesus showed another woman the kindness that I thought only I deserved. In my hurt I refused to read the letter. Instead I let Nicodemus keep it." Mary smiled. "I can see that hurt feelings are something that you and I have in common."

With each word Mary Magdalene spoke, Judith's admiration for her grew. Wide-eyed, she studied Mary and said, "Nicodemus believed that hearing your story would help me. When I first saw you, I could tell that you have the same serenity he has. I would do anything to attain it."

Mary Magdalene rested a hand on Judith's shoulder. "When I met

Jesus, I was aching inside after years of anguish. He cast out the demons of my broken dreams, and I fell in love with him. I thought I would die if he didn't return my affection, but instead he explained the soul of love to me and helped me find my true wealth as a woman."

Judith could feel her heart thundering in her chest, desperate for the knowledge Mary had. "Jesus also explains love in the letter. It moved me deeply, but there was a lot I didn't understand."

Mary lowered her voice and emphasized each word. "Jesus taught me how destructive it is for a woman to love out of the need to fill a void. We are capable of communion with the soul of a man, but until we become intimate with ourselves, we cannot love in a healthy way."

Comforted by Mary Magdalene's openness with her, Judith considered whether to reveal her pregnancy. Would Mary help her decide what to do? She almost told her, but then she hesitated and chose to speak further about the letter, about how it had shown her that her feelings for Dismas were based on need, not love. "I needed his strength to cover my weakness. Through his violence, I vented my rage at the Romans for murdering my brother. Through his wildness, I tried to escape boredom. But in the end, all I got was suffering."

Mary Magdalene took Judith's face in her hands. "Jesus can show you the way to healing. He pointed me to the source of harmony, which is God. I was attracted to Jesus' body, but he cared too much for my soul to become intimate with me. He freed me from the illusions of desire and taught me that all that is physical passes."

Judith looked puzzled. "Does this mean that Jesus doesn't believe in sex or marriage?"

Mary Magdalene laughed and set about straightening the table. "Not at all! He believes that until we find harmony within, we cannot love unselfishly. We get attached to people and try to possess them. That is not real love; it's a dreamlike state from which he wants to awaken us. By returning to our source in God, we see through the world's deceptions and our own sinfulness. His teachings give me the hope of becoming fully human, as he is. This means that, as a woman, I must develop the male in me, as Jesus has developed the female in him."

Mary Magdalene's wisdom spoke to Judith like the voice of a trusted friend. Judith knew the wisdom had to be real because she saw its effect in Mary's extraordinary power and poise. The voice in Judith's heart seemed to be urging her to trust Mary with her darkest secret. "I haven't told you my whole story," she said, her heart pounding. "I believe that I may be pregnant with Dismas' baby." She swallowed hard, choking back tears. "I can't raise a child with an outlaw like Dismas, but I also can't expect Gabriel to take me back—and certainly not in this condition. Oh, Mary, what am I to do?"

Mary Magdalene held her until she quieted. "Think about what's best for the baby. Maybe you're underestimating the depth of Gabriel's character." Mary let her go and gave her a warm smile. "You must pray and struggle to trust. This is life's greatest lesson, and no one learns it perfectly or all at once. We trust when we turn our problems and our future over to God—*really* turn them over. When we do this, we no longer worry about tomorrow, but focus on loving and being loved in the present. Then we let life happen as it will, and we can accept whatever it brings."

"But I'm a pregnant woman with no man to support me."

"You must learn from your past but keep looking to the future. To do this, you must trust the Lord and draw on your untapped strength. This is your greatest challenge; if you accept it, you will become a new woman. You can begin by going home and facing your parents. Once they know you are expecting, they will want to help their grandchild."

Judith shook her head. "My father can be very hardhearted. He may even disown me."

"If that happens, you can stay with me and my friends. We won't let you or your child become destitute."

Thankful for Mary Magdalene's advice and merciful offer, Judith smiled warmly. She wanted to ask Mary to introduce her to Jesus, but before she could speak, she heard heavy footsteps and loud voices. "Is Judith of Jerusalem here?" a husky male voice asked. "Tell us where she is, or you will all be arrested!"

What's going on? Judith got up and ran to the window.

"Don't jump!" Mary said. "It's too high."

"I must flee," Judith said.

It was too late. Two Roman soldiers appeared at the top of the stairs, their bronze helmets and breastplates flashing in the morning light, their long swords drawn. "Which of you is Judith of Jerusalem?" their leader asked.

"I am," she said, knowing she was trapped.

"Come with us," the soldier said. "You're under arrest for stealing from the Pharisee Nicodemus ben Gorion. A neighbor recognized you as the woman who broke into Nicodemus' house with a man."

Judith cried out in terror as the soldiers wrestled her down the stairs.

"You're going to enjoy Pilate's prison," one of them said mockingly. "It's full of Jews these days."

She used her last measure of strength to wrench herself around. "Please help me, Mary! Tell my father what has happened. He's my only hope!"

The soldiers pushed Judith toward the door. She could do nothing but obey.

CHAPTER THIRTY-SEVEN

MARY MAGDALENE ENTERED THE COURTYARD OF THE ONE-STORY, FLAT-ROOFED HOUSE WITHOUT KNOCKING, HER LEGS WEAK, HER BODY DRENCHED IN SWEAT. Exhausted from running the two miles from Jerusalem to Bethany, she closed the door and paused to catch her breath. Her sweat dripped onto the dusty stone floor as the events of the morning came rushing back.

After the soldiers arrested Judith, Mary feared that Jesus or his friends would be next. She had instructed Joanna, Susanna, and Salome to stay behind and continue to prepare for Passover; then she left for the home of Mary, Martha, and Lazarus in Bethany to warn of the danger.

But before she exited the gates of Jerusalem, she stopped at the marketplace to search for Judith's father. The second merchant she asked said that Nathan's spice business was well-known and gave her directions. Mary had found the shop on a busy street behind the marketplace in Jerusalem. Nathan's craggy features revealed his anguish when she told him about Judith. "My daughter in a filthy Roman prison? I must tell Gabriel," he said. "We must go to her!"

Nathan had rushed off, placing two assistants in charge of the bustling shop. As Mary turned to leave, she noticed an alabaster flask of sweetly scented nard on a stand by the counter. Though the lavish ointment cost nearly three hundred denarii, it seemed just the right gift for Jesus. She yearned to show him the extravagance of her love, but nothing purchased with money could fully capture the depth of her feelings. Only an impractical and wildly excessive gift could begin to express them. As harried as she was, she purchased the ointment and took it to Bethany, east of the Mount of Olives.

As she stood in the doorway of the home that belonged to Mary and Martha and their brother Lazarus, her breathing was returning to normal, and she opened the small homespun bag that contained the alabaster flask. As she admired the flask's rounded contours, the advice she had given Judith about Gabriel and Dismas echoed in her mind. The words were unrehearsed, flowing from a place deep within her, and reflected a greater wisdom than her own. In Judith, she saw herself two years earlier—a woman on the run, facing a life either as a prostitute or as a beggar if her relatives had not saved her.

But no longer was she attached to outcomes or trying to control them. She was learning to accept whatever life gave her—the joys as well as the sorrows—and to find extraordinary richness in them. After closing the bag, she wiped the sweat from her forehead and swallowed against the tightness in her throat. Maybe Jesus really *is* the Messiah, she thought.

She knew that she couldn't stop him from putting himself in harm's way. Strangely, his total surrender—his utterly reckless dedication to God—made him all the more attractive. *Will I ever get over him?* It seemed impossible, and, truthfully, she didn't want to, because after loving him she could never love another man. She needed at least to tell him about the soldiers that had come to the house in Jerusalem, and she also wanted to thank him for giving her new life.

Steadying her trembling hands, she started toward the faint murmur of voices. The sound was coming from the rear of the house, and as she moved in that direction, through a large sitting room filled with wooden furniture and past two modest bedrooms, the voices got louder. When she reached the dining room in back, she found Jesus reclining at a long table. The twelve disciples were there, along with the hosts, Mary, Martha, and Lazarus of Bethany. Knowing that Lazarus had been sick, she was glad to see him looking refreshed and healthy.

Jesus was gesturing as he spoke. She marveled at his hands, the fingers slender yet confident; the palms, a shade lighter than his dark skin, flexible yet sturdy. These carpenter's hands, extensions of his heart, passionate and overflowing with love, had made the lame walk, the dumb speak, the blind see. Perfectly formed, the hands appeared ill-matched to the rest of his body. He was telling stories with the casual air of a father at bedtime, and as always, his voice captivated her. The words flowed musically, a river of refreshment for her thirsty soul.

Her eyes scanned the group and fell on Judas, his curly black hair nonchalantly askew, his thick beard neatly trimmed. Her stomach turned, and she had to look away. Jesus had taught her how to protect herself from such unhealthy men, and she loved him for it, now more than ever. She drew a breath, her heart echoing in her ears.

Jesus turned when he heard her enter. "Mary, please come and join us."

The others made room at the table, but she could not move, her legs frozen. Martha, a plump woman with large, compassionate eyes, approached her. "There's more than enough food, Mary. We have a place for you." Martha slipped an arm around her and led her toward the table.

Mary Magdalene took a few steps and stopped. "Something terrible has happened," she said. "Soldiers raided the house in Jerusalem. They arrested a young woman whom Nicodemus brought to us to follow Jesus, but now she is in prison, and I fear the same could happen to all of us."

Jesus spoke evenly. "I will not let the Romans prevent us from celebrating Passover in the holy city. They think they have power, but the true power belongs to God."

Peter's face drained of color. "The danger in the city is increasing. We should stay in Bethany and not take chances."

John said, "I agree. The cleansing of the Temple inflamed tensions. I'm afraid the Romans will arrest us as Zealots."

Judas Iscariot glared at Jesus and said, "Let them think what they want. With Barabbas in prison, you are our only hope, Jesus! You must go to Jerusalem and rally our people. Prove that you are the Messiah! Lead us to victory!"

"Like the prophets before me, I will go to Jerusalem to do God's will. But you do not understand my mission, Judas. More violence will not win our people's freedom; it will only bring greater suffering. I have come not to kill and destroy but to heal and save," Jesus said.

Mary Magdalene thought of his prophetic teachings, of how he had mesmerized the multitudes, and remembered her conversation with John when she had run away. *Is Jesus really the Messiah? Could this awkward-looking man possibly save our people?* Jesus' authority seemed to come from beyond himself, as if from another world. *He is so extraordinary. Perhaps he is the one we have been waiting for.* She knew that she must honor him as the anointed one of God, and she must do it boldly, here and now, in front of everyone, especially Judas Iscariot.

Stumbling toward Jesus as in a dream, she remembered the prostitute at the home of Simon the Pharisee. *How different things are now. How much more I know about him. I must show the others who he really is.*

She held out the bag and said, "I have a special gift for you, rabbi." She withdrew the alabaster flask, removed the cork, and began to pour the expensive ointment on Jesus' head. As the honeyed fragrance filled the room, she massaged the ointment into his hair, rubbed it over his cheeks and eyelids, smoothed it over his nose and ears and beard.

Peter said, "Lord, why are you letting her do this to you?"

Jesus did not answer but closed his eyes and smiled as she lavished the ointment on his head, leaving neither a hair nor a spot of skin uncovered. Out of the corner of an eye she noticed Judas scowling, his face burning red, his eyes smoldering. She held his gaze, refusing to turn away, and then did something that surprised even her: She let down her long hair and draped it onto Jesus' feet. Then she anointed his feet with the ointment, drying them with her hair, as the woman at the Pharisee's home had done.

"When will you stop embarrassing us, Mary?" Peter sounded disgusted.

"Jesus deserves to be king," she said, continuing to rub his feet with her hair. "I anoint him to celebrate his reign in my heart. I anoint him because I see both male and female in him, the one God has sent to lead us in the ways of peace. He is not just a wise teacher but an enlightened man, the Messiah. May his light come to each of us and to all the world." Changing her focus to Jesus, she said, "I am sorry that I was jealous of the prostitute at the home of Simon the Pharisee. If I had known who you were, and all that you have come to give both women and men, I would have joined in anointing you then."

Jesus embraced her and then kissed her on the cheek. Judas Iscariot leapt to his feet and pointed angrily. "This is an outrage! Mary has wasted this precious ointment. We could have sold it for three hundred denarii and given the money to the poor!"

Jesus said to Judas, "Why do you trouble Mary? She has done a beautiful thing to me. For you will always have the poor among you, and you can show kindness to them whenever you wish; but you will not always have me. She has done what she could; she has anointed my body, preparing it for its burial. Truly I tell you, wherever the gospel is preached in the world, what she has done will be told in memory of her."

Jesus got up, took Mary Magdalene's hand, and led the group out of the house. As they started toward Jerusalem, she saw Judas walking by himself. Arms crossed on his chest, he was frowning angrily. Suddenly he stormed over and confronted Jesus. "Are you going to rally our people against the Romans or not?"

Jesus paused and steadied his gaze. "My kingdom is not of this world. We must live as if God is our ruler, not Caesar, and that means loving all people, even our enemies."

Judas shook his head in disgust. "Now I have my answer," he said, turning away. Then he took Mary Magdalene aside and lowered his voice. "Having you choose Jesus over me was hurtful enough, but when you wiped his feet with your hair, you scorned me." He moved closer to her. "You are both traitors!"

Mary watched Judas skulk to the back of the group, her heart racing wildly. As she rejoined Jesus in front, she thought, *If Judas thinks we are traitors, why does he stay with us?*

CHAPTER THIRTY-EIGHT

IT WAS THE BIGGEST DECISION GABRIEL WOULD EVER MAKE. He stood behind the counter of his market pondering it, and he wondered if everyone in Jerusalem had waited until the Thursday before Passover to shop. He feared the walls would burst if another customer entered. He was tired of the shuffling feet and anxious faces, of the shrill voices and pungent odors of horseradish, dates, and apples. His feet ached; he was hoarse from bargaining; his ears were ringing; and he was staring at depleted shelves.

Still, with profits so healthy, how could he complain? Sundown would bring quiet; he would rest then. For now, he needed to meet the expectations that had won him both neighbors and foreigners as customers. He turned the cashbox over to the bald and portly Caleb ben Thassi, a helper he had hired to get him through the holiday, and he went to the storage room to check the supplies.

Gabriel knew that he couldn't make this decision just once. It would have to be made repeatedly over days and weeks, even years, because his decision didn't concern his business or his money. It wasn't about his health or even his Jewish faith—it was about his heart.

Trying to study the long shelves that lined the walls of the boxlike room, he couldn't focus on the jars of wine or the bundles of bitter herbs and onions or any of the other seder essentials. The mixed smells of onion, herb, and grain vied for his attention, but all he could think of were Judith and Dismas, and whether he should forgive them.

He began to load seder supplies onto his wooden pushcart, his hands trembling. Talking with Nicodemus had helped him understand why Judith and Dismas betrayed him, but how could he get over the pain? He had considered asking Nathan and Gideon, Judith's father and brother, to go with him to Zedekiah's Cave to search for her and Dismas. But since Jesus had come to Jerusalem, the city was on edge, and to go to the Zealots' hiding place—with Pilate crucifying every Zealot his soldiers caught—would be foolhardy.

If only Gabriel had prevented Jesus from coming to Jerusalem! He had tried, but the Galilean wouldn't listen, and now Gabriel feared what would happen. His customers had mentioned how Jesus had been teaching in the Temple and stirring up controversy. If Gabriel had never met him, he wouldn't have believed that a Galilean carpenter could cause such trouble, but since he had seen Jesus' power to heal and win people's hearts, he did believe.

Gabriel continued to load his wares and thought about the meaning of Passover—freedom. Despite his being in a quandary about forgiveness, he knew that his heart was free. The letter had helped him to understand sexual attraction—how it involved more than one's body or feelings. Now he understood the spiritual nature of falling in love.

His longing for Judith was no less powerful than Adam and Eve's yearning for each other. Like them, he had hoped that sexual union would heal the alienation in his soul, and he had become obsessed with Judith.

But now he knew that his was really a search for the female in himself and in the image of God. He thought quickly of Judas Iscariot, who was obsessed with Mary Magdalene and would know nothing but suffering until he found healing. Judas had not only resisted this healing but was also hostile to it, becoming a danger to himself and others.

Gabriel took the supplies to the main room of the market and began to help Caleb with the customers. A tall man with a Roman nose bought flour. The man looked like a foreigner. Gabriel liked them best because they knew nothing of the shame of his wedding day. He asked about their jobs and homes and families, and answered their questions about his, without fear of humiliation. It was harder to encounter old friends or familiar customers. None of them inquired about Judith, but the pity in their eyes was crushing. He discussed their purchases, and he constantly directed the conversation to the weather, to Temple politics—anything to divert attention from him. He had begun restocking shelves when he caught a glimpse of a white-haired man in a long robe.

Nicodemus.

Gabriel noticed a scroll in his hand and hoped it was the letter. As Nicodemus approached, he held out the scroll. "Mysterious things have happened to this letter since we last spoke. Where can we talk?"

Gabriel led him to the storage room, his heart pounding in his ears. Mysterious things? *What on earth did Nicodemus mean?*

The old Pharisee began to speak. "I have news about Judith and Dismas. The Zealots were desperate to raise money, so they robbed my home. Along with jewelry and other valuables, they stole the box in which I hid the letter."

Gabriel gasped. He knew that his brother was aware of Nicodemus' wealth, but he never imagined that Dismas would rob a member of the Sanhedrin. He must have considered the Pharisee's home an easy target.

"Now my brother has turned Judith into a thief as well as an adulteress! How could he be so callous?"

Nicodemus clapped a hand on Gabriel's shoulder to steady him. "The news I have is not all bad. Judith read the letter and was so moved that she left Dismas and returned the scroll to me."

Gabriel's mind was reeling. "Did you confront her with her crimes?" His voice was shaking with emotion. "Did you tell her how loathsome she has become?"

"I was tempted to, but she explained that the letter had convinced her to become a follower of Jesus, and she begged my forgiveness. I forgave her since she seemed sincere, and I was overjoyed to have the letter back. I introduced her to Mary Magdalene and some of the other women disciples. She promised to tell Mary what she had done."

Gabriel stared at the old man, head spinning and knees weak. "Where is she?"

Nicodemus stepped back, holding the scroll with both hands. "I took her to the home of a friend, where Jesus will celebrate Passover tonight. Before you give up on her, you must read the letter yourself." Nicodemus held out the scroll. "Please take it. The letter will help you decide what to do."

Gabriel hesitated a moment. He wasn't willing to forgive as easily as Nicodemus had. Before Judith stole the letter, she had stolen his happiness, and he didn't have much hope of getting that back. Anger smoldered in his gut as he tried to forgive. Out of respect for the wisdom of the letter and because he wanted to read it himself, he took the scroll.

"I will return tomorrow," Nicodemus said, leaving as quickly as he had arrived.

Gabriel sat on a sack of wheat and breathed in the scent of nutmeg and cardamom. His throat tightened as he unfurled the letter that had brought him so much healing and began to read.

As Nicodemus had said, the letter described the purest essence of love—that this essence is the secret of life for each human soul, relationship, and community, and that the essence comes from God's love for the world and for each person. The letter emphasized that to know this love and to make it known are the only paths to happiness. Gabriel's eyes took in each word, moving slowly from line to line. After a few paragraphs, he understood why the letter had touched Nicodemus so deeply. It contained insights from beyond this world, insights about the eternal kingdom that Jesus came to reveal. As he read on, the Galilean's discussion of love and relationships, prayer, spiritual knowledge, healing for men and women, liberation for the poor and oppressed, the kingdom of God, and peace on earth challenged Gabriel's thinking and softened his heart.

Unconsciously he began to pace as he read. According to the letter, learning to forgive is part of loving as Jesus does. Holding on to hurt only makes one bitter and miserable. Forgiveness is the way out of the misery, but it will not come quickly or easily. Forgiveness takes time and work. Gradually letting go of hurt and hate and giving them to God, one is free to begin a new life. Forgiveness is not for the sake of the forgiven but for the forgiver. This is the way to healing.

Gabriel shook his head. Before he began reading, he wasn't ready to forgive, but now he knew he wouldn't heal fully until he did. The teachings about balancing the male and female within were powerful; they had made a difference already in how he saw himself and how he related to women and to life itself. According to the letter, the male and the female are one in Jesus. This union means that God's kingdom is near, manifested in healing, creativity, and joy. Gabriel couldn't have made this discovery on his own. Perhaps the letter's teachings on forgiveness were equally true. But they would be hard to follow.

His pacing slowed as he became more and more entranced. Jesus of Nazareth claimed that the greatest love had come into the world through him. If Gabriel had never seen or heard him, he would have thought that such a boast was scandalous. But Gabriel had gazed into the Galilean's eyes, sensed his serenity, witnessed his compassion, and watched as he opened the eyes of the blind Bartimaeus.

He shifted his weight from one foot to the other, struggling to understand what God's love meant for him. The letter said that you experience this love by being born of the Spirit. Through this rebirth you find your true purpose, the deeper reason you are here. You begin to die to yourself and live for God. Such self-denial means putting God's dreams above your own, which feels like a loss of control. But the letter promised that God's dreams for you far exceed any you have for yourself. By losing your life to God, you gain it back, fuller and richer than before, since those who want to save their lives will lose them, and those who lose their lives for Jesus' sake will find them.

Gabriel sat down, gripped by the power of these words. He had invested his life completely in business. Becoming successful and polishing his reputation had required all his energy. Still, he often felt empty and wondered if there wasn't more to life than work. In the letter Jesus said that being born anew can be dramatic and life-changing, or it can happen gradually, in a quieter but equally powerful way. The wind blows where it chooses, and you hear the sound of it, but you do not know where it comes from or where it goes. So it is with everyone who is born of the Spirit, Jesus said. You can receive this birth over and over, not just once. Life presents constant challenges. But even the darkest despair has lessons to teach if you keep your heart open and touch the depths of God.

Gabriel's mind raced with questions. *Is my heart open? Am I interested in spiritual matters? Do I know even the first thing about happiness?* As he kept reading, the letter provided more and more answers. It said that you must explore the depths in yourself. As you discover the truth about who you are, and who God is, you will be free. This freedom comes at the price of courage. Confronting your inner darkness can be terrifying because it reveals your selfishness, pride, and violence. You must bear the pain of knowing yourself because, if you do not, your life will be based on illusions, and you will fall victim to your hidden needs, wounds, and desires. It is not what goes into a person that destroys the soul but what comes out. For it is from within, from the human heart, that evil intentions flow.

Gabriel closed his eyes. *Do I have evil intentions? What are my true desires?* He read on. The letter affirmed that the better you know yourself, the wiser your choices will ultimately be. You will discover your light as a person created in the image of God. If your whole body is full of light, with no part of it in darkness, you will be like a lamp that gives light to the world. Knowing the truth about yourself will make you question the world's values when they clash with your own. Rather than wear a mask or follow the crowd, you will honor the person you really are, even if it makes you unpopular. And you will find the wealth of your life, for where your treasure is, there your heart will also be.

Gabriel unrolled the scroll farther. Jesus discussed the particular torment caused by sexual sins. Whether the torment was private shame or public humiliation, Jesus said that he shared the pain, for sexuality is a great mystery, and even he struggled with it in his relationship with Mary Magdalene. He revealed the nature of that relationship and how much he learned from it. Based on his own experience, he taught that sexuality should be handled with gentleness and humility. To do otherwise, to shame people or treat them as outcasts is to sin against the God in whose image they were created.

Gabriel stared at the shelves of the storage room without really seeing them. He had been condemning Judith and Dismas, even wishing for revenge. But his attitude had been very wrong. Instead of seeking vengeance, he was to seek forgiveness. He was to think of them not as evil but as weak, as people like all others—in need of the marvelous, undeserved grace that Jesus described in the letter and shared through his life. Nicodemus was right: Love meant wanting the best for another person, and Gabriel knew that he still loved Judith.

Tears burned the backs of his eyes as he recalled the scene with the prostitute at the home of Simon the Pharisee. Though she was attractive in a sensual, provocative way, she sat with her shoulders slumped, her eyes downcast, and her expression forlorn. But when she heard Jesus speak, her demeanor had changed, and when she anointed him, her face radiated joy. Others condemned her, but Jesus showed her compassion and offered her forgiveness.

Gabriel set down the letter and stood up. Crossing his arms over his chest, he leaned back, stretched, and stared at the ceiling of rough stone. Unexpected warmth ran down his spine. Slowly at first and then uncontrollably his body began to shake, and tears flowed from his eyes. He wiped at them with both hands and sat back down to calm himself. After picking up the letter, he reread the part about forgiveness being the highest expression of love and knew what he needed to do: He had to offer both Dismas and Judith the forgiveness that Jesus had offered the prostitute.

The letter promised that if Gabriel clung to his faith even through suffering, he would grow in this love. The past would no longer seem so powerful: He could leave it and begin again. He heard Jesus' voice telling him to focus on today. Dwelling on the past cannot banish regrets or recapture lost happiness. Fretting about the future will not calm fears or make a single fantasy come true. The present—this very moment—is all you have, and it could be your last. You must seek the good in this moment, even though it is hard to find, and live fully and gratefully.

Timeless wisdom was flowing through this Galilean rabbi! Gabriel wanted the qualities that Jesus was describing—the self-love that would free him from comparing himself to others; the inner knowledge that assured him of God's presence; the grace and courage to persevere through any struggle; the freedom from attachment that would bring him joy.

Jesus' teachings were irresistibly convincing. He said, "Do not worry about your life, what you will eat or what you will drink, or about your body, what you will wear. Is not life more than food, and the body more than clothing? Look at the birds of the air; they neither sow nor reap nor gather into barns, and yet your heavenly Father feeds them. Are you not of more value than they?"

Reading these words, Gabriel felt God's love rising like fresh yeast in his unleavened heart. Jesus was charting a higher path, the path toward a complete change of life through a growing faith. More than anything, Gabriel yearned to walk this path with him. He no longer wanted to strive for riches or pleasure, for knowledge, success, or fame. Rather, he would strive for God's kingdom, believing that all good things would come to him.

Now he knew what Dismas lacked: the rebirth that could free him from his violence. He also wondered about Judith. How much had the letter changed her? She had become a follower of Jesus, but what did that mean for Gabriel? Was she ready to ask his forgiveness? If so, could she truly love him? Or would she abandon him as soon as she no longer needed him?

"Gabriel ben Zebulun! Is Gabriel ben Zebulun here?" A man was yelling loudly enough for Gabriel to hear in the storage room. The voice sounded so insistent that he rolled up the scroll and rushed to see who was calling. When he reached the main room, he was surprised to see Judith's father.

"What are you doing here?" Gabriel asked.

"You must come with me tomorrow morning," Nathan said.

"Come with you? Where?"

"The Romans have arrested Judith and thrown her into prison. A friend of hers—Mary Magdalene, she called herself—came to my shop to tell me. She said that Judith broke into the home of Nicodemus ben Gorion, a member of the Sanhedrin, and the Romans have arrested her for robbery."

Gabriel stared at him wide-eyed. "Nicodemus was just here—he said nothing about this."

"It just happened; he didn't know." Nathan grabbed Gabriel by the shoulders. "With all the criminals in that prison, I fear for her. I have arranged for us to meet with the governor in the morning. We must get her out!"

Before Nathan had finished his sentence, Gabriel knew that he would go with him, and that he would bring the scroll. He prayed that Pilate would show Judith mercy. He could not imagine all that she had been through.

Or that a Roman jail would likely become the place where they would meet again.

CHAPTER THIRTY-NINE

THE BELIEF THAT LOVE BRINGS HAPPINESS IS ONLY HALF TRUE. THE BONDING OF TWO SOULS AS ONE PRODUCES A RARE FORM OF BLISS.

BUT THIS ISN'T THE WHOLE STORY.

DARK MOODS CAN SET IN. ARGUMENTS HAPPEN. SICKNESS OR TRAGEDY INTRUDES. EVERYTHING FROM HOUSEHOLD DUTIES TO THE MOST INTIMATE OF MATTERS MUST BE NEGOTIATED.

TO GIVE ONE'S HEART TO ANOTHER PERSON IS TO BEAR A CROSS. NO ONE LOVES WITHOUT SUFFERING.

MAKING A RELATIONSHIP WORK DEMANDS ONE'S DEEPEST MATURITY AND STRONGEST RESOLVE. IN ORDER TO SUCCEED, REMIND YOURSELF DAILY THAT LOVE IS NOT ABOUT HAPPINESS.

IT'S ABOUT THE EVOLUTION OF THE SOUL.

—**Brother Gregory Andreou's Journal**

Nablus

Saturday, April 13

KARIM MUSALAHA ENTERED HIS FATHER'S STUDY, CLOSED AND LOCKED THE DOOR, AND THEN SLID A METAL FILE CABINET IN FRONT OF IT, HIS HANDS TREMBLING. In the Mercedes, on the sixty-three kilometer drive north from Jerusalem to Nablus, he had hoped that this moment would come. After spending the day in his bedroom down the hall, guarded by Abdul Fattah, he had sneaked out when Abdul momentarily left his post.

Eager to e-mail Rachel after five days of home confinement, Karim sat down at his father's cluttered desk and switched on the computer. Words of lament swirled in his mind. He had lied to Rachel by withholding the truth. He had failed her as a friend and partner for peace. Worst of all, he had lost her love and respect.

As the computer began to boot, he glanced up and noticed a framed photo of his mother on the shelf above the desk. She wore a green hijab and stared out with piercing ebony eyes. Karim tried to look away but couldn't. In his mother's austere face he saw great pain and even greater depth.

He wanted neither.

Not if gaining the depth meant suffering the pain.

What he longed for as he logged into his e-mail account was the pure joy of Rachel's kisses, the thrill of her touch, the delight of her embrace. But perhaps he had no choice but to walk his mother's path. They had both fallen in love with people whose understanding of faith conflicted with theirs, and such relationships always involved pain.

As he typed Rachel's name, he wondered if his love for her was so powerful because it was forbidden. He paused and fingered the gold band that had once belonged to his mother. She couldn't leave Sadiq Musalaha because she had nowhere to go. Karim, on the other hand, could move on with his life without Rachel. So why was he unable to? Why did he keep thinking about her beauty and their unfinished quest for the truth about Jesus and Mary Magdalene?

He began to type his apology but was interrupted by pounding on the door. "Either let me in or I will get the key." Abdul's muffled voice sounded angry but matter-of-fact. It struck Karim as ironic that this severe man had saved him from Ezra Sharett. Then he remembered that Abdul hadn't always been so cruel. "Just leave me alone for a few minutes, please."

"I can't do that."

Knowing that Abdul would soon return with the key, Karim typed quickly:

Dear Rachel,

I am writing these words after many tears. I withheld the truth about Saed and about my father because I was afraid of losing you. Please forgive me! I will love you always.

In peace and hope,

Karim

As he sent the message, Karim heard a key turn in the door. He hurried to the file cabinet, pressed his back against it, and pushed with his legs as Abdul began to force the door open. Karim's back ached as the pressure grew, every muscle tensing. He pushed harder, but the file cabinet kept sliding. "You'll be sorry you put me through this," Abdul said as he strained to open the door.

Karim's head began to throb. The harder he pushed, the more ground he lost. When the file cabinet shifted sideways, Abdul burst into the room and grabbed Karim's throat, cutting off his air supply. Karim swung an arm, desperate to shake him off, but Abdul deflected the blow and tightened his grip. As the seconds ticked on, Karim felt as though he might pass out.

"Stop!"

Sadiq Musalaha entered the room and said to Abdul, "I told you to keep an eye on my son, not strangle him. Wait outside the door."

As Abdul left, Sadiq Musalaha led Karim to the faded gold couch and chairs opposite the desk. "We need to talk." Sadiq motioned Karim to sit down. Karim glanced out the window behind the couch and caught a glimpse of the shop-lined streets of Old Nablus. Nothing about the city provided any comfort, not the scent of apricots and figs, not even the green-carpeted slopes of Mount Gerizim. He stared at his father, wishing he were anywhere but here.

When Sadiq Musalaha spoke, his rage was barely controlled. "By running away as you did, you placed yourself in grave danger. You are fortunate not to be in an Israeli prison or dead."

"You know how I feel about serving in the militia, *Baba*."

"So you prefer to march in demonstrations with an Israeli woman? Have you gone mad?"

Karim leaned forward, elbows on knees. "The madness is the violence. Until it stops, no one in this land will have a decent life. No one will be safe."

"And you think that demonstrations will stop it? There have been thousands of them, and they have changed nothing. Violence is the only language the Israelis understand. We will use it until we drive them out of Palestine."

Karim shook his head in disagreement. "True freedom will only come when Palestinians and Israelis live side by side in sovereign, secure countries. I believe this now more than ever—especially after what happened to Saed."

"After Saed became a holy martyr, you mean?"

"Saed killed and injured innocent people, and his death changed nothing."

Sadiq Musalaha swung and landed an openhanded blow on Karim's cheek. "Don't speak of Saed without giving him the honor he deserves!"

Karim recoiled and met his father's eyes. "I will never understand how killing and injuring innocent people are honorable."

Before Sadiq Musalaha stood, he pressed his lips together, his posture awkward, and studied Karim. "Our *objective* is honorable—that's all that matters. We must use whatever means necessary to secure justice for our people." He raised his index finger. "There is one way you can make amends. You must devote yourself to the work of the PPA." Sadiq Musalaha strode toward the door, paused, and without turning, said, "You have no choice—you will serve in the militia. This is my decision."

After Karim heard the study door close and lock, he went to the window and looked out. His only hope was to climb down and disappear into the labyrinthine alleyways of Old Nablus. But sand had blown between the frame and the casement, jamming the window. Placing his palms at the top, Karim pushed up and succeeded in cracking the window open at the bottom. He slipped his fingers through the crack and with his other hand pushed up from the top. As the window opened, it made a loud scraping sound.

Karim heard footsteps, and then the door crashed open as he leapt onto the sill and swung his legs up, ready to jump. Before he could leap, Abdul yelled, "Stop!" Then he raced toward Karim, grabbing his arm and yanking him back. Abdul stood over him as he fell to the floor.

"I'm supposed to keep you here until you agree to your father's orders."

Karim got up and met his gaze. "Never! You of all people should understand. You used to be like an uncle to me."

"The past counts for nothing. The PPA is our family now."

Karim furrowed his brow. "The family meals, the games in the street, the prayers at the mosque—none of those meant anything to you? You've changed."

"No more than you." Abdul gave him a shove. "Until Saed died you were patriotic. Now you organize protests with Jews."

"At least I still have a heart. When I was a boy, you used to bring me candy and figs. You used to laugh and play with me—buy me presents for my birthday. Now you're hard and bitter."

"At least I care about my people, like your father and Saed."

Karim walked to the couch and then turned and faced him. "I, too, care about our people, about liberation, but we will never achieve it through violence. There's another path to peace."

"What are you talking about?"

Karim paused, willing his mouth to speak the words that he hoped would win Abdul's heart. "When I ran away, I found an ancient scroll at Qumran. It contains a letter written by Jesus of Nazareth."

Abdul smirked. "That's impossible."

"I thought so too, but the more I study the letter, the more I'm sure it's real. Jesus wrote to Mary Magdalene about how to find the harmony that creates peace in the world. I have to get back to Bethlehem to research whether the letter is genuine." Karim reached out a hand. "Please, Abdul. You've known me since I was a boy. If you still have any caring in your heart for me, let me leave. Please."

Abdul ignored Karim's hand. "Why should I help you?"

"Because the Galilean secrets taught me something."

"What are these supposed secrets?"

Karim drew a breath before he answered. "There are many of them, all related to the spiritual path of love. I know it's hard to believe, but this path is the only way to find peace within and peace in the world."

Abdul gave a dismissive laugh. “I’ve never heard such nonsense.”

Karim shrugged. “To you the secrets may be nonsense, but they hold the keys to freedom and happiness.”

Abdul walked over and sat in the chair across from the couch. “What would you know about freedom and happiness?”

Karim sat down and studied him. “When Saed killed those people, everybody was celebrating, but I felt sick inside. I thought maybe something was wrong with me. I should have been happy, but I wasn’t. And we were no better off afterward. We’ve buried one person after another. So have the Israelis. I’m tired of tears and funerals. Aren’t you?”

Abdul appeared offended, but Karim pressed on. “Violence breeds more violence. It hasn’t worked, and it will never give us our Palestinian homeland. But we haven’t tried loving our enemies and being reconciled to them, as the letter counsels. Even the Qur’an says, ‘It may be that Allah will grant love between you and those whom ye now hold as enemies. For Allah has power over all things and Allah is Oft-Forgiving, Most Merciful.’”

Abdul was silent, but Karim could see his frown softening and his eyes becoming moist. Karim thought of all the friends and relatives they had both lost, and he wondered whether Abdul was thinking of his nephew, Hakim Fattah. How tragic and senseless that seven-year-old Hakim had died in the crossfire between IDF soldiers and PPA militants in Nablus.

Quieter now, Karim said, “I want to return to the monastery in Bethlehem to continue my work and to find the truth about the letter.”

Abdul wiped his eyes. “If I let you leave, your father will demote me.”

“He needs your help too much.” Karim placed a hand on Abdul’s arm and met his eyes. Then he started for the door. “That’s why violence is so oppressive. It creates layers of stupidity that trap people in loneliness and alienation. And I’m tired of being isolated and lonely.” Karim kept walking as Abdul followed him. "This is your chance to feel compassion again. This is your chance to change things for the better, to do what's right."

Tears seeped from the corners of Abdul's eyes. He appeared torn. "Why should I?"

"Because you love me," Karim said with a shaky voice.

Abdul appeared taken aback. He bit his lip and shook his head as though trying to expel the idea, but he couldn't. Finally he waved a hand and said, "Follow me. I know of only one way for you to escape—through the tunnel below the house. Your father installed it in case of an IDF raid."

Karim opened the door. "Thank you, Abdul. I will never forget this."

Abdul nodded and embraced him. When they left the study, Abdul led him down the back stairs and showed him the way to the tunnel. Even if he no longer had Rachel, Karim would return to the monastery and help Brother Gregory find the truth, wherever it might lead.

CHAPTER FORTY

JUDAS ISCARIOT BRACED HIMSELF FOR WHAT HE FEARED WOULD BECOME AN INTERROGATION. Inside the open doors of the praetorium, he glimpsed a brooding Pontius Pilate, the Roman governor of Judea. As Judas hurried through the court called the *Gabbatha* in Hebrew and Aramaic, images of a naked Mary Magdalene erupted in his thoughts. She was dancing around his bed, stepping close to caress him, and then circling with a "come-hither" gleam in her eye. As he rose to meet her, another image interrupted: the memory of her anointing and kissing Jesus. That picture throbbed in Judas' mind, more vivid with each step he took across the polished rectangular stones. Rage blinded him, hot as burning sulfur. *You deserved her, Judas. But she was only toying with you. Leading you on like a cheap whore. She loved Jesus all along. Now they both must suffer.*

Pilate offered him hope for revenge. Judas' heartbeat quickened. He must convince him that Jesus, not Barabbas, had incited the Temple riot. No Roman governor could allow a popular rabbi to call himself the Messiah and lead a revolt. This was treason! A knot formed in Judas' stomach. If he succeeded in his mission, Pilate would free Barabbas and have Jesus arrested, scourged, and crucified. It would break Mary Magdalene's heart, and Judas would have sweet revenge.

But was that what he wanted? Or did he still want Mary's love? She had allowed him to sip her love like fine wine, only to withdraw the chalice and leave him craving more. He wished he had never become attracted to her, but now he felt he couldn't live without her. Still, as much as she had hurt him, he would marry her if given the chance.

But that chance no longer existed.

She and Jesus had trampled his heart and left him cut and bleeding.

There would be consequences.

Judas' cheeks burned as Lucius Sulla, Pilate's brawny personal tribune, led him into the praetorium. He scanned the massive pillars, domed ceiling and pink-orange marble walls, comforted by Lucius' dignified manner. Such a respected soldier wouldn't arouse suspicions about the thirty-denarii bribe he had accepted to arrange the audience. Lucius approached Pilate and said, "I present Judas Iscariot, Excellency. He has information about that rabbi who has been stirring up hostilities around the city, Jesus of Nazareth."

The sight of Pontius Pilate disgusted Judas. The firm-jawed governor had brought idolatrous banners into Jerusalem and minted coins that celebrated emperor-worship. He had even stolen from the Temple treasury to build an aqueduct and then massacred any Jews who protested. Judas considered Pilate an arrogant and treacherous man. A man who had acted savagely to solidify his power but whose cruelty toward the Jews had caused him trouble with Emperor Tiberius Caesar.

Now Judas needed him.

Seated in a high-backed chair of carved cedar, Pilate squared his broad shoulders and leveled his gaze at Judas. "How do you know the Galilean?"

Judas admired Pilate's fine white robe with red piping. He bowed low and decided he must lie to hide his Zealot past. "A friend introduced me, your Excellency."

"So you are a friend of the Galilean?"

"No, Honorable Prefect, but I have met him on several occasions and heard him teach." Judas looked Pilate in the eye and spoke confidently. "I came here because I believe in doing what is right. I fear for the security of Jerusalem."

Pilate leaned his thickset frame forward to question Judas with flashing dark eyes. "What causes your concern?"

"Jesus claims to be the Messiah, and many believe him. He rode into Jerusalem on a donkey, and they hailed him as their king, the heir to David's throne."

Pilate turned to Lucius. "If this is true, the Galilean could incite another revolt, and it would be worse than the riot at the Temple."

Before Lucius could respond, Judas said, "Jesus started that riot. It erupted when he tried to throw out the money changers." A shocked expression animated Pilate's meaty features as Judas continued, "Your soldiers arrested Barabbas and some others, but Jesus and his friends got away. Now they're planning their next attack—an assault on the Antonia on Passover."

Pilate stood and gestured angrily at Lucius. "Why was I not told of this? Don't you have men investigating plots of treason?"

Judas noticed the color draining from Lucius' round, pockmarked face. The tribune said, "I've kept you informed of the Galilean's activities as you ordered, Excellency. We've known that he has a following, but this is the first I've heard of a revolt."

Pilate began to pace. "We must arrest the Galilean immediately. I'll make an example of him, as I have of other Galilean rebels, and as Quintilius Varus did of Judas of Gamla."

Lucius held up a hand. "With all respect, sire, we must handle this rabbi differently. If you crucify him without the support of the Jews, his friends among them may lead a revolt."

When Judas heard the word *crucify,* pangs of guilt assaulted him. He wanted Jesus dead, but the horror of crucifixion hadn't set in until now. Jesus had been his friend and hadn't hurt him intentionally. Did he really want him to suffer crucifixion? Judas had a sudden impulse to flee the praetorium. Then he remembered Mary Magdalene and how he desired her. How he *deserved* her. The rapture he had felt in her arms in Caesarea Philippi came back to him—her sweet scent, the glint in her depthless eyes, the power of his response to her. But she would never be his. Because of Jesus.

Judas caught a whiff of Pilate's lemony cologne. The temptation to flee passed as Lucius went on, "You must proceed cautiously, Governor. Discredit Jesus among his own people first and *then* crucify him." Lucius paused, his expression turning sober. "With the backing of Caiaphas, you can get rid of the Galilean and also keep the peace, as the Emperor demands." Lucius dropped his voice almost to a whisper. "Remember the stakes, sire. If you antagonize the Jews as you have in the past and they rebel, you could be relieved of your command. I advise you to let Caiaphas take the initiative. It may even be to your advantage to publicly appear indecisive in this matter, so that Caiaphas and the Sanhedrin, not you, will be blamed for the crucifixion of a popular rabbi."

Judas' thoughts leapt from one scenario to another. He agreed with Lucius. Jesus' disciples and the crowd that had welcomed him into Jerusalem were fervently behind him. By laying palm branches on the road—a symbol of the Zealots—they had made a political statement. If they channeled their fervor into violence, they might spark the greatest insurrection to date.

Judas felt an infusion of glee. The entanglement of religion and politics was setting a trap for Jesus. Pilate wanted him dead for his own reasons, but to achieve that end, he needed the Sanhedrin. Judas saw where Lucius' argument was going. Pilate needed to strike a deal with Caiaphas. Only if the high priest brought religious charges against Jesus could Pilate crucify him without inciting a revolt. Since Caiaphas had been outraged by Jesus' cleansing of the Temple and his messianic claims, the high priest should be willing to cooperate.

But Pilate would need a liaison. And Judas smiled to himself as he realized he was the man for the job. He held his breath and waited for the governor's response. After a moment of reflection, Pilate said, "I see your point, Lucius. But how can I get to Caiaphas? He won't meet with a Gentile during Passover. I need someone to win the Sanhedrin's support for a plan to crucify the Galilean."

Judas threw his shoulders back. This was his chance. "I talk well, and I am a Jew who knows Jesus." Judas drew a breath and measured his words, determined not to raise suspicions by appearing overly eager. "Going to Caiaphas on your behalf is a dangerous assignment, Wise Prefect, but I'm willing to undertake it for the sake of peace."

Pilate eyed Judas and then turned to Lucius. "Can we trust this man?"

Lucius put a hand on Judas' shoulder. "He took a risk to come here. That speaks well of his character. With Passover tomorrow, we have no choice but to act."

"All right," Pilate said to Judas. "You go to Caiaphas and inform him of my intentions. If he agrees to bring charges against Jesus, tell him to send his Temple police to me. I'll bolster them with armed soldiers, and you can lead them to make the arrest." Pilate smiled without warmth. "The high priest will probably welcome the chance to get rid of the Galilean."

Judas couldn't believe his good fortune. His wildest hopes had been surpassed. The hair on the back of his neck bristled with excitement. Pilate's plan was ingenious. By using the Sanhedrin to set the Jews against Jesus, Pilate could crucify him without being blamed. The entire matter would be interpreted as a Jewish affair. The city would remain at peace, and Pilate's command would not be threatened.

Judas bowed low. "Thank you for the trust you have placed in me, your Excellency. I promise never to betray it." As Judas turned to leave, he imagined standing before Caiaphas and his father-in-law Annas. They would be grateful for his courage in coming to them. They might even pay him. All he had to do was fuel the fires of their distrust of Jesus and assure them of Pilate's backing. His mind raced with possibilities. After Jesus was discredited and crucified, the Jews would look for the true Messiah. Who better to fill this role than the man brave enough to expose the pretender? With Judas' rise to power, Mary Magdalene would finally be his.

CHAPTER FORTY-ONE

THE CRAMPED QUARTERS OF PILATE'S PRISON IN THE ANTONIA FORTRESS WERE DAMP, COLD, AND STANK OF URINE, MAKING IT IMPOSSIBLE FOR JUDITH TO SLEEP. The scant light of Thursday's afternoon sun had long since faded, leaving the oversized holding cell in shadows. She sat near the barred door, her hands and feet in chains, straining to see her cellmates, who were mostly asleep. There were more than a dozen of them—a few straggly-haired women, the rest sunken-eyed men. With so many arrests during the Passover preparations, the guards had had to put both sexes together.

Some of the men had taunted her when she first arrived. Already queasy from her pregnancy, Judith felt nauseated at the thought of the men's lechery; breathing the foul air intensified the feeling. She took comfort that the men's crimes, like hers, had been nonviolent. Murderers and insurrectionists occupied the cell down the corridor; she could hear them cursing their fate and complaining to the guards. Equally large and overcrowded, both cells had thick iron bars, making escape attempts futile and inflicting impenetrable misery on anyone locked within them.

Judith feared that the Romans might flog her in the morning, yet she doubted that any pain could surpass the torment of her guilt and shame. She had failed everyone who counted on her. Each had expected her to be brave and loyal, whether as sister, daughter, betrothed, or friend. Instead, she had been cowardly and selfish, a vain and weak-willed woman whose treachery had exacted its cruel price.

Worst of all, she had failed herself. She could have married Gabriel, a successful merchant, and presided over a respectable household while raising a fine family. Instead she had chosen Dismas and a life of lawlessness and infamy. How could she have been so foolish? The letter revealed why, and Mary Magdalene had explained further: What Judith had called love was really a dangerous dependency. A dependency that got her pregnant!

It was too late. If she had read the letter a few months earlier, perhaps she would have married Gabriel. Then she would be carrying *his* child, not Dismas', and the child would have had a future. Now the only future that awaited an unwed mother and her baby was one of poverty and shame. Feeling as if her spirit had been thrown off a cliff into the Dead Sea, she began to weep, her entire body trembling. No one would know she was here if Mary Magdalene hadn't told her father. Would he find her? And if he did, would he disown her when he learned she was pregnant?

Just then she heard a soldier fumbling with keys, and soon he and another guard entered with a new prisoner in chains. The creak of the door awakened a few of her cellmates, who fell back to sleep as soon as the guards left. The torches outside the door illuminated the new prisoner's frame. He was a tall, broad-shouldered man with a decidedly angular face. He appeared young, but his tight-set jaw and the wrinkles around his eyes reflected maturity beyond his years. He stood perfectly still, as if praying silently, until he turned toward Judith and asked, "Why are you weeping, my child?"

The question took her aback. It sounded too personal coming from a stranger. But she found the man's gentle tone disarming. "I've never been in prison before," she said. "I don't know what is going to happen to me."

"If you knew who is speaking to you, you would not weep but rejoice."

The man sounded so earnest that Judith gasped. "What gets a man thrown into prison so late at night?"

"My only crime was to speak the truth," the man said, sitting down. "But the Temple leaders would rather cling to their illusions and protect their power than listen."

She was surprised to hear such reflective words from a petty criminal. Increasingly curious about this man, she said, "I am here because I was *too* truthful."

The man spoke quietly but with compelling authority. "The truth will make you free. There must be more to why you are here."

Judith hesitated, her breathing became shallow; she was unsure what to say. The compassion in the stranger's voice finally convinced her to tell her story. "I stole from a Pharisee. I thought I was taking jewels, but instead the jewelry box contained a letter. I read it and learned about a love that—"

The man held up a shackled hand, cutting her off. "I wrote the letter," he said simply.

She drew back in disbelief.

"I am Jesus, the rabbi from Nazareth. I know that your heart is breaking, but if you remember, the letter describes the way to healing."

She tried to speak, but no words came.

He went on, "I know the burden you carry. Many women have told me of their suffering at the hands of men. I befriended a woman caught in adultery. I helped a woman of Samaria through the pain of her divorces and wounds in love. When a prostitute anointed me at the home of Simon the Pharisee, I embraced rather than condemned her.

"Men had abused these women, and they felt unclean and lived in prisons of inner torment, worse than this one of Pilate's. As in the letter, I told them that I came to bring God's love to the world. When they received this love, they began to love themselves and found a new beginning. What I said to them, I say to you: 'Come to me, you who labor and are heavily burdened, and I will give you rest.'"

Judith's heart was pounding so hard she could barely breathe. What an extraordinary twist of fate. Humiliated to be in prison, she now saw the harrowing ordeal in a new light. "What you promised those women," she said, "I experienced when I read the letter. It was as if you were speaking to me. I felt God's love in your words, and I knew I wanted to follow you. I returned the letter to Nicodemus, and he introduced me to Mary Magdalene. She explained your teachings to me, but I still have many questions."

Jesus leaned back against the stone wall, his chains clanking on the floor. "Mary Magdalene is very special to me. She will change the world because she has been deeply changed herself."

Judith raised an arm and wiped the sweat from her face on her tunic. Each ping and rattle of his chains reminded her of how alone she had been in this dank place with its fetid air. "Mary Magdalene told me that you healed her, but I am beyond healing, for I sinned against my betrothed, and now I am carrying his brother's baby. What hope is there for me?"

Jesus made a gesture of blessing. "Your sins are forgiven, my child."

She stared at him as her arms and legs became buoyant. Her heavy load had finally been lifted from her, and her heart felt warm. "But I do not deserve to be forgiven."

Jesus kept one hand raised above her head. "God is like a good shepherd who leaves ninety-nine of his flock to search for one lost sheep. You lost your way in the darkness of your passions, but you are still loved by God, and so is the child in your womb." He blessed her again and then put his hands down. "My own mother faced the scorn you will face. Trust in me always, and I will help you to overcome."

Judith nodded silently. The cell, which had been threatening, now felt safe and less confining as she yearned to hear more. "The letter spoke of a new future. How can I find it?"

He moved closer, the shadows cast by the torches outside the door dancing on his face. "In the letter I wrote about a young man who demanded his inheritance from his father and then squandered it in a distant country. He eventually returned home, but rather than punish him, the father embraced him and hosted a lavish party in his honor. Do you remember this story?"

"I remember it."

"Well, there is more, and what happened next relates to your healing. The older brother was working in the fields when the party began. He heard the music and dancing and got mad. When had the father thrown a party for *him?* He deserved it more than his loose-living brother! It seemed that his father was playing favorites, so he refused to celebrate. Do you think he was right?"

Judith needed no time to reflect. "Of course. How could he participate in such an injustice?"

Jesus spoke slowly, emphasizing each word. "Your answer shows that you care more about fairness than about healing. God forgives you, Judith, but you must learn to accept his forgiveness, to let down your defenses and *truly* accept it. You are clinging to your guilt and shame to gain power over the past, which you cannot change. There is a voice in you saying, 'You must be punished for what you did to Gabriel. You must pay for your unwanted pregnancy. You are unworthy of forgiveness.' It is the voice of the older brother, and you must hear God's voice forgiving you more powerfully than the voice condemning you. Only then will you be healed, because only then will you forgive *yourself*."

Those words made the darkness in the prison glow with light. Judith thought that the bars appeared less strong, the walls less thick, and the putrid air no longer made her nauseated. God still loved her, and nothing could change that, not even her worst sins. She must *claim* God's love and forgive herself. Not to do so would be the height of ingratitude, even arrogance. "Is this all you expect of me?" she asked.

He shook his head. "No, it is only the beginning. You must keep seeking if you want to find; you must keep knocking if you want the door to be opened. I have come that you may have life and have it abundantly, but you must desire this life each day, each moment."

She frowned, her stomach clenching with disappointment. "I have been seeking for so long, and look where it has gotten me. I just want to find . . . to find security . . . to find peace, and hope for the future."

Jesus maintained an earnest, steady voice. "The seeking of which I speak is the only kind that will satisfy your heart's desire. You must seek *first* the eternal life of God's kingdom. The kingdom is the pearl of great price, the treasure so valuable that one sells everything in order to attain it. If you make the kingdom your first priority, all good things will come to you. But entering the kingdom is difficult, for wide is the gate and easy the road that leads to destruction, and many take it, but narrow is the gate and hard the road that leads to eternal life, and only a few find it."

She was quivering with eagerness. "What must I do to inherit eternal life?"

"Become my disciple and surrender completely to God."

"I have already done this. It happened in my heart while I was reading the letter and heard your voice speaking to me."

Jesus peered at her through the gray light. "Believing in me is the beginning; you must also seek God's reign in all areas of your life. If you trust me with your whole heart, you will be able to move mountains."

Judith reached to touch him, and as he gripped her shackled hands in his, she said, "In the letter, you described the coming of your kingdom on earth. When will this happen and how?"

His tone became somber, his face pale, with a flicker of light from the torches playing off his eyes. "It will happen when I return in the future. Only God knows the day and the hour. Until then, as long as men and women are alienated from one another, the world will be filled with conflict. To make peace, they must discover the fullness of God's image in themselves. I am preparing a wedding banquet for the union of the male and female within. When we enter this union, we find the soul of love. I helped Mary Magdalene find it, and she bears witness to the power of my gospel. The lost can be found; the broken made whole; the wounded healed. This happens not through human effort but when you accept my free gift of love."

She smiled and tightened her grip on his hands. "What does your kingdom require of me?"

"You must live the truths contained in the letter. The day is coming when the rich will share with the poor, the hungry will be filled and the oppressed freed. The world will not be conquered by force but by the greatest of all loves. You must go forth and preach the good news."

Judith was trembling. "How can I do this? I am with child, and I am homeless."

Jesus stepped back, blessed her again, and said, "If the Romans crucify me tomorrow, do not forget this conversation. Trust me, and I will help you share the letter with the entire world. I pray that Gabriel will forgive you."

After Jesus finished speaking, Judith saw his eyes close as he rested for a time, his chest rising and falling with the slow, steady cadence of rhythmic breathing. He sat with his back and head against the wall, straight and perfectly still, as if anchored in that place but focused on some distant, invisible goal. He appeared so peaceful, so totally gathered within himself, that she grew calm in his presence and she, too, slept.

The peaceful respite ended abruptly with the light of morning. Judith heard the jingling of the guards' keys; the door was opened, and two soldiers entered. They seized Jesus and led him toward the door. Before leaving, he turned to her and said, "I will love you always."

When he was gone, she reflected on his urging that she seek his kingdom and try to begin anew with Gabriel. She promised herself to do both if she gained her freedom.

The watery light of morning slid through the small barred windows of the cell down the corridor, casting soft shadows over the cramped prisoners. Dismas stood alone in his irons; Barabbas, Gestas, and the fourteen other Zealots arrested before him were chained in pairs. *This is our last chance to escape,* Dismas thought, preparing to attack the guards when they approached on their rounds. "The guards will come any moment," he whispered, gagging from the stench of sweat and urine. "Either we escape or we die." His eyes were heavy from a sleepless night, his body still aching from the beating at the Temple.

"Prepare for the fight of your life, and may God fight with us." Dismas took comfort from Barabbas' voice. Its confident tone brought to mind the man's gladiator physique, ruddy face, and thick beard. This image of strength calmed Dismas. *Barabbas is capable of escaping even a Roman prison.*

"You should have listened to me, Dismas!" Gestas was continuing some inner dialogue—a fight with Dismas that he was replaying in his mind. The words stabbed Dismas. Gestas' meaty features were animated. As if unable to stop, he roared on, "I told you that soldiers would be watching the Temple at Passover. It was worse this year because of that rabbi from Nazareth. The Romans think he's one of us. His fame and your stupidity landed us here!"

Dismas scowled back, but held his tongue. Hearing Gestas mention Jesus of Nazareth sent a chill through him. Maybe his letter had been right. Maybe lust and greed and violence destroyed the soul, and maybe Jesus did offer *inner* freedom. Only now did Dismas realize that he wanted what Judith had—release from the guilt and shame of betraying Gabriel. *I will get out of here and start a new life,* he told himself. *I will leave the Zealots, beg Gabriel to forgive me, and win Judith back. We have to escape!*

He heard footsteps. Two soldiers wearing breastplates and red-plumed helmets appeared outside the cell. "Barabbas! We have come for Barabbas!"

"Here I am," Barabbas said, a note of defiance in his voice. The soldiers opened the barred door and approached quickly.

Dismas eyed them, ready to strike. When they came within an arm's length, Barabbas yelled, "Now!" Barabbas and Gestas dove at one soldier's legs. Dismas rushed the other guard and began to choke him as the Roman's partner cried for help. Caught flat-footed, the soldiers reeled back and fell as the other Zealots piled on. Dismas grabbed the keys, but as he reached to free Barabbas and Gestas, reinforcements arrived. Using their javelins, a dozen cursing soldiers drove the prisoners back against the wall. Two of them wrestled the keys from Dismas, while another held a sword to Barabbas' throat. "Did you really think you could escape a Roman prison?" The tall soldier laughed mockingly. "If Pilate didn't want you alive, I would kill you myself." He drew a trickle of blood from Barabbas' arm and then turned to Dismas and Gestas. "You two will die soon enough."

The soldier unlocked Barabbas' chains. "This is your lucky day. The crowd wants the rabbi from Galilee crucified instead of you." He turned to Dismas and Gestas. "No one but the gods can save you two." The soldier sneered and led Barabbas out of the prison.

Judith heard pounding feet and bodies crashing against each other in the cell down the corridor. Men were yelling, and she recognized two of the voices: They belonged to Dismas and Gestas! She tugged futilely at her chains as she realized what was happening. Dismas, Gestas, and Barabbas had tried to escape; now Barabbas was being freed, and Jesus, Dismas, and Gestas would be crucified. *Oh God, oh God, oh God,* she thought. *How can this be happening? Don't let the Romans do it. Please help me, God!*

Never had she felt so alone, yet through her fear and rage, the serenity she had known in Jesus' presence never left her. She prayed and remained quiet for some time, until she heard the guards approaching. When they threw the door open, she gawked in disbelief.

There stood her father and Gabriel.

They burst in and embraced her.

"We went to Pilate and told him who you were," her father said. "He demanded a large bribe, but since Nicodemus brought no charges, he agreed to release you."

After the guards had freed her, she faced Gabriel, wiping away tears. "I am so sorry for what I did to you. It was cruel. Can you ever forgive me?"

Gabriel, anguish glinting in his teary eyes, said, "Only with God's help."

As they left the prison, Judith rubbed at her wrists and ankles. The streets were flooded with people flowing out of the city.

"What is going on?" Gabriel asked the first man he passed.

"Pilate has sentenced Jesus of Nazareth to be crucified at Golgotha," the thin elderly man answered matter-of-factly.

Although Judith had expected this, actually hearing it brought acrid bile to the back of her throat, her nausea returning. She nudged Gabriel along the street. "Jesus was in prison with me last night. Dismas will be crucified with him. We must go to be with them."

Gabriel took her hand and joined the procession to Golgotha. Her father tried to stop them, but she shook loose and said, "I could not live with myself if I did not go." Nathan frowned disapprovingly and turned toward home. In spite of her exhaustion, she pressed on.

The soldiers dragged Dismas out of the cell, followed by Gestas, and wrestled them toward the courtyard. There they encountered more soldiers, several holding whips. The soldiers were unchaining a tall, broad-shouldered man from the whipping post. Gangly in appearance, he had long, dark hair and intense, penetrating eyes. Dismas had never seen a man in such physical condition, the skin hanging off his back in sections, the tissue and bone exposed.

Yet the man held his chin high, asserting a personal authority that violence and pain could not challenge. He refused to divert his gaze from those of the soldiers, his silent defiance strangely victorious.

Dismas' knees buckled. The soldiers steadied him, tied him and Gestas to the posts, and began to flog them. Dismas tried to steel himself against the impact of the bone and metal at the ends of the leather cords, but to no avail. The first blow sent white lightning ricocheting through his brain as the sun exploded on his back. He cried for mercy, but lash after lash continued to pummel his back. No mercy came.

The next thing he remembered was the soldiers forcing him to pick up and carry the wooden crossbar to which he would be nailed. He bore it on bloodied shoulders, mocked and spat on by the crowd lining the street. Some of the people were shouting words of sympathy to the man who had been flogged before him. As Dismas stumbled behind him, he heard the man's name.

Jesus.

CHAPTER FORTY-TWO

THE WEED-STREWN FIELD BECKONED JUDAS ISCARIOT AS IF IT WERE A POOL OF REFRESHING WATER. He stopped running and bent over, hands on his knees, lungs heaving, sweat streaming from every pore. He fought to catch his breath between sobs. Because he was gasping for air, the sobs sounded like retches. The morning's brilliance mocked the darkness that shrouded his heart. Seeing Jesus condemned by the Sanhedrin and led away to Pilate had overwhelmed him with guilt. He fled the city and came to this rocky patch of land called the Valley of Hinnom, rope in hand.

Through watery eyes he saw a sturdy olive tree thirty feet away. He gripped the rope and stumbled toward it. The tree's lowest branch stood ten feet above the ground. He used the large knots on the trunk to support his weight and climbed up. As he tied the rope to the branch and formed a noose on the other end, a memory played in his mind.

He was meeting Jesus for the first time, on the Plain of Gennesaret, watching him bless baskets of bread and fish and pass them to his friends.

Thin and somewhat awkward, Jesus still carried himself with a serenity and assurance that inspired confidence in others. He addressed each man and woman by name and made sure that everyone had enough to eat. But Judas barely saw Jesus. His eyes were fixed on Mary Magdalene's fathomless dark eyes, her silken hair, and the mystery behind her sensual smile.

On the heels of Judith's rejection, Judas' heart burned for Mary. When Jesus' eyes met his, Judas felt embarrassed by his lustful thoughts. But the thoughts never left him. How he wished he had known that they would lead him here, to this desolate place of rock and weed, with a rope in hand. The only person who had tried to understand was Gabriel. He spoke of the female image of God. Of how finding her heals a man and unleashes his joy and creativity. But no true man would believe such a ridiculous idea.

Judas finished securing the rope to the branch and felt his way back to the tree trunk. The earlier memory faded into a recent one: the memory of the arrest in the Garden of Gethsemane. Judas had led Pilate's soldiers and Caiaphas' police there and betrayed Jesus with a kiss. As he watched the soldiers take Jesus away, Judas felt as if a chain were wrapped around his heart, growing tighter with each step. The memory brought such pain to Judas that he nearly lost his balance. As he clung to the tree with one hand and the rope with the other, more memories intruded.

Caiaphas questioning Jesus.

The Temple police taking Jesus to prison.

Judas roaming the streets all night like a madman, wracked with guilt.

Jesus being handed over to Pilate in the morning.

The crowd yelling, "Crucify him!"

Judas' throat ached from sobbing. His ears were ringing and his vision blurry. Returning the thirty pieces of silver to the chief priests hadn't eased the pain. Nor had writing a note to Mary Magdalene and leaving it in the upper room with her name on it. Each beat of his heart had become unbearable, a reminder that he was alive even though his spirit was dead. He had lied to many people, but no lie was greater than the one he had told himself—the lie that Mary Magdalene would eventually love him. Now he knew she couldn't love any man who had betrayed Jesus.

Judas had no more hope. Climbing halfway down the tree, he gripped the trunk with one hand and the rope with the other. Then he slipped the noose around his neck and held onto the rope above his head. He wanted to ease himself out so his neck wouldn't break and he could suffocate peacefully.

When he let go of the tree trunk, he immediately felt the rope cutting into his skin. Flailing in the air, he swung to and fro, gagging. The ground began to spin like a whirlpool, threatening to suck him into the depths. He nearly bit through his tongue. A cacophony of pleas erupted in his mind. *Where are you, God? Do you care? Do you even exist? Why did you allow me to hurt so bad and to hurt others?* Suspended in space, he writhed and spit up blood, almost swallowing his tongue. He nearly passed out and became groggy and disoriented.

His nose bled, his temples pounded; his face was on fire. He managed to reach the rope and pull himself up for an instant, but then he lost his grip, and the full weight of his body slammed down. A jolting pain shot through his arms and legs. He vomited, unable to catch his breath. The putrid odor nauseated him more. His body became dead weight, his exhausted arms too weak to save him. He was defenseless against the terror.

The noose around his neck was slowly suffocating him. *Forgive me, God! Please forgive me!* His eyes were swelling shut; his body growing numb. Seeing nothing but darkness, he tried to cry out but could only whisper, "Mary Magdalene . . . Mary Magdalene . . . Mary. . ."

The strain on his neck increased.

He heard a loud snap.

The darkness became absolute.

CHAPTER FORTY-THREE

THE DREAM OF PERFECT LOVE IS JUST THAT—A DREAM. ONLY THE LOVE THAT FLOWS FROM THE HEART OF GOD IS PERFECT.

NO FALLIBLE HUMAN BEING CAN MEET ALL NEEDS AND CAUSE NO PAIN. AS FLAWED PEOPLE LIVING IN A BROKEN WORLD, WE CAN'T AVOID TIMES OF CONFLICT, ALIENATION, AND LONELINESS.

BUT WE CAN KEEP THE PAIN IN PERSPECTIVE BY FINDING CONSTRUCTIVE USES FOR IT.

NEVER FORGET THAT GOD IS WORKING TO REDEEM AND TRANSFORM OUR IMPERFECT LOVE INTO A GLORIOUS FULFILLMENT. WHEN TWO SOULS BECOME ONE, THEY HASTEN THE DAWN OF ALL THINGS MADE NEW.

—**Brother Gregory Andreou's Journal**

Bethlehem
Monday, April 15

"WHY DIDN'T YOU ASK ME FIRST?" Karim Musalaha riveted his gaze on Brother Gregory, fighting the urge to yell. The question had gnawed at him since he arrived at the monastery from Nablus the previous night. He had traversed rutted back roads and rocky hillsides in order to skirt the checkpoints of the West Bank. Then he had encountered a media frenzy outside the monastery gates and learned that Brother Gregory had scheduled a news conference without consulting him. He began to fume. "You should have talked to me before contacting the media." His voice trembled as he and Brother Gregory entered the spacious reading room of the monastery library, its tables replaced by rows of folding chairs for the news conference.

"What else could I do?" Brother Gregory appeared surprised and hurt. He led Karim across the open space and down a row of bookshelves. "It was getting too dangerous to keep the scroll. We need to make the Jesus letter public and then turn the scroll over to the authorities. I hope the publicity will generate support for an excavation of the Cave of Gethsemane. Fortunately the Government Antiquities Agency is helping to sponsor the news conference."

"Dangerous? What about the danger I will face once they discover I was the one who found the scroll?" Under his breath he said, *"Inna lillahi wa inna ilayhi raji'un."*

"What does that mean?" Brother Gregory asked.

"In Islam we use this phrase at times of misfortune. It means, 'We are from Allah and to Him we are returning.' The words are encouragement to keep everything in perspective." He shook his head. "I'm struggling to do that right now."

As Karim followed Brother Gregory, he noticed the precision with which the books had been placed on the shelves, each row in perfect order, like everything in the monastery. He found himself longing for the orderly days at Birzeit University, the predictability of his schedule, the security of his career plans. Since discovering the scroll, nothing had been predictable or secure. And it seemed possible that it never would be again.

He hurried to keep up as Brother Gregory pointed toward the

conference room in back and headed for it. Fishing in his pocket for the key, the monk said, "I didn't intend to go against your wishes, but you were unreachable."

"Couldn't you have waited until I contacted you? If my father's people hear I'm associated with a Christian artifact, my life will not be worth much."

Brother Gregory unlocked and opened the door of the small conference room. "I promise I won't mention your name. The timing of your discovery, right before the March for Peace, was more than a coincidence." He put a hand on Karim's shoulder. "Think about it. This is God's plan, to make the discovery known so that people from all countries, from all religions, can come together to learn its message of peace. This message *must* be told now, when the world is in such turmoil, and I am willing to go to jail if necessary in order to tell it."

Karim stepped into the bookshelf-lined room as Brother Gregory spread out his original translation on the center table, along with his statement for the news conference. The monk pointed to the documents. "I wanted to show you what I plan to say."

Seeing the pages renewed Karim's concern. "Even if you don't reveal my name, someone is sure to discover my association with the scroll. You saw the media outside. They will never stop until they have answers."

Brother Gregory squeezed Karim's arm. "Don't you see? When you didn't return for over a week, I had no choice but to act. No serious scholar believes that Judas Iscariot wrote to Mary Magdalene before he hanged himself. The idea of excavating the Cave of Gethsemane sounds ludicrous to them. At the news conference, I'll reveal the positive results of my tests on the scroll. We need the publicity in order to generate support for the excavation. Only by finding Judas' note can we definitively prove that the Jesus letter is genuine."

Karim pulled his arm away. "Yes, but I'm Sadiq Musalaha's son. Being too closely associated with Christianity would bring persecution to any Muslim. For me it could be a death sentence." Karim felt blood rise into his cheeks, unable to hide his anguish.

The monk pulled a chair from under the table and sat down, gentle eyes directed at Karim. "Please forgive me. I didn't mean to deceive you."

"Well, I feel deceived, whether you meant to or not." Karim scanned the books that lined the walls of the room. It felt as if Brother Gregory were plunging him deeper into chaos. His orderly past at Birzeit was gone—no words or wishes could transport him back. With Rachel estranged and the news conference planned, all he could do was live the painful present—and hope that the uncertain future wouldn't grow even worse. Spotting a copy of the Qur'an, he walked over, picked it up and placed it on the table next to the translation.

Brother Gregory stood and moved to the other side of the table.

The backs of Karim's eyes stung as he studied the Qur'an and the translation side by side. The Jesus letter set forth the Qur'an's highest ideals, which Karim found hard to practice. He returned the Qur'an to the shelf and spoke as he walked back to the table. "Promoting Christianity is a heresy for any Muslim. My father's followers will kill me if they even suspect that I'm associated with a Christian document that advocates peace and nonviolence."

Brother Gregory flashed Karim a compassionate look. "The news conference is tomorrow. Television crews will be here, as well as representatives from major museums and universities and even the Vatican. The Jesus letter has the potential to draw thousands of people to Jerusalem. The only artifact of its kind is the Shroud of Turin, the alleged burial cloth of Christ. Whenever the shroud is displayed, millions of people flock to view it. Can you imagine the drawing power of a document written by Jesus? The organizers of the March for Peace heard about it through leaks to the media and they've asked to have the scroll displayed at the culminating ceremony at the Wailing Wall. I think it's a wonderful idea. I can't help but believe that God's timing was meant to be. Besides, it's too late to cancel. You saw the media."

Karim shook his head. "After Abbot Zeno's betrayal, it's hard to know who to trust, what to believe."

Brother Gregory relaxed his shoulders and leaned forward. "True. A sacred artifact can be an ally for peace or an instrument of division. It depends on whether we use it to serve others or for personal gain."

"I have no interest in gaining anything from the scroll. All I want now is for Rachel to forgive me."

"I suggest that you write her again. Tell her about the news conference; invite her to attend. It could be your last chance to. . ." He left the words unfinished.

Karim stared at the translation of the Jesus letter and thought of how it had brought him and Rachel together. He glimpsed a few lines and remembered the compassion she had shown him, the softness of her touch, the urgency of her kisses.

The translation of the letter lay motionless, issuing a silent invitation that spoke of the power and potential of love.

No, the letter issued him a challenge.

What he had with Rachel was real, and he couldn't give up on it.

Not now.

Not ever.

Karim stood. "May I use a computer?"

"Yes, of course." Brother Gregory led Karim out of the conference room and locked the door. Then the monk took him to a cell-like room that contained several computers. "I have work to do in my apartment," the monk said, turning to go. "I'll give you some time alone."

After Brother Gregory left, Karim sat down at the first terminal, logged on and began to type:

Dear Rachel,

A news conference will be held at Holy Angels Monastery tomorrow. Brother Gregory has decided to make the Jesus letter public. I hope you will be there. I also want you to know that you gave me something beyond happiness or even joy. You gave me hope for a future in which Muslims and Jews can sit down as friends. Where war and violence are no longer committed in the name of religion.

Our love began amid terror, and love is the only way to end this violence. I believed this message before we found each other. Now I know it's true. If everyone could experience what we had together, there would be no more bloodstained streets or cries of anguish.

Compassion and forgiveness are the greatest gifts two people can offer each other. I don't understand the gifts, nor can I describe them adequately. But oh, Rachel! We must keep working for a better world for both Palestinians and Israelis. A peaceful world in which love has finally made all things new.

I pray that you have had time to reflect on what I wrote earlier, and that you will accept my deepest apology and forgive me. If you cannot, I will still love you, and I believe that someday, perhaps in the world to come, we will meet again and our souls will rediscover the oneness we shared.

Until then and forever, I am yours,
Karim

After sending the e-mail, Karim navigated to the Web site set up to promote the demonstration in Jerusalem. He began to read the latest updates but stopped when he heard the library door open. He hurried into the reading room and saw Brother Gregory running toward him, red-faced and frowning. "I just got a call from Robert Kenyon." The monk spoke rapidly, his tone urgent. "He has kidnapped Rachel. He'll be watching the news conference tomorrow, and he demands that we name him as the one who discovered the scroll. Only if we give him full credit and only if we deliver my laptop and original translation to him will he release Rachel."

Karim felt the blood drain from his cheeks. The walls of the library started to close in on him. "Oh no, not Rachel." He buried his face in his hands, trying to gather his composure. "Kenyon is known as a respected archaeologist, but he attacked me with a trowel at Qumran. There's no telling how far he'll go to get what he wants." He released a breath and shot the monk an anxious stare.

Brother Gregory said, "But I can't give in to his corruption. If I agree to this deception, the GAA could prosecute me for fraud. We must call the police."

"What leads could we give them? Did you get Kenyon's number?"

"It was blocked."

Karim threw up his hands. "I can't believe this is happening." He narrowed his eyes and spoke with exasperation. "The police couldn't possibly rescue Rachel before the press conference. With no leads, where would they begin to look? Besides, calling them would be too risky. Kenyon's probably bluffing, but we can't take that chance. You have no choice but to say that Kenyon found the scroll, and I'll deliver your laptop and translation materials to him."

Brother Gregory recoiled as his eyes darted around the room. "Perhaps you're right. But I don't trust Kenyon. He could kill Rachel anyway, and then we'd lose her *and* our credibility."

"We have no choice."

"But the truth will eventually come out, and if I get caught lying about who found the scroll, I could be accused of forging it. The media will ridicule the Jesus letter as a fake, and my career will be over. God's work will have gone unfinished."

Karim grabbed the monk by the shoulders. "If you won't meet Kenyon's demand, I will—even if it means going on TV."

"That would be too dangerous. Your face would be splashed everywhere."

"Yes, but what choice do I have?"

Brother Gregory hesitated. Then, with a nod of his head, he embraced Karim and stepped away. "You're right. What else can we do?" As if fully committed now, he began making plans. "I've compiled a lot of evidence to authenticate the scroll, but no one will believe it if I'm caught in a lie. I suggest that I lead the news conference and make the opening statement. I will answer all questions about the radiocarbon dating, the ink and linguistic analysis, and the multispectral imaging of the scroll. But I will refer the questions about who found it to you."

Karim fought to steady his knees as he followed Brother Gregory to his apartment. An image of Rachel bound and gagged stalked his thoughts. The stones on the walkway felt hot as he tried to figure out how to find her. He decided it was futile and silently cursed the rogue archaeologist who held her. He saw the television crews outside the gates, surrounding the monastery like an invading army, and heard the din of voices and vehicles. The midday sun seemed blindingly bright as he thought of these crews broadcasting tomorrow's news conference.

He could never have imagined that finding the scroll would lead to this. Part of him wished that he had left it buried at Qumran. Another part knew he couldn't go back. He only hoped that Rachel had received his e-mails before she was abducted and knew that he loved her. Then, if he died as a result of the news conference, at least he would be at peace.

CHAPTER FORTY-FOUR

IN ORDER FOR LOVE TO LAST, IT MUST BECOME MORE AN ACTION THAN AN EMOTION. A RELATIONSHIP IS ONLY AS STRONG AS THE COUPLE'S ABILITY TO LIVE OUT THEIR LOVE IN GOOD TIMES AND IN BAD.

THIS IS PARTICULARLY DIFFICULT TO DO WHEN YOU ARE ANNOYED, DISAPPOINTED, OR HURT. DURING THESE TIMES, TRY TO EMPATHIZE WITH YOUR PARTNER'S PAST WOUNDS AND PRESENT STRESSES. THEN YOU CAN BRING UNDERSTANDING TO THE CONFLICT AND LET GO OF YOUR ANGER AND THE IMPULSE TO LASH OUT IN RETURN.

WHEN WE RESPOND WITH CARING INSTEAD OF SPITE, WE OPEN PATHWAYS OF HEALING AND RECONCILIATION.

THIS IS WHEN A RELATIONSHIP BECOMES A THING OF BEAUTY, A GARDEN IN WHICH CHARACTER, NOBILITY, AND SPIRITUAL DEPTH BLOOM LIKE HIBISCUS IN SPRING.

—**Brother Gregory Andreou's Journal**

Bethlehem
Tuesday, April 16

IT WAS THE MOST MOMENTOUS EVENT THAT KARIM MUSALAHA HAD EVER EXPERIENCED. Only at the Kaaba in Mecca had he felt so engulfed by a swarm of humanity. The reporters, photographers, and television crews packed the reading room of the monastery library. Their animated conversations and the clicking of cameras created an aura of anticipation and excitement. And yet the historic news conference, in this airy but unadorned space, held little luster for Karim.

His words might determine whether Rachel Sharett lived or died.

He ran a hand across the metal edge of his front-row seat as Brother Gregory stepped to the podium. The incessant flashes from hundreds of cameras illumined the scholarly monk's face.

Fast approaching his turn before the cameras, Karim tightened his hands into fists and then loosened them, but no matter how many times he repeated the motion, he couldn't calm his anxiety. He would have to lie to save Rachel, and then he would have to hide from his father's men. Only the thought of Rachel seeing him on TV gave him solace. He yearned for her to know that his love for her was constant.

As Karim waited for Brother Gregory to speak, he thought of Judas Iscariot and his feelings for Mary Magdalene—and whether Judas had written down his feelings.

Brother Gregory nodded at the experts seated to the left of the podium and then he turned toward the scroll. It lay on the table to his right, protected by a Plexiglas cover and draped with a purple cloth. Karim sensed reverence in the man's gaze. After drawing a deep breath, the white-robed monk introduced himself and then said, "Let me assure you that as a scholar of Near Eastern languages and civilizations, I am not given to exaggeration. But in the long history of the discovery of antiquities, never has a find been as momentous as this one."

To his right Karim caught a glimpse of the dignitaries seated beside him in front—the head of the Semitic Museum, the chief archaeology officer of the Government Antiquities Agency, the director of the Society for the Prevention of Antiquities Robbery. They had the best view and didn't have to compete with representatives from major universities and seminaries, archaeological and cultural associations, and research organizations such as the National Geographic Society.

Camera operators from the Israel Broadcasting Authority and the European and American television networks were recording the event from every angle. The CNN camera was focused on the emissaries from the Vatican—three elderly men in the black ankle-length cassocks and red skullcaps and sashes of Cardinals. But as everyone gave full attention to Brother Gregory, all Karim could think of was Rachel.

"I'm old enough to have experienced the jubilation of many past discoveries—the Dead Sea Scrolls, the Nag Hammadi library, the secret Gospels of Thomas and of Judas. I have devoted my professional life to the translation and study of these magnificent texts. But never in my most cherished dreams did I imagine this day."

Brother Gregory paused to take control of his emotions and have a sip of water before continuing, "Today I have the sacred honor of unveiling an antiquity unprecedented in importance and inestimable in value."

If Rachel were with him, Karim could have enjoyed this moment and celebrated with her. With each word that Brother Gregory spoke, the monk came closer to describing the revelations of the Jesus letter, and then the spotlight would shift to Karim, who wasn't eager to speak. He barely heard Brother Gregory say what everyone in the room had been waiting to hear.

"A month ago I began translating an ancient letter written on well-preserved papyrus. The letter was addressed to Mary Magdalene."

An excited murmur swept the room and turned Karim's attention back to Brother Gregory.

"The author makes the most audacious claim: He refers to himself as 'Jesus.'" Commotion erupted at the words, forcing Brother Gregory to raise his arms and plead for order. When the reporters finally calmed down, he said, "As I translated, I wondered if the letter might be fraudulent. But by the time I finished, I believed I heard Jesus' voice in the letter—the same voice that resounds in the Gospels of the New Testament. I took the scroll to the scientists and epigraphers seated here, and the many tests they ran on it, including radiocarbon dating, multispectral imaging, and analyses of the ink, script, and linguistic styles, point to its being authentic—indeed, to its being the most important archaeological discovery in history."

Karim kept listening as he surveyed the crowd and saw the emissaries from the Vatican whispering among themselves. The representatives of many of the museums and universities exchanged glances of disbelief, but Brother Gregory kept speaking.

"The letter clarifies the nature of Jesus' relationship with Mary Magdalene, and it explains how he came to embrace and embody perfect love. The letter's revelations have profound relevance for relationships today and for our dreams of peace between Israelis and Palestinians—even our dreams of peace on earth."

Karim clasped and unclasped his hands as he observed the expressions of fascination, disbelief, and skepticism on the faces of all those gathered.

"On the same papyrus, below the letter," Brother Gregory continued with a sweep of his hand, "I also discovered the diary of a Jewish woman named Judith of Jerusalem, a friend of Mary Magdalene. This diary reveals that Jesus was not the only man who loved Mary. Judas Iscariot also loved her."

Cries of protest erupted, startling Karim. Murmurs of incredulity ran through the crowd as Brother Gregory walked over to the scroll and lifted the purple cloth in dramatic fashion.

Amid the cacophony of cameras clicking, Karim glanced at the reporters and camera operators, historians and archaeologists and continued to see the skepticism on their faces. One emissary from the Vatican passed a note to his fellow Cardinals as Brother Gregory exclaimed, "According to Judith of Jerusalem's diary, Judas Iscariot betrayed Jesus Christ out of jealousy."

Karim stiffened as he absorbed the buzz of emotions and spontaneous reactions that the monk's statement evoked.

"That's outrageous!"

"How can we believe this?"

Brother Gregory paused, raising a hand to call for quiet. He waited for the protests to die down before he went on. "Judith reveals that Judas wrote to Mary Magdalene and professed his love before he committed suicide. Judas' note is the missing piece of this puzzle. It could substantiate, once and for all, the exact nature of Jesus' relationship with Mary Magdalene. It could also verify the authenticity of the Jesus letter. Judith says that Mary Magdalene told her that she buried the note in the northeast corner of the Cave of Gethsemane. This is why I wish to raise funds for an excavation of the cave."

As soon as Brother Gregory finished, questions erupted from the reporters, sending a wave of fear through Karim that someone might ask the wrong ones.

"Why did you wait so long to reveal the scroll?"

"Didn't you know that all antiquities belong to the Israeli government?"

"Have other scholars seen your translation?"

"What will you do with the scroll now?"

Brother Gregory once again appealed for quiet and agreed to answer questions. An American reporter spoke first. The stern-looking middle-aged woman identified herself as Marjorie Stevens. "You have told us little about the content of this letter. What does it say?"

Brother Gregory stepped to the podium. "The letter disproves two prominent theories about Jesus' relationship with Mary Magdalene. One theory says that the relationship was strictly platonic; the other, that Jesus and Mary Magdalene were married and had a child. This letter reveals something quite different—that the relationship was charged with romantic feelings, but that Jesus transcended these and achieved true spiritual enlightenment. He was tempted as we all are, yet remained chaste through the marriage of the masculine and the feminine within."

Marjorie Stevens asked, "What *kind* of marriage?"

"I'm using contemporary language to describe the mystery of Jesus' enlightenment," Brother Gregory said. "As he struggled in prayer with his attraction to Mary Magdalene, he had a vision of the human soul as both masculine and feminine. He saw that a person can only become whole through the inner marriage of the two, as the two are one in God. The Jesus of both the biblical and the Gnostic Gospels was made whole in this way. His inner intimacy liberated him to speak to women publicly, which was prohibited for the men of his day. He treated all women with respect and compassion, especially those of poor reputation. He even had women disciples and on occasion used feminine imagery for God. Out of his prayer life came this extraordinary spiritual understanding, personal integration, and practical wisdom. In the letter he shares all of this with Mary Magdalene so that she, too, can become enlightened."

Another American reporter, a bald, stocky man who identified himself as P.W. Richardson, pressed the point. "Why would it have been a sin for Jesus to marry the woman he loved?"

"It wouldn't have been," Brother Gregory said. "But remaining single was the only way for him to protect Mary Magdalene from devastating pain. They loved one another deeply, but Jesus knew that his life was in danger. He was too compassionate to marry her and then leave her a widow, which in those days meant a life of poverty and despair."

Karim gripped the edge of his chair, anticipating the question that he knew couldn't be avoided. A thicket of hands shot up as Brother Gregory finished his answer. He recognized a British reporter who gave his name as Robert Dougherty, a tall, fair-haired man with wire-rimmed glasses. "Rumor has it that the scroll will figure prominently in the March for Peace tomorrow," Dougherty said. "Is this true, and if so, what security precautions will be taken to protect this priceless artifact?"

"The rumors are true," Brother Gregory said. "When the GAA and I started publicizing this news conference, word of the discovery of a Jesus letter leaked out, and the organizers of the march requested permission to feature the scroll at their event. It makes perfect sense because the letter is a symbol of reconciliation and peace among all religions. But I must refer you to Dr. Abraham Saltzman, head of the GAA, to address your question about security." He called to the podium a studious-looking man in a charcoal suit.

"I can assure you that we have taken every precaution to protect the scroll," Dr. Saltzman said. "A detail of IDF soldiers has been assigned this task under the leadership of Commander Ezra Sharett."

Karim's vision went dark at this news, as if the announcement had blinded him. Memories came back of Ezra pulling him out of Rachel's closet and trying to arrest him at the preparation rally. Karim could still see the rage in Ezra's eyes and hear the accusation in his tone, and feel the hate in his yanks and shoves. This was the man who had ordered him to stay away from his sister and who had threatened to have him shot on sight if he entered Jerusalem again. Only as Karim silently cried out to

Allah and fingered the ring that his mother had given him did his vision slowly return.

After Dr. Saltzman sat down, the barrage of questions continued. Karim braced himself as Brother Gregory called on a short woman who wore a white hijab. She gave her name as Yosri Elbaz of Al Jazeera and then said, "You have told us about your translation and about the content of the so-called 'Jesus letter,' but you didn't say who found the scroll or where it was discovered. Could you address these questions, please?"

Karim sat up in rapt attention as Brother Gregory hesitated. Then the monk said, "I'm going to call on my assistant Karim Musalaha to address this question. He knows more about the specifics than I do." Brother Gregory waved Karim to the podium and stepped aside. Images of Rachel pummeled Karim's mind as, lightheaded, he went forward, a chalky feeling in his mouth.

When he got to the podium, the room appeared even more crowded and chaotic than it had from his seat. He felt badgered by pulsating bodies, swirling cameras, and jousting microphones, but he drew a breath and said, "Only one person found the scroll and unfortunately he couldn't be here today because of illness. Robert Kenyon, an archaeologist and professor at Jerusalem International University, was exploring the caves of Qumran when he came across the top of a ceramic jar buried in a cave, about a kilometer south of the visitors' center. He dug up the jar and found the scroll inside."

"Why didn't the professor turn over the scroll to the government immediately, as the law requires?" Yosri Elbaz asked.

Karim knew that this was a complicated question, and since he didn't want to raise suspicions or implicate Brother Gregory in any way, he said, "I must refer you to Robert Kenyon. Only he would know the answer to your question."

Karim was ready to step away from the podium when one of the emissaries from the Vatican stood. A portly man of average height, he approached the microphone. "Please excuse this interruption," he said, "but I have urgent news to share. My name is Ferdinand Cardinal Mancini, and I am here as a special emissary from the Holy See and the Vatican Apostolic Library. When my colleagues and I heard about this news conference, we consulted with the Holy Father about whether the Vatican should make a revelation of its own. I am convinced that we should reveal a document that is contained in the Vatican's secret archives. Previous popes and archivists have dismissed the document as a hoax, but the revelations of the Jesus letter and Judith of Jerusalem's diary provide evidence to the contrary. When we heard about the letter and the diary, we suspected that they might provide corroborating evidence for the authenticity of the document I am about to show you."

Holding up a sheet of paper, the Cardinal said, "It is my privilege to unveil a translation of an unsigned note, the content of which suggests that the author is Judas Iscariot, writing to Mary Magdalene. Extensive scientific tests were conducted on the papyrus, and the results indicate that the note is authentic."

Karim closed his eyes and bowed his head, wonder filling him as the room fell silent. The Cardinal began to read,

> "No more can I bear it.
>
> The fire in my heart burned too hot for you, Mary.
>
> Now I am accursed, for I betrayed my friend, the man you loved, and he is condemned.
>
> I, too, must die."

Karim raised his head and opened his eyes as the Cardinal finished. The silence in the room gave way to a whirlwind of questions, but Karim heard only his own urgent thoughts. Could these really be the words of

Judas Iscariot? Karim wished that Saed had heard them. Even more, he wished that Saed had read the Jesus letter.

With a jolt Karim realized that Judas' note provided the answers for which he and Rachel had searched. The Jesus letter was real! The relationship between Jesus and Mary Magdalene was mystical in nature, revealing the path toward spiritual enlightenment, the path toward peace. Tears gathered in Karim's eyes. If only Judas Iscariot and Saed Musalaha had walked these paths. Karim would always associate their names with suicides that could have been prevented had these men learned the deeper meaning of love.

Karim longed to tell Rachel about these revelations, but he didn't know where she was. He had decided to give Kenyon everything he demanded and prayed that Kenyon would let Rachel go as promised. Then she could speak at the March for Peace as planned, and Karim could meet her there.

If only she would forgive him.

A surge of adrenaline rushed through Karim as he remembered that PPA militants would be stalking him. He had to flee immediately. With everyone still focused on Cardinal Mancini, Karim slipped away from the podium, worked his way to the back of the room and left the library.

Then his cell phone rang.

Kenyon.

CHAPTER FORTY-FIVE

ANYONE WHO LOVES MUST LEARN TO FORGIVE. WHEN HURT, OUR CHOICES ARE TO INFLICT PAIN IN RETURN, TO WITHDRAW, TO LEAVE.

OR TO FORGIVE.

SOMETIMES THE ONE WHO COMMITTED THE WRONG WILL ACKNOWLEDGE IT AND ASK TO BE FORGIVEN. JUST AS OFTEN, NO ACCEPTANCE OF RESPONSIBILITY OR APOLOGY WILL BE FORTHCOMING. HEALING LIES NOT IN EXCUSING THE MISDEED OR DENYING THAT IT HAPPENED, BUT RATHER IN FORGIVING AND ENTRUSTING THE MATTER TO GOD'S JUSTICE.

WHEN WE FORGIVE, WE BEGIN A HEALING PROCESS GUIDED BY GRACE AND ANCHORED IN HOPE. THIS PROCESS GRADUALLY FREES US FROM RAGE AND HATE, MAKING A NEW FUTURE POSSIBLE.

—**Brother Gregory Andreou's Journal**

Bethlehem
Tuesday, April 16

UNDER DIFFERENT CIRCUMSTANCES THE WORLD OF HOTELS AND TAXIS MIGHT HAVE INTRIGUED KARIM, BUT NOT TONIGHT. Not with Rachel's life at stake. He paced in front of the Three Kings Hotel, eyes riveted on each taxi that pulled up, his hand sweating as he held the straps of a paper bag. Robert Kenyon had called and demanded that he arrive at midnight—alone—to be picked up and taken to an undisclosed location. Only if Karim turned over the contents of the bag—Brother Gregory's laptop, the earliest handwritten copies of his translation of the Jesus letter, and all other computer files and materials related to it—would Kenyon release Rachel. If Karim failed to deliver the items, or if he or Brother Gregory went to the police, Rachel would die.

The thought made Karim's skin crawl. He suspected that Kenyon was bluffing, that the professor wouldn't really kill Rachel and risk losing his career and going to prison for life. But as long as Kenyon held her, Karim had no choice but to follow his instructions.

He drew the bag closer as the headlights of an approaching car nearly blinded him. When it stopped at the curb, Karim saw that it was a yellow Palestinian taxi. An older gentleman in a herringbone sports coat stepped out and sauntered through the hotel's revolving doors. Karim stayed close enough for the driver to notice him. The taxi turned left onto Manger Street, Bethlehem's main thoroughfare, headed away from Jerusalem, which lay a few kilometers north.

Karim kicked the pavement with his heel and checked his watch: six minutes past midnight. If Kenyon wanted to make him worry, he was succeeding.

When another taxi approached, Karim moved in front of the hotel door. The white sedan had a yellow Israeli plate. A nicely dressed couple got out holding hands. They had no luggage. Karim imagined them to be European tourists returning from the theatre in Jerusalem. The trim, nattily dressed man paid the driver and closed the door. Then the cab accelerated into the traffic and disappeared.

Karim checked his watch: thirteen minutes past. He set the bag down and wiped his palm before picking it up again and gripping the handles tighter. Where was Kenyon holding Rachel? Was she all right?

The next taxi was different from the first two. It was white and had yellow plates but carried no passengers. When the car stopped, the driver rolled down the passenger-side window. "Are you Karim Musalaha?"

"Yes."

The stocky man in his mid-thirties got out and frisked him for a cell phone, weapon, or tracking device. When the man had determined that Karim was clean, he said, "Get in."

Karim settled into the backseat as the driver slid behind the wheel, adjusted his red baseball cap, and waited for a break in the traffic. Then he headed south on Manger Street.

"Where are we going?" Karim asked.

The driver turned up the Israeli rock music on his radio.

Karim's temples began to throb. He rubbed them in an attempt to ease the stress, but it didn't help. As the taxi picked up speed, the lights of Bethlehem's storefront businesses and boxlike houses became a blur. The road grew hilly outside of town, reminding Karim of his life: an accelerating ride on a dangerous road that kept getting steeper. Now, if he wasn't careful, he could lose control of the speeding vehicle. His and Rachel's salvation lay with the items in the bag. By delivering Brother Gregory's laptop and translation materials to Kenyon, Karim could save Rachel's life. The harder question was whether he could save her heart.

Or his.

He grabbed the edge of the vinyl seat as the taxi swung onto a gravel road forty-five minutes south of Bethlehem. They followed this unmarked road for another ten minutes and came to an open field. The driver steered the taxi onto the grass and stopped. "This is where I was told to drop you." He came around and opened the door.

Karim stepped out and caught a whiff of sheep dung. His legs were heavy, his throat parched, his fingers tingling. "Did you receive any other instructions?"

"No." The driver rounded the front of the car and got back in.

Karim paced as he watched the taxi's red taillights disappear up the road. He could do nothing but wait in this windswept field, beneath stars that appeared farther away than usual. Feeling edgy, he pulled up his collar against the brisk wind. He kicked a stone, wishing this night were over. Kenyon held all the power. At first Karim had considered the professor's plan impossible to execute. Now he saw its cruel logic.

Kenyon wanted the acclaim and honor that would be accorded the man who discovered and translated the Jesus letter. He was a respected archaeologist and professor; now he would become an international figure, an icon, his face on the cover of *Time* magazine. Karim was a Palestinian, in Israel illegally, and the son of a man who sponsored terrorism. The GAA officials would have to believe Kenyon—especially since Karim had publicly credited him with finding the scroll. Kenyon would show the officials the computer files and other materials as if they were his own, and Karim would have to go along with the scheme. Just then a chilling thought occurred to him: Rachel could expose and destroy Kenyon, and Kenyon had to have realized this. Would he kill her to silence her?

The roar of an approaching engine broke into Karim's thoughts. He squeezed the bag's straps, trying to stifle his anger and remain calm. Headlights appeared on the road and then swerved into the field, shining in Karim's eyes.

The Impala stopped a few meters away and Kenyon rolled down the window. "Give me the bag and then go back to where you're standing."

"First I want to know that Rachel is safe."

"We'll talk about Rachel soon enough."

"No!" Karim yelled and then lowered his voice. "I want to talk about her now. Where is she?"

Kenyon held up a handgun. "If you care about Rachel, you'll do as I say."

"Don't believe his threats, Karim!" Rachel called to him from the backseat. "He can't get away with this."

Kenyon slapped the seat with a fist. "Shut up! I'll do whatever it takes to get the laptop and papers."

Karim stepped closer and peered into the car. In the darkness he could make out Rachel's face in the backseat. She was sitting up, her hands behind her back, squirming and trying to break free from the cords. A tremor rattled his bones. He held the bag away from Kenyon and said, "If you want Brother Gregory's laptop and translations, release her."

Kenyon put the car in reverse. "It's the other way around. Either you give me the bag or you'll never see Rachel again."

Karim pulled the backdoor handle, but it was locked. He shook the car. "If you hurt her, you'll never sleep at night."

"I'll sleep just fine." Kenyon began to back up the car.

Karim pounded on the glass and Kenyon stopped the car. "I'm not giving you anything until I have Rachel."

"Then say good-bye to your friend," Kenyon said, moving forward now.

If Karim didn't act fast, he would never see Rachel again. He took off after the car when he heard Rachel scream.

Reluctantly Karim held out the bag and shouted, "Let her go. Please let her go."

The car braked abruptly and Kenyon took the bag. "As soon as I make sure everything is here." He switched on the dome light and rummaged in the bag, pointing the gun at Karim.

Karim's forehead felt ready to split. "Deception never brings happiness."

"But getting credit for this discovery is worth any sacrifice."

Karim pressed his fingers against the glass. "You have what you want. Now let Rachel go."

Kenyon turned toward her. "If you breathe a word of this to the authorities, I'll tell them that Karim stole the scroll from me, and he'll go to prison. Do you understand?"

Rachel remained still. "Perfectly."

Karim heard the doors unlock and pulled on the backdoor handle. Rachel tumbled out, her hands and feet tied with cords.

As Karim untied her feet and helped her onto the grass, Kenyon said, "I know you'll keep your mouths shut. And you'll tell Brother Gregory to do the same." Then the car sped away, its tires spitting gravel.

"I was praying it would be you who came for me," Rachel said, grimacing as she stood. Her hair was disheveled, her blouse wrinkled. "That man should be—"

Karim pressed a finger to her lips. "Don't try to talk. The important thing is that you're safe." He untied Rachel's hands.

She embraced him, choking back a sob. "I've never been so glad to see anyone."

"Me either."

She pulled away, rubbing her wrists. "Kenyon really scared me. Watching the news conference... I don't know. He's just so . . . so fanatical. If you hadn't come..." Her last words got lost as her voice broke.

Karim caressed her cheek, wishing he could say what was in his heart. "There's something I need to know. Are you really glad to see me or just happy because you were rescued?"

She drew a breath and cleared her throat. "When I left Jerusalem, I wanted nothing more to do with you. But your e-mails..."

He wiped a tear from her cheek. "I would have told you about Saed, but I wasn't ready then."

"When would you have been ready?"

He shook his head. "I don't know. When we first met, I thought I would never see you again, so I had no reason to tell you. Then we got close and I was afraid you would hate me if you knew." Karim paused and met her gaze. "I'm so very sorry that I didn't tell you sooner."

Rachel moved closer. "I will forgive you if you will forgive *me* for leaving you in Jerusalem."

Karim gathered her in his arms. "I promise not to keep any more secrets from you."

"And I promise to be more understanding." She nestled her cheek against his chest. "Jesus told Mary Magdalene that love is always a risk. That's especially true for an Israeli and a Palestinian. Love guarantees nothing except that our lives will never be the same. That's my prayer for the March for Peace—that all of our lives will be changed forever."

"I thought that you would miss the march."

"Even Robert Kenyon couldn't keep me away. I'm giving a speech."

Karim pulled back and gazed into eyes as fathomless as space. He hesitated and then leaned down to kiss her tenderly. He cared little that they were standing in a lonely field with no ride to the monastery. What mattered was the canopy of stars glimmering in the cloudless sky, and even more, Rachel's soft, receptive lips. He held her close, running his hands across her back and around her shoulders.

"I love you," she said, squeezing his arms. "And this time I'm never going to let you go."

Karim smiled and nudged her toward the road. "I've been longing to hear those words, because I love you too, more than I could ever express." He wrapped an arm around her and guided her toward the highway, praying that a sympathetic motorist would pick them up.

CHAPTER FORTY-SIX

CHAPTER FORTY-SIX

WHEN GABRIEL AND JUDITH REACHED THE GENNATH GATE, HE SAW THAT SHE WAS EXHAUSTED AND COULD GO NO FARTHER SO HE PICKED HER UP AND CARRIED HER. It was Friday, the day when the lambs would be slaughtered for Passover. His arms should have ached, but as he trudged toward the crest of the Place of the Skull, he hardly noticed her weight. With one arm supporting her legs and the other her back, he held her horizontal body against his heaving chest, the scroll still clutched tightly in his hand. Her arms were wrapped around his neck, her cheek pressing against his.

He waded through the crowd, toward the three six-foot vertical posts on which the crossbeams would be erected, and felt her trembling. Twelve burly soldiers, fiercely brandishing their javelins, were keeping the people at a safe distance. He stopped in front of them, sweating in the blazing sun. The three condemned men were lying on the ground, moaning and weak, ready to be nailed to the crossbeams they had carried from the city.

Jesus appeared particularly mangled, the crown of thorns on his head skewed awkwardly to the right, obscuring an eye.

Gabriel could not have imagined an uglier place or one more eerily barren. Golgotha's eroding rock, covered with thick gray dust, looked like the head of a corpse, vacant-eyed and jagged. Treeless except for a few scrawny shrubs, the place reeked of rotting, vulture-torn flesh. The stifling hot air was swarming with flies, wild dogs howled in the distance. *Why am I here?* Gabriel felt a tremor run through him. A few months ago all he had wanted was a happy marriage and success as a merchant. His dreams had been so close to fulfillment on his wedding day.

Why should he not put Judith down and leave her to watch Dismas suffer? The answer echoed in his mind with unmistakable clarity: He was here because of the letter. The love that it described had taken hold of him. He glanced with reverence at the rabbi from Nazareth sprawled on the ground. Silently he thanked Jesus for giving him the courage to be present.

Not wanting to look, he finally saw his brother lying on his stomach. Blood was streaming from his back and mixing with the dust to form rivulets of crimson mud. Gabriel's mouth went dry, his heart stopped beating. Was this the brother he had raced against and wrestled and sparred with? Gabriel nestled Judith's head against his chest, shielding her eyes, his anger at his brother sliding away.

"What is the other Zealot's name?" Gabriel asked.

"Gestas."

He watched the compact man with meaty features struggle to break free, but Gestas' pathetic flailing was no match for the soldiers. Their whips slapped and thudded against his neck and back and shoulders. Each blow and scream caused Judith to flinch in Gabriel's arms. The soldiers beat Gestas mercilessly as he lay on the ground. A group of women approached as they subdued him. The women carried jars of wine laced with gall, a mild narcotic. As retaliation for Gestas' resistance, the soldiers denied him the drink. The women offered some to Jesus; he tasted it, but then shook his head and sent them away. Only Dismas drank the soothing liquid; Gabriel was glad for anything that would spare his brother more suffering.

The sturdy, square-jawed centurion in charge of the execution went to the condemned men and examined their wounds. He ordered the soldiers to strip the men naked and wrap loincloths around their genitals. The soldiers carried out the order and laid the men's garments at the foot of the vertical posts. With their knees, the soldiers then held the men's arms and strapped them to the crossbars with ropes.

The hulking executioner, his arms as thick as most men's thighs, approached with his mallet. He first went to Gestas, several long spikes held between his teeth. One by one he took the spikes and drove them into Gestas' palms. Gestas cursed the Romans with each blow until the curses became cries of agony.

When the executioner stood over Dismas, Gabriel whispered to Judith, "Please don't look." Dismas shrieked as sharp iron penetrated soft flesh; the spikes pierced his palms and the wood underneath. Gabriel turned away, biting back tears, the bile in his stomach rising as he witnessed his brother's torture. Then he steeled his will and turned back, determined to show Dismas sympathy and support. With each blow, Judith squeezed Gabriel's neck harder. He watched his brother's body shake as the soldiers lifted Dismas upright and fastened the crossbar to the vertical beam in the ground. Gestas, already erected, was cursing his tormentors.

Taunts and jeers erupted from the crowd.

"That will teach you to desecrate the Temple!"

"Give them a taste of Roman justice!"

"No sympathy for these criminals!"

"You filthy swine! You're getting what you deserve!"

The muscles in Gabriel's neck tensed at the sound of such cruelty, and his blood ran hot. His brother was an enemy of Rome, but no one deserved such torture. The shouting stopped as the executioner knelt beside Jesus. With three vicious wallops of his mallet, he drove the first spike through the Galilean's palm, causing him to groan. Jesus bit his lip and writhed in pain as the executioner repeated the process on the other hand.

The soldiers erected Jesus' cross in the middle, with Dismas and Gestas on either side. As was the custom, they nailed a wedge between the men's legs, helping to distribute their weight so that their bodies would not tear loose from the wood. The executioner then went from cross to cross, nailing the right foot of each condemned man over the left. When he had finished, two soldiers used a ladder to nail a placard over Jesus' head. Written in Hebrew, Latin, and Greek, the inscription read, "Jesus of Nazareth, King of the Jews."

The crowd moved in closer and some mocked him.

"You saved others; can't you save yourself?"

"If you're the King of Israel, come down from the cross now, and we'll believe in you."

"If you trust in God, then why doesn't he deliver you?"

When Gabriel heard this, he put Judith down and ran up to the soldiers, enraged. "Why do you let them mock him like that? Aren't you in charge? Rome takes pride in its laws, yet you crucify an innocent man." He shook an accusing fist at them. "May his blood be upon you, and upon your children, and upon all who use brutality to support injustice!"

The centurion swung his javelin and knocked him down. "Shut up," he said in Greek. "Or you'll end up on a cross like your friend."

The soldiers began to gamble for Jesus' clothes. They were particularly enamored of the seamless scarlet robe that they had brought from the praetorium. Finally a scar-faced soldier grinned triumphantly and said, "The robe is mine."

At this Jesus cried out in Aramaic, "Father, forgive them, for they know not what they do!"

The words struck Gabriel with such power that he fell to his knees. How could Jesus forgive those who were crucifying him? How could he pray for those who had stripped him naked and gambled for his clothes? Jesus should be hurling abuse at them! Then Gabriel remembered what the letter said—that forgiveness is a matter of the soul; that we do it not for those who wronged us but for ourselves; and that we only begin to heal when we let go of hurt and hate.

Gabriel looked up in profound admiration. The betrayal that he had endured still gnawed at him. But in comparison with Jesus' anguish, his wound seemed minor. He turned as the scar-faced soldier smugly draped the robe over a shoulder. If Jesus could forgive the soldier's greed and cruelty, should Gabriel not do the same for Dismas? And should he not give Judith another chance?

Hot tears stung his eyes. He got up and stumbled toward his brother's cross. Judith had moved to it and was standing there weeping, her hands covering her mouth, her lustrous hair disheveled, her eyes red from crying. Pale as a corpse, her body shaking uncontrollably, she fell to her knees and gazed up in horror.

Gabriel put an arm around her and looked up tearfully. Then, in a measured, deliberate voice, he said, "I love you . . . and I forgive you, Dismas."

Dismas stared down in agonized disbelief. "After what I did, how can you forgive me?"

Gabriel pointed at Jesus. "Because of him." He held up the scroll that contained the letter. "And because of this."

Judith broke away from Gabriel and fell sobbing at the Galilean's feet, his bloodstained face contorted in agony. She then approached Dismas and said, "I couldn't stay with you, but I will never forget all that we shared and how much you meant to me. Now you must think about more important matters. It's not too late to receive Jesus' peace. It's your only hope for salvation."

Dismas nodded and rolled his head back against the cross. "I wish I *had* heeded the letter," he said, his voice raspy. "All my fighting has been in vain." Dismas paused, panting, struggling to catch his breath and glancing at Gabriel and Judith. "But you two have a chance to do better." He stared directly at her. "I love you . . . and I am sorry for how I hurt you." Then he shifted his gaze to Gabriel. "Knowing that you forgive me, I can die in peace."

Before Gabriel could reply, Gestas interrupted. Echoing the jeers of the soldiers and some in the crowd, he taunted Jesus. "Are you not the Messiah? Save yourself and us!"

Gabriel marveled at how Dismas, in hearing these words, seemed to regain his strength. Barely alive, choking now on each breath, Dismas shouted at Gestas, "Do you not fear God, since you are under the same sentence of condemnation? And we indeed have been condemned justly, for we are getting what we deserve for our deeds, but this man has done nothing wrong." Then Dismas turned toward the middle cross and said, "Jesus, remember me when you come into your kingdom."

Jesus answered, "Truly I tell you, today you will be with me in paradise."

Gabriel's heart was racing, but in hearing Jesus' promise to Dismas, he became surprisingly calm. A peculiar peace descended on him, accompanied by a compelling vision: He imagined that he and Dismas were in a place of glorious light, embracing. They had died and been reunited in peace, the past forgotten, a new relationship begun. Dismas' face appeared radiant, as if illuminated by a thousand stars. Although Gabriel recognized his brother's features, it seemed that he was seeing them for the first time, and he could not turn away from their perfection. He wanted to hold the vision forever, but Judith squeezed his arm and interrupted his thoughts.

"There's something I need to tell both of you," she said, gazing tearfully at Dismas and speaking in a loud, trembling voice. "What I have to say will affect us all." She struggled to catch her breath. "You both need to know that. . ." She trailed off, her voice breaking. "You need to know that I am . . . I am pregnant with Dismas' baby."

Gabriel stared at her and then at his suffering brother. The anguish in Dismas' eyes, and in Judith's, mirrored Gabriel's own. Dismas lifted up his head and cried out, "Please forgive her, Gabriel! If you can't do it for her sake, do it for the child's. Judith was young and innocent—everything was my fault! She needs you to take care of her and the baby."

Gabriel's stomach churned as he noticed the sky darkening and began to back away. Glancing up, he expected to see clouds blocking the sun, but there were none.

"A storm is rolling in," said a sallow-skinned man nearby.

A scribe turned to a group of onlookers. "Come on, let's go before we get drenched."

Gabriel shook his head and stared at the sky, baffled. There could be no storm without clouds. Why had dusk fallen at noon? As he pondered the mystery, the light continued to fade. The soldiers lit torches in order to continue their gruesome work.

Barely able to see, Gabriel turned and dropped the scroll. He had to get away. Away from Golgotha's blood and tears. Away from Judith and Dismas, who had ruined his life. Away from Jesus, whose forgiving spirit he could not match. Gabriel did not know what the sun's strange disappearance meant or where he would go. He only knew that Judith's revelation had brought darkness to his heart. And it was thicker than Golgotha's untimely midnight.

CHAPTER FORTY-SEVEN

BY TORCHLIGHT JUDITH COULD SEE THE THREE DYING MEN ON THE CROSSES, BUT LITTLE ELSE. She took her eyes off Dismas for a moment to reach for Gabriel. Panic seized her when she grabbed nothing but air. He was gone! She had lost him in the darkness! She began to grope through the crowd, searching. "Gabriel! Gabriel ben Zebulun! Where are you?"

As she moved right and then left, she questioned whether she should have told Gabriel about her pregnancy. She couldn't keep secrets from him anymore. Nor could she let Dismas die without knowing about his child. After Gabriel rescued her from prison, she had thought that he loved her enough to understand and forgive. How wrong she had been.

She wove through the crowd like a woman possessed, her voice nearly as desperate as those moaning from the crosses. "Gabriel ben Zebulun! Has anyone seen Gabriel ben Zebulun?" Finally she got tired of hearing people say no, and walked back toward Dismas.

Near his cross she stumbled on something on the ground. She bent down and recognized what it was. The scroll! She picked it up and held it to her breast. At least she would have the letter from Jesus to comfort her. Just then someone latched on to her arm. She turned and heard a reassuring voice. "Thank God you are out of prison," the voice said. In the dim light, she made out the tear-streaked face of Mary Magdalene.

Judith held out the scroll. "This belongs to you."

"What is it?"

"The letter that Jesus wrote you."

Mary took the scroll. "How did it get here?"

"Nicodemus gave it to Gabriel. He was here earlier, but I lost him in the darkness. He left the scroll behind."

Mary Magdalene took Judith's hand. "I am so thankful to have the letter back. It will become my most treasured possession." Mary led her near Jesus' cross, and Judith recognized his mother standing there with two other women and a young, dark-haired man with delicate features. She stared at the suffering men on the crosses and couldn't stop sobbing. She had known about the Zealots' plan to cleanse the Temple. Couldn't she have tried to warn Jesus? If she had succeeded, he could have been spared this suffering. She shifted her gaze to Dismas and pressed a fist against her trembling lips. Dismas was the first man she had ever loved. Now his arms were stretched out on a cross. His hands were hemorrhaging blood, and the dreams that she and Dismas had shared were shattered forever.

Tears dripped onto her hand as she stared at Dismas. Never again would she hold those arms. Never again would she whisper secrets into those ears or gaze longingly into those eyes or hear that voice pleading for one more chance. Never again would she fight with him and then make up and make love, drowning the hurt in passion's depths. She longed to climb up and take him down and carry him home, wherever home was, and nurse him back to health. But it was not to be. She had deserted him on the eve of his greatest battle. If only she had convinced him to leave the Zealots with her . . . now it was too late.

She ran a hand through her hair, feeling partly to blame for his agony and praying that it would end soon. Kneeling down, she covered her face with her hands. She had made so many mistakes, failed so many people. But she couldn't go back, couldn't undo the mistakes or heal the hurt she had caused. She could only stay and keep her vigil.

Mary Magdalene slipped an arm around her shoulders, and Judith pointed at Dismas. "He's the man I told you about, the one I ran away with. He was arrested at the Temple, and now he's dying with Jesus. His brother, Gabriel, rescued me from prison; then he left me too. Oh, Mary, I have no one, and it's all my fault."

Mary Magdalene squeezed Judith harder. "We must be strong for these suffering men. Please pray with us." Mary brought Judith into the group. Judith recognized the women who had been in the house when she was arrested, and also the disciple named John. When Jesus saw the group clustered together and weeping and praying, he fixed his gaze on his mother. "Woman, here is your son!" Then he said to John, "Here is your mother."

Mary Magdalene and the others were embracing Jesus' mother, and Judith joined them. His mother's sobs crushed Judith's heart, yet the older woman's steady rhythmic breathing, and the firmness with which she held the arms around her, spoke of her deep inner strength. Although Judith's future appeared as uncertain as the return of the sun, she took courage from the women who included her in their circle of grief and prayer.

Jesus' concern for his mother reminded Judith of his closeness to women. How she yearned for such tender love from a man! But Gabriel was gone and might never come back. She had humiliated him on their wedding day; she was pregnant with his brother's child—perhaps he could never forgive, never believe she had changed.

And why should he believe? He probably feared that she would betray him again. Thinking about the word *betrayal* caused a knot to form in her throat and tears to form in her eyes. Betrayal was a prison worse than Pilate's. The prison had no walls, but shame kept her locked inside. And the prison was darker and lonelier than any Rome ever built.

Hearing Dismas' wailing set her body shaking, and she couldn't stop. He was suffering, and so were Gabriel and his parents and hers—on crosses of the heart. Her betrayals had constructed the beams and driven in the nails. Now she could never escape the prison inside her, never be released from the sentence of shame, never come home to innocence.

It seemed unfair that she would have to pay for her sins for the rest of her life. But as she stared into Golgotha's darkness and smelled the smoky torches, the sweaty bodies, the rotting flesh, she realized that questions of fairness were not allowed here. Crucifixion was not fair. It was evil, and here evil reigned. She, too, had done evil, and no amount of explaining could free her from the consequences of her actions.

She shivered as she thought about raising a child without a man. How would they eat? Where would they live? The questions tormented her until she remembered Mary Magdalene's words: *You are afraid because you have not learned to trust. . . .*

Judith sighed and closed her eyes, momentarily shutting out the horror of the crucifixions. *I don't want to lose Gabriel. But if he cannot forgive and wholeheartedly commit to a new future with me, I must let him go.*

Another cry rose from the cross, its strained guttural sound startling her. This time Jesus lifted up his head and exclaimed, "I am thirsty!" The plea followed soon after his words to his mother, and Judith sensed that he was pleading for more than a drink. He had spent his life thirsting for God and his kingdom, for honest relationships, for justice and peace. His lament cut to her soul, and she became aware of the chalky dryness in her own mouth.

She watched Mary Magdalene turn a cunning eye toward the soldiers and set the scroll on the ground. Mary waved Judith over, pointed to a jar of the soldiers' sour wine, and told her to grab it when the men were distracted in conversation. Judith waited until the soldiers were laughing at a coarse joke and then ran and picked up the jar, Mary Magdalene at her side. They went to Jesus' cross, and Mary dipped a sponge into the sour wine and lifted it to him on a hyssop branch. Jesus sucked the wine briefly, but when the soldiers saw what was happening, they shooed Judith and Mary Magdalene away. As they returned to the group, Jesus cried out, "My God, my God! Why have you forsaken me?"

The words tore at Judith's heart. She glanced up at Jesus and saw an expression of utter abandonment on his contorted face, his eyes clamped shut, his mouth twisted into a grimace, his chin tucked against his chest as if rooted there. Appalled and sickened by the horror, she turned away, expecting to see only darkness, but a canopy of stars covered the heavens. She lifted both fists and shook them and said as Jesus had, "Why, God? Why do the heavens appear so peaceful when there is such anguish on earth?" But her cry, like Jesus' expression of forsakenness, was greeted by an indifferent silence.

In the face of such horror, it *did* seem that God had forsaken Jesus. It was all too much. She withdrew from the women. Jesus had lost his hope; hers was gone too. She had managed to remain strong through the battles at Qumran and the conflict with Judas Iscariot and her decision to leave the Zealots, but now she had no strength left. She was estranged from Dismas, from her family, from the Zealots, from Gabriel. She needed to flee Golgotha and never look back. But as she turned to go, she felt a hand on her shoulder and heard Mary Magdalene's voice. "Judith. . . Judith of Jerusalem, don't leave. We need you—and you need us."

Judith stopped. She wanted to keep going but couldn't. The women's tortured eyes stared longingly at her. The crowd's jeering rang in her ears, crueler as Jesus neared death.

"Ha! He is calling Elijah to rescue him!"

"A suffering Messiah? What a joke!"

"Only a fool would challenge Rome! He's getting what he deserves!"

Jesus was heaving now, gasping for breath, convulsing, his voice raspy, distant. His words were indistinct, as if he were trapped in a deep ravine that was muffling his cries for help. Her own breathing became labored in sympathetic response to his, her lungs constricting in spasms of coughs and sobs. In the prison Jesus had spoken of forgiveness and said it was possible for her to receive it, even to forgive herself. She felt the crushing weight of her own condemnation and the condemnation of everyone she had betrayed. In that moment she sensed from some hidden place that Jesus understood her suffering, that in a mysterious way he was suffering with her and for her. His love ignited like a flame inside her, spreading warmth through every bone and muscle. She felt that he loved her as no one ever had or could and that the flame would never die. Golgotha's darkness and stench and brutality no longer mattered. She would stay with him.

In the next moment Jesus straightened, mustered his strength and proclaimed triumphantly, "It is finished!" The crowd fell silent, amazed. It appeared that his energy was completely spent, and he sighed, "Father, into your hands I commit my spirit." Judith let out a cry of sorrow and knelt in front of him, her head bowed, her hair wet with sweat, her eyes awash in tears. Then he slouched forward and became still.

Judith reached for the other women. She tightened her embrace around them and they around her. The earth began to rumble. Streaks of lightning flashed across the sky. Thunder boomed. Rocks cracked, the ground split in places, people dove for cover. The centurion looked up at Jesus, and when the earthquake had ended, he said, "Truly this man was the Son of God."

Judith noticed the other soldiers grimacing at their commander's words. Their expressions of disbelief increased as the darkness began to lift and the sun broke through. The centurion noticed the scroll on the ground and retrieved it. He unfurled the papyrus and scanned the letter.

"What do you have there, Longinus?" the brazen scar-faced soldier asked.

The centurion came to the end of the scroll. "Something better than the robe." He pointed mockingly at Jesus. "It's a letter from our king here."

Judith accompanied Mary Magdalene as she approached Longinus in horror and said, "The letter belongs to me. You have no right—"

"Not anymore." Longinus cut Mary off, stepping toward Dismas with several other soldiers. In the murky light and fragile quiet, they picked up clubs, preparing to break Dismas' and Gestas' legs, and thus speed their deaths. Longinus had the scroll in one hand, a spear in the other. Judith charged toward him, but Mary Magdalene caught and held her back.

"Haven't they suffered enough?" Judith fought to break free, her voice a desperate shriek.

It was no use. She cringed as Dismas cried out, "Please! Have mercy!"

Two soldiers proceeded to smash Gestas' and Dismas' legs, eliciting wails of anguish from both. As Dismas continued to moan, Judith covered her ears and closed her eyes, but she couldn't shut out the labored gurgling of a man drowning in his own vomit. The hideous sound cut through her. She shook her head in disbelief that she was really here, that this was really happening. She and Dismas had been together for only a few months, but she felt years older. In the beginning anything had seemed possible—riding into the morning on horseback, defeating the Romans, building a family together. When they ran away, she had believed in true love—believed in it as much as she believed in the moon and sun and stars—but she had lived several lifetimes since then, and the belief had betrayed her as surely as she had betrayed Dismas and Gabriel. Now it was ending in agony and death. If she could go back and start over, she would make different choices. But there was no going back.

She opened her eyes and gazed up at Dismas. Within minutes, his head slumped to his chest and he died, as did Gestas. She tried to push the soldiers away, but they ignored her and went on to Jesus, whom they saw was already dead. Longinus stabbed him in the side with a spear, causing a mixture of blood and yellow bile to gush forth. Then, barely pausing to catch his breath, Longinus and the other soldiers began to leave with the crowd.

Judith stayed by Mary Magdalene's side as she ran and caught up with him. "That letter is all I have to remember Jesus by." Mary held his arm. "Please don't take it from me."

Longinus showed no emotion and shook her off. "I lost the robe, but the letter is mine," he said, walking away with the other soldiers. Only four of his men remained behind.

The crowd was thinning, and as Judith walked back to the other women with Mary, she asked, "May I stay with you for the Sabbath?"

Mary appeared stricken, her face contorted with grief. She grasped Judith's arm gently. "Of course you may. We are going back to the upper room, where we had our last meal with Jesus. We'll spend the Sabbath there."

While Mary was still speaking, two older men approached. Dressed in the long robes of Pharisees, one of them was carrying a shroud and wet cloths, and the other, two large jars. Judith recognized the heavier of the men as Nicodemus ben Gorion. He greeted the women mournfully and introduced his friend, Joseph of Arimathea, an average-size man with a pleasant face and graying black hair.

Joseph presented the soldiers with Pilate's written order that Jesus' body be released to him. The Romans examined the document carefully and then a barrel-chested soldier told Joseph, "All right, you have permission to take the Galilean's body, but only his."

Judith went to Nicodemus and whispered, "Please, sir, may we also bury Dismas?"

Nicodemus glanced nervously at the brawny soldiers, who were sternly keeping watch. "You heard the order. We dare not."

Using the soldiers' ladders and ropes, Joseph, Nicodemus, and John lowered Jesus' body from the cross. When they had laid it on the ground, his mother cradled his head in her arms one last time. She tossed aside the crown of thorns, gently touched his eyes, and kissed him tenderly. Joseph unrolled the shroud and said, "Not all of us on the Sanhedrin approved of your son's execution. The least we can do is give him a proper burial."

The men placed Jesus' body on the shroud, and Nicodemus asked the women to help with the embalming. At first Judith drew back, sickened by the body's bloody, mangled appearance. Then she steadied herself and, along with the others, began to wash it, her stomach turned inside out, her hands trembling. She rubbed gently around the wounds inflicted by the whip, the nails, and the spear; then she took the myrrh and aloe from the jars and spread the spices on the pallid torso, the limp arms, the bloodstained legs.

Sorrow weighed on her. Each movement required such energy that she thought it would be her last, but her love for Jesus gave her the strength to go on. It seemed that she had just begun when Joseph of Arimathea noticed the sun setting, barely visible on the darkened horizon. "The Sabbath is about to start; we do not have time to finish the embalming," he said. "We must get Jesus' body to the tomb immediately."

As Nicodemus was straightening the body, Judith told him about the centurion taking the letter.

Nicodemus glared at her and frowned. "We must find that centurion and get the letter back. We need it now more than ever."

Mary Magdalene, Jesus' mother, and several of the other women from Galilee went to the tomb with the men; Judith stayed behind with Susanna, Joanna, and a few other women she had never met. When her group started back toward the city, she paused for a moment and stared up at Dismas' swollen face and bruised legs, wishing there was more they could do for him. She gazed into the marbled purple sky and remembered how the stars had looked on the night that she and Dismas had first made love. How different everything was now. How passion had led to death and despair.

Judith stood motionless, her legs weak, her head spinning. An eerie silence had fallen on the dark afternoon. Not the renewing quiet of a peaceful night, but the haunting silence of a battlefield after a war. A dog howled in the distance. The plaintive sound pierced her heart and reminded her that she was alone: Love had ended; hope had ended; happiness and freedom and dreams had ended.

The dog howled again and Judith fell to the ground, one ear crushed against the pitiless earth, the other covered with a trembling hand. She pushed hard, desperate to shut out the howling, which reminded her of Dismas' moaning. But she knew that the terror of his anguished cries would be with her forever, as would the memory of her betrayals. As his body had been crucified, so had her heart, and she feared that she would never get up, that she would die with Dismas. More than a small part of her wished she would.

Only the memory of Jesus' words to Dismas gave her the strength to stand again: "Truly I tell you, today you will be with me in paradise." Her vision blurry with tears, she placed a hand on her abdomen. Someday, when her child asked about Dismas, those were the words she would speak. Whatever he had done, however tragically he had died, in the end, those were the words that mattered. It had taken him a long time, but he had finally understood. He had surrendered to Jesus. She turned to follow the other women, confident that she would carry the words with her always, and remember them each time she thought of Dismas.

CHAPTER FORTY-EIGHT

HEARTBREAK TEMPTS US TO GIVE UP ON LOVE, TO WITHDRAW AND VOW NEVER TO LOVE AGAIN. IN THIS WAY THE PAIN CAN BE STOPPED AND THE RISK MINIMIZED.

BUT WE CAN NEVER WITHDRAW FAR ENOUGH TO BE PERFECTLY SAFE.

A BETTER STRATEGY IS TO STAY ENGAGED. LOVE MAY LOSE MANY BATTLES, BUT EVEN ITS LOSSES ARE VICTORIES FOR HEARTS THAT REFUSE TO GROW COLD. IN THE END THESE HEARTS WILL WIN.

AS GOD LIVES, THEY WILL WIN.

AND HAVE ALREADY WON.

—**Brother Gregory Andreou's Journal**

Jerusalem
Wednesday, April 17

THE MARCH FOR PEACE DREW A LARGER-THAN-EXPECTED CROWD, BUT DESPITE THE OUTWARD SIGNS OF ITS SUCCESS, KARIM FELT DISAPPOINTMENT. The feeling surprised him as he and Rachel moved with the masses toward the plaza in front of the Wailing Wall.

He had just whispered a prayer of thanks that Kenyon had freed her and that a passing motorist had taken them to the monastery. But as he caught a glimpse of the Wailing Wall and the Dome of the Rock above it, his gratitude turned to gloom. He groped to understand why.

He wasn't disappointed in the thousands of people who were marching around the walls of the Old City. The flags of nations from Africa and Asia, Europe and the Americas lifted his spirits, as did the colorful banners decorated with doves and olive branches, which inspired him to keep believing in peace. The mingling of families and college students with priests, rabbis, and imams reminded him that all people can get along. The diversity of the marchers had exceeded his expectations—Jews draped in blue and white prayer shawls, Russian Orthodox priests in long black robes, Muslim men with *kufi* prayer caps, and Muslim women wearing the *hijab* on their heads.

As Karim reflected further, he identified the source of his disappointment. Jerusalem meant "city of peace," but never did a name resound with more biting irony. This city of prophets and sages, kings and pilgrims, scholars and poets was also a city of generals and crusaders and suicide bombers.

Surrounded by holy sites, Karim sensed the clash between the dream of divine blessing and the nightmare of warfare and squandered potential, of grand possibility compromised by the endless cycle of brutality and revenge. Jerusalem struck him as a lovely bride with the heart of a prostitute. She seduced you with lofty promises of peace, only to leave you wailing when the promises were dashed upon the rocks of bloodshed and death.

The talking and laughing of this raucous swath of marching humanity teemed with multicolored richness. But Jerusalem's dominant color was beige—its walls, its streets, its sidewalks, its buildings. The scene spoke of religion itself—that when it promoted justice and compassion, religion pulsed with color and life, but when it inspired hatred and violence, it was as beige as the bones decaying in hundreds of graves in the Kidron and Hinnom Valleys.

Karim coaxed Rachel through the crowd in order to catch up with Brother Gregory, thankful that after much wrangling—and in response to pressure from Washington—the Israeli government had eased permit restrictions for the day. As they jostled their way through the crowd, surrounded by IDF soldiers with tear gas at the ready, Karim rotated the ring on his finger—his mother's ring.

Last night had been a turning point for him and Rachel. They had talked through what was left of the night, sharing their hopes, their dreams, and their fears. He had comforted her when she cried, and she had fallen asleep for a few minutes, wrapped in his arms. The experience had convinced him that he wanted her there forever.

That he would ask her to marry him.

When he turned to look at her, he was amazed at how she had recovered from her abduction. In spite of having nearly no sleep, her wholesome beauty seemed undimmed. Her resilience captivated him. "Are you nervous about your speech?"

"Of course."

"Keep focused on your message and you'll do fine." He led her forward, eager to see the scroll, but even more eager to steal a moment when he could ask the question that was burning through him: *Will you marry me?* He pushed the question aside as they neared Brother Gregory and the scroll. Public demonstrations had applied pressure on the Government Antiquities Agency to allow the scroll to be displayed at the march. Fearing a popular revolt, the GAA had relented and entrusted the scroll to Brother Gregory. It rested on a wooden pallet, carried by four monks and protected by a sealed Plexiglas cover and Israeli guards armed with automatic weapons. He glanced around but didn't see Ezra.

With Rachel at his side, Karim prodded and cajoled his way through the raging sea of marchers until he reached Brother Gregory and the pallet. Television crews were filming the scene, beaming video and audio of the event to millions of viewers around the world. Karim hoped that the images of tens of thousands of people praying for peace would inspire support for the two-state solution.

A memory of the encounter with Kenyon surfaced just then, spreading goosebumps over his arms, despite the heat of the noonday sun. He hoped that Kenyon was done causing trouble. Now that the rogue archaeologist had Brother Gregory's laptop and translation materials, he could accuse Karim of stealing the scroll and send him to jail. Karim had nowhere to hide. Alienated from his father, he couldn't go home. Nor could he stay at the monastery indefinitely or in Jerusalem without a permit. He was a man without a country.

Karim nudged Rachel. "I'm nervous about being here."

She dodged a heavyset man. "Don't worry. Where could you be more inconspicuous than in a crowd of thousands?"

Karim fingered the ring. He longed for the day when he could take Rachel out for dinner, walk under the stars, share tender moments. He wanted her by his side always, to marry her and create a family together.

But marriage seemed impossible. Their families stood between them. The animosity of Muslims and Jews stood between them. The checkpoints and pass system and separation barrier stood between them. And yet he was determined not to give up. Although his chances of being happily married to Rachel seemed as remote as lasting peace, he vowed to try. Remembering the letter's teachings about the meaning of true love, he led her out of the crowd. The only quiet place was an unoccupied set of stairs located on the plaza's upper boundary. He moved away from the marchers, Rachel at his side, and climbed the stairs. "I can't imagine life without you," he said.

"If you return to the West Bank and I stay in Jerusalem. . ." she trailed off.

"My father will never forgive my defying him. I can't go back."

"Can you stay at the monastery?"

"Not forever."

"I would let you stay with me, but it would be too dangerous. We were lucky last night at the monastery, but we'd be fools to tempt fate again."

He drew her close. "I can think of something even more dangerous."

"What would that be?"

He paused. "If we were to become man and wife."

She stared at him, surprise etched on her face. "Are you proposing to me?"

He turned the ring and remembered where it had come from, what it represented. Then he nodded.

For a moment her eyes searched his and then she became still. "You're right—marrying *would* be dangerous but not just because of our differences. We haven't known each other long."

He reached for her hand and intertwined his fingers with hers. "Doesn't the letter say that love is always a risk?" When she stared at the passing marchers and didn't respond, he realized how true the statement was. He hadn't planned to propose quite that way. The words had tumbled out spontaneously, surprising him as much as her. Now the feeling of risk settled over him like one of Ezra's threats. If she said no, Karim knew he would be crushed, but he had to take the risk. He stroked the back of her hand with his thumb.

Perhaps he should have waited. Perhaps he should have chosen a quieter place, a more romantic setting, a more opportune moment. But with all the dangers they faced, would he get another chance? He longed to take Rachel away from the strife and oppression, to find a place where they would be accepted as a couple and allowed to live in peace, but if they didn't stay here and work for change, no such place would ever exist. He would never have chosen the middle of the march as the time—and the Wailing Wall plaza as the place—to propose. He sensed that they had chosen him. With Rachel's eyes expressing all the warring emotions he felt, he couldn't turn away.

She stared down again, and for him time was passing as slowly as . . . eternity. How could he have dared hope that she, an Israeli Jew, could love him, a Palestinian Muslim? But he did hope, and now she was about to break his heart.

Finally she met his gaze and with a teary smile surprised him by saying, "I would be proud to be your wife."

A surge of relief and then joy rushed through him as he took her in his arms. He wanted to marry her here and now, before she changed her mind, before their world exploded into violence again. "When can we set the date?"

"As soon as we can find a rabbi to perform the ceremony."

He kissed her tenderly. "And an imam?"

She pulled back and laughed. "Yes, of course, *and* an imam."

Karim slipped the ring off his little finger and held it up. "This ring belonged to my mother. I want you to wear it."

Rachel hesitated, eyeing the ring as if caught off guard. "But the way your mother died . . . there are painful memories associated with that ring. Are you sure you want me to wear it?"

He took her hand. "The best way to forget sad memories is to replace them with happy ones." He slid the ring onto her finger. "Let's make the future better than the past."

She admired the ring. "How would your mother have felt about having a Jewish daughter-in-law?"

"Horrified." Karim gave her a wide smile. "But the horror would have ended the moment she met you."

Soaring applause almost drowned out Karim's words. With the ceremony underway, they rejoined the vast crowd. Rabbi Jonathan Meltzer was speaking from the elevated platform that had been set up in the unrestricted area in front of the Wailing Wall. He was affirming the hope that the State of Israel offers to Jews all over the world, and he lauded the country's achievements in education, business, health care, and the arts. But when the applause died down, he emphasized the dire consequences of failing to make peace. "A one-state reality would emerge with disastrous consequences not only for Israel and Palestine but also for the entire world."

"Rabbi Meltzer is almost finished," Karim told Rachel. "You had better get to the platform." As Karim glanced to his left, he noticed a familiar face.

The square-jawed man in the IDF uniform was standing at the northern wall of the plaza with two other soldiers, tear gas rifles in hand.

Ezra Sharett.

Karim pointed him out to Rachel.

"I just hope he remains calm," she said.

Karim ducked behind a tall balding gentleman in front of them. "We'd better separate so your brother doesn't see us together."

She was about to leave, but he stopped her. "I love you, Rachel Sharett."

She nodded once, eyes teary. Then she was gone. Karim weaved through the marchers to join them near the platform. He watched as Brother Gregory and the monks, guarded by the soldiers, set the scroll beside the podium.

Rabbi Meltzer finished his remarks by praising Rachel as a founder of the Abrahamic Peace Initiative and introducing her. The crowd applauded as the rabbi embraced her.

When she stepped to the microphone, she had to wait a full two minutes for the applause to die down before beginning her remarks. "We are here to call for an end to violence and oppression!" Rachel's fervent cry elicited an energetic roar from the crowd, sending a swirl of energy through Karim. When the noise receded, she continued, "We know that the fighting will only end when Palestinians and Israelis live in sovereign states with secure borders. The leaders on both sides know this too. Today we invite them to dream with us and begin to heal our individual and collective suffering. No political, economic or military opposition can prevail against this unifying force. The day of victory is drawing near."

Another roar surged through the crowd. When the furor subsided, a college-age woman holding a banner in front yelled, "How can we succeed when all past efforts have failed?"

Rachel held up her hands and motioned for quiet. "Let me tell you a story. There was once a great civilization built along the banks of a mighty river. The people thrived until they polluted the river and began to die from the diseases it spread. Their only hope was the pure water of a deep lake at the top of a nearby mountain, but the lake's tributaries were clogged with debris and couldn't be cleared because of the extreme danger involved.

"A young man climbed up to the lake and successfully opened a passage through which the water could flow. But he was swept downstream and killed in the process. The people found his body at the bottom of the mountain and buried him with honor. On his tombstone they wrote, 'Greater love has no one than this—to lay down one's life for others.'"

Karim kept his eyes riveted on Rachel, as did everyone in the crowd.

"What does the story mean?" the slender young woman asked.

Rachel spoke from the depths of conviction. "Justice is the pure mountain water. When it rolls down like a mighty stream, it gives life to everyone in the land. But justice has a cost. It requires that we lay down our lives for others. And who can do this? Only those who have love in their hearts. This love is the foundation of all ethical religion. I'm talking about religion rooted in equality, truth, freedom, and peace. The United Nations can't manufacture this religion or impose it, nor can any nation. Religion that heals and unites arises from honest, open hearts. It inspires courage, self-awareness, and deep repentance. Its spiritual essence confronts the darkness in us all and brings it into the light."

"We want peace!" The cry in Arabic came from Karim's right. When similar chants arose in Hebrew, and then in English and French and German, goose bumps climbed up Karim's arms. The crowd applauded with such fervor that it sounded like thunder.

"Only the two-state solution can transform religious bigotry and violence into justice that flows like a mighty stream," Rachel said, her thick, lustrous hair falling forward.

Karim noticed the crowd growing silent as she pushed her hair back and pressed on.

"We've come to a turning point in history. The Israeli-Palestinian conflict not only causes untold suffering in this land but also fuels the fires of terrorism around the world. The window of opportunity for solving this conflict is closing, and if we don't succeed, terrorism could be visited upon the world for generations to come.

"I've found a new resource for addressing the cause of the hatred and violence. It's a letter that Jesus of Nazareth wrote to Mary Magdalene, and it addresses the spiritual alienation at the heart of the problem." She pointed to the scroll. "This letter was recently discovered and is here in front of me. We know that the letter is genuine because it has been thoroughly tested. Even the Vatican has authenticated it. The letter's insights shed new light on the meaning of religion for these times. As a Jew I regard Jesus as a spiritual teacher. He is also a prophet in Islam. Somehow we Jews and Muslims must learn to make peace. And I believe that this letter can help us."

When murmurs arose in the crowd, Rachel said, "I know you must be wondering what Jesus and Mary Magdalene have to do with Jews and Muslims. Let me explain." She held up her hands for silence. "Jesus' struggle with his love for Mary Magdalene led him to an encounter with the creation story accepted by Jews, Christians, and Muslims. He received a revelation of God's image in him as male and female. The integration between the masculine and feminine in Jesus was essential to his spiritual genius. The gifts of his feminine side are available to all people today—creativity, compassion, a capacity for relationship, a nurturing spirit, the ability to feel and express emotion. But in order to receive these gifts, we must encounter the fullness of God.

"Here lies the mystery and challenge for Judaism, Christianity, and Islam. Our revelations of God are weighted in favor of the masculine. We primarily see God as powerful, rational, and authoritative; therefore these are the qualities we revere in ourselves. If God is a warrior, we can justify our warlike tendencies and shun the work of peacemaking. Only by honoring and embracing the feminine dimension of the divine can we restore the balance that will make us whole. Then we'll care for one another's children as if they were our own, and we'll stop killing in the name of God. The Jesus letter has been discovered now when we most need it. May its wisdom become a vital resource for Christians, Muslims, and Jews in our joined quest for peace."

As Rachel finished, she invited the marchers to join hands and sing:

Hand in hand we'll start the journey that will lead beyond the past.
Hand in hand we'll find the peace that's strong enough to last.
Divided we will surely fail; there'll be no peace at all
Just wars and confrontations, just barriers and walls.
Beyond the far horizon, someday we'll understand
That we must walk together hand in hand.

The crowd's singing morphed into chants of "Peace, peace, peace!" in many languages. Pride welled up in Karim that the woman he would soon marry had evoked such fervor from the marchers. He wanted to join in, but then he remembered his brother Saed's tragic, senseless suicide attack, and a tightness in his throat silenced him. Karim yearned to catch Rachel's eye, to receive some sign of her love. He moved forward, never taking his eyes off her.

As he drew close enough for her to see him, he noticed a man in front quickly move toward the platform. Rachel flashed Karim a radiant smile, reminding him why he was willing to risk everything for her. But he had no time to savor the gesture because the man climbed onto the platform. Alarmed, Karim hastened forward. The marchers applauded Rachel's speech, their chanting reaching fever pitch. She waved to the throng and backed away from the microphone. As Karim drew near, he recognized the man who was now on the stage.

Robert Kenyon.

Karim pushed through the assemblage, ignoring the shouts of anger, but he couldn't reach Kenyon before he stepped in front of Rachel and spoke into the microphone. "My name is Dr. Robert Kenyon. I'm the archaeologist who discovered this scroll. The Government Antiquities Agency should never have allowed it to be here. The scroll belongs in a museum and should be returned immediately."

A middle-aged woman who wore an orange *hijab* said, "That scroll gives hope to *all* people, not just Christians and Jews, and not just men. It gives hope to Muslim *women* too."

"No!" Robert Kenyon shouted, and then grabbed the podium as several march organizers and guards tried to lead him away. He resisted, throwing fists and elbows, until they finally subdued him. Rachel appealed for calm, but five men wearing the Roman collars of priests were making their way to the podium. One of them, a burly, round-faced man with reddish hair, pushed his way in front of the microphone. He caused a commotion among the monks when he said, "We agree with Dr. Kenyon. The scroll doesn't belong here."

Karim felt a sinking sensation in his chest as the priests and monks faced each other. Pushing and shoving erupted in the crowd, jostling him forward. Seconds later he heard screams as Jews fought Muslims, and Christians fought Jews. He glanced at the stage and saw Rachel trying to break up the scuffle between the priests and monks. Then, out of the corner of his eye, Karim glimpsed Ezra Sharett and the soldiers as they prepared to fire tear-gas canisters. Ezra raised a bullhorn and warned the crowd to disperse, but the fighting escalated until he gave a final warning. It was lost in the melee.

Seconds later, shots erupted and tear-gas canisters were detonated among the fighters. One canister landed on the stage, shrouding it in smoke. The marchers began to flee, coughing and gagging. Some of them fell. Others, blinded by the tear gas, tripped over them. The running and falling bodies created a scene of chaos on the plaza, the smell acrid, the shrieks and cries fever-pitched. Brother Gregory and the monks shielded the scroll as the fight intensified.

As the smoke cleared, Karim heard a shot and watched as Rachel slowly collapsed onto the stage floor.

No, no, no! Please, Allah, no! The prayer echoed in Karim's mind as he pushed toward the platform, more a demand than a request. As he climbed onto the steps, the demand became an attempt to bargain. *I will do anything for you, merciful Allah. Anything! Just let Rachel live.*

He wanted the prayer to be about her, but it was also about him. About the thirst of a man running out of water in the desert. About his slow death beneath a sky without stars. He had to get to her, had to help her. She was all that lay between him and a life of heartbreak and loneliness.

Karim felt the scorching sun burn through him as he ran toward Rachel. She was on her back, holding her chest where the bullet-like tear-gas cylinder had hit, her white cotton blouse wet with blood. He knelt beside her and stroked her forehead. "Rachel, it's Karim."

"Please help me." Her words were strained, barely audible.

Karim waved and shouted to the medical personnel stationed near the platform. "Help is coming. I won't leave you. I love you."

Rachel squeezed his hand, her fingers covered in blood, and spoke in a raspy voice. "I love you too."

The platform shook. Karim glanced up and saw the soldiers approaching, saw—Commander Ezra Sharett.

"Oh, my God, no!" Ezra waved the three emergency medical workers over and knelt beside her. "Please, Rachel, you can't die." Then he glanced up and gestured toward Karim. "Arrest this man! He's in the city illegally." Two soldiers grabbed him.

"*Nooo!* I can't leave Rachel." Karim tried to shake off the soldiers. Staring into Ezra's furious eyes, he yelled, "You did this. You shot her. You're the one who should go to jail!"

Karim could hear Rachel groan as the soldiers yanked him up. He fought them, twisting left and right, planting his feet and pushing against their weight. "No, no, Rachel! Don't die . . . I love you!"

Out of the corner of his eye, Karim glimpsed Ezra kneeling at her side as the emergency workers attended to her. The soldiers handcuffed him, hustled him out to the street, and turned him over to the Israeli police.

CHAPTER FORTY-NINE

WHEN JUDITH WOKE ON THE SABBATH OF PASSOVER, SHE KEPT HER EYES CLOSED AND LAY PERFECTLY STILL. If she shut out the light, perhaps it would go away. Perhaps she could fall asleep again and escape her anguish a little longer.

Or never wake up.

But the light penetrated her eyelids like an attacking intruder, and the stronger it got, the more her dread increased. It was a new day—the day after the crucifixions of Jesus and Dismas. Her head was spinning, her stomach upset, her energy drained. *Why couldn't I die too?* She sat up, squinting against the light.

The slant of the sun told her that it was nearly noon. She glanced around and remembered where she was—in a bedroom of the house where the soldiers had arrested her. After neatly folding the bedclothes, she moved to the window to hear the voices of the women in the courtyard below. They were carried up to her on a crisp spring breeze, its freshness in jarring contrast to the stench of death in the air the day before.

She stepped to the window, straightened her soiled tunic, and ran a hand through her tangled hair. Memories of Golgotha tore at her, evoking self-loathing. She gripped the window ledge to steady herself. Denying that the events had happened would accomplish nothing. She had to face them and somehow accept that life would never be the same.

Her only hope came from the words that Jesus had spoken to her in the prison. He said that God had forgiven her, and that she would find new life by forgiving herself. At Golgotha he had pleaded for forgiveness for those who crucified him. She knew she was one of them. Remembering how she had supported the Zealots and sinned with Dismas, she whispered a prayer for mercy. Now she needed to follow his teachings and show her gratitude by sharing them with others. Perhaps his closest followers would take her in. If so, she would help them in any way she could, for she felt as if she had become one of them.

She walked down the stairs, through the living quarters, and out to the courtyard. There, gathered around a wooden table, were Mary Magdalene and the other Mary, along with Susanna, Joanna, Salome, and Jesus' mother. They were combining lamb with some vegetables for the Passover meal.

"We knew you were exhausted, so we let you rest." Mary Magdalene gave Judith a faint smile, her face pale and streaked with weariness. Mary appeared different today—smaller, almost frail, as if she had been sick and was losing the battle to regain her strength.

"Where's John?" Judith asked.

The sandy-haired Susanna looked up. "He's out searching for Jesus' disciples."

Salome, a slender woman with a ruddy complexion, cut a piece of lamb and placed it on a plate. Judith marveled at the quiet courage with which the women were bearing their sorrow. When Mary Magdalene went into the kitchen, Judith followed her. "I desperately need to bathe. May I before we eat?"

Mary Magdalene interrupted her preparations and led Judith to the bathing area on the bottom level of the house. Judith slipped off her tunic, which was grimy from the prison and Golgotha, and slid into the cool water. To her surprise, Mary Magdalene stayed and rubbed her back with a soft sponge.

"You are being very brave," Mary said.

"It only appears that way. I've cried so many tears that I have none left."

Mary's voice became quiet and strained with sadness. "Nor do I, and tomorrow we must go to the tomb early and finish embalming Jesus' body."

Judith turned around abruptly. "Oh, Mary, what will we do without him? We don't even have the letter to remember him by."

Mary squeezed water from the sponge. "It angers me that the centurion took it. I didn't even have the chance to read what Jesus wrote. My only consolation is that if we live by his teachings and love as he did, he will be with us always."

"I *need* Jesus to be with me." Judith splashed water on her face, whispering a silent prayer for Dismas and Gabriel. "And with my child."

Mary turned her around again and resumed rubbing her back. "Then you must find your mission and live it as bravely as Jesus lived his. He's closest to us when we follow his example." Mary cupped water in her hands and poured it over Judith's shoulders. "Jesus was more whole than any man I have known. He helped me to become whole too, and find my inner wealth."

Judith rinsed her arms with water, puzzled by what Mary Magdalene had said. "How can a single woman be wealthy?"

"When she first finds happiness with God." Mary scooped water onto Judith's neck and back. "Jesus taught me that. Now I love him even more—with a love that goes beyond physical attraction. He taught me to claim my untapped power and truly become independent. Taking that step was frightening, but I needed to do it to grow, and he couldn't have taught me these things as my lover, only as my friend and guide."

Judith washed her face with soap, thinking about Mary's words and pondering her feelings for Gabriel. "I don't have as much courage as you do."

"It's not so much courage as a commitment to my own well-being. If we choose to have a relationship with a man, we must enter into it freely and joyfully, not out of need. That means we must draw on our deepest strength, and, unfortunately, strong women often threaten men. The way to reassure them is to help them grow too. When they become whole and free, as Jesus was, they will no longer fear us. Then men and women can relate to each other as equals, and they can finally achieve God's highest dreams for them."

Judith rinsed off her face. "If you didn't read the letter, how do you know its teachings so well?"

"I learned them from Jesus himself."

Judith swirled the water aimlessly with her hands. "I wish that Gabriel had learned them better—he left me, and I don't know if he will ever come back."

"Gabriel is having trouble accepting your pregnancy, as any man would." Mary Magdalene gently massaged Judith's neck. "The only way he can really come back is by growing. Perhaps you should write him a letter that expresses how you feel. Nicodemus will join us for our meal; he could deliver it to him."

Mary brought Judith a clean tunic, whispered a few more words of support, hugged her warmly and left. Judith stayed in the water and thought about writing to Gabriel. Written words seemed inadequate, but she finally decided that she needed to do it. She stayed in the water for a while longer, composing the letter in her mind.

All at once men's voices in the courtyard interrupted her thoughts. After stepping out of the water, she dried herself and put on the clean tunic. Returning to the courtyard, she recognized John and Matthew, Peter and Andrew, but she had not met the other men. John was explaining that he had found some of the disciples at the home of Mary, Martha, and Lazarus in Bethany. Others were staying in Jerusalem with a wealthy woman and her young son, John Mark.

Nicodemus and Joseph of Arimathea, wearing clean robes and carrying jars of myrrh and aloe, arrived as John was speaking. Mary Magdalene and several of the other women volunteered to go in the morning to complete the embalming. Judith stared at the floor, unsettled by the prospect of seeing and handling Jesus' crucified body again. But when Mary Magdalene asked her to join them, Judith sighed and, feeling obligated for all that the women had done for her, reluctantly agreed.

When the Passover meal was ready, Jesus' mother invited everyone upstairs to the room where the disciples had shared their last supper with Jesus. Judith reclined next to Nicodemus at the long table as Mary Magdalene brought in the lamb and vegetables. After Joseph of Arimathea gave the blessing, they began to eat in silence. Judith studied each face, the morbid expressions, all eyes red from weeping.

Mary Magdalene tried to lighten the mood. "I'm glad that all of you came. Jesus would want us to be together."

Peter did not take any food. "This is my last meal with you," he said without looking up. "I'm going back to fishing."

"Please don't leave us," Jesus' mother said. "We need your leadership, now more than ever."

Peter shook his head. "I let Jesus down. He predicted that I would deny him, and I did." Peter's voice broke. He grabbed the edge of the low table to steady his trembling hands. "When Jesus needed me most, I ran away." Peter swallowed hard, straining to speak. "Please let me go quietly. Forget that I ever came here. Forget that you ever knew me."

Matthew, heavyset and bearded, tried to comfort him. "I am no better than you. I ran away, just as you did."

Judith took a deep breath, her chest tightening. "I have something to tell all of you," she said, remembering the gift of her forgiveness and wanting to share it. "Jesus was in prison with me on the night of his arrest. I told him about the people I had hurt and betrayed, and about the deep shame I felt." Her lips trembled slightly. "He did not condemn me. Instead, he pleaded with me not to condemn myself. He said that my only hope was to love and forgive myself, as God already had." She paused and waited for Peter to look up before adding, "That is your only hope too."

Peter studied each face. "I will never recover from my shame as long as I live." He crossed his arms, lowered his head, and wept bitterly. When Mary Magdalene put a hand on his shoulder, he looked up. "I will stay here tonight and then leave for Galilee in the morning."

Moved by Peter's despair, Judith stood. Although a newcomer among the disciples, she had an important message for them and mustered the courage to speak it. "We are all terribly distraught right now, but we have to keep believing in the future." She swept her gaze around the table and met each set of eyes. "I had only begun to follow Jesus when he was crucified. My sins are many and deep, but he told me of a love greater than even the worst of them. Knowing that God loves me and will never give up on me, even when I give up on myself, has made me strong enough to go on." She looked at Peter. "God hasn't given up on you either. What you see as a terrible failure may be the beginning of a miracle in your life. It was in mine."

Judith sat down, her face hot from the stress of sharing something so personal. She glanced at Mary Magdalene across from her. Mary kept eating in the awkward silence that followed, and then put down her wine and cleared her throat. "I want you to know that Jesus wrote me a letter in which he shared his secret knowledge of love and relationships. He said that mysterious things would happen to the letter, and they have. I set the scroll down at Golgotha and a centurion called Longinus took it. The only way to get it back is to appeal to Pilate." Judith's heart was beating wildly as Mary turned toward Nicodemus and said, "Are you willing to make the appeal? You and Joseph persuaded Pilate to give you Jesus' body. Perhaps you can convince him to demand the scroll from Longinus."

Nicodemus' eyes glinted fiercely. "Yes, I will go to Pilate. We *must* get it back."

Judith squeezed Nicodemus' arm. "Thank you." She leaned closer and dropped her voice to a whisper. "And I have decided to write to Gabriel. Will you deliver my letter to him?"

Nicodemus gave her a reassuring smile. "Of course."

After they finished eating, Mary Magdalene led Judith away and gave her a quiet place to sit. Judith was ready to begin a new life but not on the shaky foundation of her old one. She had deeper wisdom to build on, the wisdom of Jesus that had made Mary Magdalene so strong and free. *I must help Gabriel to see that I have changed, that we could still have a future.* She picked up the stylus and began to write.

CHAPTER FIFTY

THE LAST TIME GABRIEL HAD PLANNED TO KILL SOMEONE, IT WAS HIMSELF. This time it was a Roman soldier. Consumed by anger, he had lost himself. And forgotten all that he had learned. He held a bleating lamb against his chest, concealing the dagger beneath his tunic. The Sabbath crowd swept him into the Temple as if he were a pebble in rushing water. Since leaving Golgotha, he had reflected on his heartbreak and realized who was the ultimate cause of it—the Romans! They had murdered Judith's brother and turned her and Dismas into outlaws. They had crucified Dismas and an innocent, righteous man, Jesus of Nazareth. Now the Romans would pay!

The throng led him into the Court of the Israelites, his temples pounding, his palms sweating. Lost in the madness of his fury, he ignored the smoky air and barely heard the Levite choir singing. Only when the priest took the squirming lamb for the sacrifice did the lyres, harps, and trumpets catch his ear. The soaring melodies and crashing cymbals at the words, "God's mercy endures forever," reverberated joyfully, but not for him. Nothing about the Temple—not the majestic courts nor the sweet-smelling incense nor the elaborate pageantry—could alter his plan for revenge.

Gabriel slipped away from the crowd and headed for the stairs to the high walkway. The last time he climbed here, he had tried to jump. This time, he would make the soldier on patrol his first victim.

He took the stairs two at a time, glancing furtively in each direction. Reaching the top without being noticed, he stepped behind a pillar and waited. He could hear footsteps. He reached for the dagger.

Then he looked down. The Temple's dazzling white marble, filigreed with silver and gold, gleamed in the late-afternoon sun. The rooftops of Jerusalem sparkled like a field of jewels. He remembered his horrendous wedding day, the ache in his heart, the terror in his gut. And he thought of Nicodemus, the man who had saved him.

Had the old Pharisee really taught him the secret of happiness? Or had Nicodemus' wisdom been folly? And what of the letter from Jesus? Gabriel had discarded it at Golgotha, and now he regretted it. Nicodemus had entrusted the letter to him, but it belonged to Mary Magdalene; she deserved to get it back.

Gabriel froze, paralyzed by remorse. Mary had tried to help Judith, and how had Gabriel shown his gratitude? By throwing the letter away like worthless litter. Attacking the soldier might mean never knowing what happened to it. His life would be changed forever—he could end up crucified like Dismas!

He gripped the dagger, unafraid to kill, but wondering whether he truly wanted revenge. The soldier drew near. Gabriel must lunge now, if ever. Then he remembered Jesus' lament from the cross: "Father, forgive them, for they know not what they do!"

Gabriel felt dazed, the lament echoing in his mind. He left the dagger in his belt and let go. The soldier walked past. Gabriel leaned against the pillar and drew a deep breath before descending the stairs. He would go immediately to Nicodemus' house, tell him about Judith's pregnancy, and explain what had happened to the letter. He owed Nicodemus that much for saving his life.

Jerusalem's streets were quiet. Gabriel sprinted along them, trying to convince himself that he was not a coward or a disloyal friend. By the time he reached Nicodemus' house, the Sabbath was ending. Fresh from his evening prayers, Nicodemus invited Gabriel in and said, "It was hard to pray tonight.

"Jesus' crucifixion was a terrible injustice." Gabriel followed him through the courtyard, remembering the shrieks of horror and the stench of death at Golgotha. When they reached the upstairs dining room, he withdrew the dagger from the belt inside his tunic. "I wanted revenge," he said. "I thought I'd use this on one of the soldiers at the Temple."

Nicodemus stepped away from the sharp blade. "I know how you feel. Joseph of Arimathea and I tried to defend Jesus in the Sanhedrin, but we lost. You want to lash out—I'm glad you thought better of it."

Gabriel tucked the dagger back into his belt. "I made things worse by throwing the letter away at Golgotha."

Nicodemus' expression turned grave. "Mary Magdalene told me that a centurion named Longinus now has the letter."

"I came to apologize for—"

Nicodemus waved a hand dismissively, interrupting. "Judith explained everything."

An image of Judith's terrified face came back to Gabriel, and his knees went weak. He hadn't planned to leave her at Golgotha, to run away like an impulsive child, but seeing his brother suffer on the cross had been too much to bear, especially when Judith confessed she was carrying Dismas' baby. Gabriel had become confused and needed time to sort out his feelings. He knew that he still loved Judith. His heart leapt when Nicodemus mentioned her name. But did he have a heart big enough to forgive her? He gathered his strength and straightened his knees. "How is she?" he asked.

"As well as can be expected. She took it hard when you left, but she still hopes that you will go back to her."

Gabriel shook his head. "I don't know if I can."

Nicodemus gestured toward the storage chamber and then led him to it. Once inside, Gabriel saw the dinnerware, the candelabras, the long robes and the parchments. Nicodemus removed his shawl and folded it; then he peered at Gabriel and said, "What you don't know is that Judith and Dismas were in this chamber when I was talking with you about your broken heart. She understood how deeply she had hurt you and what a mistake she made. She wants to start a new life."

Gabriel frowned. "But now she's pregnant with Dismas' child. I could never—"

Nicodemus put up a hand, interrupting. "Maybe, maybe not. The pregnancy could also be a blessing. Do you still love her?"

"I thought I did, but when she told me she was pregnant . . ."

Nicodemus became reflective. "Do you remember Jesus' discussion of Adam and Eve in the letter?"

"About their being one?"

Nicodemus put a hand on his shoulder. "They had to cope with betrayal. Eve acted deceitfully, and they got expelled from the Garden of Eden. God placed cherubim and a flaming sword at the entrance of the Garden so that they could not return. Adam and Eve had to venture into unexplored territory and build a new relationship outside of paradise. For any couple to find true love, they must do the same. The letter affirms that we only learn what love is by persevering through the hard times, and if we do not, we will spend our lives alone, because we cannot get back into Eden."

A sudden gust of anger battered Gabriel's heart, and he turned to leave. "I'd be happier alone—or with another woman."

Nicodemus held his arm. "Perhaps, perhaps not. You care deeply about Judith—otherwise you wouldn't have been so hurt when she left, and you wouldn't have wanted her back. The pregnancy is the problem. You're not sure you can raise your brother's child, and I can't resolve that question for you. I only know that if you accept love's challenge, it will take you places you never imagined going."

Gabriel stopped and turned around, his head aching with confusion. Judith was his first love, the woman whose smile had sent a shiver down his spine, the woman he had dreamed of lying with on their wedding night and raising a family and growing old with. His head pounded harder as he thought of how the dream had been denied. "I don't know if I still love Judith."

Nicodemus left the chamber and then returned shortly with a sheet of papyrus. "I hope this will help you decide what to do." He handed him the papyrus. "It is a letter from Judith."

He led Gabriel into the courtyard, offered him a chair, and lit some candles. Gabriel sat down and began to read:

My dearest Gabriel,

I haven't stopped thinking of you. Although you have every right to throw this letter away, I hope you will read it and give me one last chance to tell you what is in my heart. I can't undo the pain I have created, and nothing can justify the shameful way I treated you. If I had known on our wedding day what I know now, I would have married you, and joyfully! There was a lot I needed to learn—lessons about true love.

Everything changed for me on a Sabbath afternoon when Dismas and I overheard the conversation that you and Nicodemus were having in his dining room. We were hiding, stealing from this good man, when you came in. We escaped when you left suddenly. What Nicodemus said was meant to help you, but it also helped me. I saw—really saw—how much I had hurt you, and I began to understand sexual attraction, and why we get so swept up in it.

I read the letter that Jesus of Nazareth wrote Mary Magdalene, and I now know that this attraction involves the soul. When two people remain unaware of this mystery, the attraction becomes powerful enough to overwhelm them.

This is what happened to me, but God's voice spoke through the words of Jesus, assuring me of forgiveness, affirming my worth, lifting the burden of my shame and guilt. On the night before his crucifixion, Jesus and I were imprisoned together. In those desperate hours, he told me to forgive myself, a lesson I'm still trying to learn. I recognized what an extraordinary man he is, how perfectly the male and the female are unified in him, and I saw his deep serenity in the face of death.

I also met Mary Magdalene, and she brought me further understanding. She shared with me how Jesus taught her to claim her worth apart from that of a man. I am learning how to become strong and independent by finding the untapped power within me. I am also learning that I don't need a man in order to survive, but if I choose to love again, I believe I could do it in a healthy way.

I only wish that I had learned these lessons earlier, and that you had been spared the pain I caused you. I could spend a lifetime making it up to you, but penance would do neither of us any good. I want to be done with guilt and shame and get on with my life. I have found the way to healing, and I hope that you will too. In fact, I hope that I can become part of your healing. From our mutual suffering, perhaps we alone can give each other joy.

I love you, Gabriel, and I'll never stop. I want to laugh and cry with you, and nurse you when you're sick, and hold you when you're scared. Most of all, I want to be your friend and share your dreams, until one of us closes the other's eyes.

But in order for us to be together, you must become as whole as I am becoming. Our marriage would work only if our souls are both growing. We must be true equals and bring out the best in each other. Only then will we redeem the past and become the strong, caring parents that my child needs. You must decide if an equal marriage is really what you want.

I'm staying with Jesus' disciples. Nicodemus knows where. If you're ready to forgive, please meet me there. If you don't come, I will make my own way, knowing what you have chosen. No matter what happens, I will always want the best for you and pray for your safety and happiness.

Judith

Gabriel stared at the letter for a long time, his eyes moist. He knew what he had to do.

CHAPTER FIFTY-ONE

A SENSATION OF NUMBNESS RIPPLED THROUGH JUDITH WHEN MARY MAGDALENE SHOOK HER AWAKE. It was early on the first day of the week, and still dark outside. Terrified by the thought of seeing the crucified Jesus again, Judith felt paralyzed. But when Mary Magdalene tightened her determined grip and intensified her impassioned whispers, Judith had no choice but to keep her promise: She would go with the women to finish the embalming. She got up, hastily brushed her hair and put on her sandals and cloak. Mary held her hand and guided her down the stairs by candlelight.

In the courtyard Salome, Susanna, Joanna, and Mary, the mother of James, were waiting with jars of embalming spices and ointments. Careful not to wake the disciples, they led Mary Magdalene and Judith out of the courtyard. Judith surrendered to their grim procession, her legs wobbly and her eyes downcast, like those of the other women.

Jerusalem lay quiet, the air brisk. Judith caught a whiff of hibiscus and almond blossoms, but the spring freshness seemed more cruel than welcoming, mocking her grief with hope. She dreaded the task of embalming Jesus' body, of seeing his gruesome wounds again, of touching his death-stiffened frame. Pausing, she let the others go ahead. Before the crucifixion, the only dead person she had ever seen was her four-year-old brother Reuben.

But now he was gone.

Forever gone.

So was Dismas. And Jesus. And Gabriel.

And she was alone.

She realized that Jesus wouldn't want her to dwell on these thoughts, but she couldn't stop them. Oh, why had she promised to go with Mary Magdalene? Why had she not insisted that the others finish the embalming? With so much on her mind, how could she relive the numbing horrific events? She wanted to find somewhere to hide and never come out, but when Mary Magdalene glanced back at her, Judith ran to catch up and walked with the women through Jerusalem's empty streets beneath a silent blue-black sky.

As she and the women retraced their steps from three days earlier, Golgotha's forbidding outline came into view. Judith noticed a glimmer of light on the predawn horizon; she heard a cock crowing in the distance; she watched as a few pigeons landed nearby with a single squawk. The stillness was interrupted only by the songs of birds welcoming the day. Ever so slowly, the light expanded, coloring the horizon pinkish orange. She felt as if her heart were expanding too, as her hope struggled to return. Her breathing quickened. In order for hope to sustain her, she would have to nurture it like the child in her womb.

The dawn reminded her of Mary Magdalene's promise to help. Like the sun, Judith would rise again. Regardless of what Gabriel did, she had no choice—she had to care for her baby. She promised herself to do so and to help Mary Magdalene and the disciples keep Jesus' legacy alive. If only they had the letter! It would remind them of Jesus' teachings and make it easier to spread them. Perhaps Nicodemus could convince Pilate to order Longinus to return it.

Judith paused at Joseph of Arimathea's garden, staggered by the rich colors and dizzying fragrances. The fig trees hung heavy with the green fruit of spring; the terebinths stood tall and broad, as if guarding the treasures of Eden. Red roses and white lilies and pink almond blossoms—they were all startling in their untamed virgin freshness. And yet amid all the glories of the earth, Judith sensed a foreboding of something yet to come. Her temples throbbed in anticipation as the gentle breeze died and the air became stagnant and the birds stopped their joyous singing.

Suddenly the ground began to shake. "Earthquake!" Judith's entire body shook and she had to fight to steady herself. The trembling increased and she was thrown down. She dug her fingers into the dusty ground, desperate to hang on, terrified of being swallowed alive. The rumbling went on for minutes. As she tensed every muscle, the ground gradually became still and the garden quiet. She got up and stared at the tombs, their entrances carved into the craggy stone hillside. The front of the middle one, where Joseph and Nicodemus had placed Jesus' body, appeared as dark as a starless night.

Something was wrong.

No stone was covering its entrance!

The women ran to the tomb. Along with the others, Judith peered cautiously inside and then entered, her pulse racing. Where was Jesus' body? A young man was sitting on the right side, his face shining like the sun, his robe whiter than bleached wool. The women were terrified and bowed their faces to the ground, but the young man greeted them and said, "Do not be afraid; I know that you are looking for Jesus who was crucified. He is not here; for he is risen, as he said. Come, see the place where he lay. Then go quickly and tell his disciples, 'He has been raised from the dead, and indeed he is going ahead of you to Galilee; there you will see him again.' This is my message for you."

Judith was shaking. Raised? How could it be? Had the Romans stolen Jesus' body? Had they sent the young man to cover up their treachery?

Mary Magdalene threw her jar of spices into the air and took off running. Joanna reached out and grabbed her by the tunic, slowing her until they were running side by side. The jar hit the rocky ground with a crash and broke open, but no one stopped for it. Judith clung to Salome and they lurched forward together. Mary, the mother of James, was sprinting away from them; they strained to keep up.

Judith raced through the early dawn, legs churning, arms pumping, lungs burning. As she pulled even with Mary Magdalene, she heard a man's voice from behind. "Wait! Someone is calling us." Everyone stopped and turned.

"Greetings!" the man said with a distinctive resonance.

She saw who was standing there. It was the man who had come to her in prison. The man who had healed her of shame and guilt.

Jesus!

He was standing right in front of her, his face brilliant, his arms outstretched. She recognized him and began to tremble, the color draining from her face, her feet freezing in place. The other women recognized him too. Immediately they all fell at his feet. "Do not be afraid," he said. "Go and tell my brothers to go to Galilee; there they will see me." Then he was gone.

Judith and the others arose and began to run again, but she noticed that Mary Magdalene had stopped, tears streaming down her cheeks. "Mary, come with us!"

Mary Magdalene waved dismissively and shook her head no. Judith couldn't understand why Mary wasn't coming with them, but she also couldn't wait for her—she had to tell the disciples the shocking news.

Judith sprinted through Jerusalem's streets, dodging merchants and laborers who were opening their shops or going to work. *How could Jesus appear to us?* Questions catapulted through her mind as she trembled in fear and amazement. She had seen him with her own eyes and heard him with her own ears. He was alive!

As the women entered the house, she asked, "How can we tell the disciples? They will never believe us."

"Never believe what?" Peter came into the kitchen, concern in his voice.

John was close behind him, alarm written on his face. "What is all the noise about?"

Susanna began to speak, but suddenly went mute, unable to describe the wonder. Judith blurted out, "It is Jesus. We went to the tomb and found it empty. An angel spoke to us!" Giddy with excitement, she could barely get out the words. Tears were streaming down her cheeks. "The angel said that God has raised Jesus from the dead! We came running to tell you, and Jesus himself greeted us. We have seen the Lord!"

Joanna put an arm around her and smiled triumphantly. "You must believe her," she said, her voice surging with joy. "Jesus is not dead but alive!"

Peter shifted his gaze to each of the women, scrutinizing them with disbelief. "Are you mad? Why have you come here talking foolishness?"

The rest of the disciples rushed in to see what the excitement was about. When Matthew heard the news, he said, "Must you tell idle tales at a time like this?"

The thin-faced Bartholomew grimaced and shouted, "This isn't funny!"

"Women! They cannot be trusted!" Andrew said, shaking his head.

"They talk utter nonsense!" Thomas said, throwing his hands up in exasperation.

While the disciples were expressing their displeasure, Mary Magdalene opened the door, her face so radiant that Judith stepped back when she saw it. Every eye was riveted on Mary. She explained that the mystery and the terror had exhausted her, that she had slowed down to catch her breath. "Then Jesus appeared to me again, and I ran all the way here," she said. "He is alive! Go see for yourselves!"

Peter and John leapt up and ran out the door. The women gathered around Mary Magdalene in the kitchen as the remaining disciples shook their heads and went upstairs to pack for home.

"Jesus really *did* appear to me. He told me he will love me forever; then he reminded me of the secret of his eternal love, and commissioned me to proclaim the secret fearlessly." Mary folded her arms on her chest and gripped them to stop her shaking. "Why would I tell tales about something so serious?"

Judith embraced her. "I believe you, Mary."

Mary Magdalene smiled and said, "Let the men think what they want. We must trust our own experience and speak boldly of what we have seen and heard."

"But what will we tell people?" Judith asked. "If they didn't know Jesus, why would they care if he is alive?"

Mary became still for a moment, deep in thought. "People will care because his resurrection gives hope to everyone. If he conquered suffering and death, how can we doubt that he is with us? He took the worst evil and transformed it to new life; so can we. His resurrection tells us that darkness never wins. Today a new era of light and love has dawned."

As the women began to prepare breakfast, Judith spoke to Mary Magdalene. "It may seem selfish at this wondrous time, but I'm still worried that I have lost Gabriel."

Mary Magdalene looked at her with understanding and squeezed her hand. Just then Salome reentered the kitchen and said, "Judith, you have a visitor."

Salome was smiling broadly as she led Judith to the kitchen door. When Judith saw who was standing there, she stepped back.

Gabriel.

He hugged her and whispered, "I missed you. Your letter meant so much."

Mary Magdalene hugged them both and said to Gabriel, "I'm so glad you found her, and I hope you'll never let her go. Now I must catch up with Peter and John."

As Mary rushed out the door, Judith gazed at Gabriel, unable to turn away. "I'm so glad you came. This morning has changed everything."

"Can we talk somewhere?" Gabriel asked.

Judith took his hand and led him into the sitting room. After he had shut the door, he said, "There is so much I want to tell you." But instead of speaking, he took her in his arms and kissed her. She submitted freely, savoring his gentle embrace and the soft contours of his lips.

At last she stepped back and gazed into his moist tawny eyes, so warm that they almost shone. "Oh, Gabriel, I have wanted you so, and I thought that I had lost you forever. I love you, and I'm so glad you came back to me." She led him to the long couch.

Gabriel sat down and pulled her beside him. "I'm so sorry that I left you at Golgotha. It was all too much, and I acted like a coward. When I got away and thought about everything that had happened, I realized how angry I was at the Romans and wanted to attack a soldier. Fortunately I found Nicodemus instead. He's a very wise man. He helped me with my anger and explained what love really means. After I read the letter you wrote me, I had no choice but to come find you. What you said in the letter confirmed everything that I learned from Nicodemus. I, too, want to start a new life with you based on Jesus' teachings." He reached for her hand. "Please come with me."

Judith gazed into his vulnerable eyes and wondered how to tell him about the events of the morning. She feared he wouldn't believe them. "Everything has changed. The women and I went to the tomb at dawn, and we found it empty. A strange man told us that God had raised Jesus from the dead. Then, when we were running back to tell the disciples, Jesus himself greeted us, and he appeared again to Mary Magdalene. He is alive, Gabriel! Even the cross could not defeat him!"

He furrowed his brow. "How do you expect me to believe that?"

"I know it sounds impossible, and I cannot explain or prove it, but I *know* that God raised Jesus from the dead. I experienced his presence."

While she was still speaking, shouting erupted in the kitchen. She grabbed Gabriel's hand and they ran to see what was happening. The women and the disciples were running out to the courtyard. She and Gabriel followed them, and once outside, they saw Peter and John.

"It's true," Peter said. "The tomb is empty!"

John spoke in a hushed voice. "I saw Jesus' shroud and grave wrappings with my own eyes. They were all he left behind."

Everyone in the courtyard fell silent, awed by reports too disturbing and wonderful to fathom. Judith noticed how pale Peter and John appeared, as if they hadn't seen the sun for weeks. They were nervously wringing their hands, their eyes wide.

Thomas became impatient. "Peter, you are acting as strangely as the women," he said. "So are you, John." He headed for the street and then turned to face the group. "When people die, they stay dead. To believe otherwise is the height of stupidity."

When Thomas left, it was as if he had given everyone permission to speak again. The courtyard came alive with conversations about the empty tomb and Jesus' appearances and how mysterious it all was. Judith glanced at Gabriel and saw confusion in his eyes. Her lips dry and her breathing shallow, she wondered if he was ready to follow Thomas. Did he believe her story? Did he think she was lying? It was important for her to know. "Some of the men think they have heard an idle tale. What do you think?" she asked.

Gabriel threw up his hands. "How can I be sure? You've told me what you saw and experienced, but honestly . . . it's hard to accept."

Her eyes remained locked on his. "Then you must see for yourself." She took his arm and guided him toward the street.

CHAPTER FIFTY-TWO

GABRIEL STIFLED QUESTIONS HE DARED NOT FACE AS HE FOLLOWED JUDITH TOWARD JOSEPH OF ARIMATHEA'S GARDEN. He knew that their future depended on what the tomb revealed. Skeptical of her story, he didn't say a word as they hurried through Jerusalem's crowded streets, dodging pilgrims headed home after Passover. What if she were lying? If Jesus' body were still in the tomb, he could never trust her again.

A cold chill crawled up his spine as Judith led him into the garden. She moved confidently, as if she owned it, jaw firmly set, lips pursed so tightly that her cheeks twitched. Gabriel watched her out of the corner of his eye, captivated by her resolve but certain that he could not stay with any woman given to deceit.

Gabriel approached the hillside below Golgotha and caught his first glimpse of the tomb. He froze in disbelief. The tomb was indeed open. Judith glanced at him. His heart turned over as she grabbed his hand and broke into a run. He resisted, but she yanked his arm so hard that he was compelled to follow.

When they got to the tomb, she led him inside. The morning sun was shining in, illuminating the ledge where Jesus' body should have been. But Gabriel saw only a linen shroud on the ledge, along with some wrappings and a cloth napkin folded neatly at the far end. He drew back, terrified. "I suspect foul play." He rushed to the entrance of the tomb and cautiously peered out.

Judith followed him. "What kind of foul play?"

"Someone must have stolen the body, or the Romans may have moved it to discourage Jesus' followers from coming here."

"Then why would they have left his grave clothes behind?"

"Because they wanted to make it mysterious so that everyone would wonder what happened."

Judith threw up a hand. "That makes no sense. The Romans crave peace. To raise questions about Jesus' body would only stir up controversy."

Gabriel went back to the slab where the grave clothes lay. He wanted to believe her, but his mind raced with questions. "Criminals don't think logically. How can we understand their motives?"

Judith moved between Gabriel and the slab. "You're not thinking logically either. The miracle is not only that Jesus' body is gone but also that he appeared to me and the others. We saw him with our own eyes. He spoke to us and we felt his presence. In order to refute that, you'd have to say that we all had delusions at the same time. That's highly unlikely."

Gabriel stared at the grave clothes, unable to move or speak. He understood her point, but accepting it would mean that he would have to believe in a miracle. As much as he wanted to believe and to continue their relationship, his mind rebelled against the idea. Then, before he realized what he was doing, he reached out and touched the wrappings. Their thin, tightly woven fabric felt rough against his skin. He stared at the ledge, mesmerized, unable to turn away from its emptiness or to release the shroud.

Warmth surged through every fiber of his body. He smelled hibiscus mixed with the gingery scent of the embalming spices—the sweetness was intoxicating. He could no longer tell where his fingers ended and the shroud began, as if his skin had become part of the fabric. It seemed that his mind and body were merging with the earth of the tomb, the sweet spring air, the dusty floor, and with Judith too.

He sensed that someone unseen was with them, and that this presence was part of him and he of the presence, filling him with total peace. The experience was like passing through an ocean storm in a small boat when suddenly the winds grow calm, the rain ceases, and the cresting waves fold down into themselves to become a sea of glass.

Judith was not lying. Something miraculous *had* happened to her and the other women—he could trust that now. The evidence of her joy, combined with his own peacefulness, convinced him that Jesus' resurrection was, in some mysterious way, true. This Galilean rabbi who had unlocked the mysteries of his soul, this healing counselor who had taught him the meaning of forgiveness, this radical prophet who had been crucified and buried, was with him still.

Gabriel turned, took Judith in his arms and held her. Neither said a word. She surrendered to his embrace, turning her head and laying it against his chest. He rocked her back and forth, his eyes closed, the words of her letter repeating in his mind:

I want to laugh and cry with you, and nurse you when you are sick, and hold you when you are scared. Most of all, I want to be your friend, until one of us closes the other's eyes.

His throat grew tight as he leaned back and measured her through watery eyes. She was weeping too. In her tears he saw sincerity and knew that he could love her—*and* her child, always.

He lowered his head to kiss her, but before their lips met, he heard footsteps outside the tomb. Stepping back, he seized her arm and pressed a finger to his lips. Whoever was out there might not like their being inside. He moved to the back of the tomb and, holding Judith tightly, braced himself for the worst.

CHAPTER FIFTY-THREE

THE STONE ON THE FAR WALL FELT SHARP AGAINST JUDITH'S SHOULDERS. This morning had been full of surprises; now here was one more. Had the other women or the disciples followed her and Gabriel to the tomb? Had word about Jesus' resurrection spread so that people were coming to see for themselves? She heard not only footsteps but also several thuds, as if someone's belongings were being dropped on the ground. What could be happening? She looked at Gabriel and he shrugged, perplexed. Then she heard two men talking.

"Let's seal the tomb right away. Pilate doesn't want the Galilean's friends snooping around and telling stories."

"Then Pilate had better silence the guards who were here earlier! They're saying that an earthquake rolled the stone away. Then they saw a bright light and heard voices."

"One of them told me something even stranger. Apparently several women arrived at dawn to embalm the body, but it was gone."

"Let me check inside. With all the rumors, it's hard to know what to believe."

As soon as the conversation ended, a Roman soldier appeared at the tomb's entrance. Judith held on to Gabriel, shocked by this turn of events. When the soldier saw them, he drew his sword. "What are you doing here? This tomb is closed by order of the Roman governor, Pontius Pilate!"

Gabriel stepped forward. "We came to check on our friend's body. There are rumors that it had been disturbed."

The soldier held out his sword. "You can see that there is no body here." He shook the sword threateningly. "Stay where you are!"

Judith saw that the soldier was well-built, with a square jaw and wide-set eyes. She studied him intently and recoiled in disbelief, recognizing the man. Longinus! He was the centurion who had stabbed Jesus with the spear. He had taken the scroll and refused to give it back to Mary Magdalene. Apparently he and another soldier had been assigned to the tomb after the first guards ran away.

She met Longinus' gaze and refused to flinch. Under her breath, she whispered to Gabriel, "I know this man." Gabriel glanced at her incredulously and held his ground, not saying a word. She had heard rage in Longinus' voice and seen hate on his face, but the longer she studied him, the more his hardened features seemed to soften and a glimmer of recognition appeared in his eyes.

She decided to take a risk and stepped toward him, letting go of Gabriel's hand. "You remember me, don't you?" she said, stopping a few feet from him.

He shook the sword again. "Why would I remember you?"

"Because my friend Mary and I confronted you at Golgotha when you took her scroll. Your name is Longinus, isn't it?"

When he heard her say his name, Longinus lowered his sword, and the tension drained from his darkly handsome face. "Yes, I remember you." He sounded almost apologetic. "I can't believe you're here. Everything is different now."

"What do you mean?" she asked.

A shout came from outside: "Longinus, what's taking so long?"

"I'm coming," Longinus said, motioning Judith and Gabriel to follow him. Then he whispered, "I've been searching for you."

She walked out of the tomb, puzzled by Longinus' statement, her hand in Gabriel's. The other soldier, a younger, shorter man, saw the three of them emerge and drew back, wide-eyed. The soldier reached for his sword, but Longinus grasped his hand and prevented him from drawing it. "You won't need that, Marcellus. I know this woman. She and her friend came to pay their respects to the Galilean. All they found were some linen wrappings, and they didn't disturb them."

Marcellus backed off, shaking his head. "They'd better not have disturbed anything." He stepped inside the tomb, glanced around and came out. "If we neglect our duty, Pilate will have our heads. Now help me move the stone back to cover the entrance."

Longinus laid his sword on a canvas bag of supplies next to the entrance; then he crossed over and joined Marcellus in trying to roll the stone. The stone would not budge. Longinus asked Judith and Gabriel to help, but even with their added strength the stone remained immovable, so Longinus ordered Marcellus to get more soldiers.

After Marcellus left, Longinus picked up a satchel that lay next to the bag of supplies. Judith stood with Gabriel and waited. Longinus finally came over and peered at her. "I have the scroll in here," he said, holding up the satchel. "I have been wanting to return it to your friend. Is she the woman called Mary of Magdala?"

"Yes," Judith said.

"Will you take it to her?"

"Of course."

"I would like to go with you . . . to meet her, if you would let me." Judith stifled a cry of joy and waited for Longinus to continue. "I will tell you why." Longinus removed his helmet and wiped the sweat from his face. "When I got home after the crucifixion, I read the letter. It was as if Jesus of Nazareth was speaking to me, and I couldn't get his voice out of my mind. The remorse I felt for stabbing him . . . well, it was unbearable." Longinus stumbled on the words, his voice choked and faltering. Judith put a hand on his shoulder, and he went on, "I could not sleep that night, and I cried out in agony for forgiveness. A deep peace came over me, and I knew that I must return the scroll and meet the woman to whom it was addressed. I also knew that I could never be cruel again; I stabbed Jesus with a spear, but he healed me with his love."

Longinus began to weep. Judith embraced him and said, "This morning he appeared to some other women and me; now I have seen inside the tomb, and I know that the same Jesus who was crucified is alive again!"

Longinus shook his head skeptically. "This is too unbelievable."

Judith let go of him, silently agreeing. But it was true. She had sensed extraordinary power in Jesus. He was a healer not only of people's bodies but also of their souls. His disciples had found this healing. Even Dismas, in his dying moment, had been healed. Now her eyes were bright with tears as she fully realized that Jesus had offered healing to the man who had driven a spear into his side. "You must truly surrender to Jesus, Longinus, and you, too, will believe."

Longinus reached into his satchel, withdrew the scroll and handed it to her. "I'll start by returning this scroll; then, if you and your friends will have me, I will do all I can for the cause of the Galilean."

Judith told him how to get to the upper room and promised to meet him there, to introduce him to Mary Magdalene that night. She hugged him before taking the scroll and leading Gabriel away from the tomb.

Then she held out the scroll and said, "In this letter Jesus has given us the secrets of love and relationships, but the story of his struggles with Mary Magdalene and Judas will be lost unless someone writes it down. I intend to be that writer. The story affected you and me and Dismas so profoundly. I must share both the pain and the healing, that others may know that grace is real—the greatest of God's miracles."

The sun suddenly appeared, radiant in the cloudless sky, waiting until that moment to show its true glory. Drawing in the bracing freshness of spring, Judith delighted in the earth's awakening. When she and Gabriel reached the edge of the garden, he stopped and wrapped his arms around her. "I will provide you with the stylus at my store. Perhaps you should also record the name of our baby. What do you suggest?"

Silent for a time, she finally looked up and met his lips with hers. Afterward she smiled and said, "I'm hoping for a boy, and I would like to name him Reuben, after my brother. May he grow up to be a man of peace."

They began to walk away, but after a few steps she turned and glanced back at the open tomb. It was the loveliest of sights, the large rectangular opening surrounded by a garden ablaze with color. *They can seal the entrance, she thought, gripping the scroll firmly, but no stone can keep Jesus buried now.* She turned to Gabriel. "Will you stay with me always?"

He kissed her forehead and tightened his arms around her. Just then a flock of doves took flight nearby, a flurry of wings lifting them into the endless canopy of sky. "Until forever," he said.

CHAPTER FIFTY-FOUR

Qumran at the Dead Sea
One Year Later

As Judith rocked her fussing baby in her arms, she was struck by the contrast between his untamable energy and Mary Magdalene's declining health. Holding Reuben to her breast, Judith fought to banish from her mind images of Mary's sweating and shaking, her body swollen and fever-ridden. The disease Mary had contracted several weeks earlier while working among the crippled and infirm had progressed quickly and mercilessly. But Judith didn't want to remember how this extraordinary woman looked on her sick bed. Mary had left such a mark on her and on so many others. Judith wanted to remember her as vibrant and stunning as she had been when they first met.

Along with Judith's marriage vow to Gabriel, her promise to Mary Magdalene to hide the letter was the most sacred pledge she had ever made.

Now she had to keep it.

As Reuben fussed and finally latched on, the rising sun cast Mount Nebo as a silhouette against the orange-red of a Qumran dawn. Gabriel was packing up their supplies and belongings after a restless night. Soon they would start the long journey to Antioch in Syria. There they hoped to escape the persecution led by the fanatical Saul of Tarsus in Jerusalem.

The persecution had begun after what had come to be called the day of Pentecost, when Peter and the other disciples proclaimed the gospel boldly, and many believers were added to their number. They met secretly in one another's homes, praising God, breaking bread together, and caring for the needy. But whenever they preached in the name of Jesus, Saul threatened them with death.

Judith hoped that she and her family would find safety among the believers in Antioch, but before they could continue their journey, she needed to finish feeding her baby. As she nursed him, the promise she had made to Mary Magdalene as she lay dying looped through her mind. On her deathbed Mary had sent for her. Judith could still see the dark circles that ringed Mary's half-closed eyes, the jaundiced skin and the heaving of her chest as she labored for her last breath. Mary revived a bit when she recognized her and, propping herself up on her elbows, pointed to the scroll that Judith had returned to her.

"You must care for the scroll," Mary said. "It contains the only words Jesus ever wrote to me. The Romans want to be rid of him forever—if they knew about the letter, they would seize and destroy it. You must hide the scroll for future generations." She gasped for breath. "And there's something else you must know. Before Judas took his life, he left a note in the upper room for me. I wept when I read it, as I often do when I think of Judas. Then I buried the note in the most fitting place I could think of—the Cave of Gethsemane, where Judas betrayed Jesus. When you write the story, as you have promised you will, you should mention the note, and that it's buried in the northeast corner of the cave."

Gently patting Mary's heaving chest, Judith said, "Please, you must rest."

Mary lay back, gripping Judith's arm. "I will rest only if you promise to take the letter. You must also write the story of what happened between Jesus and me and Judas so that others can learn from it. You must hide these writings so that, in God's timing, they will be found when the human family most needs them." Mary was sweating profusely, her words interrupted by bouts of coughing. "Do you promise?"

"Yes, I promise. I will write the story on the same papyrus and hide it where no one will find it for a long time."

Even before Judith finished speaking, she had decided on the perfect place: Qumran. It was fairly near the city and secluded enough so that the scroll would not be found soon, but accessible enough so that it would eventually be discovered. She bent to tell Mary Magdalene, but her breathing had stopped and she was still. Judith held her hand for a moment, and said a prayer of thanksgiving for all that Mary had been to her.

Now Judith needed to keep her promise and bury the scroll in these forbidding hills, which were as rugged and parched as she remembered, as well as make peace with her past. After Reuben finished nursing, she covered herself and set him down. The tall ceramic jar that contained the scroll lay at her feet. She removed the scroll and opened it, carefully laying aside the strips of linen in which she had wrapped it. The papyrus had aged somewhat and appeared soiled in places, perhaps from the fingers of the many believers who had read the letter, along with her diary entries. She admired Jesus' handwriting one last time.

Gabriel had lit a torch and was burying the dying embers of the campfire. As she watched him, she was struck by the strength in his features.

Had it not been for the letter, she could have been crucified with his brother, and she feared that Barabbas, whom she had heard was organizing a new uprising with the Zealot leader Menahem, son of Judas the Galilean, could still meet that horrific fate.

She put the thought out of her mind. The time had come. After rolling up the scroll, she placed it in the jar and sealed the top. With one arm she picked up Reuben, and with the other, she took hold of the jar. Gabriel grabbed the shovel that he had brought from home and, torch in hand, led her toward a cliff above the plateau on which they had camped.

Up a narrow ledge, they made their way into a cave cut into the craggy rock. Once inside, she set down the jar and held the torch as Gabriel began to dig a hole. He stabbed at the dusty ground with the shovel, loosening the hard-packed earth until the hole was deep enough for the jar. When he had placed the jar in the hole, they used their feet to cover it with pebbles and sand. "It will be a long time before anyone finds the scroll," he said, satisfied.

She pressed Reuben against her breast. "I only hope that by the time someone finds it, the world will have learned Jesus' way to peace."

Gabriel left, but Judith stood for a moment, staring at the spot where the scroll was now hidden. She knew that she had buried her past with the jar. It had been a long journey back to Qumran. She had touched depths so low that few people return from them alive, and those who do are changed forever. Her failures had shown her how powerless she was to heal herself. Only because the unexpected happened was she among the living. Jesus had visited her in prison. Mary Magdalene had befriended her. With their help, she had begun to forgive herself.

Running a hand over Reuben's bald little head, she offered a prayer of thanksgiving that in Gabriel and Reuben she had found the true meaning of love. The discovery was a homecoming, a return to everything noble and endearing in life. She prayed that whoever found the letter would experience the union of the male and the female within. If so—and if they shared the letter with the world—future generations could be healed and grow into the fullness of their creation in God's image.

Judith peered into Reuben's large eyes, which were the color of molasses, and knew they would always remind her of Dismas. Pressing Reuben's face against her cheek, she shuddered as she considered what she would tell Reuben about his father. She wouldn't emphasize Dismas' life as a Zealot, but rather how, in the end, he had asked for Gabriel's forgiveness and pleaded with him to love his wife and child.

As she admired her perfect baby, she knew her future lay with him and with Gabriel. But she would never forget Dismas' crucifixion, his dying words and Jesus' reply, "I tell you the truth, today you will be with me in paradise." She repeated these words out loud, kissed Reuben, and followed Gabriel into the morning.

CHAPTER FIFTY-FIVE

NO MATTER WHAT HAPPENS, ALWAYS BELIEVE IN THE POWER OF LOVE. EVENTUALLY EVERY FORCE THAT STANDS AGAINST THIS POWER WILL FADE INTO AN ABYSS OF FORGOTTEN MEMORIES.

LOVE'S INFLUENCE IS LIKE A TINY GLIMMER OF LIGHT IN A DARK ROOM. AS MORNING COMES, THE LIGHT GROWS AND DRIVES OUT THE DARKNESS.

ALIGN ALL THOUGHTS AND ACTIONS WITH THE LIGHT. DRAW POWER FROM THIS SOURCE OF NOBILITY, COURAGE, AND JOY. HEARTS THAT SURRENDER TO THE LIGHT OF LOVE WILL BE INSPIRED AND TRANSFORMED.

BEGINNING THIS VERY MOMENT.

—**Brother Gregory Andreou's Journal**

Beit Jala, Israel
Friday, April 19

AS THE THREE MEN BACKED KARIM INTO A SECLUDED CORNER OF BETHEL PRISON, AN UNBIDDEN THOUGHT ENTERED HIS MIND: *I HAVE NOTHING TO LIVE FOR. Why not let them kill me?* The stench of urine and the prison's gloom made the thought toxic enough to choke on. The bars that ringed the indoor recreation area were behind him. He had seen the attack dogs and iron gates outside. There was no escaping.

"You look even uglier in jail than you did on TV," the rawboned, darkly bearded Rivca said.

Three days earlier, when Karim entered the prison, he had met Rivca and his friends Marwan and Yasser. "How would you know?" Karim asked.

Rivca narrowed his eyes. "Because I saw your news conference before I got arrested."

The scowls on the men's faces blew terror through Karim. Even with their wrists handcuffed and their ankles in chains, these Palestinians could injure or kill him. Such was life in an Israeli prison, where the guards ignored the violence, and where smuggled cell phones and information from family visitors kept the prisoners abreast of—even involved in—events outside. Through this secret network Karim had learned of Rachel's death, and it left him in no condition to fight.

Or to do anything else.

He spoke the only words that came to mind. "What you heard on TV—that wasn't the whole story."

"Which story?" Yasser said, jutting out his pointed nose and thick chest. "Are you speaking of you becoming a Christian, or of you marching with Jews?" Yasser cupped his hands and swung with a chopping motion.

Karim blocked the blow with an arm. Thrown off balance, he reeled backward and Marwan, scar-faced and swarthy, kicked him. Karim fell and considered staying down, letting them beat him.

Kill him.

He despised the thought, but after the horrendous ending of the march—and after losing Rachel—he felt tempted.

"Leave him alone!" The voice spoke with such authority that the three attackers froze. Karim glanced up at a broad-shouldered man with wide-set eyes. "He's Sadiq Musalaha's son," the man said. "If you ever want out of here, you'll leave him alone." The man stepped in front of the attackers. "His father is negotiating a prisoner exchange with the Israelis."

Yasser spit on the floor. "They'll never do it. The Israelis raise our hopes and then dash them every time."

Karim got up as the broad-shouldered man said, "This situation is different. The Israelis have never captured the son of the PPA's leader. They're using him as a bargaining chip to pressure Musalaha to release their IDF soldier." The man pushed the attackers away. "From what we know of Sadiq Musalaha, he'll bargain for more than his son's release. He won't give up an IDF soldier until the Israelis free us too."

Rivca backed away. "I still don't like this man sympathizing with Christians and Jews, and I bet his father doesn't either."

Karim gave Rivca a disapproving stare. "That attitude is the reason we're in here. Even if we're freed, our spirits will be in prison until we see all people as equals."

Rivca smirked and walked away with his friends. Karim leaned back against the bars, rubbing his forehead. He had avoided the pain of a beating but couldn't escape the greater anguish of grief. Tormented by the memory of Rachel lying motionless in front of the Wailing Wall, a tear-gas cylinder in her chest, he raised a prayer of lament. *Yu Allah!* She was too young, too beautiful, too *good* to die—especially at her brother's hand. Karim's eyes blurred as a lump swelled in his throat.

She was gone.

Forever gone.

And he could do nothing to bring her back.

He shook his head and slapped the bars with a hand, tears dripping on the floor. Then the siren blared, signaling the end of the exercise session. As he started back to his cell, a guard approached. "Are you Karim Musalaha?"

"Yes."

"Come with me. You have a visitor."

Karim followed the muscular guard through a set of electronically controlled steel doors. The guard led him into a transfer corridor that had another set of identical doors at the far end. They clanked and squeaked as they opened. The noises had already become familiar to Karim, making him feel strangely at home. As he walked through and saw yet more bars and locked doors, he understood why he was comfortable: Israel, the West Bank, and Gaza were larger versions of this British-mandate-era prison. He had lived in such a place all his life. His mother and brother had died in such places. So had his wife-to-be and her father.

He swallowed against the lump that rose in his throat. He and Rachel had tried to find a path to freedom, and for a brief moment, through the Jesus letter, the path had become clear. But with Rachel's death, darkness had closed in again, more ominous and forbidding than ever.

The guard ushered him down a windowless hallway. "The room at the end is usually reserved for interrogations," he said. "But because you're Musalaha's son, you're being allowed to use it." The guard opened the door and Karim walked into a drab room that contained only a gunmetal gray desk and three wooden chairs. In one of the chairs sat Brother Gregory Andreou, his chin cradled in his palm.

After the guard left and locked the door, Brother Gregory stood and embraced Karim. "I've been so worried about you," he said, his voice trembling.

"And I about you." Karim patted the monk's back and studied the dark circles under his eyes. "If only Rachel were with us . . ."

"She is."

"What do you mean?"

"A miracle of sorts has happened." Brother Gregory's voice took on new urgency. "The footage of Rachel being shot was broadcast on TV and all over the Internet. It became an international human interest story—how a sister and brother chose opposite paths after their father died in a suicide bombing. Hearts broke all over the world when people saw the brother, an IDF commander, fatally shoot his sister, a peace activist, with a tear-gas canister. It also became known that the suicide bomber was Sadiq Musalaha's son—your brother. As a result, there have been calls from both Israeli and Palestinian leaders for new peace initiatives, and the United States is seizing the opportunity to bring the sides together. Your father is talking to the Israelis about a prisoner swap."

As Karim reflected on these surprising developments, another question arose in his mind. "What happened to the scroll?"

Brother Gregory's expression turned sober. "It's in the hands of the Government Antiquities Agency. I learned a painful lesson from the trouble it caused."

"About security, you mean?"

"No, about so-called 'holy' things—artifacts, sacred books and sites, even this land." Brother Gregory shook his head and crossed his arms on his chest. "When material things are called 'holy,' people become obsessed with them. These things seduce us away from the spiritual essence of our religions, and once we begin to fight over such things, the bloodshed never ends."

"And what about Ezra?"

Brother Gregory ran a hand through his flowing white hair, a glimmer of wonder in his eyes. "I don't understand it. He was such a hardliner; I thought he would always remain that way, but I'm astonished by how he has changed." Brother Gregory hesitated, his eyes wet. "Ezra told me that he doesn't blame you for Rachel's death, only himself. He resigned his commission in the army. Now he wants to make amends with you." The monk took hold of Karim's arm. "I brought him here. He's waiting outside . . . if you're willing to see him."

The room became stuffy, its walls closing in on Karim. He began to pace, his heart throbbing in his ears. How could he ever speak with Ezra again, let alone forgive him?

"I'll understand if you refuse to see him," Brother Gregory said. "I only hope you'll remember the lessons of the Jesus letter and of Judith of Jerusalem's diary." Brother Gregory's face was flushed. "Miracles happen every day. Don't you think you deserve one? Don't you think Rachel deserves one too?"

Karim felt dizzy, his legs weak. "I don't want to see Ezra." He threw his hands forward as if tossing an object on the ground. "I can't do it."

Brother Gregory grew very still. "This is the hardest decision of your life. But while you ponder it, let me tell you about a dream I had last night. I was at the ceremony celebrating the founding of the new nation of Palestine. The leaders of every Arab country were there, along with the president of the United States, the prime minister and the president of Israel, and many other dignitaries and heads of state. Everyone was standing in Jerusalem and nothing was happening. They looked bored and perplexed, not knowing what to do. Then Rachel entered the city from the Mount of Olives, through the Golden Gate, and everyone stood and applauded. They hugged one another and the bands played and the ceremony began. I think the dream is telling us that we need Rachel and her message of healing faith in order to create a new future. Perhaps she will accomplish even more in death than she did in life, and her work of reconciliation must begin with you and her brother."

Karim felt the blood rush to his cheeks. His hands shook. Beads of sweat formed above his upper lip. He closed his eyes, and then with a sigh he opened them. "All right," he said. "I will see Ezra."

Brother Gregory went to the door and knocked. When the guard answered, the monk asked him to show Ezra in. A moment later Karim saw his bitter enemy walk through the door. His army uniform gone,

Ezra wore only a white shirt and black slacks. His eyes red and lips quivering, his expression exuded unbearable sadness.

Karim stood beside the desk and said nothing. As Ezra approached, a host of images played across Karim's mind. He wondered if Ezra saw them too: bombed-out buildings and bloodstained streets, razor-wire fences and plumes of tear-gas smoke, rock-throwing youths and soldiers on the march. Karim sensed that he, Ezra, and Brother Gregory were not the only ones in the room. The memories and sorrows of Jews, Christians, and Muslims through the ages were there with them—the tear-streaked faces of mothers wailing for their lost sons, the wrenching chants of crowds carrying coffins, the shrill cries of orphans searching for parents who would never return.

Brother Gregory broke the silence as he grasped both of their hands. "You are the two bravest men I have ever known."

The two stared at each other in silence. Finally Ezra said, "I have come to express my deepest sorrow over my hateful actions and over Rachel's death." Tears pooled in his eyes. "Will you please forgive me?"

Before he could respond, a siren went off. Karim glanced around in confusion as did Ezra and Brother Gregory. The door opened and the guard came in. "We have just received word that the prisoner exchange has gone through. The Palestinians incarcerated here must leave immediately." The guard held the door open. "Follow me."

The three men walked down the hall and into the transfer corridor, where they joined several hundred Palestinians flowing through the open front gate. Blinking against the midday sun, Karim beheld a chaotic scene. Television crews were broadcasting live as the families and friends of released prisoners swarmed around. Karim heard someone in the crowd call his name. He looked and saw Abdul Fattah waving to him. "Come on, Karim! Your father wants you to join him at the peace talks."

Ezra held up a hand. "Give us a minute." He took Karim aside, reached into his pocket and withdrew a ring. Holding it out to Karim, he said, "Before Rachel died, she gave me this ring to return to you. She said that she will always love you, and that she will wait for you in the next life. Please receive this ring as a sign of my deepest remorse and a plea for your forgiveness."

Karim stared at the ring. He would take it, of course, but he didn't know if he could or even wanted to forgive Ezra. Would it betray Rachel to forgive the brother who had killed her? Or would forgiving him be the deepest act of loyalty to her?

Karim searched Ezra's eyes and saw longing there, the passionate longing that he had seen in the eyes of *Rajiya,* the little girl whose image was painted on the separation wall at A-Ram, clutching enough balloons to carry her over.

Karim took the ring and studied its inscription: "True Islam is peace." That was the message his beloved mother had left him. It was also the message that Rachel had taught him to live. Now he would inscribe two more words inside the ring—"True Islam is peace *and forgiveness.*"

Ezra reached for him, tempting Karim to turn away, but he saw the longing again and opened his arms. Then Ezra did what Karim had never expected an Israeli to do in a Palestinian's company, let alone in his embrace.

He wept.

From The Day the World Changed
Copyright © *2063*
by Karim Musalaha

BEFORE THE CHANGE CAME, THE ONE THING THAT EVERYONE KNEW ABOUT ISRAELIS AND PALESTINIANS IS THAT THEY HATED EACH OTHER. And they used religion to justify their violence. The hypocrisy only ended when all the children of Abraham—Jews, Christians, and Muslims—began to uphold justice and practice compassion.

Looking back, I see that the roots of peace were there all along, but the bombings and the blood and the tears had blinded us to them.

It took Rachel Sharett—the courageous Israeli whom I will forever love—to give us a new vision. Now, after the founding of the nation of Palestine, after Israel's separation barrier came down and the pass system ended and the checkpoints got dismantled and the matters of the settlements and the status of Jerusalem were resolved, her legend continues to grow.

Her vision came from history's most famous love letter—written by Jesus of Nazareth to Mary Magdalene. No one could have imagined that the letter would start a revolution, least of all me, the runaway university student who discovered it.

But it did.

And the revolution continues today wherever love enters and makes enemies friends.

This revolution, I believe, is the world's only true hope.

Beginning with you and me.

AUTHOR'S NOTE

WHEN I REFLECT ON WHY I WROTE THIS NOVEL, I AM HAUNTED BY A MEMORY FROM JUNE 2006. As I visited Ground Zero with my son's sixth-grade class, hundreds of people swirled around the observation deck in lower Manhattan. Some stared through tall iron bars at the vast crater where the twin towers of the World Trade Center once stood. Others studied photographs and timelines of the September 11 attack. Still others snapped pictures or strolled with their tour groups, some of them speaking foreign languages.

Then I heard singing.

"Our Father, which art in heaven, hallowed be thy name" lilted over the crowd and into the gaping crater as if on the voices of angels. I recognized Malotte's arrangement of "The Lord's Prayer" and wove my way toward the multicultural youth choir. By the time I reached them, they were singing, "Thy kingdom come, thy will be done, on earth as it is in heaven." The sprawling choir infused the words with such emotion that I felt as if I were hearing them for the first time.

I kept thinking about the monstrous evil that had been visited on Ground Zero, and how violence is humanity's most virulent disease. Given the facts of history, thinking that a cure will ever be found seemed impossibly naive. But in that moment I was also flooded with hope. In the Lord's Prayer, Jesus instructs us to pray for the coming of God's reign on earth. With this coming, the glory of eternity will break into time, and all things will be made new. Christians serve humanity as a way of embodying this prayer.

The Galilean Secret is about the love that gave birth to this hope. I wrote the novel out of my belief that Jesus Christ fully actualized divine love. His decisive actions flowed from an enlightened spiritual awareness —an awareness of God's concern even for the sparrows, and for every hair on our heads. As God's love flowed through him, it became a creative, transformative power, healing bodies, captivating hearts, and posing a dramatic challenge to the religious and political establishments of his time. Not only did this love embrace tax collectors, prostitutes, and lepers, but it also compelled Jesus to forgive those who crucified him. Based on his example, he exhorts us to love others—even our enemies— as he has loved us.

I wanted the novel to reflect the connection between the personal and the social implications of Jesus' ministry. If God's reign on earth doesn't come to us personally, it will remain forever unreal, a fantasy with no basis in experience. For Jesus, the love that inspires hope for us all became personal. Christians who emphasize his divinity may say that his astute spiritual awareness was eternally part of his being. As a novelist, I am more interested in the human Jesus—in what we might learn from his struggle to comprehend and live the fullness of love.

I wondered about the influences that may have shaped his awareness. The New Testament and other early Christian writings don't give a definitive answer. We know that he was raised a Jew by working-class parents in Nazareth, and that he had brothers and sisters. But no reliable source tells us how these people, or anyone else, molded his thinking or his character.

I began to wonder if Jesus' radical way of relating to women might provide a clue. Against the conventions of his time, he included women among his companions, spoke to them publicly, and showed them compassion. On occasion he even used female imagery for God. How did Jesus develop this unusual sensitivity? *The Galilean Secret* dramatizes this mystery. The novel raises the question of whether Mary Magdalene had a powerful influence on him, and whether these two first-century Galileans discovered the secret of love, which can speak to our troubled times today.

The Gospels of the New Testament offer only sketchy details about their relationship. Of the twelve times that Mary Magdalene appears, eleven are in the scenes of the Crucifixion and Resurrection. That Mary stays with Jesus during his agony is significant, as is her role in all four Gospels as the first witness to his resurrection. In the Gospel of John she even has a personal conversation with the risen Lord.

All of this suggests a very close relationship.

Some passages in the ancient manuscripts discovered in Nag Hammadi, Egypt, in 1945 support this view. More than forty in number, these manuscripts include some of what have become known as the Gnostic Gospels, as well as other genres of literature. These Gospels were written by religious seekers known as Gnostics (from the Greek word *gnosis,* meaning "knowledge") because they associated spiritual development with secret "knowledge" or experiential insight more than with belief in doctrines. Along with the Gospel of Mary, a Gnostic text found a half century earlier, some of the Nag Hammadi manuscripts mention Jesus and Mary Magdalene.

Written during the second century or later, these references portray

Mary as the constant companion of Jesus who has special insight into his teachings and the meaning of discipleship. She is even exalted above Peter, leading some scholars to conclude that she and Peter symbolized the conflict between Gnosticism and orthodox Christianity, with Mary standing for the former and Peter the latter.

Among these writings, the Gospel of Philip contains perhaps the most provocative verse: "The companion of the [Savior] is Mary Magdalene. The [Savior loved] her more than [all] the disciples, [and he] kissed her often on her [mouth]." Since the text discovered at Nag Hammadi is missing words in the places designated by brackets, we may never know exactly where Jesus kissed Mary. (Translators have suggested the words in brackets as guesses, based on the themes and vocabulary of the Gospel. Jesus may just as well have kissed Mary on the forehead, the cheek or the feet.)

Drawing on this Gnostic tradition, some novelists and filmmakers have portrayed Jesus and Mary Magdalene as married and the parents of a child, with a bloodline that continues to this day. The vast majority of New Testament scholars and historians of early Christianity don't accept this view, and the longstanding tradition of the church is that the relationship was strictly platonic. Roman Catholicism even requires its priests to remain celibate, based on the belief that Jesus refrained from any intimate relationship with a woman.

I find both extremes hard to accept. On the one hand, the idea that Jesus and Mary Magdalene were married is based on conjecture, with no direct support in either the canonical or noncanonical sources. On the other hand, if Jesus were celibate, and if he never struggled with his sexuality, he would have been less than fully human, a contradiction of the creeds and historic teachings of the church.

I wrote this book in the belief that the most fruitful place of discovery is the middle ground. In *The Galilean Secret* the letter from Jesus to Mary

Magdalene is fictional, but even if the scenario it describes didn't happen, it contains insights that are true to the teachings of Jesus and to the larger framework of biblical revelation. We cannot know whether he and Mary shared physical intimacies, but we can ponder what may have happened between them—and how what they learned from one another affected the people around them.

This exploration of the middle ground illuminates one of the great mysteries of being human—our masculinity and femininity. Although we cannot completely fathom this mystery, we gain insight into it by learning how the masculine and the feminine components of our personalities relate within us, as they related within Jesus and Mary. The deeper we go into this spiritual work, the better we will understand the Galilean secret of love. Not only will this secret reveal the wonder of our creation in God's image, but it will also give us resources to use in friendships, dating, and marriage.

In the novel the relationship between Jesus and Mary tells us something about the evolution of love. Their struggle becomes an extraordinary quest to establish intimacy with the gender opposite in themselves. This spiritual approach reminds us that only the divine lover of our souls can bring us ultimate fulfillment. When a person fails to learn this lesson, as was the case with Judas Iscariot in the novel, the consequences can be catastrophic. Even those who do learn to love—Judith and Gabriel, Karim and Rachel—suffer in the process. And yet the pain is worth the price because love brings transformation.

The work of unifying the masculine and the feminine and thus maximizing the power of love is a critical need today. The Abrahamic religions —Judaism, Christianity, and Islam—are dominated by male images of God and by men in positions of leadership. To evolve beyond this one-sided paradigm would be liberating for both women and men, and a huge step forward for humanity. Our tendency to set up dichotomies and become captives of their limitations robs us of the richness of integrating opposites and finding the creativity in the tension between them.

We can hardly imagine a world in which men no longer exploit or abuse women and in which women no longer distrust or fear men. The work of building such a world begins within each of us. If we fail to do this inner work, we will always live in a divided world.

Today interpretations of the Hebrew Bible, the Christian scriptures, and the Qur'an that are disconnected from love incite division, violence, and terrorism. How will this change if we never learn to reconcile the opposites within us? Are we doomed to create bigger, more destructive weapons to defeat those whose religiously inspired hatred threatens the security of the world? The Abrahamic religions also contain traditions that advocate peacemaking rooted in justice for all. Part of my purpose in writing this novel was to dramatize this tradition as articulated and embodied by Jesus of Nazareth. His teachings and decisive actions give voice to the social dimension of hope.

The Galilean Secret has both historical and contemporary plots that involve violence fueled by religion. I want readers to experience the clash of religion and politics in first-century Jerusalem and in Israel/Palestine today. The clash inevitably breeds upheaval in people's lives and in the larger society. In today's world, religion is often used to catalyze regional and international conflicts rather than resolve them. The novel's historical plot bears witness to the perennial nature of this problem.

This is where fiction holds unique potential in our current situation. In Judaism, Christianity, and Islam we have traditions that have been handed down for centuries. In hindsight, we can read our scriptures and identify traditions that have divided rather than united people. How can there ever be greater understanding, let alone reconciliation and peace, if we don't find more creative ways of interpreting our traditions?

For example, the Jews have been singled out and blamed for killing

Jesus. In a post-Holocaust world, it seems inconceivable that novelists or filmmakers would create art that perpetuates this fallacy. In *The Galilean Secret,* I tried to show that there are other alternatives. The Gospel of John records that Judas Iscariot brought Roman soldiers with him to arrest Jesus. Where could he have gotten these soldiers if Pilate hadn't given the order?

The Gospels present the Roman governor as vacillating and indecisive, but we know from the historian Josephus that Pilate could be ruthless. Fiction provides a way to balance the picture. It allows us to understand the Gospels in light of history's tragedies, which is the first step toward healing and preventing them in the future.

If we don't take this approach, how will we ever create a better world? At present, religion is often used to support oppression and to inflict suffering, but will this always be the case? Part of the solution lies in taking our understanding further and learning to read our scriptures critically. The old paradigm of winners and losers is untenable in today's world. With everything so interconnected, if one group or nation loses, we all lose. We must learn to communicate with respect for one another's religious traditions, and we must become secure enough in our beliefs that we no longer demonize those who disagree with us.

I wrote this novel to lift up the kind of religion that promotes personal and social healing. I love the Christian faith in which I was raised, but I long for it to become more of a force for peace. In order for this to happen, a transformation must begin from within. By seeking the oneness of the masculine and the feminine as Jesus and Mary Magdalene did, we will better find the secret of love that inspires hope. Then we will give thanks for the spiritual progress we have made and for the light that is penetrating even the darkest places.

ACKNOWLEDGMENTS

I OWE MY DEEPEST THANKS TO MANY PEOPLE WHO MADE THE PUBLICATION OF THIS NOVEL POSSIBLE: To the incomparable Robert Gottlieb, chairman of Trident Media Group, for persevering valiantly until he found the right publishing match, and for his friendship, vision, and professional expertise; to Linda Raglan Cunningham, editor-in-chief of Guideposts Books, for seeing the potential of this project and taking a chance on a first-time novelist; to David Morris, senior editor, for his constant encouragement and savvy editorial guidance; to Carl Raymond, director of marketing, and to the entire editorial and sales team of Guideposts for their hard work, enthusiasm, and creativity.

I am also grateful beyond words to Carol L. Craig for her extraordinary editorial skill and unfailing encouragement; to Marjorie Hanlon for her wealth of experience and keen sense of what was working and what wasn't; and to Judy Kellem for reflective feedback early in the process.

To my wife, Carol, and my sons, Evanjohn and Peter, for persevering with me on this long journey and for bearing the strains of living with a writer.

To my friends Lou Quetel, Mike Burch, Stephanie Merrim, Dave and Anne Burnham, Hank and Fran Pedersen, Jeana Whittredge,

Shlomit Yusifon, and Jon Almond. Thanks so much for reading the manuscript, for discussing it with me, or both.

To Peter Miano of the Society for Biblical Studies, Ghada Abdelqader and Barbara Martens for sharing your knowledge of Israeli and Palestinian society.

To members of my writers group: the late A. D. Van Nostrand, Joan Pettigrew, Scott Allen, Dick Upson, Keith Cooper, David Howard, Jan Molinari, Kathleen Tremblay, Pat Trodson, and John Patrick. Your substantive suggestions made this book much better than it otherwise would have been.

To my spiritual guides Paul Sanderson and Roberta Cote. You lived the intricacies of this story with me and made the process of writing it a matter of prayer and spiritual exploration.

To publishing professionals Marie Cantlon and Roy Carlisle for your gracious interest and helpful advice.

To Kelly Hughes of the Dechant-Hughes Agency for her stellar work in publicizing the book.

To attorney Eric Raymon for his friendship and wise counsel.

To Lana Romano for assistance with preparing the original manuscript for publication.

To the congregation of Community Church of Providence for your encouragement and support.

To the staff of Canonius Camp and Conference Center for your warm hospitality.

While I drew on too many scholarly books to mention all of them here, I want to acknowledge *How Good Do We Have to Be?* by Rabbi Harold S. Kushner as the source of the interpretation of the Hebrew word *tsela* used in this novel. I am also grateful to the late Lewis B. Smedes for his books about forgiveness and to the Swiss psychologist C. G. Jung and his modern interpreters John A. Sanford and Robert A. Johnson for their psychological insights.

I owe you all a profound debt of gratitude!